GW00836658

Praise for the first
ZIPPERED FLESH anthology

Zippered Flesh

Tales of Body
Enhancements
Gone Bad!

Edited by Weldon Burge

"If director David Cronenberg edited an anthology, this would be that book."
—HORROR WORLD

"Hardcore studies of shocking monstrosities that will enthrall and entice even the most hardened horror fan." —FANGORIA

"I *loved* this anthology. Reading it was like riding a rollercoaster in a haunted house." —READER'S DEN

"There are some real high points in this collection, and the authors have all attempted to approach the subject matter from very different and interesting angles." —THIS IS HORROR

"This anthology will not let you down!"
—Blaze McRob's TALES OF HORROR

DEDICATION

For the editors and fellow writers who provided support and encouragement to make Smart Rhino Publications possible.

CONTENTS

ACKNOWLEDGMENTS

Thanks go to Shelley Everett Bergen for her amazing cover illustration, to Scott Medina for designing the cover, and to Terri Gillespie for her excellent proofreading skills.

I must also point out that, although most of the stories are original to this volume, a number are reprints. Carson Buckingham's story, "Skin Deep," was originally published in the *Masters of Horror* anthology (published by Triskaideka Books, 2010). Kealan Patrick Burke's "Underneath" first appeared in *Shivers III*, edited by Richard Chizmar, Cemetery Dance Publications, 2004. "Clockwork" by Shaun Jeffrey was originally published in *Wicked Karnival #7*, 2006.

THE MODERN ADONIS

BY BRYAN HALL

Firm.

Firm, but not rock hard. Not the kind of muscle a real man should have. The kid had a long way to go, but even I had to admit he was off to a good start.

He was standing in the back corner of the gym, over past the free weights, flexing and taking a good long look at himself in the wall-to-wall mirror back there.

Doubts. If you've got that need to check yourself out in public, it means even you know you've got a lot of work to do. I know. I was there once, just starting to fill out and excited as hell at what I was achieving.

I thought about going over and letting the kid know that he'd hit a plateau. That no matter how hard he worked, he'd hit the point where the body simply can't convert anything else to muscle. It's a weight ratio thing. Your body is only designed for a certain amount of muscle mass; anything beyond it is impossible.

Fuck impossible. There are ways. People don't wanna talk about them. Don't wanna admit to them. But the simple fact is that there's a limit to what the body can produce, and once you hit it there's no damn way to go any higher on your own.

On your own being the key phrase there.

I didn't bother telling the kid. He'd find out on his own eventually, if he stuck with his regimen. Then he'd have to make a decision.

Me, I had my own worries. My own decision.

Seems there's a natural plateau, and there's one designed all on its own, one that you can't eclipse no matter what. It's frustration is what it is. A real synthetic son of a bitch. You push and you shoot and you lift and you work and you just don't get any more gain.

I'd spent two months languishing at that ceiling, trying everything I could. Talking to everyone I knew. They all said the same thing.

"Sorry, Al. You've hit it, man. No way to get bigger."

"Christ buddy, look at you. You're a fucking specimen. What else do you want?"

More.

That's all. Not too much to ask. But I'd hit the point where I realized me and that kid had something in common.

I watched him flex and smile and posture and go try to strike up a conversation with a pair of blondes on the treadmills. I chuckled to myself and left.

Home was a little house in an upscale neighborhood outside Atlanta. Away from the junkies and the thugs and the drunks. Tucked in a nice pine grove, not a skyscraper in sight.

Upchuck was at the door, same as every day, little nub of a tail wagging like crazy. They say a man's dog is a reflection of himself, and we were proof of that. He was a boxer-pit mix—a mongrel, just like me. Shorter than a boxer but with that square chest and shoulders that a badass pit bull has. Pure muscle—not an ounce of fat on his seventy-pound body. Part of it was his own genetics, but he owed a little to me, too. I mixed in a few supplements with his dinner, and made sure to buy only the best dog food. No soy. No fillers. Red meat three days a week.

If you're gonna have a pet, you treat it like you would want to be treated. And I treat myself well.

2

Upchuck followed me through the house to the weight room. I dropped my gym bag in the corner and went to the shelf in the center of the far wall, took the metal toolbox off it. The combination to the padlock was 265—my own season weight goal. Pro bodybuilders separate their weight from their off-season and on-season numbers. Off-season, you're usually heavier since you start training harder during competition time. You gain a little when you're not pressing yourself as hard, or at least most do.

Not me. I've always stayed right at two hundred forty-five, or within a couple pounds of it. I don't gain fat. I gain muscle, or I don't gain at all. If you treat every day like you're in competition, you'll stay hard.

Built.

Ripped.

Toned.

Two hundred sixty-five was a good number to shoot for. Realistic, achievable. Until my body decided to impose that goddamn two-hundred-forty-eight ceiling. I couldn't climb above it. No matter what. I guess I could stop working out, start eating processed shit and drinking milk shakes until I turned into a chubby blob. That would put me up to two hundred sixty-five. Past it, really.

But I wanted two hundred sixty-five in muscle. Pure muscle. Sure, my bones and organs and skin would all help add to that weight, but most of it?

Muscle. Just the way it should be.

I unlocked the case and slipped out the bottle, the vial, and a fresh syringe. Drew out a dose of testosterone cypionate first. After a while you don't even feel the needle's little prick. After a while, your muscles are so tight you don't even bleed.

After that was the Winstrol. Little pill with a big punch. Took two of them dry, then put everything back into the box and put it back where it went. Upchuck watched me like he had a thousand times before. He never got his own shot, but I swear sometimes his eyes were begging me to give him one.

I went to the study, Upchuck padding along behind me. One wall was lined with trophies, photos of me at different competitions, newspaper clippings. Stuff like that. Rhonda had taken most of the pictures, back before she said the bodybuilding was getting in the way of our relationship. We never married, so she couldn't take any of my money. But I missed her. After nine years of being with someone, you can't help but miss them.

I dialed Ricky's number and waited. I needed something else. Something better. I'd doubled the doses on both of the chems, but nothing had happened in the last two months. Not a single pound of change in my weight. Normally I stacked, running through the cycle the way you were supposed to. But two months with no change at all called for doubling up. Ricky yelled at me the last time I talked to him and told me I was gonna do it. He's an asshole, but he can get what you need.

"I'll be damned, Al. I expected you to call me from a hospital," he said as he answered the phone. His nasal voice sounded happy that he'd been wrong.

"I told you I'd be okay."

"Small miracles, man. Small miracles."

"Listen ... I need something else."

The line was silent for a long time. When he spoke again, all joy was gone from his voice. "I can't do that, man."

"Why not?"

"I've sold you too much. You're stacking and cycling like a madman, Al. I don't want you to hurt yourself. And besides, I've gotta cover my own ass. You kill your damn fool self with all this juice and it gets traced back to me somehow ..."

"It wouldn't. And I won't. I'm a fucking brick wall, man. The stuff I'm on now doesn't even speed up my heart. It doesn't do shit, in fact. That's the problem."

"Have you looked in the mirror lately, Al? You get any more ripped, your muscles will probably split through your skin."

The thought actually made me grin for a second. Then reality crashed back in. "I can't get any more ripped, damn it. That's why I'm calling you."

He hesitated. "No. I can't, man. Not in good conscience. It's too dangerous."

"Fuck your conscience."

"Al, man. There's no need to—"

"And fuck you, too." I hung up the phone. Thought about throwing it across the room, let it smash into the wall. But, as much as

4

Ricky may not want to admit it to his other clients, I knew damn well that there were plenty of other chemical fish in the sea.

I switched on the computer and listened to it hum to life. I like computers. They're so goddamn useful it's amazing anyone got by without them. So much information, so easily obtainable. Plus, they're like a human. You can keep upgrading them, adding new RAM and hard drives and video cards. There's always something else you can do to make them a little better.

I had a few bookmarks stored, online shops for different chems. But I'd tried most of them through Ricky over the last months. There had to be something else.

An hour into the search and I was starting to lose hope. Vague searches weren't working. Things like *Steroids Online* or *Muscle Building Supplements*. Finally, my Hail Mary play turned up something. I searched for something simple—*Buy Steroids in Atlanta*. Hard to get more direct than that.

And it worked.

The top results were the same bullshit sites I'd seen a dozen times, but I combed through them and on page six of the results, right about the time I was starting to give it up, I saw a result that looked promising. I clicked it and watched as a knockoff version of Craigslist filled the screen. Shady shit on there, things like *Evening Companions* and *Help With Your Problems* buried alongside *Electronics* and *Collectibles*.

I'd never seen anything like it, but after you see some of the shit the internet is home to, it's hard to be surprised.

The listing I found was too perfect to believe.

Gain muscle mass! No matter your size or figure, bulking up is possible! Get the body you want—no side effects!

It was followed by a local number that was practically begging me to call it.

So I did.

I got an answer on the third ring. A lot quicker than Ricky had ever answered my calls.

"Yes?" The voice was nothing special. A man, impossible to tell the age. Just a common baritone.

"I'm calling about the ad online?"

"Which one?"

"The one for muscle mass?"

5

"Oh. Well. What is it you want?"

"I need to get bigger. I've hit a plateau and the stuff my usual guy's giving me isn't helping anymore."

"Okay. Well, I can probably help you. But it's costly."

"I'll pay."

There was a long pause. "How much do you want this?" The voice had dropped to a near-whisper.

"More than anything."

Another pause. "You're sure?"

"Yes."

"Do you have someone close to you? A brother, a lover? Even a pet?"

I glanced at Upchuck. He'd plopped down in front of the trophy case and was licking his balls like they were ice cream. "Yes. A dog."

"Bring it. And five thousand dollars."

I hesitated, but only for a second. "Okay. No problem."

He gave me the address and told me to be there in two hours, then hung up.

It was a long wait. I left twenty minutes early and did fifteen over the speed limit all the way there. I expected a business, some run down little shithole in a bad part of town. Instead, I ended up parked on the sidewalk in front of a house that looked a hell of a lot like mine. A little suburban community, first home on the left. Two stories, manicured lawn. I double-checked my GPS to make sure it hadn't led me astray, then checked it again on my cell phone with the maps application. Everything said I was in the right spot except my gut.

I tucked the envelope with the guy's cash into my waistband, clipped Upchuck's leash to his collar, and we climbed out of the car.

The door opened before I was able to ring the bell. The guy standing in the doorway looked like a skeleton. He was thin to the point of being disgusting—I could probably fart and knock him over. His skin was like chalk, eyes sunk back into his head and sitting atop purple bags that were bigger than his biceps. His gaze jumped from me to Upchuck and back again.

"I'm here about the—"

"Come on in." He moved to the side and I started into the house. Upchuck had other plans. He barked twice, then let out that low growl that dogs do when they're about to bite. He didn't like the look of the guy any more than I did.

I dragged him into the house anyway. He'd never been a fan of strange places—or people—so I was pretty much used to it. The guy didn't seem to give a shit either. He didn't give Upchuck a second glance and motioned for me to follow him.

"You okay, man?" I asked as we walked down a bare hallway. I had to pull Upchuck every step of the way. "You sick or anything?"

"I'm fine. I just don't sleep a lot."

I glanced through the open doors we passed. Nothing remarkable. A den with a recliner and a midsized TV. A bathroom with seashells on the shower curtain. The hallway ended at a closed door, with an open one on the right. The man led us through the open door.

It was a bedroom he'd converted into a kind of home office. Three computer monitors lined a desk, with a matching trio of computer towers visible underneath it. The desk was cluttered, lots of notes scattered among wires and wire cutters, bulbs and screwdrivers. A pair of envelopes that looked a lot like mine—one of them a lot thicker—sat to one side of the desk.

"So ... advertising online. That's not risky?" I'd never felt the need in my life to break the ice, but the guy's nonchalant, disinterested demeanor was starting to make me feel a little like Upchuck.

He shrugged. "No risk, no reward. Besides, cops have more important things to do than try to bust people on a web site offering blowjobs for twenty bucks a pop."

I held out my hand. "I'm Al."

He stared at my palm a moment, and then leveled his eyes back to mine. "Mark." He didn't bother shaking hands; he just sat there, looking back and forth from me to Upchuck and back again.

"So ... here's your money." I offered him the envelope and he tossed it to the desk beside the other ones.

"You're willing to do anything for this?"

I nodded.

"I need your dog. And I need you to wait here. You should say goodbye."

My breath stuck in my throat for a second. "What? Say goodbye to who?"

He jerked his head slightly, gesturing toward Upchuck.

"No. You can't have my fucking dog, man."

"Why did you think I told you to bring it, exactly?"

"I—" What had I thought? The truth was, I hadn't. I didn't give a shit. The muscles. My body. Those were the things that mattered. When he'd said to bring Upchuck along, I hadn't given it a second thought. The allure of his promise held too much sway. "No. I can't give you my dog."

He studied me a moment, then nodded. He pushed the envelope back across the desk. "Okay then. Have a good day."

"You're serious?"

He nodded.

I looked at Upchuck, who'd sat down beside me and was staring up at me, waiting to leave. He'd been a hell of a good dog. My companion, especially after Rhonda had left. She'd tried to take him but I promised her that she'd get the house before she'd get the dog, which was to say that there wasn't a chance in hell of her getting either one. But he'd been a fifty-dollar pound rescue. As much as I liked him, it seemed like an investment in my body that I couldn't pass up.

I've heard of alcoholics and crackheads stealing their momma's jewelry to get the money for their next drink, their next hit. I know a guy who used to be the world's biggest homophobe who now trades his ass to any man willing to give him twenty bucks or a dime of good meth. I'd never understood how you could let something get hold of you like that until I looked at my dog and realized that, if he could help me hit two hundred sixty-five, letting him go made sense.

"You guarantee this will work? That I'll break this ceiling and start gaining muscle again?"

Mark shrugged. "If that's what you really, truly want. Then yes. It will work. You'll get what you want."

"Guaranteed?"

"Guaranteed."

I bent over and hugged Upchuck, stroked under his chin the way he liked and nuzzled his face a minute, then offered the leash to Mark. He slid the envelope back to the pile and walked around the desk.

"Wait here. *Right* here," he said as he took the leash. It was the first time since I was a boy that I remember actually crying. Not much—just a couple of tears that I rubbed off in a hurry—but still, they were there.

Upchuck was muscular, and it took every ounce of strength Mark had to pull him out of the room. I was expecting my dog to bite his scrawny ass, but he surprised me.

Mark got to the closed door at the end of the hallway and glanced back to me before opening it.

A moment later, he was able to drag Upchuck through the door and close it behind him.

The house went quiet, but only for a few minutes. Upchuck's barks punched through the walls, short vicious ones I'd never heard him use before. Angry, threatening barks.

The feel of the house changed. The scent of metal rushed in, the sweet, metallic taste of copper filling my mouth. My ears popped as the pressure changed, and each breath became a struggle. I was pulling air in, but it was so thin it barely seemed to have any effect on my screaming lungs. There was a sound like air rushing through the window of a car on the highway. Upchuck stopped barking and let loose a long, high-pitched whine that died with a yelp.

All the sounds and scents receded, plunging the house back into an abominable silence. The sound of the doorknob turning almost made me scream, and Mark came back into the room.

Without Upchuck.

In his right hand, where the leash had been moments earlier, he was clutching something else.

He walked back around the desk and sat down, then placed the item in front of me.

A syringe. Identical to the hundreds I'd used in the past, except for its contents. It was filled with a fluid blacker than used motor oil. Five ccs of pure darkness.

"That's it?" I said. "You take my dog and my money and expect me to inject myself with whatever the hell that is?"

"I don't expect you to do anything. I've seen so many different kinds of people that I know you can never count on them to act the way you expect."

"This is a fucking joke. I want my dog back. And my money."

He shook his head. "That's not possible. This is yours. You bought it. It's not for anyone else."

I leaned forward, flexing my neck muscles and slapping on my most intimidating snarl. "Give me back my dog."

"Your dog is gone." His right hand rose up from behind the table and pointed a handgun at my chest. I wasn't much on guns, but I'd seen enough TV to know it was a 9mm. And that no matter how ripped I was, that bullet could tear through my muscle and organs like a chainsaw through a birthday cake.

We stared at each other for a long while. I was three of him. Maybe four. But that little candyass hunk of metal in his hand gave him the advantage, and we both knew it. I stood and backed toward the door.

"The needle," he said. "Take what's yours."

"I'm not using that."

"You came here for it." He smiled. "I suspect you will. But whether you do or not, you'll take it with you."

Another minute stretched out to seeming days. I took the syringe. It was like picking up an icicle—the cold stung my skin. I didn't let Mark see the pain, though. It hadn't bothered him. It damn sure wouldn't bother me.

He followed me out and, twenty minutes after I arrived, I was back on the road for my house, alone and more pissed off than I could ever remember being.

I stared at that goddamn syringe for three hours when I got home. Put it on my own desk in my study and watched it as if it was going to grow wings and fly away. If I'd been a drinking man, I would have gone through a bottle that night. As it was, I only had a bottle of water to help me ponder my options.

It looked like tar. I knew the side effects of the chems I used. I knew the risks. This stuff? Pure mystery. An enigma as deep as it was dark. One that had cost me five grand and my best friend.

Was it worth risking more? My health?

I weighed myself a dozen times that night, never expecting a change but still compelled to look for one. If a single pound had been added, I probably would have thrown the needle away.

Left deciding between life as I was and the chance of improving even more, there was no real choice to make.

I uncapped the needle and slipped it into the ball of muscle above my hip. A moment's hesitation, and I depressed the plunger.

The cold slid through me, spreading in tendrils like an oil spill caught in a tide. My legs went numb first, then my stomach. It crept upward until it coated my skull, shards of pain splintering my mind. There was an instant where my panic washed away, replaced by a sense that I was no longer alone. No longer a mere mortal.

And then my mind succumbed to the darkness.

I woke on the floor, sore and stiff but otherwise unaffected by the injection. Sunlight blazed through the windows, casting the tan carpet in shades of gold.

Food.

It was my only thought—the only purpose I could concentrate on. I'd never before been so famished.

The raid on the refrigerator was legendary. My strict dietary plan was forgotten in that instant, and before I'd sated the hunger I'd cleared nearly two shelves. There was no counting calories, no monitoring protein levels. It was all fair game and I the hunter.

Once I filled my belly, I felt better than I had in years. I've never been lazy, but the energy was phenomenal. And for the first time in months, I felt confident that the plateau would be erased.

The trip to the gym was ecstasy, each lift a revelation. My body burned with pleasure, demanding more. I obliged, until finally the manager told me they were closing for the night. I drove home, shuddering. My body felt alive—each muscle and tendon singing in harmony.

I gave in to the urge as soon as I woke the next morning and climbed onto the scale. It announced two hundred forty-nine and I nearly screamed with joy. The ceiling was broken. The plateau nothing but a runway I'd used to sail off of, upward toward that mythical number. That magical goal.

The hunger was nowhere as profound as it had been, and I let myself go back to my diet plan. I knew it was pure muscle I'd added—there was no doubt that the calories from my buffet the day before had been burned away by my workout.

The next trip to the gym was no less a marvel, though this time the initial amazement had diminished. It gave my mind time to wander, to remember.

Two questions bored into my brain, blossoming wider the more I thought about them.

What had happened in that room?—the first and obvious one. A sacrifice? Whether financial or physical, spiritual or scientific, a trade had been made.

The second hinged on the question Mark had asked me during that initial phone call—*Do you have someone close to you? A brother?*

Would people actually trade those they loved for some promise within a syringe?

If so, and if these were the rewards from a dog ... what would it be like if a human was offered up in that sacrificial room?

It took will power, but I left the gym early that evening and went home. I logged back into the classified web site and started searching other listings.

I found the one I'd responded to easily enough, with a dozen more.

Plastic surgery results without the surgery! Roll back the years!
Escape the clutches of cancer without medicine or surgery!
Rebuild your self-esteem in days!
Enlarge your penis—no pumps, pills, or exercises!
Lose weight without dieting or exercising! Real results, real fast!

And more, all of them followed by the same local number.

If that's what you really, truly want. Mark had said. *You'll get what you want.*

My mouth was dry, my brain reeling with excitement. He offered perfection in all its forms. A chance to become glory incarnate, beauty made flesh. For a price, but what didn't have one attached to it these days?

I drove back to the mouth of the subdivision Mark lived in. I found a strip mall about a mile from the house and left my car there. I was still in gym clothes, so I wouldn't look out of place as a jogger.

I can run a mile in just under six minutes, but I kept my pace slow and Mark's house came into view as the sun began to fall. I ran past until night had taken hold of the world and then doubled back. The darkness enveloped me and I crept around the corner of his house, well in the shadows.

I waited until after midnight, when the lights inside the house had switched off, before I gave up.

The days went like that for a week. Each evening after my workout I'd make my way to the house and hide, waiting and hoping for some other soul in search of salvation.

On the ninth day, one came.

She was middle-aged, pretty but not beautiful. Her thick lips and upturned eyes proclaimed her affection for cosmetic surgery. Nothing to be ashamed of, in my opinion. If surgery can help you look and feel better, why not? But it wasn't as kind to her as it could have been. It was obvious. A good surgeon will do work you'd never be able to pick out of a crowd. I know. I bought Rhonda a lot of work and she left looking far better than when we'd met.

The man that she brought into the house must have been close to ninety. Frail, hunched over from the weight of life itself, a walker leading him into the house. I wondered if he knew he was making his final march, if he'd volunteered his last days to help the woman or if he was ignorant of what lay inside for him. Her father? Grandfather? Some poor old bastard she'd wooed with her fake tits and plastic smile?

I listened as their movements thumped and creaked and groaned through the house. I circled to the rear and found the room I'd made the deal in. Mark apparently cared little for privacy. The windows weren't curtained and I could see him at his desk, talking to the mismatched pair across from him.

The conversation was short. The woman slid a stack of bills across the table, no envelope. It looked much thinner than my own had been. But of course, she'd brought a bigger prize.

Mark stood and led the man back out of the room. The old man followed willingly.

I tried to follow them as well, tracking them back along the rear wall of the home. I found what I was looking for as I rounded the corner. A window, painted black except for a few flaking spots near its bottom. The paint had begun to chip away there and, while it was barely more than a pinhole, I could see the room inside when I pressed my eye tight against it.

A large room, probably a master bedroom at one time, lay within. It was sparsely decorated or furnished; a half dozen cages of various sizes sat against the far wall, while the center of the room held a large oval drawn on the bare wooden floor. Around the oval was a series of symbols and letters, each so peculiar I couldn't even begin to fathom just what they meant or symbolized. To one side of the oval, a table held a thick tome and an electric device that looked like a mixing board in a recording studio. A table on the other side of the oval held a bastardized lab device. A glass funnel protruded out of the table and just over the edge of the oval, its furthest extremity supported by a steel rod set in the ground. The funnel narrowed quickly, its tip ending over a small rack on the table. The rack held syringes, their plungers removed. Ready to be filled.

Mark was positioning the old man in the center of the oval, whispering into his ear as he did so.

The frail old man teetered there, almost fell, and then righted himself as Mark went to the tome and switched on the machine. Immediately the man went rigid.

I felt it outside, too. The same sensation as before, only much more intense now that only a thin sheet of glass separated me from it. Mark was reading from the book, but I couldn't hear him. The air warbled, like a thin sheet of metal caught in the wind. The rushing of air was starting to come as well, along with the metallic odor.

I had to fight the urge to remove my eye from the hole. The sensations were overwhelming, making me want to vomit.

But inside, the show was beginning.

The ceiling of the room changed, shifted, began to dance. It rolled like ocean waves, a square body of water barely held in check by the walls. It darkened in places, grew brighter in others. Colors pitched and swirled and oozed like a massive lava lamp designed to defy the laws of physics.

It was more than a color show, however. Behind the nebulas and vortexes there was something else. Something organic. Huge.

The sliding shapes made it impossible to see it all at once, and as each part appeared it seemed to recede, then return, closer then further away, here then gone, obscured then revealed.

It squirmed and writhed, a single body made up from many.

Snouts and fangs, claw and tentacle. Hair and scale, skin and slime.

Legion.

Glory.

Alpha and Omega.

The old man's screams cut through the din and his body snapped backward, nearly folded in half. It rose up off the floor, suspended by some unseen force, and then began to spasm.

He fell to pieces. His skin and tissue came off in chunks, tendons popping and veins drooping like ropes of spaghetti. Organs shook free from their mortal imprisonment, a kidney here, a liver there. Bones splintered and shattered into powder and fragments. The blood rained a crimson monsoon, but not a drop of it reached the floor. Nothing did. Each atom of his being was sucked up into the nightmare kaleidoscope above. Each bit of flesh that found freedom from the old man's body was absorbed into its new home in that fabulous beyond.

The sacrifice claimed, the infinite being became harder to spot. The nebulas spread, blotting out the view and turning the ceiling into a rippling, black pool.

From that impossible surface salvation began to flow. A stream of black liquid dribbled from the ceiling into the funnel and rolled down into the syringe waiting below.

The blackness shuddered, the liquid slowed to a drip, and then the world righted itself.

Mark turned off the machine, bowed his head in some kind of prayer, and then took the syringe, reinserting the plunger before he left the room.

My ears popped; the dizzy-sick feeling subsided. But my mind and body were coursing with adrenaline. With excitement.

I'd witnessed a miracle. In fact, I was a part of that miracle. It coursed in my veins. Beat inside my heart.

But I could have more.

15

Two hundred sixty-five? It was a fool's dream when there was so much more potential to be tapped here.

The path to perfection lay before me.

I had only to follow it.

The woman left five minutes later, a smile stretched across her face and a syringe of perfection in her hand.

The lights inside went out fifteen minutes later.

I waited an hour to make sure he was asleep. It was hard to be patient, but necessary. He'd already said that he didn't sleep much. Which meant he was probably in there somewhere, awake. Staring at the walls. Thinking of the miracle he had dominion over.

The door was the problem. He locked it. Windows, too. It's a habit that everyone has, but the fact is that if someone wants inside your house, they'll get in.

And I wanted in pale, sickly looking Mark's house.

I opted for the window in his office. I knew I was strong enough to kick in the door no matter what type of lock was on it. But the noise would be tremendous. There would be no questioning what he'd heard. With the window, there would still be a lingering "what if" in his mind. A hesitation. A doubt.

And I needed him to have that tiny doubt.

I wrapped my hand in my shirt and punched through the glass, then undid the lock, climbed into the room, and hurried across to the door. It took no more than thirty seconds, but before I'd reached my post I heard soft footsteps and saw distant light spill beneath the door into the office.

The next minutes stretched into hours. I heard him in the hallway; saw his shadow dance in the glow on the floor. Heard the doorknob twist and watched as the door swung open. It stopped inches from me, concealing me behind it.

Through the crack in the door, I watched him enter the office slowly, the gun out in front of him as if he were clutching a cross before a vampire's attack. I waited for him to switch on the light, to step into the room, to see the open window.

Then I was on him before he had time to react. My left arm wrapped around his head, enveloping him in the muscle. I squeezed tight, cutting off the air. My right arm grabbed his wrist and twisted.

The bone snapped almost at once and the gun dropped to the carpet. I could feel him try to scream against my arm.

I waited for him to stop his feeble struggle. It was a short wait. When his body went limp I moved my arm and gave him back his breath.

Everyone wakes up from being knocked unconscious differently. Scrawny Mark didn't do it peacefully. His legs twitched and he sat up with a scream, looked around with wide eyes to try to figure out where he was and what happened. As his synapses started firing off and it came rushing back to him, his pale face flushed.

We were in the sacrifice room. I'd put him into one of the larger cages on the wall and secured the closure with a lock that had been dangling from one of the others.

"What the fuck do you think you're doing?" He spat out the words.

"I'm impressed. I expected you to shit your pants as soon as you woke up. You sound pissed. Maybe you're more of a man than I thought." I gestured to the room, to the strange oval. "Not enough of a man to deserve this, but still ..."

"You're a goddamn idiot. You have no idea what this is."

"I know enough. I may be big, but I'm not stupid. I know you're wasting this chance for a few dollars."

"I'm not wasting anything."

"Look at you. You sell the chance to be perfect to anyone willing to pay. And you haven't bothered to even try to improve yourself. You're weak, emaciated, pale. Ugly. You could be a god. But you're too pathetic to even see it."

"This is beyond that."

"What is it?"

He said nothing.

"How did you find it?"

"I looked."

"These cages ... for the animals people bring?"

He shrugged.

"What is it?" I asked again.

He shook his head, smiled smugly.

"Doesn't matter." I grabbed the cage and dragged it across the floor. Once I left it in the center of the oval, his resolve shattered.

17

"Please, no. No. I'll tell you what I can. This won't work!" he was crying already, blubbering and pleading and wailing. "It won't work. Strangers barely give you anything. The person has to know them. Love them."

"But I do love you, Mark. You gave me the greatest gift in the world." I switched on the machine. It emitted a low, pulsating warble. I didn't bother with the knobs or dials.

"Please!" He cried out.

The book was in another language, one I'd never seen. I sounded out the words phonetically in my mind before I started speaking them.

"Chryu alanion Dis! Ralo U Sym Dantalion! Pepe! Pepe! Carthun Chryu alanion nu! Kesto, Kesto Dantalion! Pepe!"

It happened. The sounds and the scents and the change in the air all came at once. I sucked deep breaths to fill my lungs, trying to focus on what was happening. The room itself blurred, bent as the ceiling transformed.

Mark's screams reached a crescendo. He rattled and thrashed in the cage, trying to escape. He lay on his back and kicked at the door. The thin metal wires bent, but it was no use. Already the thing of a million faces was drifting through the display overhead.

Mark rose off the ground, touched the top of the cage, and carried it up with him. They hovered in the air for a moment, and then his screams of terror took a different timbre. They were wails of agony. The shrieks of the damned.

He flailed once, twice, and then his body went rigid. Then the convulsions took him. He came apart much like the old man had, though the cage made it worse. His body shredded itself, but the chunks were too large to escape the cage bars. He was sucked upward, his body splitting and squeezing and pressing through the bars in thin sheets. The blood had all left for the beyond while half his body remained in its confines. It twisted and crunched, a pink and white and gray mess that bore little resemblance to the scrawny, pathetic thing it had been moments earlier.

The cage crashed to the floor and the miracle above abated.

The air thickened, breaths came back to me in gulps. I fell to my knees, staring and wondering and so grateful for what I'd been given.

I checked the syringe. Half full—2.5 ccs. Not much, but a start toward something great.

The ads could stay up on the web site. Even one customer a week would be enough. They wouldn't even have to bring a loved one with them anymore, either. Not where they'd be going.

So, two hundred sixty-five would be easy to hit. And after that goal was attained, there was still so much more to change, to mold, to sculpt.

Whatever my heart's desire.

I could be the pinnacle of man.

Adonis.

Perfection.

TAUT

BY SHAUN MEEKS

It was getting cold, or at least she felt it was. Her body swayed slightly, nausea coming in and moving out in waves. Tina didn't want to throw up, what little there might be to bring up, afraid of dehydration as much as anything else. The sick feeling was a combination of a few things. No doubt, keeping her eyes closed wasn't helping anything. Yet she didn't want to open them; didn't want to face the reality before her.

The reality was, she was going to die.

Cold.

Alone.

Her back throbbed and she bit back the pain she felt rippling across her body, bile burning the back of her throat. She wanted to cry out, scream, but there was no hope. Screaming and crying wouldn't do anything but make her feel worse. There was nobody around that would hear her, so it would be useless to expend the energy.

Tina wondered how James had found this place; an old, beat-up warehouse that stood like a decaying tooth in an equally rotting mouth. From the outside, the building was something from a bad horror movie, a lost building that seemed as though it would be haunted with malicious memories and putrid souls.

When they had pulled up to it in James' old sedan, Tina looked at the place and told herself there was no way she was stepping foot into a building that undoubtedly housed rats, bugs, and one or two homeless people. Some people would look at her dreads, piercings, brandings, and surface implants and think *"A freak like her lives for places like this."* Those people, she thought, are idiots. Her body modifications didn't mean she liked the macabre; she wasn't into horror movies or shock value. Tina altered her body for spiritual reasons.

James knew that. So why he had brought her out to this warehouse close to nightfall was beyond her. He had told her he had a surprise for her, an early birthday present.

Right.

"Here we are," he said. He pulled his keys out and got out of the car. "You coming?"

"You're kidding, right?"

"Come on, T. You'll love it!"

James smirked at her, giving Tina that look that he knew melted her resolve.

Bastard.

She looked back at the building, a husk of its former self, appearing both too dark and too luminous in the fading light. Turning to look at James, she felt a trust in him that she had never felt in another, and had no idea why. He was no fairy tale, though. A string of fuck-ups led up to this moment, and he was sucking up large.

Below her now, James is only visible in parts, where the moonlight breaks through broken window, walls, and a dilapidated ceiling. What she is seeing is enough though, as his destroyed body is being visited by a family of raccoons. She sways and can hear what she is happy not to be able to fully see.

Wet sounds.

Hungry sounds.

The sounds of noisy eaters, feasting on meat; feeding on her boyfriend. Even though she can't see it, hearing the sounds, just able to make out his body jerking in and out of the shadows as the little animals tear away bits of him, would have been enough torture for her. She closes her eyes again, wishing she hadn't trusted his smile; she blames herself almost as much as she blames him. It's not like it was the first time he dragged her into a bad situation. Like the time he

22

convinced her to climb over a chain-link fence to watch the meteor shower in a clearing and they were chased by a shotgun-wielding farmer. Or like the time they went skinny-dipping in a large stagnant pond and came out covered in huge leeches. She'd never forgotten how it felt to pluck the slippery, fat bodies off her, leaving tiny little wounds behind.

Her back and legs cry out in protest, screaming at her for her stupidity. She knows her mother would tell her she deserved this, that it was her punishment for making some pretty stupid choices.

When Tina had first gotten into body modification after meeting her first boyfriend, she told Tina that she was a freak. And that had only been a lip piercing. The more she did, the worse her mother's reaction had been. She was "an abomination in the eyes of God."

Her mom didn't get it, though. Most people didn't.

The things she did to modify her body weren't about looking a certain way, and definitely weren't about fitting in with any group. It was about how they made her feel. For Tina and many others, it was a spiritual thing—a way to be pulled out of her body and see and feel things most people never do. Each new piercing, tattoo, alteration of skin and flesh brought her one step closer to something greater.

Something more.

Yet as soon as each incision was closed, or the hot pink of a brand faded and healed, came a feeling of not enough. Never enough. She began reading up on different religions and cultures that used body modification to reach spiritual enlightenment and wanted nothing more than to experience each one, to feel it for herself.

Now, hanging in the dark, her body cold and numb in places and alive with pain in others, she sways over the partially devoured body of her greatest love, contemplating the cost of her lust for hooks.

James had known about her obsession with enlightenment, had joined her on many of the same paths. But there was one thing she had been seeking, one that seemed to be the ultimate release. It was so attractive in that it seemed impossible to achieve. Her body, she was sure, could do it. But it was pretty hard to find people who knew how in this little town.

Then, fast forward to the dirty warehouse and the "surprise" he had waiting for her. "Oh my god!" Tina gasped, standing in the open doorway of the old building. "How the hell did you set this up?" She was already forgetting the state of the building's exterior, now that she could see the guts.

"I take it you like?"

"What do you think?"

The interior of the building was a shock; almost medically clean, the smell of bleach still strong in the air. It wasn't perfect; there were holes in some of the outer walls, smashed windows, and spots missing out of the ceiling. But otherwise, it was cleaner than she could have imagined, as though an army of Molly Maids had stormed in and performed their magic.

It wasn't the cleanliness that amazed her, though. It was the apparatus and gear in the middle of the room that she was focused on. It was her dream come true.

"Now, I set up a small generator here, too, but it won't last long. We won't really need it too much anyway, T. This will be your first time, so I don't think it will be a long one."

"Who's setting me up?"

"I am."

Tina had raised her eyebrow at that. James was deep into modifications himself, but she knew he'd never performed any before. Especially not something this complicated.

Below her, as James continues to be eaten, chewed on by the shadowy animals, she tells herself that she should have listened to her own reason, knowing that James was a complete novice. Totally untrained. She wishes the stink of bleach, the wet sounds below, and the throbbing in her back would just go away. As she grits her teeth, biting back at the bursts of red-hot pain exploding across her flesh, she shifts to try to bring relief. It's no use. And it wouldn't be an issue if she hadn't been so damned excited about what James had done for her.

"I've been reading up on this and checked out some videos and documentaries. I even did some messaging to make sure I don't dick it up on you, T. Trust me; this is going to be amazing."

She had smiled at him, walking over to the set-up, admiring the amount of work he had put into it all, which he begun to explain. "Cleaned it all myself. That alone took over eight hours, and you know how much I love to clean."

"Yeah, right!"

24

"Exactly. So everything after that was a cakewalk. The main chain and crank was easy enough, but I had to climb all the way up to that beam to set it."

She looked up as James pointed out the "I" beam close to the ceiling, nearly forty feet up. "When we get going, you can go as low as you want, or just below that. You'll know what feels right."

"I want to feel like I'm flying. I want to feel so free!"

She looked at the rest of it—the cords, the frame, and the hooks. There were ten in all—six thick ones for her back and four thinner ones, two for each leg. When it came to suspensions, the hooks scared a lot of people, but the pain was the key. Sometimes you have to push your pain threshold to its limits before you can let go and find out who you are. And there was pain, but nothing she couldn't tolerate, nothing unbearable.

She stripped down to her panties, and laid down on a tarp James had brought, beginning breathing exercises before he started.

Then the first hook pierced her back. She took a quick breath in, and then out as James pushed the point of the metal into the skin he was pinching. Tina was already so in tune with herself, so close to a peaceful state, that she was even able to hear the popping sound of the hook as it broke through the other side.

"You good?"

"Perfect."

Each hook went in.

Quick breath.

Pop!

And with each one, she felt more and more relaxed, feeling a release from the world around her. The warehouse began to fade around her, as though it was set on a dimmer switch. The only sounds she could hear were James, her own breath and heartbeat, and that of the hooks going in.

She could sense how close she was to that place she had always sought, her personal Nirvana. After the last hook was in, she stretched her arms out and waited.

"I'll go slow. Tell me when you're ready for me to stop."

Tina said nothing, but gave him small nod, not wanting to lose her headspace. She heard the crank turning, took in a deep breath, then almost forgot to let it out again. Never in her life had she felt what she had at that moment. Her bond with the earth was suddenly gone, like an umbilical cord being cut; she was free of the womb that once held her and kept her safe.

She was flying.

She was free.

Tina was everything and nothing all at once.

Around her, everything became instantly silent and dark, her mind totally absorbed in the moment. She felt the pain as she rose in the air, but only so much as someone is aware there are other planets or galaxies above them. To her, the pain became her air; a tool of necessity to get beyond the physical.

She closed her eyes, began to breathe meditatively and flew on her physical and spiritual plane.

It was glorious.

Then, suddenly, the feeling was lost.

"Shit!"

Tina opened her eyes and she looked down at James, fifteen feet below, standing at the crank and looking pissed off.

"What is it?"

"Something is wrong. You're jammed. Damn it!" He looked up and the problem was clear. "Looks like there's something wrong up top. If you want higher, I have to clear it."

"Make it fast!" Tina called out and bit back laughter. Her body was filling with endorphins and she was feeling a huge natural high. Light-headed and giddy, the pain was evaporating.

"I'll try."

Tina's body hummed with an electricity she'd never felt in her life. Each nerve ending seemed to pulse, to throb with its own pleasant heartbeat, slowly moving toward a unison that she knew would be the final key to finding her true self.

Throb. Throb. Throb. Throb. Throb. *Close.*

She could sense it, feel and see in her mind's eye, her dream coming true. Her own inner heaven was about to be seen.

Then, James screamed.

Loud and abrupt.

Her eyes shot open in time to see her boyfriend of three years, the man she loved and trusted—hit the concrete almost directly below her.

THE HUNGER ARTIST

BY LISA MANNETTI

"The ultimate effects of starvation are identical whether the process be gradual or rapid, occupying days or years, and death results when the body has lost six tenths of its weight."
~William Gillman Thompson, 1905

"Many serial killers are pathological liars."
~Dr. Jack. Levin, Criminologist,
Northeastern University, 2012

1973

All this time and there were still the dreams. Iva heard the wind soughing in the pines, heard the pines themselves creaking, listing like shipboard masts when they swayed. It was summer, but it was terribly cold; the damp that settled on everything—tables and blankets and floorboards and skin—fled inward to her bones. There was never any moon lighting up these dreadful nightscapes, but she always saw her sister, Callie, standing barefoot by the lake, white gown plastered against the skeletonized frame of her body, hands rapidly opening and closing like a pair of gobbling beaks.

"I'm hungry, Iva," she mourned. "I'm so cold and so hungry."

And it was always a shock when Iva went toward her, and—moonlight or no—underneath the white cotton gown, she could clearly see and count her sister's ribs.

Then Iva would wake shivering under the hospital blanket. Sometimes she rang for the nurse; sometimes it was enough to turn on the lamp and watch her fingers pinching the healthy flesh of her own hip or arm. Knowledge—certainty—that she was no longer the prisoner starving in the New England woods sixty years ago was balm that warmed her—to a point. Nothing, no one could soothe her completely; after all, her beloved Callie was dead.

Everything had gone wrong back then; two years that Iva still envisioned as a meager handful of dull, feathery ashes. No gust or exhalation ever stirred or scattered them. Sometimes she might forget the hideous physical ordeal when scenes from the trial intruded on her consciousness. Sometimes, recalling the shame and the heart-pounding fear that surrounded the weeks in court—when she was afraid Gretchen Burkehart would be acquitted and win—upset her equilibrium so badly, that visions of her own suffering and Callie's extremis seemed almost benign by contrast. Both events were terrible. And the memories that were ashes lay eternally unmoving in her palm, she thought, because one day when they laid out her body (her elbows crooked, snugged to her waist, her hands crossed) they'd be pressed against her heart: that had been burnt past charring, too, during those black, seemingly endless two years. Ashes to ashes.

1912

"Just tell us in your own words, Miss Fredericks ..." Thomas Vining began, one hand gently curving the rail in front of the witness box—as if just by standing close to Iva the prosecutor could steady her nerves.

She swallowed, but there was no spittle to moisten her throat and her voice was thin. "I saw an ad in one of the Boston papers for what sounded like a wonderful rest cure. Callie—she—maybe I indulged her too much, but she was my baby sister and our parents were dead; Callie was only twelve when Mother died, still a little girl ..."

1973

"Is that you, Maggie?" Iva turtled (her breasts had shrunk to the point where they were no longer an inconvenience), smoothly rolling onto her back to look up at the face of a young woman whose hand lightly skimmed her own. "No, of course not," she said, "Margaret was twenty years older than I am and she's been dead a long time. And your skin is soft ..." Iva paused, aware that she was looking at short brown hair, asymmetrically cut. Bareheaded. No cap. Instead of crisp whites, a peasant blouse. "You're not a nurse."

"Jill Davis. I'm a reporter. Well, a stringer, really."

"Come to unravel something?"

"A stringer is a sort of freelance journalist—"

"My dear. I'm merely old, not ignorant."

"Of course. I meant ..." She stopped, cheeks reddening.

In the brief silence that ensued, Iva pressed the electric button near her right hand and the top third of the bed glided upward until she was sitting, and now she could see the girl was wearing blue jeans. Sandals. Every year since she'd turned 99, about a week before her birthday the local paper sent someone to interview the oldest woman in Melton Lake. When she hit a hundred, there'd been articles written up in *The Portsmouth Herald*, *The Manchester Union Leader*—even *The Boston Globe*. But an old woman was old news, she guessed. So here was this hippie—this *stringer*—to ask the same tedious questions about whether she drank liquor (a weak champagne cocktail at five p.m., a glass of wine with dinner), smoked cigarettes, (only when she could cadge one; these days, alas, they gave her indigestion); exercised (absolutely—on warm days she pushed a wheelchair in front of her and walked to that pathetic little fountain out back, then sat and read a book in the sunshine—and that was surely exercise aplenty when you hit one hundred two); what she ate (anything that didn't hurt her teeth when she chewed); what she did for amusement (the main thing was avoiding the nursing home's idea of arts and crafts which consisted of gluing a mirror in the center of a paper plate, cementing macaroni around the rim, then spray-painting the whole shebang gold and attaching string to hang the monstrosity); and most importantly what did she—Iva Fredericks—believe was the secret behind achieving her great age?

But Jill Davis surprised her.

"I'm supposed to be writing a spec piece for the *Millerton Record* about the root causes of anorexia; and then, you know, throw in some historical background about turn-of-the-century fasting girls, tie it into new trends in teenage fad dieting—but the feature editor over there has about as much imagination as a humphead wrasse. I did some digging, read about the trial back in 1912 and—"

"And I guess you found out the term aphorism is a complete misnomer," Iva said. Jill pulled out a pack of Tarreyton 100s, extending it toward the old woman, and Iva took one. Jill lit them both. Iva dragged on hers but merely let the smoke roll around her mouth briefly before she exhaled. "Truth is hard to come by, lies are easy. Maybe I wasn't 'too rich'—but I was definitely 'too thin.'"

Jill nodded, absently blowing tarnished gray smoke downward toward the steno pad perched on her knee. Iva caught the wink of a small gold ring on the pinky of the hand the reporter used to rapidly flip through what must have been fifty pages of notes in tiny, precise handwriting. "There's something missing. I must've read a thousand damn articles on microfiche *and* the court transcript, and the story's out of whack—completely off-kilter." Her eyes were ink-colored and Iva saw herself haloed inside their hard, bright shine. "And that's before you take into account that despite the murder charge, Gretchen Burkehart was convicted only of manslaughter, before you consider that she was pardoned by the governor and that she only served two years out of twenty."

Jill had wheeled Iva's chair outside to the grounds of the small, old-fashioned hospital, while Iva clung to the younger woman's arm and ambled slowly alongside before sitting down where they'd parked under a huge maple.

"What's missing," Iva said, "was stricken from the official record."

"Well, I just assumed *that* naturally; but what's really goddamn odd is that usually you can get a whiff of what happened or what was said from books or newspapers—especially contemporary newspapers."

Iva shook her head. "Money can buy a lot, Jill. A lot more than someone your age truly realizes. I paid—or, rather, through me my lawyer paid—a great deal to keep the details you so cleverly inferred from showing up anywhere—"

"Bullshit."

"Did you know that after Lizzie Borden's trial, Lizzie bought up the entire edition—the entire printing run of thousands of copies, that is—of a book called *The Fall River Tragedy*? Lizzie was rich, but I had a great deal more money than she had." Iva saw Jill's gaze n arrow and she could read that the younger woman was considering the idea. *Local scribes, okay, no problem. Guys who, back in 1912, earned maybe ten bucks a week and were probably bought off regularly by hometown politicians for a few beers, a whiskey, a good meal; but what about reporters from Boston or New York? Could she have scuttled them, too? She had the means, though ... not to mention the Wren county prosecutor said there wasn't enough money to go to trial, so Iva picked up the tab.*

"So what was the big, deep, dark secret you suppressed, Iva?"

"It's very easy to grind someone into submission when you're starving them," Iva said. "And it's even easier to hem them in if you convince them—if they believe—you have occult power."

1912

"Miss Fredericks, can you tell us about this picture?" Vining asked, handing it to her.

"That's a picture of me and Maggie. Margaret Woodbridge. When Callie and I were growing up, Maggie was our nursemaid, and even after we were adults she stayed on with us. She was like a second mother, really. And ..."

The photo had been taken a few weeks after Maggie had come all the way from Australia to rescue her and Callie. The telegram. Callie sent it—somehow sneaked it out of the filthy cabin they shared at Lakemere Rest Sanitarium. Maggie, bless her, had sailed immediately, but she wasn't in time, because Callie's weight had dropped to 40 pounds. Iva felt her face flush. Is that what *she* looked like almost a month *after* Maggie had taken her away from that terrible place?

Her face was nothing more than a skull thinly layered with dark flesh. The eyes themselves were vacant, glittering; her gaze, empty—as if impossibly remote and infinitesimally tiny stars had been caught inside the deeps of her eye sockets and flickered there indifferently ... meaninglessly. Her cheeks were smudged hollows with the sere look of ancient parchment. Her pale hair lay in knotty clumps, barely concealing huge bald patches. Her starched dress—size four—had been pinned, but it was still so oversized it appeared as if it might fall from her slight frame the instant she stood up.

Vining passed it to the jurors and Iva could see them cringe with revulsion. Looking at the picture was like looking at a ravaged mummy that had been spelled back to half-life. Worst of all, Iva clearly remembered how she carefully primped—so she'd look her best.

His voice startled her. "Miss Fredericks, how did you come to be in this condition? In this photo you weighed sixty-eight pounds—not kilos, *pounds*. And before you began "treatment" with Mrs. Burkehart, your weight—completely normal for someone who stands five feet, two inches tall—was one hundred four pounds. How did it happen, Miss Fredericks?"

Iva's chest heaved, her stomach knotted, but she took a deep breath. "She advertised—the only *doctor*, she called herself—who was a licensed fasting specialist. She advertised that she'd cured everything from syphilis to ulcers to blindness. Over and over, she told us and stated in writing, 'All functional disease is the result of improper diet,'" Iva said. In her mind's eye, grim sequences and flashing images unspooled.

Callie unwrapped the pamphlet with such excitement, she tore the paper.

Iva read it, but Callie studied the damn thing and within hours of its arrival could quote whole passages verbatim. Iva knew that some of their relatives thought the girls had too much money and too much time and that, as a result, hobbies and interests became fads with them. Aunt Caroline said as much when the girls refused meat at her table: "Being a vegetarian is a luxury—those who work for a living can't pick and choose what they eat. If you girls were shipwrecked, you'd soon enough be eating fish and fowl."

So, when they decided to take the fasting cure, they told no one.

Gretchen Burkehart professed to be uncertain about whether they were candidates for her cure. Callie told the osteopath she had a tipped uterus that caused awkward pains. Iva complained of a feeling of torpor in her limbs.

They expected massage and a carefully controlled but bracing diet that would cleanse them. They expected to be in a lakeside rest home with awning-covered balconies. They got nothing but a cup of watery broth made from canned tomatoes served twice a day and hot water enemas that lasted six hours at a time. Within a few weeks, neither of them could really walk ... they were stinking, wasted scarecrows lying on narrow cots listening to the rain patter against the metal roof of the "cabin" that was really a shed, listening to Gretchen Burkehart and her "nurses" rifle their trunks for clothes, shoes, jewelry, books—anything they could lay their hands on. But even that wasn't the worst of it ...

1973

"I know one of the medical doctors testified that you and Claire would have needed to drink fifty quarts of that broth a day—just to survive. And I'm not sure he was taking into account those enemas," Jill said. "It's pretty clear Gretchen was a klysmaphiliac—you know, someone with an obsession for enemas."

"Humiliating." Iva shook her head. "And worse was having her or one of her assistants check the contents—like someone sieving for precious metals." In her mind's eye she felt the rude shock of the rubber tube, the onrush of the hot water, heard the ugly spatter of liquid feces pouring into an enamel pail.

"In her books, she called them 'enemata'—trying to sound high-flown," Iva shrugged. "And you're spot on about her obsession, because people who are starving have chronic diarrhea."

"What about the other symptoms?" Jill asked.

Iva looked up at the canopy of leaves over her head. "Funny how your mind plays tricks. Sometimes I could only notice what was happening when I looked at Callie—as if the same things weren't happening to me. The hair is pouring off your head, but you grow a kind of thin fur over your body—"

"Lanugo," Jill said. "I read about that. Survival at its most basic, the body's attempt to stay warm."

"I drooled all the time, but I couldn't chew," Iva said. For a moment she put her hands over her face. "My God, it was awful ... cried all the time because I wanted to eat and I couldn't."

"This was after Margaret came from Australia, after Callie died?"

"Some part of me saw how much worse it was for Callie—when she lay on her back, the bones of her spine could be seen through her abdomen. I doubted I'd actually seen it; I looked a long time—years and years—before I found a picture that showed how someone's spine *could* be visible when they lay face up. You know where I finally found it? In a book that showed piles of corpses in Auschwitz." Iva winced. "My sister. She was like a carcass that's been picked clean by scavenger birds."

1912

Gretchen Burkehart was going to take the stand that day and because she and Maggie might be called as rebuttal witnesses, naturally they weren't allowed in open court, but there were pictures in the newspaper and the prosecutor would be telling them about her testimony. The accused wore an elegant narrow-waisted brown merino dress with a high lattice collar, and a huge hat cascading with pheasant feathers that was straight out of the most recent edition of *Ladies' Home Journal*. Undoubtedly, Iva remarked drily, the money for the fancy togs had come from Gretchen's depredations on Iva's own bank account. By then, both Iva and Maggie knew not only that Callie wasn't Mrs. Burkehart's first victim, but that she'd managed to seize assets — jewelry, valuables, and property—from other patients she'd killed as well. Hell, it turned out the land for Lakemere Sanitarium came from one of her former patients.

On direct testimony, with her lawyer jollying her along, Gretchen wove a charming tale fraught with outright lies.

"The tomato broth was merely a hot drink between meals. The Fredericks were allowed *all* the food they wanted to eat. But they refused everything my nurses cooked for them," she began. "It was very sad, but then, you know Callie told me other doctors had given up hope on her case, so she and Iva came to me as a last resort," she said. Nearby, artists sketched her face, the fluttering feathers on her hat, and the fan she coyly flashed at dramatic moments.

Callie, she declared, had absolutely given all the jewelry to Gretchen and the nurses as gifts. Callie had known she was dying, and appointed Gretchen as Iva's guardian because Iva was insane —and had been deteriorating mentally for several years. Callie had not died of starvation—but from an organic colonic disease that originated in her childhood and, according to Gretchen Burkehart, nothing and no one could have saved the young woman.

"In fact, Callie was so grateful for the fact that I prolonged her life beyond what was expected, she changed her will."

Pens flew across reporters' notepads; the court reporter's typewriter beat the rhythm the scratching nibs kept time to. Gretchen Burkehart appeared calm, but even the reporters could see that as her testimony was drawing to a close, more and more frequently she glanced over at the prosecutor—and he was clearly itching to take her to task.

"Mrs. Burkehart," Vining said.

"*Doctor*—" Gretchen interrupted. "I prefer to be called doctor."

"You have no medical degree, *Mrs.* Burkehart," the prosecutor said. His smile was knife-thin and everyone knew he was about to tear her to shreds.

1973

"All right," Jill said, "I know Vining got a graphologist—a handwriting expert—who proved that Burkehart was full of shit. Callie never wrote that codicil to her will; Gretchen Burkehart did. And he brought in experts who testified about her other cases—not once when she performed the autopsy on one of her patients did she list starvation as the cause of death. It was always some half-assed diagnosis like paralyzed intestines—but plenty of other doctors completely contradicted her—her and her paid stooges. Those so-called nurses who backed her up."

"There was only one who slipped—and it was her testimony that was expunged from the record," Iva said. "There's a hint about Gretchen Burkehart's power over people in what Maggie said, too. She told the court that even though she knew the tomato broth was made from canned goods, Gretchen actually convinced *her* at times that everything was farm fresh ... that the tomatoes had been raised locally—not purchased at some market—and therefore each serving had even *more* nutrients. That was impossible, of course. Tomatoes can't be harvested before the end of August in New Hampshire, and we began treatment at the end of February; Callie was dead by May." She watched Jill scribble the date and went on. "There were days, Maggie said, she had to fight off what Gretchen was saying: that I was improving—had improved tremendously under her care—that Maggie *must* recall how deranged I'd been before the treatment started. How ill I'd been and that Callie had been even sicker than I was ... Maggie said she made herself remember that Gretchen was lying through her teeth by reminding herself over and over that two other patients—also young women—begged her to take them away from Lakemere because they knew they were starving to death, and after the first ten days they were already so weak they couldn't get away on their own."

"Disgusting ... that woman was disgusting."

"Evil," Iva said. "Of course, you know that when Maggie arrived Gretchen Burkehart showed her someone else's corpse and said it was Callie." Iva herself had been too weak to make the trip to the funeral home or to the funeral—so her last memory of Callie was at her sister's deathbed; Callie's eyes starting from the sockets, her fetid breath rattling, claw-like fingers grasping a thin cotton sheet drawn over the wasted body.

Jill nodded. "Tried to foist off the wrong body on a woman who raised the girl practically from birth. That was stupid—but we know she was very smart, so what made her think she could get away with it? Was her ego that overblown? Was she drugging Maggie's tea or the broth she served you?" Jill lit a cigarette. "That'd be really rich—she detested pills so much she would've been the queen of the '60s antidrug contingent."

"Maggie wasn't the only one who thought Gretchen Burkehart had some kind of hypnotic power she could use to force people to do what was against their own better judgment."

1911

"You're looking ever so much stronger, Miss. The doctor says it won't be long now before you're up and walking!"

Iva lay on a makeshift mattress on the bathroom floor. It had once really been a mattress she thought, but maybe rats had gotten to it and now it was little more than lumpy cotton batting wadded in a nest shape and covered with oilcloth. Above her hung a pail and a rubber hose. The end of the tube was in her rectum. She no longer had the strength to stand up and evacuate, so the oilcloth served as a sluiceway that disgorged her stinking brown water into an old privy hole. Didn't have the energy to get herself to the porcelain toilet, and the doctor still insisted the enemas were crucial to her treatment. Her nurse was prattling about being able to walk—as if Iva had been wheelchair-bound for a decade. Was it only last summer that she and Callie had trekked to Mount Kilimanjaro? It was painful lying on her side. Her bones—ribs, pelvis, and knee—dug into what was left of her flesh. If only she could see Callie, but they had separated the sisters, and the nurse, Marina, said she was too weak to leave her cabin next door. Last week Marina had carried Callie—the way a child carried a doll in her arms—over in the evenings. Could Callie have gotten so much worse so quickly?

"Tub time!" Marina said. Iva wasn't sure how long she'd been lying on the floor and drifting, but at the sound of the nurse's voice, she felt herself being hoisted upward and then pushed into scalding water. She began to scream.

Gretchen Burkehart's voice boomed from the doorway. "You're not clean. Your stool is malodorous, your breath is foul. And, since you refuse to walk—"

"I don't refuse—" Iva was crying, but there were no tears; her dehydration was too extreme.

"You refuse to walk," Gretchen interrupted, "so the tub baths need to be hot." She put her own hand in briefly and Iva registered that it emerged the boiled red of shellfish—and that was merely the osteopath's hand—not her whole body. "Gordon," she directed, "add another bucket. And scrub her down, she's dirty."

"No," Iva said, feebly trying to cover her breasts. *"No!"*

1973

"Gordon Fields," Jill said, nodding. "He and his girlfriend, Marina Slade—the so-called nurse—both testified that he only lugged water to the cabin, that he was just a hired hand and never in the room when either you or Callie were given those baths—or the enemas."

"He and Marina were both Spiritualists."

"They don't sound very spiritual to me."

"I'm not sure you understand." Iva shook her head. "Give me another cigarette ... and damn, is it almost five o'clock? I'd like a drink before I tell you about what happened next."

Jill looked up at the slanting sun, shielding her eyes, and then glanced down at her watch. "It's been five o'clock across the pond for at least five hours. Close enough for me." She opened a brightly striped wool shoulder bag she used as a tote and pulled out a mayonnaise jar she'd filled with Almaden wine. "Look, it's not the greatest and I don't have glasses. I planned on snatching a couple from the hospital cafeteria."

"A lady knows when to forego niceties. Hand it over." Iva swigged, wiped her mouth with the back of her wrist, and passed the jar to Jill.

"If anyone—curious or otherwise—comes over here, this is a urine sample I'm bringing to *my* doctor," Jill said. "So don't get caught swilling."

They both began to laugh.

1911

"It's very simple," Gretchen Burkehart said. "Marina is not only a nurse, she's a talented medium. You'd be helping Callie, of course. She's still grieving for your mother and she'll be stronger emotionally. It may be her best chance at getting well."

Iva looked at her sister, blade-thin, propped on pillows and seated at a small, round table between Marina and Gretchen. Gordon Fields sat opposite. In the center of the table, a pair of slates—like the ones used by school children—had been hinged together. Just now they were lying open with a piece of ordinary white chalk lying on the one on the right.

"Let's try. Please, Iva?"

There was nothing to lose—or so Iva thought.

Gordon Fields closed the slates and latched them shut.

The lights were extinguished and Marina admonished them not to be frightened and to keep holding hands. She recited a prayer and asked Rose Fredericks if she would come and make herself known to her daughters. A long while passed and then suddenly, in the pitch black, the sound of scratching on the slates could be heard.

1973

"When they lit the candles, Callie opened the slates and the words *Flower Girls: Calla and Ivy* were written in chalk. My mother called us her flower girls," Iva said.

She motioned for the jar of wine and Jill handed it to her saying, "I drank ninety percent of this. There's only a sip left; go ahead and finish it." Iva nodded. "Go on," Jill said.

"After that, that's when I started seeing Marina wearing Callie's silk robe, and Gretchen wearing a diamond ring that had belonged to Mother."

"Do you think Callie told them—even accidentally?"

"I think one of them found those words written in Callie's red leather diary. It was one of the things that was gone. Even Maggie couldn't find it."

"So they tricked her into thinking your mother was there and communicating."

"Oh yes—all the usual japes and shenanigans. From trumpets floating in the air, to ectoplasm, to more and more detailed messages written on the slates."

"Did you believe it was real, Iva?"

"I was out of my mind with hunger, cold, and fear."

"Did you think it was your mother?"

"I was certain Callie came back to me."

Jill flipped through her notebook and read, "In 1926, Harry Houdini wrote, 'Distressed relatives catch at the least word which may remotely indicate that the Spirit which they seek is in communication with them. One little sign even, which appeals to their waiting imagination, shatters all ordinary caution and they are converted.' Is that what happened to you?"

Iva lowered her eyes and shook her head.

Callie. The dreams. Callie barefoot by the lake, shuddering with cold. "I'm hungry, Iva." She mourns. "I'm so cold and so hungry."

"But you know that Gretchen Burkehart stole from you and others—she took money and jewelry, property. You know that she killed many, many patients—ten or fifteen others. She was arrested for practicing medicine without a license even after she served time for murdering Callie."

Iva gave a thin smile. "Maggie told me those same things—over and over—all the rest of her life. Callie was starved to death, and I was nearly dead—but I'm still alive. I'm one hundred two and still alive because Callie has never left my side."

44

SKIN DEEP

BY CARSON BUCKINGHAM

It all began innocently enough with the removal of a single unsightly wart.

Lucinda Parker had been begging her mother for years to take her to someone who could get rid of "the immense-by-any-standards" growth next to her nose.

"Mother, it looks like I have three nostrils," she would wail, and her long-suffering parent would then give her the same, half-listening broken record response, "When you're older."

To which Lucinda's broken-record rejoinder was, "I'll never be 'older' because I'll kill myself before then!" This was invariably followed by stomping down the hallway and slamming her bedroom door—often more than once.

"The difficult years have arrived," Mrs. Parker could be heard to mutter as she dried another dish.

The difficult years. Lucinda was twelve. She had had exactly one menstrual cycle, thirty-two (she counted them) pubic hairs, and one training bra which she wore night and day. She was already shaving her underarms and legs, though not out of necessity, and was experimenting with make-up. Her best effort to date made her look, if you squinted, like Lady Gaga; her biggest failure, a cross between Alice Cooper and Tammy Faye Bakker.

The hairstyles are not to be mentioned, much less discussed.

In short, Lucinda felt that she was now a Grade-A, one hundred percent woman, and she wanted the perks that went with it; but before they could even begin to kick in, she had to do something about her face.

Everything would be perfect if I could only get rid of this tumor next to my nose. It dwarfs the Empire State Building, for cryin' out loud!

Mr. and Mrs. Parker remained unconcerned for most of that year, chalking their daughter's antics up to number one, a phase, and number two, hormones.

However, as Lucinda's thirteenth birthday neared, things shifted dramatically.

"Lucinda, it's Saturday night. Why don't you go out to the movies with your friends?" Mrs. Parker asked.

Her daughter looked up from her copy of "Marie Claire" and rolled her eyes. "I don't have any friends."

"Oh nonsense. Of course you do! Call one and go out—my treat."

Lucinda sighed and picked up the phone.

Ten minutes later, there was a soft knock at the front door.

"Must be Lu's friend," Mr. Parker muttered behind his newspaper.

Mrs. Parker, ever cautious, glanced into the peephole. "There's nobody there, George."

"Damned kids. You'd better see if they left a bag full of dog crap on the stoop, hoping that you'll step on it."

"George Parker, *really*!"

"We did it when I was a kid. Doubt things have changed all that much."

"Haven't," Lucinda said, walking in. "Except now they set fire to it to make sure you step on it."

"How charming," Mrs. Parker said. The word "disgust" could have actually appeared across her forehead and no one would have been surprised.

"Aren't you going to open the door?" Lucinda asked.

"There's no one there."

"Sure there is." She swung open the door and there stood six-year-old Charlie Foley from next door. He was so small that he didn't show up in the peephole.

46

"Oh, I'm sorry to keep you waiting out there, Charlie," Mrs. Parker said. "Does your mother need something? Eggs? Sugar?"

"No, m'am. I'm here fer Lucinda. We're goin' on a ... uh ... what was it again?" he asked Lucinda.

"A 'date,' Charlie."

"Thassit! A date. Whassa 'date,' Mrs. Parker?"

Eleanor Parker was too flummoxed to reply. George Parker, on the other hand, was laughing quietly behind the sports section—you could tell because the paper was shaking.

"Charlie, a 'date' is when we go to the movies and stuff ourselves with popcorn and candy and soda!" Lucinda said, tickling his tummy. She would have tousled his hair, but in honor of the occasion, it was so plastered down that she was afraid she'd stick to it.

Mrs. Parker turned to her daughter. "May I see you in the kitchen, Lucinda? Oh, and *do* come in, Charlie. You can have a nice chat with Mr. Parker. We won't be a moment."

Mr. Parker sighed, folded his paper, shot the missus a dagger-filled look, then put a smile on his face and turned to their little guest.

Once in the kitchen, Lucinda's mother rounded on her. "What are you trying to prove, Lucinda?" she hissed. "Do you think you're funny?"

"No, just funny-looking."

"What?"

"I don't *have* any friends my own age, Mom. I keep trying to tell you that—and it's all because of this ... this ... whatever it is on my face!"

"But why Charlie?"

"He's too young to care about how I look. He just cares that I like him and treat him nice. He's the only real friend I have. We were walking home from school the other day and one of the football players called me 'the Wicked Witch of the West.' Well, Charlie ran right up to him and started punching his leg." Lucinda smiled, tears welling up at the memory. "It was as high as he could reach, Mom, but he did it without a second thought. He did it for me. That linebacker could have made him into a stain on the sidewalk, but Charlie didn't care. So, yes, Mom, I'm going to the movies with Charlie Foley, my little knight in shining armor and red Velcro sneakers. Are you driving us, or is Dad?" Before her mother could reply, Lucinda dried her eyes and left the room.

Mrs. Parker was floored. "I had no idea things were as bad as that," she murmured before joining everyone in the living room.

Mr. Parker looked up, an expression of wonder on his face. "Eleanor, this little guy knows more about the Yankees than I ever did—every stat on every player! A fine young man ... just fine." He reached over to tousle Charlie's hair, thought better of it, and settled for a manly pat on the back.

"I brought all my saved 'lowance, Lu, and I'm gonna buy you a humongous bagga popcorn—all by myself!" Charlie was really good at saving his money—even at age six. He had big plans, that one; but he understood the importance of gratitude, as well, and it didn't take a chain saw to get him to part with some cash when it was appropriate.

Lucinda kissed Charlie on the cheek. She knew how hard he worked for that fifty cents a week—it wasn't just handed to him. "You are the sweetest man in the world, Charlie Foley, but my mom's paying tonight. Save your money, kiddo. Someday I'll want a car ... or maybe an elephant."

"Or a giraffe?" Charlie giggled.

"Nope, no giraffe. Costs too much when they get a sore throat."

"What are you two going to see tonight?" Mr. Parker asked.

"Oh! 'The Incredibles'! Pleeeeeeeeeeease, Lu?"

"Absolutely."

Mr. Parker stood. "I'll drive. Let's get going. Coming, dear?"

"No ... no. I think I'll stay here, thanks."

Twenty minutes later, Mr. Parker stepped back through the door, chuckling. "We had to stop next door so Charlie could put his bag of quarters away. He's such a nice little kid—no wonder Lu likes to baby-sit for him. Smart, too, that one, and ... what's the matter, El?"

"I thought she was going out with Charlie to defy us or to make some obscure pre-teenage point, but she wasn't." She recapped the kitchen confrontation for him and when she was done, Mr. Parker sat back in his chair looking thoughtful; but when at last he opened his mouth to speak, it was his wife who voiced his thoughts.

Mr. Parker just smiled and nodded.

It was a glum Lucinda who sat at the table with her parents two weeks later. An angel food cake with thirteen candles blazed before her. Her loot this year consisted of an iPod and a gift certificate to download music onto it. She'd wanted just that, but nothing much seemed to make her happy anymore, and though she did her best to appear ecstatic, she knew from her parents' reaction that her attempt had fallen flat. She also knew that money was tight in the house these days and that they really didn't have cash to spare on such expensive gifts, so that added guilt to guest list of her pity party. Depression had already arrived.

She was really starting to hate birthdays.

"Now, make a wish, Lu. Make it a really good one, and I bet it comes true. Thirteen is the most magical birthday of all, or so I've heard," Mr. Parker said.

"Dad, I'm thirteen, not three. Wishing doesn't work."

"Humor me. Close your eyes and concentrate."

Lucinda sighed as only a thirteen-year-old can, closed her eyes, wished, then blew out the candles, eyes still closed. She didn't care if she blew them all out or not, but when she opened her eyes, she saw that she had, and that there was an envelope in front of her with her name on it.

Her parents looked at each other, secrets dancing in their eyes.

She tore the envelope and out fell a rectangular card. She picked it up and looked at it, more to indulge her parents than her curiosity; but as she realized what she held, her face transformed.

It was an appointment card ... for her ... at a cosmetic surgeon's! She searched her parents' smiling faces. "Really? *Really?*"

"Yes, honey, really. Not that we don't think you're beautiful exactly the way you are; but you don't and that's what needs to change," Mrs. Parker said.

"I'd just hate to see you get so tied up with outer beauty that you lose the inner, most important beauty that you already have in spades, my little girl. Promise me you won't," Mr. Parker said.

"I promise, Daddy."

The surgery cost the Parkers close to four thousand dollars, so as an economy measure they put off replacing the old clunker that Mrs. Parker was driving. This was done not with resentment, but with love and good grace. The old car would surely limp along for another year or two until the surgical bill was paid off.

Since Lucinda's birthday was July fifteenth, she had plenty of time to recover from her surgery before returning to school, to eighth grade, in early September.

When the bandage finally came off, Lucinda looked in the mirror and couldn't believe what she saw.

She looked normal.

Actually normal.

A little pretty, even.

Possibly slightly beautiful.

She gazed at herself for over an hour.

Her face was perfect ... or would be, if it wasn't for that bump on the bridge of her nose. Now that the distraction of that Oldsmobile-size growth was gone, it was easier to notice what else needed fixing.

But it would do ... for now. At least she didn't have to hide in the house anymore, and the teasing at school, hopefully, would let up, too.

Lucinda pulled a pad and pencil out of her desk drawer, reluctantly laid the mirror aside, and made a list of the shortcomings that required repair as soon as possible:

> *Bump on nose—plane down bone*
> *Too thin lips—collagen injections to fill out*
> *Faint forehead lines—botox?*
> *Weak chin—chin implants*
> *Flat cheeks—cheek implants*
> *Moles on neck and left ear—remove*
> *Earlobes too big—reduction*
> *Hair too thin—hair implants*
> *Imperfect teeth—bright white implants necessary*
> *Laser eye surgery—get rid of glasses*
> *Bright blue contact lenses to have blue eyes*

Watching the cosmetic surgery channel for the past year had really paid off. She knew exactly what she'd need to have done, and by God, she was going to look like Heidi Klum if it was the last thing she ever did.

Now that she knew what had to be done to achieve facial perfection, she needed a plan to get there; and that plan required money and lots of it. Lucinda knew that her parents wouldn't allow her to make any major changes, so she'd have to wait until she turned eighteen for those. However, she thought she could talk them into paying for some of the minor surgery she wanted—like the mole removal and maybe the earlobe thing. Perhaps even the blue contacts that would transform her fog gray eyes. It wouldn't cost all *that* much, and her father had been talking about getting a second job anyhow; plus her mother was working at the flower shop and now doing custom sewing on the side, too, so there should be plenty of extra cash to go around.

In any case, she knew how to get her way now.

All she had to do was mope around and act suicidal and they'd shell out for sure. She could even insist on helping with the finances, and turn over all her baby-sitting money and any other money she raised. It would be so much less than the surgery would cost, but they wouldn't feel that they could turn her request down after that.

She knew them way too well.

Now the question was, outside of baby-sitting, what could she do? There was dog walking, car washing, leaf raking, and snow shoveling. She could also help around her own house more—cleaning and such— and put her parents even further in her debt.

Oh, that's a fine plan—everyone gets something out of it—especially me, Lucinda thought.

That afternoon, she launched into "Operation Operation" and biked over to every grocery store and pharmacy in town. She posted a list of jobs she could do and the prices for each, along with tear-off flaps with her phone number on them. In no time at all, she was up to her eyeballs in work.

She still didn't have any friends at school, but this time it was her choice not to. She had far too much to do to fit friends into her big picture. No, she figured that once she was perfect she'd be at least eighteen and she'd find a rich man to marry her and be set for life. After all, why play with boys when what you really wanted was a man, right? A boy can't take care of you and give you what you want.

The only thing that didn't change in her life, at least for a while, was her monthly movie "date" with Charlie, her one true friend. She'd never forget that.

Lucinda smiled, remembering Charlie's reaction when the final bandage had been removed.

He had been perplexed and said, "You don't look any diff'rint to me."

"But Charlie, don't you remember the big ugly thing that was right here?"

"Nope. I don't 'member that."

"But it was there. Don't I look beautiful now?"

"Sure, Lu. You were a'ways bootiful."

Lucinda smiled. "You'd have noticed it if you were older."

"Nah, I don't care 'bout stuff like that. All I know is when you have somethin' cut off, it means there's less of you left, and I like as much of you as can be, Lu. Maybe you should gain some weight."

Lucinda had laughed and hugged her little friend, feeling sorry for him that he was so terribly naïve about the way the world *really* worked.

Her plan went along perfectly until one chilly day in January. When she got home from baby-sitting that evening, her mother and father were sitting at the kitchen table, waiting. If their expressions were any indication, things were not looking good for her.

"Hi you guys. Hey, I have to tell you the cute thing that Mrs. Dillard's kids did. You'd have—"

"Lucinda Ruth Parker, you will take off your jacket and you will sit yourself down and explain this, please," her mother said.

No, not good at all.

Once Lucinda sat, her mother pushed her report card across the table. She stared at it and the Ds and Fs stared back. Her highest grade was a C minus, and that was for Physical Education.

"I don't understand, Lu," her father said. "It's always been As and Bs with you—and mostly As. What happened?"

"Oh, I'll tell you what happened, George. It's all this work she's been doing—running here, running there. It's no wonder her grades have slid. She doesn't have time for homework—even though she's been telling us that she's finished it every night."

"Don't talk about me like I'm not here," Lucinda said.

"Then explain, Lu," her father said.

In answer, Lucinda stood. "I'll be right back. I have to get something out of my room."

"We want an explanation, young lady."

"That's what I'm going to get, Mom."

Lucinda smiled. This couldn't have been better timed if she'd planned it for a year. She reached under her bed and drew out a chipped gray-green metal strongbox the size of a hardcover book. She opened it with the tiny key she wore around her neck, then took it back to the kitchen with her.

"Here's why," she said, handing the box to her father.

"What's this? Please tell me it's not drugs, Lu."

"Just open it."

Mr. Parker flipped open the box. Then he handed it to Mrs. Parker.

"Where did you get all this money, Lucinda?" Mrs. Parker demanded.

"From working. I know things are pinched around here financially, so I thought I'd help out. That money is for you."

They melted immediately, just like she knew they would.

"But honey," her father said, counting the cash. "There's over five hundred dollars here. You earned all that baby-sitting?"

"Sure, and doing other chores for people. It's amazing what people will pay someone else to do because they're too lazy to do it themselves. I just wanted to help you guys out, that's all. I mean, we're a family, right? And family members should help each other—at least, that's how I feel about it. So please, take the money. I don't want it."

Her father sat back in his chair. "You are one impressive girl, you know that? How many other kids would try to help out their parents like this?"

Report card forgotten. Mission accomplished.

Her mother just shook her head in wonder. "I wish we could tell you to put this money away and that we don't need it, but we really do. With Dad's hours cut at the plant and mine at the flower shop, we're a month behind on the mortgage, and this will catch us up. Are you sure about this, sweety?"

"Absolutely, Mom."

"Then thank you, love. Thank you ever so much." Her mother stood and gave her a warm hug, followed by her father.

Oh yeah, they owed her now, boy.

Over coffee, milk, and pie, a détente was reached in which Lucinda would cut back on her after-school jobs and pull her grades up where they belonged. A workable schedule was arrived at that everyone could live with, and that was the end of it.

That night in bed, Lucinda smiled, happy that her backbreaking after-school odd jobs were now over. She hated working that hard, but she had to accumulate as much money as possible quickly, because she knew that once that report card showed up, it would be coming to an end—which was the plan all along.

She'd continue to babysit Charlie and run errands for Mrs. Habbershaw, a kindly widow with six cats and one Chihuahua named Max—who was a nervous wreck—probably because the cats were all bigger than he was. Mrs. H. needed cat food and litter almost every day, and hauling that junk was hard enough work, as far as Lucinda was concerned.

She put on her depressed act for exactly one week before approaching her parents about the blue contact lenses and getting the unsightly moles on her neck and ear removed. The tinted lenses cost four hundred fifty dollars and the procedure for the moles another eleven hundred, but Mr. and Mrs. Parker didn't bat an eye. After all, who had a better daughter than they did? Mrs. Parker would drive her old car for an additional year.

Over the next few years, as Lucinda learned more about manipulation, her parents learned more about state bankruptcy laws. She managed to get a number of the more minor surgeries done — dusting, cleaning, and tweaking as Lucinda called it—pouring additional bills over the heads of her already fiscally drowning parents, who just could not say no to their darling girl.

Talk about a huge ROI on a measly five hundred.

Just before her eighteenth birthday, Lucinda's mother sat her down in the kitchen for a "little talk."

"Lu, honey, I know you were counting on that earlobe reduction for your birthday this year, but frankly, we just don't have the money for it. We're still paying off all the other surgeries, and you're graduating this year. There's nothing left for college, Lu, much less more plastic surgery."

She studied her mother. The more Lucinda's looks improved, the worse her mother's became, it seemed. She was stick thin and gray. "Oh, don't worry, Mom. It's okay. I know you and Dad are struggling. There's no reason why I can't go to work and help out ... again."

Mrs. Parker hung her head. They'd once been such a happy little family. Where had all that gone? "If you could do that, Lu, just until we're back on our feet, it would be a godsend."

"Of course, Mom."

Lucinda's father, a proud man, wasn't happy about the idea of further financial assistance from his teenage daughter.

They discovered him hanging in the basement the next morning.

His life insurance policy and his will were in his shirt pocket.

There was no note.

Her mother was crushed into catatonia, so Lucinda made all the calls necessary, as well as the funeral arrangements. She opted for cremation, since it was much easier on the pocketbook, and skipped the casket in favor of a cheap pine box in which the Parker patriarch would be committed to the flames. The funeral director had looked askance, but Lucinda was past caring. Her father's will had read: "To my dear wife goes seventy percent of my estate remaining after my funeral expenses and to my dear daughter, thirty percent in hopes that she will use it to further her education." If it was to be thirty percent, then she wanted that figure to be as high as possible, and she wasn't about to waste resources on incinerating a casket costing thousands of dollars. After all, funerals were nearly as expensive as cheek and chin implants, and there wouldn't be funds enough for both.

What a shallow little bitch!

Her mother was never quite the same after they scattered her father's ashes over Sunset Pond, where he liked to fish now and then. Since Lucinda had skipped the embalming, the urn, the burial plot, and the memorial service, disposing of her father's body had cost a grand total of six hundred dollars—after the social security death benefit. Though her mother would not have a burial plot to visit and adorn with flowers, she could always sit at the edge of the pond and put flowers into the water if she wanted to, couldn't she? What was the difference?

The following week, after the life insurance check was divvied up, her mother caught up on back bills and just managed to save the house from foreclosure.

Lucinda made a surgery appointment.

It was during her recovery at home that Mrs. Parker's relic of an automobile, the one that should have been replaced years ago, finally gave out. The brakes failed, and in her panic, she lost control of the vehicle and hit a two-hundred-year-old maple tree head-on. She made it through with only a broken leg to show for it, but when they took her to the hospital for a CT scan, they found the cancer.

It was everywhere.

She had, at most, three months to live.

When she gave Lucinda the news from her hospital bed, her beautiful daughter managed to summon up a tear or two, then rushed home and dug out her mother's life insurance policy and will—which left everything to her.

It was hard for Lucinda to be too upset with that kind of a windfall staring her in the face.

She met with her mother's doctor the next morning to discuss her mother's illness and her final days. As the doctor was walking her out, he inquired about family medical history, since her mother was alternately too sick or too upset to discuss it.

"Has anyone else in your family ever had cancer?" he asked.

"Oh, sure. One of my uncles died of it a few years ago."

"A blood relation?"

"Yes. My mother's brother. Why?"

"I'm concerned that you may have a predisposition for cancer."

"What does that mean?"

"That because it runs in your family, you would be more likely to get it than someone whose family is clean of it. What sort of cancer did your uncle have?"

"Colon cancer, I think."

"Then you should be sure to get a colonoscopy at least once every two years.

Lucinda was alarmed. "And what kind of cancer does my mother have?"

"Well, since it's spread so far, it's a little hard to say, but from what I've seen in the scan results, I'd guess it started somewhere in the reproductive tract."

"I had an aunt who died of ovarian cancer."

"Mother's side or father's?"

"Father's."

"Oh, then you have a predisposition for it on both sides of your family. Any breast cancer?"

Lucinda nodded miserably. "Two cousins. Both dead."

"My advice to you, then, is to get a PAP smear, mammogram, and colonoscopy every year, like clockwork," the doctor said. "My dear, are you all right?"

Lucinda was sheet white and trembling all over.

"I understand that you lost your father recently, too. I'm sure the stress of that and your mother's situation is taking a huge toll on you." The doctor pulled his prescription pad from his pocket. "Ever taken Valium?"

"No."

"Well, you're going to start. This will at least allow you to get some sleep. Under no circumstances are you to drink alcohol with this medication—do you understand?"

"Yes. But I don't drink. It's really bad for the skin. Ages it, you know? I can't have that. Thank you, doctor." Lucinda took the slip from his fingers, and then left the hospital.

As the doctor watched her walk away, his eyes narrowed slightly. *The only time she showed any emotion at all was when I explained predisposition.*

Lucinda sat in her-father's-now-her-car on Level B of the hospital's underground parking garage and stared into space. *I finally got my face and neck looking perfect. There nothing more that has to be done for another five years, and now I could get cancer and die? I don't think so! I've invested too much money in this perfect face to be dying any time soon.*

Lucinda firmly believed there is a way out of every problem, and so she reclined her seat a bit and thought.

And it didn't take long before she had a solution.

A perfect solution.

As it turned out, her mother didn't have three days left to live, much less three months. She passed peacefully, or so they told Lucinda. Her mother's body met the same fate as her father's, even though she had specifically requested embalming and burial in her will. Lucinda rationalized that she'd want to be with her husband, and so it was the pine box and the pond for her, as well.

Between her mother's insurance policy and what was left of her father's, Lucinda had $65,000 to her name, as well as a house and a car. It was time to put her plan into action. She picked up the phone and dialed.

The next day, she met with a surgeon to discuss a double radical mastectomy.

"May I ask why you want this procedure if you don't have cancer? You're very young and this operation is most disfiguring."

"I have a predisposition to breast cancer, so I figure no breasts, no cancer. It's one less thing to worry about," Lucinda explained.

"Here, let me show you some photographs of post-mastectomy patients. You should know what you're asking for." He rolled open a file drawer, extracted a folder and handed it to her.

They didn't have the desired effect. The mutilated chests moved her not at all. "This doesn't bother me, doctor. I still want the procedure."

"May I ask why you are so worried about this at your age?"

"I have, over recent years, paid out approximately $150,000 for facial cosmetic surgery. I have no intention of dying of cancer now or for a long, long time and losing that investment."

"If that is your reason, then I must respectfully decline to perform this surgery."

"Okay. I'll keep looking until I find a doctor who will. You're certainly not the only one on my list. Good day."

Lucinda met with four more doctors before she found one who was glad to help her. The surgery was scheduled for that weekend, and went off without a hitch. Lucinda Parker, at age nineteen, had traded in her 34C breasts for two flat round masses of bumpy scar tissue.

And she was satisfied.

While recovering at home, she received the final bill for services rendered. This bill, added to the partial invoices already delivered, came to just over forty thousand dollars. That left her with fifteen thousand, a house, and a car. It also left her with two more procedures that had to be done ASAP.

While recovering, she applied for a second mortgage on the house. She was happy to discover that it was closer to being fully paid off than she had realized, and so had little trouble securing a six-figure equity line of credit. No sooner was she fully recovered from the breast surgery than she was doctor-shopping the next.

"I understand that you want to schedule a complete hysterectomy. And it says here on your paperwork that you're, what, twenty years old?"

"Yes, that's right."

"Are you having problems with heavy bleeding? Cramping?"

"No, not at all. I have a predisposition for cancer, and if I have a complete hysterectomy, that eliminates three cancer possibilities. No uterus, no ovaries, no cervix, no cancer. It's three less things to worry about."

"That may be true, but do you realize that you will never be able to bear children after this operation?"

Lucinda sighed. "Doctor, with a face like this, do you really think I want to spend my time chasing children around? All kids give you is wrinkles and gray hair."

The doctor looked astonished. "My dear, you will not be able to avoid either of those things forever."

"With hair dye and plastic surgery, I'm damned well going to try. Now, will you be doing this procedure, or not?"

"'Not' young lady. I'm sure you know the way out."

This time it took twelve turn-downs before she located a willing surgeon, and the bills were much higher and the recovery time much longer and much harder. It took most of her loan to pay for the hysterectomy, and she still had one more expensive procedure to go.

What to do, what to do?

Well, she'd think about it—she had a month or two of convalescing to go through. She was sure to come up with something.

A knock at the door roused her from her thoughts. It was Charlie Foley, fifteen now and working at Harkin's Market delivering groceries.

"Hi, Lu. Here's your groceries." He strode in and set the box on the table. "See you."

"Hey, wait a minute! Where you off to in such a rush? I haven't seen you in ages."

"I've been around. Not my fault you haven't seen me. Though every time you come back from the hospital, you look and act so much less like you that I don't know who you are anymore."

"I'm still me, Charlie. Still the same old Lu who used to take you to the movies."

"I really miss the old Lu. The old Lu cared about people. The old Lu loved her parents and honored their wishes," Charlie said. "You're not her—not anymore."

"Oh, sure I am, Charlie. Please stay a while and talk. I get so lonely."

"How could you possibly be lonely, Lu? What happened? Your mirror break?" With that, her former knight in red sneakers shook his head and took his leave.

"How could he treat me like that? After all I did for him! Who the hell does he think he is to say things like that to me? Me! Well, if that's the way he feels, good riddance, I say." Unconsciously, she reached for her hand mirror.

After a few weeks of weighing financial options, Lucinda finally came up with a foolproof way to cover her surgery costs and get back at Charlie and his attitude at the same time.

Once she was fully recovered, one Monday morning she walked to the end of the lane where the mailboxes were and waited in the tall grass.

It wasn't long before she heard Mr. Foley's pickup truck roaring down the narrow road. The final turn out of the lane was blind, so Lucinda stepped out into the road just before Mr. Foley rounded the corner.

When he appeared, she looked fearful and stepped slightly off to the left. The fender clipped her just where she had planned for it to — the right hip. She also didn't see any harm if some of her previous stitches pulled out and added a little more blood to the mix.

She never expected a broken hip to hurt quite as much as it did, but as her father used to say, "You can't make an omelet without breaking a few eggs."

Police and an ambulance were summoned and Lucinda played the incident for all it was worth.

And to make matters worse for poor Mr. Foley, he had whiskey on his breath. He had downed a shot that morning to treat a heavy cold. Back home, in Ireland, that was how it was done, and had always worked well for him.

This time, it worked well for Lucinda. She sued him for everything he had, and by the time the case was settled, she owned his joint bank account, his truck, his wife's car, and their house and everything in it. Oh, also Charlie's savings that he planned to use for college.

When she was being wheeled out of court that day, Charlie Foley walked up to her and spit on the ground at her feet.

But she'd won, and soon she'd have plenty of cash to get that final procedure done, once the Foley assets were liquidated, and that was the whole point, wasn't it?

By the time she'd recovered from her "accident" and sold off everything the Foleys had, there was more than enough money to cover the next procedure.

"You want a colostomy? Why?"

"I have a predisposition for colon cancer. It runs in my family. So, no colon, no colon cancer. It's one less thing to worry about."

"Are you aware that you'll have to wear a colostomy bag for the rest of your life?"

Lucinda flashed her perfect white teeth at the man. "I understand. I still want it done. Will you do it?"

"I'm afraid not."

This time, it took months before she found a willing doctor. He seemed a little sketchy and his credentials weren't the best, but he was ready to operate the next day, so the deal was sealed.

This surgery took everything she had to pay for—or, rather, everything the Foleys had had. Lucinda heard that they were living in a shelter downtown, and that Charlie's job at the grocery store was all that was feeding and clothing them. But, Lucinda reasoned, they had a roof, a bed, and food, so what more could they ask for? She thought about them less and less as time passed. A new kid, Justin now delivered her groceries. Harkins must have given Charlie a new route for some reason.

Lucinda was finally happy, finally satisfied. She had eliminated all the cancer risks that ran in her family and threatened her to take her life and, therefore her beauty, away from her. She stared into the mirror for hours on end, secure in the knowledge that, with regular surgical maintenance, she would be looking this way for a long, long time to come.

The food stamps, social security, and disability checks she was now collecting from the government covered food, her new mortgage, and miscellaneous other bills.

She never left the house.

Why should she? Who out there would appreciate her beauty as much as she did? Better to stay home.

Things were wonderful for many months—until the phone call.

Her father's last remaining brother had died.

Lucinda panicked.

She had no more money left.

The 911 call came in later that afternoon from Justin, who had come by to collect for the week. He'd received no answer to his knock, and seeing her car in the driveway and finding the door unlocked, had gone looking for her thinking she might need help.

The police found her on her bathroom floor in a pool of her own blood.

"She peeled off her skin. Got as far as her waist before she died of shock and blood loss," the M.E. said. "But she didn't touch her face or her neck. She'll be a good-looking corpse once she's dressed."

"Damnedest suicide I ever saw in my whole life," Officer Donnelly said to the M.E. "Was there a note or anything?"

"Yeah. She's looking right at it. It's a weird one. All I can figure is that it was supposed to remind her about something while she was ... doing this." The M.E., who had seen more horror in his professional life than he cared to talk about, shuddered over this latest one.

Donnelly followed the body's vacant gaze. Indeed, there was a note, of sorts, that she'd taped up to the tiles directly opposite her line of sight. She must have been looking at it right until the moment she died.

One less thing to worry about!

THE SUN-SNAKE

BY CHRISTINE MORGAN

In Kukmatlan, the Great City, the Festival of the Sun-Snake neared its culmination.

For thirteen days, the People had celebrated with banquets and sacrifices, dancing and games. Trade goods and tribute came from every province, from the small coastal villages to the remote settlements in the cloud-forests. The marketplace bustled with activity. Artisans demonstrated their crafts, displayed and sold their wares. Poets, speech-givers, and riddle-makers entertained the crowds.

For thirteen days, travelers had come to the Temple of Kuk, which climbed skyward in a stepped pyramid to a high platform where rayed- and serpentine-engraved stelae marked the calendrical and astrological positions of the sun.

For thirteen days, ritual bloodletting was done, stingray spines or threads-of-thorns piercing lips, ears, cheeks, and tongues, the heels of new infants, the foreskins of boys becoming men, the labia of girls becoming women. The scarlet drops fell upon corn paper, which was then burned to let the wafting smoke carry these offerings of nourishment and devotion to the gods.

For thirteen days, the Hom, the sacred ball court with its high walls and stone rings, had resounded with the whack and thud of pokatok. Just as each province sent its tribute, each province sent its team, made up of their best young athletes and warriors. When one team emerged victorious, its individual players competed against each other in contests of speed, strength, sport, and skill.

Now, only two remained standing.

They were not brothers, but could have been, both of an age and of a height, straight black hair cropped to equal length, muscular brown bodies gleaming with sweat. Barefoot, unadorned by jewelry, they wore only white loincloths bordered in embroidery of red and yellow.

Makchel and Tlinoc exchanged proud, anxious smiles.

Whichever of them won this final challenge, they knew they had already brought great honor to their families and their village.

Spectators looked on from the seating areas above the walls. These were the nobles of Kukmatlan and the wealthiest provinces, richly dressed, stylishly tattooed, teeth glittering with inlaid disks of crystal and precious stones.

The God-King himself was there, ancient and wizened in a jaguar-skin mantle, his face seamed like the shell of a nut but his wise eyes keenly alert beneath his quetzal-feathered headdress. His wives, sons, daughters, and grandchildren sat with him, flanked by slaves holding woven shades on poles.

There, too, aloof and untouchable, were the Corn Maidens.

Only the most beautiful of noble-born girls, whose heads swept up and back in flawless elegant lines from skull-binding since infancy, whose eyes crossed the most appealingly from having strung baubles suspended between them, only they would be selected.

Their garments were long, loose huipils of gold-beaded strands hung from collars of stiff green maize leaves. More gold hung in bangled clusters at their earlobes, around their necks, and at their wrists and ankles. In their hair were ornaments of gold, jade, and feathers of green and yellow.

A temple priest approached the young men. He carried a turquoise-decorated wooden box containing the ceremonial atl-atl and javelins. The target, a painted deer hide stretched over stacks of bundled grass, had been set up at one end of the ball court.

Tlinoc threw first. It was a good throw, good form, good distance and aim. The javelin's gilded tip struck the edge of the second sun-circle. The onlookers murmured their approval.

Makchel threw next, with three short running strides and a powerful heft of his arm. The javelin traced a smooth arc and lodged just within the boundaries of the innermost sun-circle.

Amid cheers, Makchel and Tlinoc fell together in a hearty embrace of congratulatory back-slapping. Women tossed flower petals. Men scattered fistfuls of dried tobacco. A few daring children scrambled down the walls, rushing to try and touch them for luck.

More priests emerged to lead the young men out of the Hom. The nobles, God-King's family, and Corn Maidens followed. Warriors armed with spears and fringed shields cleared a path through the immense and busy Sun Plaza. The procession grew as others joined in, forming an excited throng.

A steep flight of shallow steps climbed from the temple pyramid's base to its height. At the top, awaiting them, stood Yaxcoatl ... the High Priest of Kuk, the Guardian of the Sun-Snake.

Though short of stature and squat of build, round of face and of belly, bowlegged, Yaxcoatl nonetheless presented an imposing figure, resplendent in his mantle embroidered with patterns of interlocking red and yellow winged snakes. The fiery gold of his headdress blazed in the brilliance of the summer sun nearing its zenith.

A living sun-snake, scales shining, draped in sinuous loops and coils around the High Priest's neck. Its slim, forked tongue flicked at the air. A feathery frill surrounded its head, and more feathers made winglike ridges in twin lines to either side of its body.

Makchel glanced back down, dizzied by the view. The steps plunged away at a severe angle toward the crowded plaza below. All around him were the buildings of Kukmatlan—the God-King's palace, temples to the other gods, the Law Court, the houses and monuments, the walls and stelae covered in glyphs that told the grand history of the People.

He could not recognize any friends from their own village in the mass of upturned faces and colorful clothing, but knew that they would be there. They had come bearing tribute, and they would go home bearing word of this glorious honor.

One of the priests guided him to a spot between two tall sculptures, winged snakes that faced inward with chunks of rough crystal gripped in their fanged jaws. The crystals flashed in the strong noon sunlight. Makchel stood feeling the sun's strong rays on his bare shoulders.

Tlinoc went to the altar and lay down upon it. He turned his head once to grin with delight at Makchel, then lifted his chin to the sky. A deep breath of pride swelled his chest.

Yaxcoatl's powerful voice rang out in prayer. His teeth, the incisors filed to points and studded with disks of crystal, sparkled. The sun-snake at his neck writhed and slid. Four strong temple priests took hold of each of Tlinoc's limbs, while a fifth held a basin at the ready. The Corn Maidens chanted a song of praise.

Obsidian glinted glass-black. The knife parted Tlinoc's flesh. A single cut, sure and swift, opened from breastbone to armpit. The blood had barely begun to gush when Yaxcoatl plunged his hands into the gap of the ribs.

A choked gasp erupted from Tlinoc's throat. His eyes bulged. His back arched. His legs tried to kick but the priests held his ankles.

With a wet sound like the ripping of sodden, heavy cloth, Yaxcoatl wrenched a pulsating knot of muscle, gristle, and spurting veins from the ribcage. He thrust it aloft toward the sun, shouting to Kuk.

The heart throbbed wildly in the High Priest's grasp. Red blood ran down his arm and rained in thick splatters over Tlinoc's shocked face and aware eyes. The sun-snake, with another quick flick of its tongue, sampled the offering and found it acceptable.

More blood gushed up from the gaping hole in Tlinoc's chest, coursing over the carved stone sides of the altar, trickling along channels in the platform's floor. His head rolled to the side again. His gaze found Makchal, his expression a mix of exaltation and bewilderment.

Then he went limp, staring past Makchal into a world the rest of them could not yet see.

They burnt Tlinoc's heart in the basin, burnt it to blood-ash and charcoal.

To this, they added a liquid made from fermented corn paste, the venom of a sun-snake, sea salt, water from a sacred cenote, and medicines gathered in the deep jungles.

It tasted of life and death.

Makchel's mind reeled. He laughed. He screamed. He wept. He moaned.

His perceptions both sharpened and dulled.

He saw each fine line of the feathers in Yaxcoatl's headdress in the tiniest, clearest detail, but the sun and sky overhead melted into a glimmering puddle ... he heard each subtle golden bead-clink as the Corn Maidens moved, but the sounds of the Great City were far away and distant as the sounds of the sea ... he smelled the strange, cold, spicy scent of the snake but not his own sweat ...

... and he felt every deft slice of the sharp, brittle blade ...

... but it did not hurt.

There was pain. Makchal knew that there was.

How could there not be pain as the obsidian knife slit his leg in a single long, shallow stroke from the top of his inner thigh to the sole of his foot?

How could there not be pain as other incisions were made, leading out crossways from the first so that a flap of skin could be peeled up like a damp leaf, peeled up and folded back, revealing raw muscle that seeped sluggish blood onto the bed of corn paper underneath him?

How could there not be pain as the same was done to the other leg, the skin flap of that one peeled and folded the other way?

He felt it, every thin cut, every flaying and peeling sensation.

He felt it when they slathered the exposed flesh with an ointment boiled from bakalche bark, herbs, and rubber-tree sap ... gluey, sticky, stinging like fire nettles, soothing like the cool balm of aloe.

They pressed his legs together and pulled the skin flaps taut to seal the joining seams, the Corn Maidens stitching the edges with needlework more delicate than the finest embroidery. Priests wrapped him from hips to toes in a plaster of cloth strips and clay.

Makchel dreamed while waking and spoke while sleeping. The skies wheeled above him, light and dark, sun and stars, the gods of the Thirteen Heavens passing in rapid succession. The Lords of Night stalked him, hungry jaguars with jaws poised to rend and devour.

The priests split his tongue. They did not pierce it with a stingray spine, or pull a thread-of-thorns ... they split his tongue's end with the obsidian knife, so that it forked and curled.

Through shaving, plucking, and scouring by porous stones, all the hair of his head and body was removed.

Where his eyebrows had been, and through his lips, they affixed rows of tiny golden hoops.

The outer cartilage of his ears, they trimmed off, so that only a small ridge remained around the openings. They did the same with his nose.

When they broke the dried clay plaster and unwrapped the cloth strips, his legs had melded together into a single limb from the loins and buttocks on down.

Next came the scarification, more deft knife-work, hundreds of small semi-circular cuts in his skin ... the cuts then packed with a gritty powder of ash, gold flecks, and ground corn ... the scars healing into raised marks in a pattern of scales.

More hoops of gold were pierced through his foreskin, and rounded gold beads inserted beneath the skin of the shaft, until the length and swelled girth of his manhood was knobbled, textured like ripe maize.

As he'd climbed step by step to the temple's great height, now each new cut, scar, and piercing was another step, bringing him closer and closer to the gods.

So was each feather, as they embedded the pointed quills into him one by one. Scarlet and yellow and orange ... set into his naked scalp to form a crest of bright, fiery plumage ... tracing his jawline to make a feathery frill ... in rows along the backs of his arms from shoulder to elbow to wrist.

He was the Sun-Snake.

The god embodied.

His joined legs could support him to balance upright, but not walk. Temple slaves carried him from place to place on a litter. He slept in a luxurious bed heaped with rushes. The nobles of Kukmatlan brought him rich gifts.

The Corn Maidens served him banquets unlike anything Makchal had ever known in the humble village life he'd led before. He feasted at dawn on porridge sweetened with agave and honey, at noon on rare fruits, at dusk on meat and fowl and shellfish, and at night was given all the frothed brew of spiced cacao he could drink.

The Corn Maidens bathed him and oiled him, sang to him, danced for him, and eagerly saw to his other needs as well. His split tongue plied and savored their succulent flesh; the penile hoops and beads enhanced each thrust's intense pleasure.

On sacred days, he breathed the smoke of burnt offerings to speak divinations. He listened at the Law Court as judgments were passed. He appeared with the God-King when ambassadors from other empires visited, or when conquered enemies were sacrificed.

He was the Sun-Snake.

The god embodied.

The warm summer went on, the rains regular, the weather favorable.

In the milpas, where the field workers toiled with their digging sticks, the corn and amaranth grew tall. The beans thrived.

On their vines, squash and melons fattened toward ripeness.

In their temple chambers, so did the Corn Maidens, bellies great with child.

The harvest was plentiful.

The dry season came. The lakes fell. The rivers shrank.

Atop the Temple of Kuk, the priests tracked the movements of the sun. They followed how it rose and set in relation to the positions of the stelae, and the winged-snake sculptures, and the rays engraved into the stone.

They kept the calendar.

The days shortened.

Each one saw the sun's rising and sinking paths passing closer to the solstice markers.

Until the shortest day of the year.

In Kukmatlan, shadows lengthened. Darkness pooled in the streets until only the tops of the highest structures remained touched by daylight.

A crowd filled the Sun Plaza.

All that day, they had fasted and prayed. They had taken no tobacco. All that day, they had gone without washing, without cleaning their teeth with salt and charcoal. They dressed in their simplest clothes and flimsiest sandals. They wore no jewelry. Even the God-King and his family appeared as humble as any peasants or slaves.

Every lamp and cookfire in the Great City had been extinguished. Every clay oven for the baking of maize cakes had been left to go cold.

The temple priests chanted and the Corn Maidens sang, swaying into a frenzy as the smoldering red-gold ball descended. Yaxcoatl led them, overcome with such fervor that the tears poured from his eyes.

He uncoiled the snake looped around his neck, holding its body aloft. With his filed, crystal-set teeth he severed the head, whipping the flailing body by the tail so that its blood sprayed out and fell like red rain.

For this was the moment ... the cycle ... the year's end ...

To bring back the light, or be cast into Night forever.

Makchel raised his feathered arms and lifted his face to the last rays of the setting sun as it came perfectly poised in the center of the solstice marker's engraved stone ring.

Gold gleamed and flashed from his facial piercings, from the crown of gold hoops at the end of his jutting, engorged erection.

He was the Sun-Snake.

The god embodied.

The oils with which the Corn Maidens had anointed him ignited.

Fire swept over him, surrounded him in a blazing corona.

A cry of exultation burst from his throat.

A powerful push of his serpentine lower body launched him from the high platform into the open air, arms outstretched as extended blazing wings.

He hung there a moment as if suspended.

Then he arced into a long dive, trailing streaks of flame.

His burning body plunged into a mound of kindling, dried grasses, and corn paper sprinkled from the sacrificial bloodlettings.

It flared into a conflagration, a sudden roiling heat, sending sparks and embers spinning up in a whirlwind.

The ancient God-King, supported by two of his wives, came forward to light a ceremonial cornstalk torch from the bonfire. He touched it to the torches of his sons, who then turned to touch theirs to others. The nobles of Kukmatlan, the chiefs and the warriors, the wealthy merchants ... torch by torch, the fires increased ... spreading outward through the plaza like sun's rays, branching off into the streets like snakes of flame ... until the entire Great City glowed its defiance against the Night.

And the People celebrated the rebirth and the renewal of another year.

KNOWLEDGE

BY KATE MONROE

They say the eyes are the window to the soul. Ever since he had first peeled back his eyelids from the bionic replacements that now sat resplendent beneath them, however, Peter Smith had come to know the agonizing and incredible truth behind that oft-used saying.

Peter was an accountant. The foundations of his delightfully uninteresting life were logic and rationale. As a child, he had been taught that everything had a steadfast, scientific explanation, and he had built his life with that sole thought in mind. He was employed in the same reliable job since the age of eighteen. Each month, without fail, he had squirreled away his wages until he was able to afford the house he aspired to.

His house was neat and tidy, a carbon copy of every other one in his neighborhood in all respects save one—of the house's five bedrooms, three had never been occupied. He and Marie slept separately in two rooms these days, but the other three had never been filled.

He had long ago come to terms with the only black mark on his life's plan. The doctors had told him the reason why his wife could never conceive, and he was satisfied with their emotionless explanation. So long as he understood why something could or could not happen,

Peter was satisfied. He thrived upon constancy and reason, and his dull life provided that in abundance—until recently.

He defiantly refused to believe in the claptrap and mumbo jumbo about auras or the soul that others parroted as if it were fact. We live, we die. There was nothing more to it. Yet what could not be denied was that, since his new eyes had been fitted, he had seen much more than he had ever known it was possible to see.

The eyes. Therein lay the problem.

Peter's new eyes were a window to everyone else's souls.

It all started one week ago. Since the children he and Marie so studiously saved for had not arrived, they now had a surfeit of money. So, when one of his clients visited the office to rave about his new bionic eyes, Peter's logical mind concluded he should get a pair for himself. With a quiet word from the client he had helped without censure for twenty years, the next day he entrusted his sight to the skilled cut of the surgeon's knife.

His trust had not been misplaced. In return for the many thousands of pounds now lining the surgeon's pockets, Peter's vision was far superior to anything that nature could create. Functions previously limited to mechanoids and soulless technology were his to command. With just a blink of his eyes, he could zoom in to faraway items or focus upon even the tiniest of objects, and the sheer clarity of vision was truly astounding.

However, the one side effect that had consumed his thoughts ever since had not been mentioned in the gleaming brochures that the clinic handed out like sweets to gluttonous children. Peter had scanned it over and over with his newly enhanced vision, desperate for some rational explanation for what he was experiencing, but no peace of mind could be found within its coaxing words. He hadn't dared mention it to anyone, for who would possibly believe someone who said they could see the color of everyone's souls?

Peter could hardly believe it himself. At first he had attributed it to nothing more than a temporary disturbance, a mere quirk of the technology as his neural pathways adapted to the bionic technology that had replaced his flesh. Taking it all in stride, as he always did, he neglected to mention it to the surgeon when the initial checks were performed—after all, work awaited, and he wanted no delay in returning to it. He convinced himself that any oddities would surely settle down within days.

They did not. To the contrary, he found the more people he encountered, the stronger his newfound ability became. Each soul was unique and ever-changing. So far as he could tell, the soul's aura was fluid, a constant reflection of its owner's moods and deepest, most private thoughts. Perhaps one more sensitive than Peter to such things would be better able to interpret the colors he saw, but he had always kept his emotions and intuition on a tight leash. The habits of a lifetime were difficult to shake, for they were now the one constant in a world that had irreversibly shifted around him.

"Mr. Smith?" A smiling, perfectly made-up receptionist tapped her heel against the polished floor of the clinic as she glanced down at her clipboard one more time. "Mr. Smith, the surgeon will see you now," Emerald said.

Almost without realizing, he had begun to mentally refer to each person he met by the predominant color of his or her aura. The receptionist's was a dazzling emerald green, interspersed by sparks of incandescent white and a dash of turquoise that danced merrily around her head. It really is remarkable, he mused, how much happens around us that we are blithely unaware of until something sparks off a new level of consciousness. If this truly was a side effect of the bionic eyes, then he simply could not understand why the clinic did not advertise it. People would surely pay millions to experience this!

Had *he* known what would happen, though, he was certain he would not have been one of them. This was too jarring, too unfamiliar; the polar opposite to all that he had made his life become. Peter did not like change. That was why he was here today.

Remarkable as they were, the eyes had to go.

With that conviction burning inside his mind to provide something to focus on, he rose to his feet and strode toward the door that Emerald indicated. His heart was thudding; an indicator of the nerves that he unaccustomed to feeling. He didn't know how the surgeon would receive what he had to say. But, after another sleepless night tossing and turning, he realized he would have to confide the truth to his surgeon, to explain why he wanted the revolutionary eyes removed despite the dazzling optical improvements they possessed. Most likely, the enhancement was a side effect they had simply neglected to mention, and once he explained that he was uncomfortable with it, the clinic would make no difficulties about removing them. A brief mention of medical negligence would smooth over any reservations, no doubt.

The surgeon sat behind his desk. His aura steadily pulsed, dominated by tones of the same bright green his receptionist possessed. The cool, soft blues connoted an innate confidence that Peter could not help but admire. Soothed by the notice on the wall concerning doctor-patient confidentiality, something the medical profession held sacred, Peter pushed the door closed behind him and took the seat that the younger man indicated.

"What can I do for you today, Mr. Smith?"

Peter did not believe in small talk. "I want the eyes removed," he said bluntly. "I don't like what they've done to me. It isn't right, and I want them out."

The surgeon's easy smile faded. "To have a part of your body replaced by bionics is a lot to get your head around, Mr. Smith. If you want to talk about it—"

"I don't want to talk. I simply want to have the eyes removed." Peter absently touched his nose before realizing that his spectacles were no longer there to be pushed back up. He missed them. He sighed under his breath before forcing a calm and implacable smile as he met the surgeon's narrowed eyes. "I'll pay. That isn't a problem. I understand that you have operating costs, so if you could tell me how much it will be to have them removed, I'll transfer the money to your account now and we can schedule the operation."

"But why do you want them out, Mr. Smith? Surely you've seen by now how vastly superior they are to your original eyes." Dark streaks of muddied pink shot through the surgeon's aura and Peter tensed.

"That's the problem. I ... I see too much. I don't know why your clinic didn't mention it before, but I can see *far* too much. I see people, I see what they truly are, and I don't like it. Some might say that knowledge is power, but to me it's a curse."

"I don't understand, sir. Knowledge of what?"

The surgeon seemed to be genuinely at a loss to comprehend what Peter was talking about. His worst fear was perilously near to being confirmed—perhaps this was *not* normal, this new insight the bionic eyes had given him. For the space of a pounding heartbeat, he hesitated, but he had come too far to stop now. "I see what they can't hide. I see their souls," he said, so quietly that the sharp-suited surgeon leaned forward to hear him. Saying the words out loud for the first time was the final, incontrovertible acceptance of what had happened to him. The words were like a leaden weight, descending upon his chest and threatening to steal away his breath.

Even more oppressive, though, was the younger man's reaction. A tiny, disdainful smile played at the corners of his thin lips. He clearly struggled to suppress the faint note of rebuke in his voice when he finally replied. "Perhaps you would benefit from a complimentary session with our clinic's psychologist, Mr. Smith."

Peter recoiled in horror. He had never been affiliated with anyone who worked in mental health, and he didn't intend to start now. It wasn't that he had anything against those who needed their help, but the disorders they treated were the very definition of abnormality. His bionic eyes darted resentfully from side to side, seeing with a painful clarity the amusement upon the surgeon's face as he pushed back in his high-backed chair.

"Mr. Smith?"

"*No!*" Peter said, surprising even himself with the new venom in his voice. "I don't want to talk to your quacks, doctor. I just want the damned eyes out!"

"You don't need the eyes removed, Mr. Smith," the surgeon said firmly. "I assure you, I have fitted near a hundred pairs and they have all been flawless—as are yours, whatever you think you're seeing. What you need is a nice quiet talk with our psychologist. She's a lovely lady, and I'm sure you'll get on well with her—"

But Peter had already leapt up from his seat and was backing toward the door. He would not get the help he sought here, that much was plain. He certainly did not need the censure and derision that he saw on the other's man clinically enhanced features.

His chest was tight and it was a battle to catch his breath, but he let nothing hold him back from rushing through the clinic's glass doors and out onto the bustling London street. His eyes, far superior to those of near everyone else around him, easily picked out a path for him and guided him to his destination, to the tube train that would take him back to the one place that was his own—home. Once there, he could gather his jumbled thoughts and try to see a way forward. He knew he could no longer live with this.

All around him was a dizzying blur of color that wove and spun around each soul streaming past him. Peter blinked furiously and clung to the rails of the escalator as it descended to the platform. The world around him no longer made sense. It was a mercy that he had travelled the route from central London so many times before, for he lacked entirely the clarity of thought to navigate unfamiliar streets where the auras of everyone he passed dazzled and tormented him. As it was, though, he stole every chance he could to close his eyes and defend himself against the world until, finally, he found his feet traveling down the familiar path of the street where he lived with Marie.

Sanctuary was so near, and with a loud, agonized cry, he opened his eyes long enough to thrust the key into the lock and turn it with fumbling fingers. Glorious, unbound relief exploded inside him as he burst through the front door and slumped against the wall. Marie froze in the doorway to the kitchen with two empty, red-stained wineglasses in her hands.

"You're back already, Pete? I ... I thought you were going back to work after your appointment!"

She had changed. When Peter had given her a mechanical kiss good-bye that morning, her aura had been a bright, crimson red, far more vibrant than he had seen it before and centered around her core. Now, though, the red had faded to a murky pink overlaid by a gray storm cloud that seemed to battle to close the truth of all she was away from him.

Though he had only his woefully underused senses to rely on, some primal instinct told him with an unerring certainty that Marie was consumed by deceit—a deceit that, given the *two* used glasses in her hands, could have only one cause.

All his life, Peter had sought to control everything around him. Now it was all spiraling out of control. He could withstand it no longer. His stomach churned as he staggered past her into the kitchen, his eyes tightly shut to block out all that he could not bear to see. He didn't need his vision to find what he sought. Nothing had changed position in their house since the day they had moved in and studiously unpacked every neatly labeled box.

The cutlery drawer was six paces in front of him. With unerring certainty, he reached out and seized the handle to wrench the drawer open.

"Pete! Pete, what are you doing? It's not what you think!"

Yet neither her pleas nor the shattering crash of the twin wineglasses as they hit the tiled floor could penetrate the fugue of Peter's mind. The emotions he had kept repressed for half a century erupted as violently and uncontrollably as if Pandora's Box had opened inside him. With his path laid out clearly in front of him, he spun toward the sound of his wife's scream and lunged.

He slashed the knife through the air in a clean, precise movement borne of a lifetime spent practicing and honing his self-control. Even with his uncontrollable rage surging through his body, he still retained the presence of mind to draw the blade across Marie's throat. He issued the ultimate punishment for the infidelity that his eyes had witnessed.

In unseeing bliss, he dropped to his knees. She crumpled to the floor at his side. Her blood gushed from her throat to stain the once-pristine tiles. The blood ran around his feet, soaking his trousers, but Peter only smiled in grim and rueful acknowledgment of the truth he had spoken to the surgeon.

Knowledge truly was a curse.

As Marie's gurgling, shallow breaths finally ceased, he opened his eyes again and held the bloodstained knife in front of him. Sunlight bounced off the gleaming contours of the serrated blade, its reflection far more brilliant when seen by the bionic eyes. It was unnatural, and he no longer wanted any part of it.

The terrified, racking sobs of his wife's best friend, who had only dropped by for a glass of wine and some gossip, receded through the still open front door.

Peter lifted the knife to his face. He steadied his hand to begin the task that the surgeon had refused.

PROSTHETICS

BY DANIEL I. RUSSELL

Dr. Bowman met Jim's eyes. He seemed nervous, but remained smiling.

"You ready?" she asked, taking his hand. She sat next to him on a plush sofa.

"I ... I guess so," he said.

"Good. Don't try too hard. This should come naturally. Now ... squeeze!"

Fingers clamped down on the doctor's hand, and she cried out, pulling back. Jim held on, staring down.

"Jesus," Bowman moaned and squirmed her fingers. She worked them free from the iron grip. Pain blazed in her hand, like she'd trapped it in a door.

She slid free and massaged the skin, smoothing out the agony.

"Any harder and it would be *me* that needs a new one!"

"I'm sorry," blurted Jim.

"It wasn't your fault," said Bowman. "It's a new technology and needs a little fine-tuning. Let me take another look."

She held the prosthetic, now a tight fist, and ripped a Velcro strap free. The gloved hand fell away, revealing the fleshy stump beneath. She swallowed and pulled the glove off.

Jim snorted. "You must see this kind of thing every day, yet this," he held up the deformed hand, "this disgusts even *you*."

"It's nothing," she said. "It's the prosthetic I'm disgusted with."

Jim's injured hand turned her stomach. He'd been on the receiving end of a meat slicer accident. The machine had taken most of his right hand, cutting from the base of the thumb up to the knuckle of his little finger. The injury itself didn't sicken her, but the puckered pink flesh at the trauma site did. She knew she had a bad attitude, especially for someone in her position, but the disgust remained. She preferred nice, tidy stumps, not blood and scars.

"You don't have to worry much longer," she said. "Once I get this fixed, it'll be like having your old hand back."

Jim sighed. "I appreciate your ... enthusiasm, doctor. But you can't understand what this feels like to just ... well, lose a part of you in a split second."

Bowman pried the fingers of the hand open.

"Really?"

She reached down to her ankle and hiked up her trousers a few inches. Beneath, the silver head of a bolt glinted, embedded in pink plastic. She lifted her foot from the floor, and the hinge moved.

"Whoa," said Jim, clutching his injured hand.

"Car crash," said Bowman. "Twelve years ago. My leg was crushed, and they amputated below the knee." She tapped her shin. It sounded hollow. "Why I got into this area of medicine."

"I'm sorry," said Jim.

Bowman smiled. "No problem."

"But you don't even have a limp!"

She winked. "That's how good we are here at Bloom Memorial." She studied the hand. "Ah, I see what happened. A fuse has blown." She reached into the inner workings and snapped the offending part free. "Our engineer is in today, so he should be able to fix this right up."

"You don't build them?"

"Steve builds them and I fit them. Our system works." She stood. "Make yourself comfortable, Jim. I'll just be a minute."

"Right," he said, looking a little more reassured. "Thank you, doctor."

Bowman crossed the pastel-toned patient suite and through the door at the rear. The temperature seemed to drop ten degrees on entering the workshop. The windowless room, from the thick carpet and views of the patient suite, was oppressive. Beneath the bare bulbs, various limbs hung from rows of shelves. Legs stood in racks, like umbrellas. Hands sat in rows, robot spiders waiting to be used. It reminded Bowman of a puppet maker's workbench.

"Steve?" she called. Her voice echoed. "Steve are you back there? I need a new fuse for a TN500."

Silence greeted her.

"Damn. You on your lunch?"

She headed deeper into the room, passing more body parts. She had no idea what the building had been used for previously. The hospital had seen their work, offered positions at the facility, and given them the use of the building, set within the hospital grounds. The workshop contained a small washing area and the remains of a ward. Various bits and pieces had been left behind, the larger objects covered by sheets. Bowman had nagged Steve about shifting it all.

She approached the washing area. Steve had emptied the cupboard under the sink, and a black leather bag stood next to the rusted metal sink. Bowman glanced at her reflection in the streaked mirror.

"Steve?"

Nothing.

She opened the bag and peered inside, catching a hint of metal. She reached in.

"Eugh!"

She pulled out a scalpel, studied it, and dropped it back. It emitted a small clink, striking other instruments.

"Steve! I told you to get rid of all this!"

She turned away.

"Guess I'll have to find the fuse myself."

She walked down the old ward, scanning the cluttered shelves and work areas. Saws, drills, hammers, and other vicious objects littered the place.

"Health and safety nightmare," said Bowman, wishing for the comfort of the patient suite. She stopped. "And what the hell are you doing with this?"

85

A metal chair lay against the wall. Its seat, complete with head and foot rest, had been formed from a sheet of bent aluminum and polished to a dazzling finish. It sat on a short column, also fashioned from metal. An intricate pattern adorned its surface.

Looks like you've been renovating this. But why?

Something tapped her left foot. She looked down.

A fuse rolled and stopped.

Bowman picked it up.

Must have knocked it off something ... Bit of luck. And it hit my left foot and not my right!

The wet fuse slipped within her fingers, and she wiped it on her blouse. The tiny cylinder vibrated in her palm for a second.

"Odd." She examined it closer. Nothing out of the ordinary. "Must just be me."

She glanced at the chair and shivered. She'd never claimed to have any sixth sense, but the chair raised goosebumps on her arms and back. She wondered if anyone had died in it.

Right, Steve. As soon as your belly's filled, you're getting rid of this chair. That bag, too.

Turning her back on the piles of junk and the hideous chair, Bowman headed back through the workshop. She stopped, her heels scraping on the floor.

Something. Something behind her.

She glanced over her shoulder.

Nothing moved. The chair sat in the old ward, like a still life painted by Giger.

We need more lights in here. Place is getting to me.

Shaking her head, Bowman strode through the workshop, thankful as she entered the patient suite.

"Here we are, Jim," said Bowman, joining her patient back on the sofa. "Sorry about the delay. Steve's on his lunch, but I managed to find a fuse."

Jim shifted forward, perching on the edge. "We trying it again, then?"

"One more time, at least to check the fit. We'll make an appointment for next week so we can start your rehab properly." Bowman flipped the prosthetic hand over and clicked the fuse into place. The fingers twitched, and Bowman nearly dropped the attachment. "Must have some discharge," she said, and ripped open the Velcro. "Don't worry. You won't get a shock!"

Jim offered a nervous smile and slowly held out what remained of his severed hand. Bowman slid the fixture over the torn skin and fastened it tight.

"There we go."

Jim frowned. "It feels strange. All tingly."

Tingly?

"That's normal," said Bowman, frowning. She looked at the clock. Aware of her next appointment, she decided to cut the chat. "Just like before. Try to make a fist."

"Okay," said Jim. He closed his eyes.

"Ready?" said Bowman. "One ... two ... three!"

Thin blades shot out of the metal fingertips with a sharp *ping*!

Bowman flinched.

What the——?

"Did it work?" asked Jim. He glanced down.

The hand shot up, fingers closing in a claw. The five blades punched through Jim's throat, and blood shot across the sofa.

Bowman screamed and jumped to her feet.

Jim gurgled, wide-eyed and falling back. Crimson poured down his chest, blossoming on his white shirt. The fingers embedded in his flesh jerked and flicked, trying to dig deeper. Jim clutched it with his good hand.

"Oh god," Bowman moaned, retreating. "Oh god!"

Jim pulled the hand away for a second, but, not to be denied, it surged forward in another frenzied attack. The force knocked Jim's head back.

Bowman fled to the front door.

The sounds of Jim's thrashing and the whirring from the hand stopped behind her.

The doctor froze, her hand on the door knob. She peered over her shoulder.

Jim lay back on the sofa, his body still. His head had tilted back, revealing the carnage beneath his chin. Blood trickled down his front from pulsating tissue, which hung from his throat like glistening candy shoelaces. The remains of a crushed, mangled tube poked out of the pulpy mess.

The hand had vanished.

"Oh shit," said Bowman, and covered her mouth. The carpet seemed to tilt, and her vision blurred. She blinked the patient suite back into focus.

"No," she cried. "Oh no!"

She yanked the door handle.

The hand dropped from the ceiling and onto her arm. Bowman jumped away from the door and beat at the prosthetic. It clung on like a metal tarantula, crawling for her shoulder. The blades had retracted.

Bowman tripped on a rug and toppled onto her knees. Her leg cracked, and the fake limb came free. It hung loose within her trousers.

The hand crept along her collarbone, impartial to her thrashing.

She screamed and grabbed it. The metal throbbed within her grasp.

"No!" she yelled, prying it free.

It held onto her blouse, refusing to budge. Bowman's fingers slipped, and the metal hand darted to her face.

She snatched it with both hands and pulled.

A finger, containing tiny pistons and wires, hooked toward her mouth. The tip brushed her lips.

"Get ... the fuck ... off me!"

The hand emitted a loud click and fell away. Bowman threw it across the room just as the detached finger slipped into her mouth. She clenched her teeth, clamping the loose digit that squirmed like a swollen maggot. It curled, and the tail end flicked against her nose.

Bowman fell forward and coughed. She pressed against the probing finger with her tongue. It pushed further in, metal squeaking against her teeth. Bolts of pain shot through her tight jaws. She grabbed for the probing digit.

It slipped all the way inside and jabbed the back of her throat.

Bowman gagged and wailed.

The finger seemed to grow, and a sharp point pressed into the roof of her mouth.

The blade!

Realization fueled her panic, and she hooked the metal with her fingertips. They slid over the saliva-slick intruder and failed to find purchase.

The flesh at the back of her throat parted, and the finger dug up toward her brain.

Bowman managed a final cry and fell forward, twitching on the carpet. Her left leg jerked and kicked the hanging prosthetic.

Laura studied the mangled flesh of her elbow for the thousandth time.

You ruined everything!

She squeezed her missing hand into a fist and almost felt the fingers close. The limb remained in her mind. It gave her hope the hospital was right about Dr. Bowman's prosthetics that responded to muscle contractions. Laura knew she'd never play the guitar again, but to be able to lift a cup to her lips, or to pick a flower, the thought carried her.

And if it looked real enough, to stop the stares and whispers. That would be amazing.

She breathed in the sweet scents of hospital garden. The sun winked through hanging canopies, creating a dancing pattern of light and shadow on the path. Further along, a man in a dressing gown occupied a weatherworn bench. Laura pressed on, sure the prosthetic center lay at the end of the path.

She greeted the man as she passed. He threw biscuit crumbs on the path for the birds.

"Good afternoon," he said, returning her smile. His gaze lowered to her left arm, and his lip twitched.

Laura hurried past, her good mood evaporating. She hid her arm as best she could.

Why can't people stop staring? I'm not a freak!

She rounded a sweeping bend in the path, leaving the man behind and out of sight. She checked her watch.

One minute till two. Think that's pretty punctual.

Laura headed down the remainder of the path to the hospital building. A sign on the door read:

Dr. S. Bowman and Mr. S. Bennet
Prosthetic Center
Bloom Memorial Hospital

Laura knocked on the door.

A thump sounded from the inside, and Laura leaned forward, her ear close to the wood.

What was that?

It sounded again, closer, like someone had dropped a sack full of clothes.

Laura knocked once more. The door swung open, and she stepped back.

On the threshold stood a woman of around thirty in black trousers and a white blouse. Dark hair cascaded around her shoulders in thick waves. She coughed, covering her mouth.

"Yes?" the woman said. She seemed to check the contents of her hand before lowering it. "Can I help you?" She studied Laura with deep, brown eyes.

"I have an appointment with Dr. Bowman?" said Laura. "Is this the right place?"

The woman stared past her for a moment and seemed to snap her attention back.

"I'm Dr. Bowman. Laura, isn't it? Two' o'clock?"

Laura nodded.

"Step inside," said Bowman, smiling and holding the door open. "I was just cleaning up."

Laura entered, pleased by the warm, light room. It contrasted to the sterile, bleak corridors of the rest of the hospital.

"Nice place. Not what I expected."

Bowman closed the door and stared toward the rear of the room. Another door stood open.

"The treatment can be a challenge at the best of times. We like everyone to be as relaxed as possible." The doctor remained frozen, attention held by the far door. "Take a seat," she said.

Laura walked around a rug, which was rolled up and left in the middle of the room. A throw draped a sofa. Laura sat, sinking on the plush cushions beneath.

90

"I'll just be a moment," said Bowman, not looking in Laura's direction. "Make yourself comfortable. Today might change your life."

The girl sighed.

I hope so.

She glanced down at her stump.

Bowman, unblinking, crossed the room and vanished through the rear door.

Laura exhaled and settled back, listening to the gentle tick of the wall clock.

She seems nice enough. A little distracted, though.

Hope she's as good as her reputation.

Minutes passed, and Laura's attention wandered from her stump to the window, to her stump to the clock, and back to her stump. She knew her arm would never grow back, save for some miracle breakthrough. Even the thought of having a guy's arm grafted on appealed. She'd be more of a freak, but at least she could play the guitar.

Back to the clock. Ten minutes had gone by.

Ten minutes! What the hell is she doing? Should I check on her?

Bowman entered the room.

"I'm sorry about that," said the doctor, out of breath. "I was conferring with my engineer about your new arm. May I see?" Bowman sat on the sofa and smiled, holding out her hands.

Laura offered her disfigurement and looked away. Bowman's fingers rubbed and stroked the smooth, pink ball of skin at the end.

"Mmm ... good. Muscle tone largely intact. Yessss ..."

Laura glanced back. Something had crackled in Bowman's voice, like a short blast of electrical static.

"Should make an upgrade easy ..."

"Doctor?"

Bowman peered up. Her left eye shimmered emerald.

Laura blinked. "Wow."

The doctor frowned.

"Your eye," said Laura, and studied the wall. Her cheeks burned. "I guess I didn't notice earlier."

Bowman released Laura's arm.

"I'll go get your new attachment. Then we can begin."

The doctor rose in silence and strode out of the room.

Laura grinned.

Attachment? Makes me sound like a vacuum cleaner.

Heat flashed in her face once again. She realized how she'd been transfixed by the doctor's eye.

Must be human nature to stare. Damn it! I'm a fucking hypocrite!

The hands of the clock crept around.

Laura tapped her foot. A few magazines on a coffee table in the corner seemed the way to go.

She glanced at the clock. The time had reached twenty past.

"A third of my hour gone and nothing. Forget the magazines," Laura hissed. She stood. "Dr. Bowman?"

Silence and darkness lurked beyond the open door.

"Dr. Bowman?" Laura called.

She crossed the suite.

I shouldn't be doing this. Might be off limits to patients.

Hell. It's my time she's wasting!

Laura reached the door and peered inside. The deep, wide room, lit by hanging bulbs along the far side, lay cluttered with shelves and boxes. Her eyes adjusted to the murk, and a maze of plastic limbs emerged.

"Jesus," she said, studying the hanging arms. A box of protruding legs looked like crazy modern art.

"Dr. Bowman?"

She ventured further.

From the other side of the room, something clattered on the floor.

Laura stopped behind a rack of synthetic arms fitted with hooks.

"Thank you," the doctor said. Her voice echoed in the cold room. "Let us begin."

Laura opened her mouth, ready to call out, but paused. The doctor's voice had regained the strange static sound. The girl gazed around the rack.

At the far wall, the doctor stood before a sink, staring at her reflection in a grimy mirror. Bowman lifted her hand and examined the contents.

Laura crept forward, keeping close to the rack of arms. She crouched behind a workbench and peered around the side.

Bowman still studied the object she held. It appeared to be a small lightbulb, the size of a large marble. She turned it in her fingers for a second and placed it beside the sink. A leather bag sat beside, and the doctor reached in.

What is she doing?

Bowman removed a scalpel from the bag. The blade glistened between her face and reflection. She stared at the instrument, moving it closer and closer, the point heading for her eye.

Laura opened her mouth, a scream trapped in her throat.

Bowman plunged the scalpel deep into her pupil. It made a sound like squashing a grape.

Hands clamped over her mouth, Laura froze behind the workbench, transfixed by the doctor's reflection.

Bowman's eye, now a punched, sagging membrane, slid down her cheek in a slug's crawl. She sliced the attaching scarlet fibers with a flick of the blade. Her eye plopped on the floor.

Laura's throat tightened. She held her breath, fighting the gag.

The doctor tucked the flaccid tissue back into her empty socket, ignoring the blood and aqueous humour pouring down her cheek. She picked up the tiny bulb.

Blue worms, needle-thin, emerged from the metal plug and wiggled in the air.

Laura gasped.

Bowman neared the bulb to her empty socket. The tendrils took hold of her eyelids, and the bulb eased itself inside. She blinked once, twice, and opened wide. Her new eye glowed a radiant green.

"I know she's here," the doctor buzzed, her lips barely moving. "Leave it to me."

Laura sprang and burst into a run for the door. A protruding false leg tripped her, and she fell forward, landing hard on her hand and knees. Keeping her momentum, she jumped back up, legs pumping.

Dr. Bowman blocked her escape.

"Leaving so soon? I thought you wanted your new arm?"

Laura backed up, aware Bowman still held the scalpel. The doctor smiled and inched forward.

"You've gone quiet. Maybe a new tongue is also in order?"

"Stay away," said Laura. She swept up a hammer from a nearby shelf. "Don't come near me!"

"But isn't that why you're here? So I can touch you ... rebuild you?"

"You're ... what you just did ..."

"What I just did was amazing!" said Bowman. "I mean, look at me!" She, too. approached the shelves and selected a dusty saw. She pressed the teeth against her hip. "Think of the endless possibilities ..."

Laura turned and ran, darting between boxes and workbenches into the shadowed depths.

Under a bulb, framed in a stark halo of light, sat a polished, metal chair.

"Stop her!" Bowman screamed.

Laura ducked to the side.

The chair hummed.

Laura dashed past more shelves and cried out as she flew upward, held her up by the waist. She thrashed in the grip and pulled at the squeezing noose around her middle. A glance down revealed a shiny, thick cable. The metallic tentacle eased her backward. She kicked in the air.

"Bind her ..." said Bowman.

Laura crashed into the chair. Intimate snakes of metal laced around her limbs.

"No!" she wailed.

Snap!

Something clamped around her waist and punched the air from her lungs.

Snap snap snap!

Leather straps flew from the chair and bound her tight.

Bowman approached. Blood gushed from her hip from beneath the saw blade.

Laura screeched.

"Quiet down. You should be grateful. Look at you, such a freak. I was a freak once, but I upgraded. Look at me now ..."

"Please. Please just let me go!"

"But you came here for treatment. You want a new arm, don't you?"

"I just want to go. Please! I won't tell anyone."

Bowman held up the bloody saw.

"You'll tell the world. You would even write a song about this, if you could still play. You didn't think I knew about that."

Laura wailed. "Please don't kill me."

"We don't want to kill you." Bowman walked over. "We only want to help." She touched Laura's stump. "How many years? How many stares and comments? You could be more than any of them."

Laura howled at the tightening straps.

The doctor began to unbuttoned her own trousers.

"No," screamed Laura. "Please!"

Ignoring her pleas, Bowman slid the garment down her legs.

Laura stared. "You're ...?"

"Yes," said Bowman, caressing the joint of her prosthetic leg. "Just like you, but more." She popped the leg free. Metal winked. Pulling the plastic free, the doctor revealed a second leg hidden beneath. "Incredible, isn't it?"

She pulled the false leg away, and the new spidery limb slid further from her torso. It glinted with the metal chrome of the chair. The double-jointed leg pounded the floor with a sharp point. Blood tricked from the haggard stump where metal met flesh and bone.

"You can have all this and more. Think of the potential. You can be like me."

Laura fought the chair. Her own stump pounded the shiny top.

"Think about it," Bowman said. "The world lies in your palm."

She walked to one of the workbenches, bent over and slid a door open. An arm flopped out from the dark and hit the floor with a splat. Most of the fingers were missing from the hand.

"And don't worry. We have lots of spare parts!" The doctor approached the throbbing chair, her new leg clunking on the floor with each step. "Now," she said, leaning in close. "Shall we begin?"

95

AFTER DARQUE

BY M.L. ROOS

I'm half the man I used to be. Literally. When I was twenty-eight, I was six foot five and weighed two hundred pounds. Now, six years later, I've lost three feet and seventy pounds. Well, two feet ... ok, two legs. And you want to know how. Get yourself a coffee and pull up a seat. It's going to take some time to go through it. I could give you the condensed version, but that would do the story injustice. You need the nuances, the subtleties, and the intricacies of what was going on in my head at the time. Without it, this becomes a sad story about a meaningless man and his even sadder obsessions.

Six years ago, my life was pretty normal. I had a great job doing what I loved. In Winnipeg, I was one of the youngest investigators in Violent Crimes, and we were working on this major case involving human trafficking. It was a special project that sprang up overnight because of media attention. You know how that goes. The vilest crap can be happening in the world, but unless the media or politicians pick up on it, it won't see the light of day.

With this piece, a journalist happened to discover a story about a young girl who had been sold as a prostitute several times to different people. She ended up being bought by a minister and his wife, who used her as an indentured servant and sex slave. She was a thirteen-year-old then. Because the minister also happened to be embezzling funds and running a scam in his church, he got caught with his hand in the cookie jar, and "Lucy" became the charity case du jour. Project Eve was created, and I was selected to work on the task force.

I had girlfriends. I dated. That part of my life was fine. I had several great friends both on and off the force. Being single, I had lots of time on my hands to do research into the sex industry and human trafficking. Eventually, this led me to several people including judges, lawyers, politicians, even a few actors. We can write the laws, enforce them—but damn, can we follow them? Select people will always feel entitled, whether it is to church funds or sex with a thirteen-year-old. Don't matter. Some men are ruled by their genitals and their hands; whatever they can grab with either, it's theirs.

Another road led through Organized Crime, including a huge syndicate in Toronto and another in Vancouver with connections in Winnipeg. Aboriginal girls were being sold as quickly as they were picked up, and sold across the country. But the most interesting and dangerous connections were the clubs. They were in every city all across Canada, probably all across the world. These were connected to Organized Crime and the porn industry as well, and if I told you who was involved in them, you wouldn't believe me. Let's just say there are some doctors in this city I wouldn't want touching my testicles, knowing where their hands have been.

Anyway, one day in September, I ran across a note in a file about a club called After Darque. I had heard references to this place. You see, I visited these clubs on weekends trying to make connections with people and seeing if I could make some inroads. I needed to find the girls—who they were, where they came from, and where they ended up. To do that, I had to fit in. So, I had to act the part. I dressed the part; I interacted with the clients and, before you ask, I did participate in the events. I had to make them believe I was a part of them. I had to gain their trust and, without engaging in the sex, I would have been suspect. Besides, it was all legal. No drugs were involved and there was nothing to do with children in these clubs. Just sex. Sex like you cannot imagine.

There were groups, bondage, role-playing, S&M, voyeurism, you name it. It was a heady mixture of people, objects. OK, I won't get into details. Suffice it to say those were the most intense experiences of my life. For a few short months, I can say I was on top of the world. And I lost focus. I became so wrapped up in wanting to be accepted into the scene that I forgot the reason I was there in the first place. If I am really honest with myself—and I can do that after a few bottles of JD—I lost who *I* was. I was no longer a detective in Winnipeg looking for stray girls and saving them from the horror their lives had become. I became a man looking for sex, became nothing better than the creeps that bought and sold these girls like pieces of meat.

But the crash. Man, that was hard. Have you ever known or seen a drug addict who was trying to go cold turkey? While you are chasing the dragon, it is the most exhilarating experience of your life. Colors are brighter; sounds are sharper; your thoughts race, but they are crystalline drops of the most intelligent ideas you have ever had. I mean, you can solve all the world's problems in a single morning! But it takes more, you know? With drugs and with sex, it always takes more.

Soon, the research became less and less important and the clubs took over my thoughts. I couldn't concentrate at work anymore. People were starting to comment. Even my boss noticed. I shook it off and fought back. One weekend, I took some files home. I had decided that I would stay focused and work. Do actual work, not go out, not get involved in this dark world. I had full intentions of turning on TSN, cracking a beer, and leafing through the files, maybe make a few notes. Then, I see this scribble in a margin of a file. All it said was *After Darque*. Didn't know what it meant at the time, but then I realized a couple months back I was at XTC and one of the regulars there mentioned an underground club he had been to, only he referred to it as AD. He said it was by invitation only and you had to know someone to get in. Some real secretive and clandestine place. I thought at the time he was bragging, but what if he was trying to pique my interest? If he went, he could be my invitation, right?

I jumped in the shower, got dressed, and raced out the door. Fridays he was at XTC. I got there just after eleven. The room was dimly lit and on stage there were a couple of people giving a show for the crowd, people stood around applauding and cheering. Others were engaging in their own show at various tables around the room. I walked through the smoky haze, my curiosity getting the better of me, and glanced at a few of the scenes on display. I know, sounds sick, right? But actually, in these kinds of places, people like me fit right in. Watching is expected, encouraged. Some folks just want an audience, know what I'm saying? I saw this one girl in black leather, thigh-high boots, a black thong, and red corset, standing over a prostrate guy chained naked to a floor-level rack. Well, naked accept for the giant ball gag and anal plug. But I digress. Nudge me if I fade a bit. I tend to get lost in fond memories.

I saw "Joe" in the back, standing by the bar. I grabbed him and asked him about After Darque. He told me I wasn't ready and walked away. I tried to follow him, but I lost him in the crowd. I went back, week after week after week. Joe was never there. I lost interest in the clubs. I lost interest in the sex. I lost interest in my life. Just didn't give a damn anymore. All I thought about was After Darque. I didn't even know what it was, but I needed it.

I spent my days working, halfheartedly, on files and entering data about cases I really didn't care about, and my nights looking for Joe or other people who could tell me about AD. Or walking aimlessly.

Sex become mundane, boring, an existentialist's cage bound by social conventions and mores. I understood the dilemma Charlie Sheen faces and why he feels the need to visit his "lady" friends. I think he's looking for the same thing I am; the next experience, a new level of feeling, a new rush. I mean, when you get down to it, how many times can you suck, fuck, lick, or insert your body parts into someone else's and have it be exciting? Yeah, it feels good and it's a time waster, but seriously. Admit it. Where is the excitement? Where is the life-or-death struggle? Where is the intensity? Maybe I was looking too hard or maybe I was missing something. I mean inside me. Maybe there is a chemical or a gland or an organ that is missing or defective. Or have the majority of people reached a level of complacency they are happy with? I felt defeated.

One day, I heard a knock on the door. When I got up, there was no one there, but there was an envelope on the floor. I opened it up. Two words: *You're Ready*. I looked at the card stock. At the bottom of the note were two letters: AD. This was it! This was the invitation. But where? There was no address, no phone, no discernible clue as to where this place was located. Finally, after all this time, it's here and I couldn't pry myself from bed to answer the door. Dammit!

I decided to go to XTC to track down Joe. I would wait there all night if I had to; I was determined to get into After Darque tonight. I had to. I got there around midnight. There was standing room only.

Apparently tonight was the Cirque de Soleil of Sex. I have never seen so many naked bodies in one place. I felt like I was looking at Dante's Inferno. No matter where I looked, it was another act of debauchery and madness. The Marquis de Sade would have blushed. Makes me feel sad for the human race.

I scoured the room, trying to make out Joe's face in the sea of naked flesh. I felt a hand on my shoulder and turned around. Mr. Ball Gag held out an envelope to me. He couldn't speak. Hell he could hardly walk but he was doing the best he could as his lady friend tugged on her leash and dragged him away. I looked at the envelope and immediately wanted to sterilize my hand. I shuddered involuntarily and ripped open the seal. Inside was another postcard on the same card stock as before—60lb cream vellum paper with gold lettering, the initials AD, and an address. Finally, success. I ran to my car, switched on my GPS, and headed off to paradise—or, as I call it now, paradise lost. Ha.

I ended up in the warehouse district. Nothing around for miles except big, gray buildings, the occasional streetlight, and wide-open spaces. I checked the address again and ran it through my Garmin and, yup, I was right where I was supposed to be—a huge, deserted, run-down building on the outskirts of town. I drove around the structure and could not find a discernible door. I decided to circle it one more time to see if I missed something. After all this time, I felt like this was a taunt. What the hell, I mean, I deserved this, dammit.

I slammed my fist against the steering wheel and accidentally hit the horn. A red light came on over top one of the doors in the building. It was faint, but in the darkness of the isolated area I was in, it was easy to see. I got out of my car and walked toward the light, looking at the door, a steel rectangle with no handle, no keyhole, nothing. I heard the sound of metal on metal and a small circle of light appeared at eye level. I saw dark brown eyes looking at me. I could hear music and mechanical noises coming from within. Brown Eyes glared at me. "What?" He spit the word out as if it burnt his tongue.

"I don't know if I am in ..."

"Probably not. Card?" he asked.

"I, um, yeah I got a card," I sputtered.

"Show it to me, genius," he said, snickering.

I pulled it out of my jacket and held it to the slot.

The slot slammed shut with an audible clang and the door opened. I stepped inside and could not make out a thing. Black curtains hung, making a dark tunnel about twenty feet long. I could hear the whirring of machinery, tools hitting metal, music, and nothing else. Was this shop class?

Brown Eyes looked me over and said "Follow the music. You'll find it," and walked away.

Must have been the Welcome Wagon's day off. I walked through the darkness feeling like I was being pulled through a birth canal by invisible hands. My stomach ached and my legs felt weak. I don't know if it was from the excitement of finally being there or if it was a warning. Hindsight is always 20/20. Regardless, I pushed on and reached the end. And found more black curtains and cordoned-off areas, individual black wombs. I kept walking, not knowing what I would find, but really not expecting this cavernous, black-curtained hamster trail. Still could not hear voices, which was odd. I was expecting the same atmosphere as XTC—you know, the typical nightclub experience with music, throngs of people, laughter. But this emptiness was unnerving. I continued forward, pushing my way through the black womb, still completely unsure of what I was getting myself into, the rock in my stomach growing heavier and heavier and my mind screaming at me to get the hell out.

But the dim lighting and the black walls were eerily calming, and maybe they were also absorbing the sound. And some of the madness as well? Yeah, that must be it. Isn't it comforting how you can lie to yourself and buy into it? Ah, the great human need to want what it shouldn't have and to justify it with deception. You know what I mean, right? The way you look at the neighbor's wife and visualize her lying naked on your bed, begging you to take her now because no one is a bigger stud than you? Come on, I know you've done that at some point in your life. And then you tell yourself it is harmless because you are only thinking it and not doing it, right? And besides, the neighbor is an asshole and he doesn't deserve a fine piece like her. I can tell you had those thoughts. I can see it by the look on your face. Yeah, your secret is safe with me.

Anyway, where was I? Oh yeah, in the womb of the earth or the bowels of hell, considering what I left behind. Should have listened to my gut. Instead, I was led by my morbid curiosity. I kept going deeper and deeper into the cavern and finally came to a central room. It was beautiful in a haunted kind of way—red-velvet couches and settees; a roaring fireplace; crystal lamps; low, black tables. But not a single person. I sat on a couch, still debating if I should run. But it took so long to finally get there, and I lied to myself once again, telling myself I was there for the missing girls and not the distorted sex. What a schmuck, but it gets you through the night, right Charlie?

So I waited ... and waited. Finally, Ball-Gag man appears, looking a bit more dignified in a suit and tie than he did with that anal plug, I'll tell you.

"Welcome to After Darque, Mr. Stice. What can I offer you to drink?"

"How do you know my name?"

"I know a great deal about you, Detective. I have my own version of ... surveillance. No one comes here by chance. Everyone here has been hand-chosen." He grinned at me, his teeth a brilliant, unnatural white. An instance of feral anger flashed across his face, but it was so fleeting that I thought I had imagined it. "My name is Kane and I am here to fulfill your desire, whatever that may be." He chuckled. "Now, about that drink. I believe your libation of choice was Jack Daniel's, but that is so common. How about absinthe? A delicacy in Europe." He snapped his fingers and suddenly a woman appeared, carrying a silver tray with a tall, crystal glass containing a green, smoking liquid. She set the glass down on the table and left as silently as she entered.

"Now, about your desire, Mr. Stice. Shall we discuss what brings you here to After Darque? I suspect there are reasons even you are not aware of that drive you to our group."

"I am looking for a real experience, something better than what I can imagine. Does that make sense?"

"Go on, Mr. Stice," said Kane. He looked at me and smiled. I saw the hardness in his steel-gray eyes, along with an odd twinkle. His manicured hands templed and rested against his lips. In this dark, cave-like room, with the fire going, I could almost see the contract, written in blood, asking for my signature, could see Kane holding out the quill, waiting. It was only my soul I was selling, right?

I gulped down the licorice-flavored drink in one swallow, the wormwood warming my esophagus and cascading into my gut, becoming a sleeping, green dragon in my belly. Sparks flew from the fireplace, floating in the air, a myriad of tiny glowing embers in the stillness.

"In my head, sex is incredible, intense, a gestalt of emotions, sounds, smells, and feelings that goes on forever. But, when the real thing happens, it is the black-and-white version of the colored thing I created. Does that make any sense? I want that intensity, that experience, to be real. I want to forget I exist and just revel in the experience." I was rambling, I knew, but I had to convey what was impossible to explain.

Kane chuckled to himself. "I believe, Mr. Stice, I can offer you what you are seeking. But, are you willing to travel down that path? Once you begin this journey, you cannot go back."

"If you can give me what I am looking for, I won't want to go back." I knew I was lost and I did not care.

"Well, then, I believe we can begin." He stood and motioned me to follow him. I did, oh God, I did. I knew I should turn back, but I kept going. You know why? Because I was going to be the genius that could take this experience, use it, play with it for a while, and not get my hands dirty. Because I was smart, smarter that anyone else. I was brighter and cagier than any lost soul who walked into this place, and I *could* outplay the Devil. I could get my soul back any time I chose. Now I know nothing is more deluded than the man who believes he is in control of his own life.

We walked into another dimly lit room, cushions all over the floor, candles, soft music. Against one wall were basins and rolls of something I could not make out—but then I wasn't paying too close attention to my surroundings. The absinthe was making me a little foggy, and I suspected there was more than wormwood in the green liquid. Naked men and women relaxed on cushions, slowly caressing each other. In the middle of the floor was a low platform, and this is where I was led.

"Last chance, Mr. Stice. One more opportunity, of your own free will, to go home." Kane's eyes had a faint glow to them, boring into my head, piercing my brain.

"No, I'm ready. But this better not be just some group sex thing. I want intensity, like we talked about, Kane. I want to remember this for the rest of my life."

"Don't worry. You will never forget this moment, I promise you that."

I stretched out on that platform, never once thinking about what I was doing or what I was giving up. I blame that on the drink, because I can't believe I would willingly do it on my own.

People drew closer to the platform, and I heard the clang of metal on metal and the rip of plastic tearing. Hands were all over my body removing my clothes, rubbing my legs, massaging my head. I closed my eyes and took it all in, waiting for the moment when this would be different. So far, this was like all the rest.

Someone sat me up and removed my shirt. I watched her and she bent down to kiss me. I started to kiss her back and realized she had no tongue or teeth. Her mouth was a gaping cavern. I pulled back, a spike of fear piercing me—but too late. She grinned, and then slammed me down on the platform. I felt straps being tied to my ankles as hands held me down and more straps were tied to my wrists and shoulders, a ball gag shoved in my mouth.

I looked more closely at the group surrounding me. Every one of them was missing some body part—dear God, missing hands, lips, ears, noses, fingers, legs, every single one of them.

I tried to get up, to scream, to fight, but all I could hear was the whirring of a saw blade and Kane laughing in the back of the room. Hands caressed my legs and stroked my inner thigh. Other hands grabbed my arm and held it steady while soft lips wrapped around my penis. The feeling was exquisite! While the gentle sucking continued, I could feel the cold steel blade sever a finger from my hand. I saw stars, and my orgasm exploded beyond an intensity I could have possibly imagined. I couldn't breathe, and I drifted in a sea of darkness that went on forever.

And that was the beginning, my friend. I went back, month after month. It was hard explaining the missing body parts to coworkers after a while. Neuralgia due to a training accident was good for the missing finger. Then there was the unfortunate incident with the chainsaw that took my hand. Things got truly weird when I lost my leg. That's when they put me on administrative leave, made me see a shrink. Guess they didn't buy the flesh-eating disease story. So now I wait, and I try to conserve because I am running out of me. I figure I have about three or four more visits left before I won't be able to continue anymore.

And I need to save my hand—my thumb and one finger to hold the razor blade.

THE AFFAIR OF THE JADE DRAGON

BY RICK HUDSON

The body had been brutally abused both before and after death. It would be unseemly and prurient to give greater detail; let me just say that—even by London standards—this was an abominable and abysmal murder.

"Gangland, Inspector Lestrade?" my sergeant asked.

"No doubt."

The body of the scrawny man had been discovered sprawled in the bath of his small apartment in a tawdry district of the city. I did not need to turn on the ratiocinator to know that this man had been both a user and a dealer of narcotics. The accoutrements of drug use were openly scattered about the apartment with no attempt to disguise them—syringes, pipes, spoons, everything. The stuff itself wasn't even imaginatively hidden. The fellow was probably dealing off turf, and this had been not only a punitive killing, but one meant as a caution to others who would consider transgressing the trade boundaries established by the city's crime barons.

I reached up behind my right ear and pushed down on the small area of flesh that covered the ratiocinator implanted in my skull. As the device stirred into life, I returned to the disordered living room of the addict's den. My eyes scanned all the details so the optic circuitry could feed the miniature electrical device in my head. As always, some neural anomaly caused me to experience the olfactory illusion of heavy tobacco smoke when the ratiocinator was in action.

I scanned the cluttered table, the grubby shelves, and the dirty sofa. The ratiocinator hungrily devoured the visual data. Before long, I heard the familiar cold, analytical voice in my head.

Ah, Inspector, you have obviously deduced that the body in the bath is that of a minor dealer in narcotics who has contravened the rigidly enforced strictures placed upon such fellows by their underworld moguls?

"I have."

And you have no doubt also noted the preponderance of oriental souvenirs and mementos that clutter the mantelpiece, bookcases, occasional tables, and so on?

"Yes, dealers like this spend a great deal of their time in Thailand and places like that. I was not surprised."

But would it surprise you, Inspector, to know that these remembrances and curios are all Indonesian in origin? Javanese, to be precise.

"That I didn't know."

Yes. And what is more, a recent monograph published upon the Aether-Telegraph concerned itself with a new strain of opiate that is finding itself transported from Jakarta to this city in considerable quantities.

"Really?"

Yes. I read it while you were concerning yourself with a more mundane piece on police procedure. This new opiate is a powerful and extremely addictive substance, and is therefore greatly prized by dealers of such substances. It has been given the grandiose if rather hackneyed appellation of jade dragon. The drug lords are feverish with excitement about its existence. They stand to make a great deal of money from this particular drug. Now, show me the body.

I walked into the bathroom and allowed the ratiocinator to examine the bloody room and the wretched corpse in the bath.

Inspector, the pattern of the blood and injuries would indicate that this unfortunate was dragged and dumped in the bath before any of the actual wounds we see were inflicted upon him. He was obviously tortured with some large blade before being executed by that slash to his throat. Then his body suffered further indignities.

"I'd reckoned as much."

An elementary conclusion, to be sure. Nonetheless, a telling one as the perpetrators had no wish to disguise their identities. Indeed, they wished to advertise the fact.

"And ...?"

One of the Chinese gangs, to be sure. One with its origins in Shanghai, I'd venture.

"But how can you be so specific?"

The wounds are indicative of a particular Chai—or dagger—that is peculiar to the eastern seaboard of China. The injuries and desecrations to the body are horrific and yet precise. I'd be bold enough to state that the murderers are members of the Three Talon Brotherhood. They are renowned for delighting in such elegant atrocities. If memory serves me correctly, they operate out of a food wholesaler's in Limehouse, catering for the oriental restaurant community.

Sergeant Watson and I returned to Scotland Yard in an electric hansom, and I soon took a seat at my desk and powered up the analytical engine. Its screen blinked into life and I quickly accessed the Aether-Telegraph Network. Whilst I scanned its resources, I plugged a cable from the device into one of the sockets at the top of my spine so that the ratiocinator could search other areas of the information network.

Everything the ratiocinator had deduced fitted with what I read on the ATN pages. What deeply worried me was the Three Talon Brotherhood's reputation for being one of the most powerful and brutal of all the Chinese gangs, operating not only in London but around the globe. Drugs, extortion, prostitution, white slavery, smuggling, and all manner of crimes came under the Brotherhood's remit, and they were on the rise.

The ratiocinator's findings only added to the frightening picture of a vicious gang increasing its power base in London.

It would appear that the Brotherhood is increasing in power since it aligned itself with a western man of great intelligence. His identity is unknown, but he must be an individual of great intellect and capability. The Chinese gangs do not usually welcome European associates. I fear that the Three Talon Brotherhood will be a doubly fearful adversary now that it is in allegiance with this shadowy mind.

I did not question the ratiocinator's speculations. Over the next few weeks, ruthless and savage executions swept the London underworld. The Three Talon Brotherhood was doubtlessly expanding its narcotics empire by assassinating the foot soldiers and leaders of rival gangs. Watson and I attended one crime scene in which an Irish crime boss was impaled against a warehouse door with a stevedore's bailing pike. On another occasion, we witnessed the grisly sight of a butcher's cold storage vault in which Thomas Hewitt—a known senior member of the Scarlet Eye gang—and his entire family were suspended from the ceiling on meat hooks. The executions became ghastlier and more frequent. Beheadings, disembowelments, and disfigurements of all kinds became all too familiar in the wharf districts of London.

And then the true damage of jade dragon made itself known, the ratiocinator reported to me:

This terrible drug has crept out of Limehouse like an invisible miasma or infectious vapor. The streets are littered by stumbling or supine addicts as if a dreadful listless plague had hit the city. But it is not just the unfortunates of the warehouse and slum areas that fall to this horror. The drug has found its way into the salons and parlors of the wealthy and comfortable—particularly those who considered themselves to be somewhat bohemian, or members of the faster set. More than one heiress and several Right Honorable sons of families with solid reputations have been carried to asylums, hospitals, and mortuaries.

Neither I nor Watson had any idea about what to do next. I thought that we would pay a visit to the wholesalers that were suspected of being the center of the Three Talon empire. If we were to go during daylight hours, I wouldn't have to worry too much. Curious white men in Limehouse playing tourist or slumming it were a frequent sight before dark, as were those in need of jade dragon. Watson took his revolver.

It would have been a lie to say that we were welcome in Limehouse, but we were not subject to open hostility, only smirking derision. We were obviously two *Gwau-Lai* on the hunt for opiates, whores, or some other shameful pleasure. The business premises took up the ground floor of a building that had once been a corn warehouse. We could not guess what went on in the many stories that towered above it—and, to be truthful, we did not want to.

On entry, we found the interior to be a large, bare, wooden-floored area crowded with shelves and cabinets crammed with all manner of alien foodstuffs. Sacks of rice and less-familiar nutriments hindered our wanderings through this warren of foreignness. I was fascinated by much of what I saw, and I did not have to feign my role of a bewildered and intrigued sightseer too greatly. Watson, too, though he had seen much of the East in his former military career, found himself gawping with astonishment at the string sacks of chicken and ducks' feet that hung from the ceiling.

The proprietor and his underlings mocked us with their quiet smiles and dark eyes, but feared little from the two naive fools who browsed through their stock that—while mundane to them—was a fascinating treasure trove of wonderment to European sensibilities. However, no matter how odd and outlandish the trader's produce was to our eyes, there was nothing to suggest any criminality or links with sinister gangs of thugs.

It was not until we left that the ratiocinator spoke in my head.

Did you observe the tattoo on the proprietor's wrist, Inspector?

"Yes, a swallow in flight, and what I took to be Chinese characters."

Indeed, you saw it. But, as usual, you did not observe it. The swallow, whilst an innocent enough creature in itself, is an identifying mark of members of the Three Talon Brotherhood. And the characters translate roughly as "pledged to the emperor of crime."

"The emperor of crime? That's a little overblown, is it not?"

Grandiloquent, certainly. But not necessarily inaccurate. It obviously refers to the shadowy mind that has aligned itself to, or perhaps from, that phrasing and taken leadership of the Brotherhood.

Both Watson and I agreed that a raid of the wholesaler's was in order, yet we needed something a little more substantial than a tattoo to gain the Commissioner of Police's approval. He, I, and the ratiocinator stayed up most of the night searching through the Aether-Telegraph Network in independent directions, desperately seeking anything that would aid us in this case.

It was, however, a more visceral source that provided us with our next clue. The following morning, the body of another crime lord rival of the Three Talon Brotherhood was discovered. This evil unfortunate had been found executed in the "Blood Eagle" style of the ancient Norsemen. His arms and legs had been stretched apart and he had been nailed alive through the palms of his hands and ankles to the base of a wooden cart. He had not died, however, until his sternum had been sawn through and chest opened so that his ribcage took on the appearance of two wings. After death, or in the process of dying, the contents of his torso had been removed and placed in a bloody, mucoid halo about his person. It was the symbol that had been scribed upon the corpse's forehead in its own juices, however, that stirred the ratiocinator into activity. It was a single letter M.

I could have been forgiven for thinking that the ratiocinator gave a start at that moment when the presence of the M was brought to its attention, and could almost believe that the cold, clinical voice betrayed something resembling emotion. But I was unsure what that emotion was—excitement, fear, even admiration seemed to underscore the tone the device's voice took.

Interesting, most interesting, Inspector. We have already established that some ominous, lurking figure is directing the actions of the Three Talon Brotherhood. We may be a step closer to establishing the identity of that individual. We may even be able to link this anonymous mastermind to a greater and wider campaign of criminal activities and evils.

"How so?"

In my research, I have encountered a suggestion time and time again that a single agent of some genius is the invisible puppeteer behind much of London's felonious enterprises. I have always considered this possibility with suspicion, for I have never uncovered anything of suitable significance to authenticate the existence of this architect of corruption. This individual I have always considered to be nothing more than a product of criminal folklore or the wild imaginings and mythologies of London's darker streets. And yet, this shadow may be gathering substance before our eyes. This unseen, malevolent hand and the engineer behind the Three Talon's rise may be one and the same.

It seemed so farfetched, and yet was it any more incredible than any of the oddities I had encountered in the preceding weeks? I pressed the ratiocinator on the matter:

"How have you come to suspect that these two mysterious individuals are one and the same?"

Because, my dear Lestrade, if this underworld suzerain is ever referred to directly—and that does not happen frequently—he is referred to by one of two titles. He is either denoted rather enigmatically as "the Professor," or simply signified as "M."

Although it was hardly within the bounds of legitimate police work, both Watson and I agreed to a proposal put forward by the ratiocinator. To be blunt, we would break into the Chinese wholesaler's one night and search the place and see what we would find. In dark clothes and with torches in our pockets, we took a cab as far into Limehouse as the driver dare take us. We continued on foot through the menacing alleys and streets, and, while we were subject to intimidating glances and verbal scorn by the neighborhood's inhabitants, we thankfully arrived at our destination unmolested.

The sergeant and I slinked down an alley that ran down one side of the building and found a low window, which Watson forced open. The two of us scrambled in and found the place in total darkness. There were no sounds that suggested anyone was on the premises. Snapping on our torches, we discovered we were in a storeroom of some sort. We commenced a search of the ground floor. After some time, we were confident that this level contained no office or similar room that would betray any illicit activity, so we made our way up a concrete stairway to see if the upper stories would be more profitable.

The ratiocinator had been quiet, and I hoped that it was engaged in deductive cogitations. Now would be a poor time for its Reichenbach circuits to be failing. We moved from the staircase onto the next floor through a pair of heavy wooden doors to find ourselves in a corridor that extended a considerable distance ahead of us. Similar sets of doors were placed at regular intervals down both sides of the corridor. Watson and I walked on, not really sure what we were looking for, but trusting our intuitions to guide us. It was when we were halfway down the passageway that the Three Talon hoodlums fell upon us. They burst from doors ahead and behind us, wielding a fiendish array of blades and cudgels. Watson fell to a blow from one of these despicable fellows, but I was not to learn of his fate at that time as I, too, was struck upon the head by a weapon that was part chain and part iron bar. I fell painfully into unconsciousness.

Equally painfully and wracked with nausea, I came to my senses some indeterminable time later. The pain of my awakening was doubled by the white glare that blazed into my eyes, as I had regained consciousness in a savagely lit room. I was bound to a chair and unable to move. A hand, its wrist tattooed with a swallow and Chinese characters, went to my forehead and put fingers to my throat, checking my vital signs.

"Unlike your Sergeant, Inspector, you are alive," said the man, I assumed the proprietor of the establishment.

As my faculties slowly returned, I realized that I was in the most unlikely of environments. I was in a large room with the appearance of an operating theater. Indeed, on a nearby table lay a smartly dressed but otherwise nondescript European man. I could not tell if he was alive or dead. A masked surgeon and gowned assistants wheeled in a second table from an adjoining room.

"Yes, we need you alive, but only long enough to remove that interesting device from your head and place it in its new host. It will be interesting to see what information he has gleaned from the databanks of Scotland Yard. What secrets, I wonder, has M uncovered for us?"

And in that second, I was convinced I heard the cold, black chuckle of the Napoleon of Crime in my head.

THE FUTURE OF FLESH

BY JM REINBOLD

At the bar at Garibaldi's, Mike Gambone hunched over his beer. He kept his eyes on the big screen TV. A waitress brought a bacon cheeseburger to a guy at a nearby table. The smell made Mike's mouth water. He sipped his beer and made a face at the flat, stale taste. He'd finished off the peanuts an hour ago, but the bartender hadn't refilled the dish. Mike checked the Absolut clock on the wall behind the bar. One minute to eight. Wait for it ... the minute hand hit the 12 ... the houselights dimmed, the sports channel switched to music videos. The glorified beer jerk turned and stared at Mike's glass. Time to order another or move along. Mike swallowed the last of his warm beer and reached for his jacket, dreading the five-block walk back to his room in the bone-chilling February wind.

He had one arm in a sleeve when a blonde walked up to the bar, unsteady on her five-inch heels. Mike let the jacket slide off his arm and sat down. She wore a red dress so tight it looked sprayed on. The blonde turned in his direction, ghost pale with smudgy, dark eyes. She opened her mouth and ran her tongue over plump lips, glossed a shiny, shocking, wet red. Embarrassed, Mike looked away.

Man, oh, man, she was hot. Mike couldn't stop himself sneaking another look. A guy in a sharp black suit sidled over to the blonde. A few minutes later, by the time the bartender brought their drinks, the two were chatting like old friends. The blonde sipped her drink; the guy finished his in one swallow. She smiled at him between sips. Never taking her eyes off his, she stroked his arm. The guy put his hand on her back. She moved closer.

Mike did not need to see this. He looked away and caught the bartender smirking at him. Mike glared and turned back to the couple just as the guy's hand slid down the blonde's back and over the curve of her ass.

Mike winced at a cramp in his chest. He clenched and unclenched his fists, but the knot only got tighter. Sweat beaded his forehead. He watched as the blonde climbed into the guy's lap. Her dress couldn't have been more than two inches below her crotch. The guy slid his hand up her dress. The blonde rocked her hips. Mike stared, every nerve on fire. It took a few seconds before he realized the guy was looking right at him. A flash of panic lit up his brain. He ducked his head and stared into his glass.

When he looked up again the guy and the blonde were gone. What the hell had just happened? He shoved the empty glass away and grabbed his jacket.

"Mike Gambone! How you doin', man?"

Startled at hearing his name, Mike jumped. He turned to find the guy in the black suit standing behind him.

"Do I know you?"

"Phil Demartini," the guy answered with a grin. "From the old neighborhood."

The Phil Demartini Mike knew had buck teeth that could open beer bottles and a beak like a toucan. This guy looked airbrushed perfect, like he'd stepped off the pages of GQ. Mike pulled on his jacket and dropped a quarter on the bar.

"Yeah, right," Mike said.

"Come on, man, we were best friends back in the day."

Mike snorted. He didn't know who the hell this guy was or what he wanted, but him claiming to be Phil was bullshit.

"The Phil Demartini I knew never looked nothing like you."

Phil laughed. "Just messin' with you, dude. I knew you wouldn't recognize me. I had some work done."

Mike squinted at the man claiming to be his childhood friend. "Work?"

"Yeah, you know ... cosmetic surgery." Phil slid onto a bar stool one away from Mike's.

Mike stood. "I'm outta here."

"Hold up, man. I'm telling you, it's me. Ask me something nobody but us could know."

Mike hesitated. He and Phil had been best buds until Mike's dad died and his family moved back to Jersey. What could it hurt to hear what the guy had to say?

"Okay," Mike said. "Aunt Augusta."

Phil chuckled.

Mike scowled. "What's so funny?"

"I'm not laughing at you, man. I knew you'd pick Aunt Gussie, our deepest, darkest secret." Phil leaned toward Mike and whispered in his ear.

Mike gaped. No one except Phil knew the truth about Aunt Gussie. About what they'd done.

"Well, Mikey, did I pass?"

Wide-eyed, Mike stared at Phil. "What the hell happened to you? Your voice doesn't even sound the same."

"I told you, man, cosmetic surgery and a little nick on the cords. Changed my life."

"No kidding," Mike said. "That smokin' hot blonde, she your girlfriend?"

"Nah, we're just friends. Her name's Star. She's something, isn't she?"

Mike licked his lips. "Oh, yeah."

Phil chuckled. "When we go out we play this game sometimes, like we're strangers. You know what I mean?"

"Man," Mike said, "you are one lucky jabroni."

"What're you drinking, bro?" Phil asked.

"Lucky's."

"Jesus," Phil said. "They serve that shit here?"

Phil caught the bartender's eye, waved him over and ordered a couple of expensive lagers.

Mike sipped the lager, savoring it. The liquid felt heavy on his tongue. Compared to this, the stuff he'd been drinking tasted like warm water. He licked the foam from his lips. "Thanks."

"My pleasure, Mikey." Phil took a long swallow. "How's your mom doing?"

"Gone."

"You mean ..."

Mike nodded.

"I'm sorry to hear that, man."

The lump in Mike's throat made him choke on his next swallow of beer. Phil waved at a waitress and pointed at the empty peanut bowl. She smiled and tossed her hair as she swung by.

"How about an upgrade?" She slid a basket of wings with dipping sauce in front of Phil.

"Thanks, babe!" Phil flashed Hollywood-bright teeth. He watched as she ducked and dodged through the crowd, her tray held high above her head. He sighed and passed the wings to Mike.

"Hey, thanks!" Mike grabbed a fat wing. He ignored the sauce, tearing the meat off the bones with his teeth.

"No problem, bro. So, how long you been in Delaware?"

Mike bit into one wing after another. He answered Phil between mouthfuls.

"Came here for a job a couple months ago. It sounded like a sure thing. Then I meet the guy and all of sudden there ain't no job. I pick up some one-shot day work in construction here and there, so I stuck around, but if I don't get something permanent soon, I'm gonna be sleeping at the mission."

Phil didn't say anything for a minute or two, then asked, "Can you drive a delivery truck?"

Mike shrugged. "Sure. I got my CDL. But I can't get nothing."

"I'll see what I can do. I might be able to get you something with my company."

Caught of guard, Mike couldn't help but look surprised. The last time he'd heard anything about Phil, he'd been working at some crummy pizza joint for minimum wage. "You have a company?"

"Well, yeah. I mean, I don't own it. But I'm the regional manager. Surgical supplies." Phil winked at Mike. "That's how I met Star. She's a surgical nurse in a private hospital. You seeing anyone?"

Mike narrowed his eyes and gave Phil the look. The one his grandmother called il malocchio.

"Whoa!" Phil said leaning away from Mike. "What's that for?" He crossed himself. "God bless me."

"What do you think? I look like an ape and you ask me if I'm seeing anyone? Did they take out your brain when they fixed your face?"

Phil sucked air through his teeth. "No need for talk like that. Get a little work done."

"A little work? Are you kidding me? No offense, man, but you look like you had a whole fucking body transplant." *Must have cost millions,* Mike muttered under his breath.

"Hey," Phil said, "take it easy."

"So, how much did it cost you?"

"It cost me nada."

"Now I know you're shitting me."

"No, man." Phil said, shaking his head. "I know a guy."

"And he does this for free? How does that work?"

Phil shrugged. "I help him out from time to time. And ... I let him try out some new stuff on me."

"What ... like ... experimental?"

"The doc is always coming up with new procedures and he has to test them."

"You let him use you like a lab rat?"

Phil ignored the question, answering brusquely as if Mike had offended him. "He's a professional, man. Worst case scenario, you don't turn out quite right and you look a little funky until you heal enough for him to go back and make adjustments. No big deal."

"So, who is this guy?"

"Dr. Fleischman. He's in the industrial park over by the B&O Lanes."

"Industrial park? You gotta be kidding me."

"No, man ..."

Mike waved Phil away. What the fuck? How could that be legit?

Phil stood up. He pulled a card from his inside pocket and pushed it over to Mike. "It was good seeing you again, Mikey. Keep in touch, okay?"

Mike nodded. "You got it."

"Listen. You change your mind and you want me to hook you up with the doc, let me know." Phil clapped Mike on the shoulder and headed for the door.

Mike stared at Phil's card. There it was in black and white: Philip Demartini, Regional Manager, TSR Surgical and Hospital Supply, business and cell numbers.

Phil looked like a million bucks. And Star ... Star ... saliva pooled in Mike's mouth. It sounded crazy. It was crazy. But, what if Phil's "guy" could fix him? If Mike could look like Phil, there'd be no more being treated like a retard. No more "disappearing" jobs. No faces twisting in revulsion. No stench of desperation on him.

If he turned out even half as good as Phil, he could get a girl like Star. Shit, he could get any woman he wanted. So what if the guy experimented on him. Could he look any worse? Mike's whole life could change, like Phil's had. Wouldn't it be worth it? The bottom line was: What did he have to lose? The answer was easy: Nothing.

It had taken a while, but Mike finally found Dr. Fleischman's office in the last building at the back of the industrial park. It just figured. And the door was locked. He jabbed a finger at the doorbell. While he waited for someone to let him in, he saw a Rolls-Royce pull up to the front of the warehouse. The security doors rumbled up. The car drove in and the doors rumbled down. He was about to push the bell again when the lock clicked and the door opened.

"Mr. Gambone, please come in. I'm Miss Dare, Dr. Fleischman's assistant."

Mike wondered how she knew his name. He had an appointment, sure, but so did lots of people. Then again, maybe a doc like this didn't see many patients.

"Follow me, please." A platinum blonde, Miss Dare had that ethereal glow of a 1940's Hollywood starlet. She walked ahead of him at a leisurely pace. Mike admired her tiny waist and the side-to-side sway of her heart-shaped backside. She led Mike down a wide hallway. The only light came from lamps high up in the ceiling. Tall shelves covered with plastic sheeting lined both sides of the aisle. Mike tried to see what was on the shelves, but the plastic was almost opaque. All he could see were indistinct shapes.

"Can I ask you a personal question?"

Miss Dare turned, eyes narrowed, a tiny crease between her eyebrows. She gave him a sharp look. "You want to know if I look the way I do because of Dr. Fleischman?"

"Yeah," Mike said. "That's it."

She smiled. "From top to bottom, inside and out. Face, ass, boobs, everything."

Her breasts got Mike breathing hard. He was a breast man and hers were magnificent. A flume of blood rushed to his face. Mike nodded, wishing he'd kept his mouth shut.

Miss Dare laughed. They started walking again and came to another door. Miss Dare used the tip of a red-lacquered nail to tap in a code. As they went through, her cell phone chimed.

"Excuse me, I need to take this. Have a seat, Mike. Relax, get comfortable. Dr. Fleischman will be ready for you shortly. He has a little emergency he needs to attend to."

Miss Dare stepped out of the office and Mike sat on a divan upholstered in cream-colored leather. A desk, a chair, a floor lamp were the only other furnishings. Mike looked around for a magazine. Not a one. What kind of doctor's office didn't have magazines? He watched the second hand on the wall clock go around in circles and hoped she wouldn't be long.

About ten minutes later, Miss Dare returned. "Just a little while longer, Mike. Can I get you something? Coffee? Perrier?"

"No, thanks. I'm good." He didn't feel good, though. Now that he was actually here, he had a case of nerves; his stomach felt like it might heave.

"Would you like to see my before and after pictures?"

"Yeah, sure," Mike said.

Miss Dare unlocked a drawer in her desk and removed a thick album. She sat next to Mike, opened the album and flipped through the pages.

"Here I am." She turned the album toward Mike.

Mike's jaw dropped.

Miss Dare laughed softly. "Amazing, isn't it?"

Mike looked again at Miss Dare's before picture, then at her after picture, then at Miss Dare herself. Her before picture showed a chinless woman with stubby ears, invisible lips, and a flat, shapeless nose.

"That's not possible. That's ... but," Mike was at a loss for words.

"That is the genius of Dr. Fleischman. He's not just a cosmetic surgeon, he's a flesh artist."

"My friend Phil Demartini told me about him."

"Oh yes, I remember Phil." She flipped the pages of the album. "Here he is."

There was the face Mike remembered. And next to it the face that now belonged to Phil Demartini. Mike felt a strange exhilaration. His heart felt like it was expanding in his chest, and he realized that what he was feeling was hope. Mike hadn't felt hope in so long he'd almost forgotten the sensation.

"When can I pick out my new face?"

Miss Dare closed the album. "It doesn't work that way."

"I don't understand."

"Dr. Fleischman will explain."

Miss Dare's phone chimed again. "Dr. Fleischman will see you now."

Mike stood up. Miss Dare took him through a door behind her desk.

"Dr. Fleischman, this is Mike Gambone, Phil Demartini's friend."

Mike didn't know what he'd been expecting, but the doc looked like a regular guy: curly salt-and-pepper hair, friendly smile, in good shape for an older guy.

"Of course," Dr. Fleischman said. "Sit down, Mr. Gambone." The doctor waved Mike into a chair in front of his desk. "Thank you, Miss Dare."

She nodded and left. The pocket door whispered shut behind her.

Mike looked around. Just as he thought, this guy hauled in the bucks. Thick oriental carpets covered the floor. The furniture was heavy, made of solid wood, real wood. One wall displayed Dr. Fleischman's diplomas pressed between thick plates of glass, secured with gold screws. On another wall were photographs. One showed Dr. Fleischman surrounded by exotic fish, scuba diving near a coral reef. In another, the doctor, dressed in a tux, chatted with a famous actress at what Mike guessed must be a film premiere.

"You *know* her?" Mike asked.

"We're acquainted."

Holy shit, Mike thought. *Who is this guy?*

Could Angelina Jolie be one of Dr. Fleischman's patients? Mike was going to ask when another set of pictures caught his eye. In one, a grinning Dr. Fleischman kneeled behind an enormous boar. Mike looked at Dr. Fleischman.

"Hogzilla," Dr. Fleischman said.

In another, the doctor stood on a crate beside a monster shark. In the third photograph, Dr. Fleischman stood over a creature that looked like a giant dog with wings.

"Holy crap," Mike said, "what the hell is that?"

Dr. Fleischman laughed. He looked pleased at Mike's astonishment. "That is a Chupacabra."

"No shit," Mike said. "You killed those things?"

Dr. Fleischman chuckled. "Well, just between you and me, Mike, no, I didn't kill them. Those pictures are ... for fun. A little amusement for me and my patients."

Mike shook his head. "You had me going, doc. For a minute, I thought those things were real."

Dr. Fleischman cleared his throat. "Well now, Mr. Gambone, tell me, how I can help you."

"Are you serious?" A nugget of anger ignited in Mike's gut. "I look like a fucking ape. People think I'm stupid. Women won't come near me. They treat me like shit. I want women to beg to have sex with me, not look like they're gonna puke when they see me coming. I want what you did for Phil and Miss Dare."

Dr. Fleischman leaned across his desk. "Most people have no idea of their true form, their inner selves. I am very good at discerning the 'real you' and bringing that individual to the surface. That's what I did for Mr. Demartini and Miss Dare. I strive for positive outcomes for both my clients and myself."

"You fix me up like Phil and that's my positive outcome, Doc."

Dr. Fleischman leaned back in his chair, his steepled fingers pressed to his lips.

Sweaty and anxious, Mike hadn't meant to get in the doc's face.

123

What if the doc decided to kick him to the curb? "Look," Mike said, "I got no money for this, but—"

"Money isn't an issue, Mr. Gambone. I have no end of clients who pay me very well for services they can't get anywhere else."

"You got my permission to use me like a lab rat. What else is there?"

"Not a thing, Mr. Gambone, not a thing," Dr. Fleischman said, his dark eyes boring into Mike's with laser precision. "Let us move along to your physical evaluation."

"Now you're talking," Mike said.

In the white-tiled and stainless-steel room, the examination table was the only piece of equipment Mike recognized.

"Step behind the screen, Mr. Gambone, and remove your clothing, then get on the exam table and we'll weigh you."

Mike stepped behind the portable screen and undressed. "Hey, doc, there's no gown?"

"No gown," Dr. Fleischman replied. "I need access to your entire body."

Mike shrugged. As far as his body was concerned, he had nothing to be ashamed of, at least in the muscle department. The hair was another matter. But, Dr. Fleischman would take care of that.

"Lie down, please, Mr. Gambone. We can't weigh you standing up."

Mike stretched out on the exam table. Pretty sophisticated stuff. The platform whirred and whispered as it did its job.

"Please excuse me, Mike," Dr. Fleishmann said. "I've forgotten something. Just relax. I'll be right back."

Before Mike could reply, the pocket door shooshed open, then shut.

"Two hundred ninety-three pounds. All muscle. Not an ounce of fat."

"What the—?" Mike sat up. He hadn't heard anyone come in. A nurse stood at the end of the exam table. She was smiling, and when Mike realized what she was smiling at, blood rushed to his face.

"Sorry," she said as she draped a sheet over Mike's legs and chest. "I've seen a lot of those, but yours is a showstopper."

"Thanks," Mike muttered.

When her mobile computer station beeped, she turned and Mike saw her in profile.

"Hey, I know you ... from Garibaldi's. Star. You were with Phil Demartini."

Her eyes narrowed. "You have a good eye, Mike. I'm called Stella here. Star is the other me."

"The other you?"

"Star does all the things Stella would never dream of doing."

"That sounds ..." Mike stopped. He didn't want to insult her.

"Crazy?"

It was crazy. But Mike wasn't going to say that.

"Star is the real me," she said. "Stella just hasn't caught up with her yet. It takes a while after all this." She swept a hand over her face and body. "You'll understand what I'm talking about after you're done."

"I get it," Mike said, not sure he really did.

"I need to do a blood draw," Stella said.

Mike watched as she prepared a syringe, tube, tap, and six vials.

Jeez, Mike thought, *Dr. Fleischman must have a thing for blondes.* Even in her scrubs, Stella looked like she should be on a fashion runway, not working in some below-the-radar doctor's office doing preop exams.

Dr. Fleischman returned and Stella pulled her cart to the head of the table and out of Mike's sight.

"Mr. Gambone, if you're ready, we will begin."

Mike looked at Dr. Fleischman and said with more confidence than he'd felt in a long time, "I'm ready, Doc. Do your worst."

Stella, syringe in hand, moved to the side of the table, lifted Mike's arm and examined it closely, tapping her fingers here and there along its length.

"What are you doing?" Mike asked.

"Looking for a vein," Stella said. "Here we go." She slid the needle in with such precision that Mike didn't feel it.

"Wait," Mike said, "what's that? I thought you were going to draw blood."

"I am," Stella answered, "in just a minute."

"Okay," Mike said. "But, what's that stuff?" Mike blinked. Did he just say something? He couldn't remember. He could hear sounds, but he had a hard time recognizing them. He stared at the ceiling. His vision narrowed and blurred. He felt the room closing in on him. He tried to speak. His tongue lay in his mouth like a dead thing. He tried to move his arms, his legs. He was paralyzed. A great weight settled on his eyes; he couldn't keep them open.

"He's quite a specimen is he not, Stella?" With Mike heavily sedated, Dr. Fleischman could do an exhaustive examination and plan Mike's transformation.

"I've never seen anything like him," Stella said.

"He's a throwback to an earlier age. Rare these days, very rare. Truthfully, I never thought I'd see one in my lifetime."

"Poor guy," Stella said. "Can you fix him?"

"Revealing his true nature is a challenge worthy of the effort. When I first saw him, I had a vision. One day there will be no concept of ugliness or deformity. We will not be bound by uncontrolled genetic hocus-pocus. One day there will only be perfection of the individual form. Mr. Demartini, Miss Dare, you, even Mr. Gambone, you are all the future of flesh."

Dr. Fleischman pulled open a drawer and removed a pair of calipers. "Take this sheet away and record these measurements, please." He moved around the table, measuring every inch of Mike's body, calling out the numbers. Drawing out this man's true form would demand every skill, every technique he'd developed, and some not yet in his repertoire. Dr. Fleischman smiled. He would need to consult a geneticist. Mike Gambone might prove to be his greatest work, perhaps even his crowning achievement.

Mike's eyelids rolled open. Fluttered. Shut. Then opened again. It was an effort to keep them open at all. Where was he? He tried to think, but his thoughts flitted around his head, then flew off somewhere before he had a chance to make sense of them. His mouth was dry, so dry. The inside of his cheeks felt swollen. He tried to move and couldn't. His vision was blurry, but he thought he might be in a hospital. Had he been in an accident? After a while his vision cleared enough that he could see his immediate surroundings. He saw why he couldn't move; his entire body was wrapped in bandages.

"Ah, Mr. Gambone, I see you are awake."

With his eyes, Mike followed the sound of the voice, a man's voice.

"You're disoriented, yes? That's to be expected. Do you remember where you are?"

Mike tried to answer. He tried to say, "No," but a dry rasp was all he could manage. He shook his head.

The man nodded. "That's an unfortunate side effect of the sedatives. Your surgery was done in stages. But even so, each stage was extensive and we've had to keep you in a semi-comatose state."

Mike tried to speak, again only rasps and croaks were the result.

"Would you like a sip of water, Mr. Gambone?"

Mike nodded.

"Stella, please bring Mr. Gambone some water."

A woman appeared at Mike's side with a plastic cup with a straw in the lid. She held the cup near Mike's mouth and bent the straw so he could reach it. It was all he could do to suck water through the straw and into his mouth. Swallowing was torture. After the first time it was easier.

"Not too much," the man said. The woman pulled the straw out of Mike's mouth.

Stella. Stella. Mike remembered Stella. His nurse. Stella with the great ass. Stella ...

He looked from Stella to ... he couldn't remember his name ... the doctor. "How long?" was all he could get out before his throat closed up again. When he spoke, it felt like two pieces of sandpaper rubbing together.

"How long have you been here?" the doctor said.

Mike nodded.

"Nearly six months."

Somewhere in his foggy thoughts Mike felt alarm. But it was like the clanging of a distant bell, and a few moments later he no longer remembered why he was upset.

There was Stella beside him again. Where had she come from? She adjusted some tubes that ran from a pole down to his arm. She patted his shoulder.

"Dr. Fleischman is doing your last surgery today."

Then whatever was dripping through that tube into his arm shut him down like an on/off switch.

Mike jolted awake, or maybe he was only half awake, gripped by a dream he couldn't shake loose. His eyes were open and he was marginally aware of a room, of a presence, but within seconds of that awareness the images, the emotions going on behind his eyes overtook him.

Mike ran, ran for his life; ran from the thing that roared behind him. He ran in the dark, over unfamiliar ground. He stumbled and fell. Nearly hysterical, he scrambled to his feet, only to find his legs had turned to columns of concrete; he could barely lift them. Struggling with the terrible weight, he dragged one foot then the other an inch at a time, always aware of the thing pounding after him, overtaking him. Without warning it smashed into him, forcing him to the ground, its bulk pinning him down, hot, foul breath choking him. Mike's brain sent adrenaline-fueled commands to his limbs, but they responded like so much dead wood. The muscles in his jaws convulsed, but his mouth would not open, leaving a scream trapped in his throat.

When Mike opened his eyes again, he was staring into a wide, blue sky. Sunshine warmed his face. Birds sang. He rolled his eyes right, then left. They felt gritty, sandy. Above him the tops of evergreen trees swayed in a summer breeze. His head hurt and his thoughts wer e fuzzy. Why was he having such a hard time remembering things? Mike struggled to sit up. He felt stiff and awkward. He pushed himself up with his hands. His hands! Mike felt a stab of panic in his gut as he stared at hands that could not be his and yet we re attached to his body. He saw thick, knotty fingers and heavily muscled forearms covered in long, unkempt hair. He froze, terrified. Mike's brain stuttered like a car stuck between gears. The strong, pungent scent in the air was a stench coming from him. Mike staggered to his feet and in doing so, could not avoid looking at his body. Coarse, shaggy, tangled hair covered him. He screamed an inarticulate, inhuman bellow.

Dr. Fleischman lowered his rifle. "This really is beautiful country, Henry," he said to his companion. Snowflakes drifted around them as they crossed an ice-crusted stream at the shallows and walked to the body that lay sprawled on the opposite bank. Professo r Henry Trabant bent down and removed the tranquilizer dart embedded in the creature's coarse hair.

"Forgive me, Henry," Dr. Fleischman said as he passed his field camera to his friend and placed his foot on the creature's back. "Do you mind?"

Trabant shook his head and took the camera. "Really, Leo, this a bit much."

"I admit it's a cliché, but it's my little amusement."

Trabant took the picture, then another. "That should do it," he said. "Now, we'd better hurry. That tranquilizer won't last long."

"I'm surprised we had to capture him this way," Dr. Fleischman said.

"He's adapting better than we anticipated. Much better. He's hunting deer like he was born to it, and he's hiding from people."

Dr. Fleischman pushed apart the hair on the creature's neck until he exposed skin. He took a large needle from his kit and used it to insert a chip. He wiped away the blood and painted the wound with liquid skin, followed by an injection of antibiotic that would stay in the body for at least a month.

"That chip is state of the art," Trabant said with obvious pride, "and no bigger than a grain of rice. You can't imagine the data we'll have access to."

"The sedative is starting to wear off," Dr. Fleischman said. "He's moving. Go, go."

The two men retreated across the stream to the far bank, then further until they reached the tree line.

"I never thought it possible," Trabant said, "a living, breathing Sasquatch. You've outdone yourself, Leo."

Dr. Fleischman smiled. "I have, haven't I? I revealed his true nature. He had no idea what he really was. None at all."

The creature raised its head, rolled, and heaved itself to its feet. It shook itself, tilted its head upward, sniffed the air, and turned in their direction.

"He's seen us," Dr. Fleischman said.

The shaggy giant stared at them for a few seconds, and then moved away with increasing speed and a rolling ape-like gait, long arms swinging at its sides. It looked over its shoulder one more time before it disappeared into the cover of the trees.

WE'RE ALL MAD HERE

BY E.A. BLACK

"But I don't want to go among mad people," said Alice.
"Oh, you can't help that," said the cat. "We're all mad here."
- Lewis Carroll

Catherine "Cat" Dean held Frankie as close as she could, her face buried deep in his chest. She loved the smell of soap and the finest cologne emanating from her one true love. Her heart swelled with love as she wrapped her arms around him. She had never loved anyone as much as she loved Frankie. He snored as he slept, a habit he'd had since he was young. She tweaked his ears, and he growled as he turned away from her. She rubbed his belly in response, and he curled into her shoulder, content as can be and completely oblivious to what was going to happen to him in the morning. Cat felt so guilty over his future she fed him his favorite swordfish dish for dinner that evening.

Frankie was going to have his balls snipped.

Frankie, or more accurately, Catsahaulics Cinco de Meow of Frankincense and Purr, had already fathered several prize-winning kittens from pedigreed Ragdolls that Cat had specially selected. Only the finest Ragdolls would share Frankie's bed. Ne'er would a local stray diddle with her pwecious Fwankie-Wankie. The laid-back Ragdoll had spread his magnificent seed for catkind, and Cat had the blue ribbons and first-place trophies to prove it. It was time for her resplendent pussy to retire and enjoy the golden years beyond his short stint as a stud.

Hence, the snipping. No respectable plastic surgeon in the state would dare to give Cat the surgeries she needed for both herself and Frankie, so she was forced to rely on a backstreet cosmetic surgeon who wanted to be paid in cash. Whilst poor Frankie would be rende red an "it" after his neutering, Cat couldn't allow her best breeder the humiliation of castration. Oh, no, she insisted the surgeon insert fake testicles called Ballz into her cat's nut sack. Of course, the surgeon knew this surgery was done more to appease Cat's guilt feelings than any real humiliation the cat might have felt over being rendered unmanly, but at $250 per nut, he wasn't complaining.

The surgery didn't stop there, though.

This surgeon also transformed Cat from an overweight, jowled fifty-three-year-old woman into his finest masterpiece. Not content with the body she was born with, she sought to nip it here and tuck it there until she looked beautiful beyond belief. Today, Cat treated herself to another eyelift and cheek implants.

She paid good money to transform her own face and body into the image of Frankie. Catherine Dean wanted more than anything in the world to look like a cat.

Cat took multivitamins each morning to look and feel her best for her latest surgical enhancement. She felt healthier than ever! Her body hummed with energy! She took dance lessons so that she would lose the clunky gait she grew up with. She exercised more and lost that spare tire she'd taken years to grow. The over-the-counter diet pills she had been taking helped whittle away those extra pounds, and she wanted to show off her new, streamlined and feline body. She felt like a cheetah, all sleek and graceful. Granted, liposuction did most of the work, but Cat made an effort to do her Pilates and eat well.

As Cat left the drugstore after purchasing her monthly supply of Lose It Fatty! diet pills, she nearly collided with Joanne Brockheimer, an acquaintance Cat knew before she first went under the knife. Cat didn't acquire friends, since she rarely let anyone get close enough to know her. People frightened her. She disliked feeling judged and falling short of other people's expectations, so she took herself out of the modern world. Joanne was an exception, but Cat barely tolerated her. Joanne and Cat compared surgeries. Joanne had so much plastic surgery done she set off the scanner at the local Piggly Wiggly.

"Good morning, Cat. You're looking as ... *fine* as ever." Joanne looked down her snub nose at Cat. After a half-dozen facelifts, her skin took on a sheen like that of an overstretched balloon. Botox had wiped every expression from her face, giving her the drooling visage of a plastic baby doll covered with an inch-thick layer of makeup. She droned on, her voice a nasal whine caused by her deviated septum, which no amount of surgery ever seemed to fix. "So you're off for another lift, dear? You need to go easy on the Botox. You have that startled look you get from surgeons who don't know what they're doing." She waved one manicured hand over her face. "I had my eyes and chin tucked. You can't even see the scars. Jean-Pierre is so impressive. I'm only forty-five years old and I don't look a day over thirty."

"In dog years," Cat muttered.

"What was that?" Joanne didn't give Cat a chance to respond. "You really should give Jean-Pierre a call, but I know you can't afford him. So you've had to settle, although I don't think Jean-Pierre would approve of making anyone look like a cat. He's above that sort of thing."

Cat wished she could completely avoid Joanne, but the woman insisted upon mingling with her if only to chat about silicone versus saline and the emotional benefits of chin tucks. She walked away, calling over her shoulder, anything to give herself distance from the annoying woman. "It's nice talking to you again, Joanne, but I must be off. Things to do and people to see."

"TTFN!" Joanne waved her fingers as she teetered down the street on her five-inch heels, her superior attitude following close behind. Cat sighed as the woman wiggled her way down Central Avenue, marinating in her perfume as she walked.

"I hate the living ..." Cat groaned.

Cat preferred her dozens of felines to that peculiar species known as homo sapiens. Cats were honest. They didn't ditch her at the last minute for dates, leaving her sipping dry white wine at a restaurant table in full, embarrassing view of everyone else in the place. Cats lived life on their own terms and they didn't answer to anyone. They were selective about who they let into their lives, whether feline, animal, or human. They did not have ulterior motives, unlike her good-for-nothing uncle who cozied up to her before her wealthy mother died, hoping for a piece of the inheritance pie. When he didn't get it, he left Cat alone at long last. She felt relieved but disappointed that yet another man let her down.

Frankie never let her down. When Cat felt lonely, Frankie made his way to her lap. When Cat needed a good cry, Frankie was there, purring and rubbing against her until the tears stopped falling. She returned the favor, and she was always there for her favorite kitty. When Frankie wanted a cuddle, he jumped in her lap. When he wanted his breakfast, he awakened her at 5:30 each morning with a tap of his claw on her face. She happily fed him the best cat food money could buy. When he wanted attention, he dropped books on her head or stood in front of her computer staring at her until she gave in to his demands. She spoiled her cats, especially Frankie, and they in turn gave her the love and attention she craved.

Cats were straightforward, unlike humans. They were also not judgmental. Her father and younger sister criticized her over her crowd of cats. They fussed about the smell and recoiled when one of the twenty kitties approached them. Her sister Prudence complained about allergies, although she owned a cat herself. No one, not even family, could talk Cat out of her horde of felines. Things were so bad between Cat and her family that they stopped coming around to visit. They stopped calling and they didn't even bother to check in. Cat didn't notice she received no birthday cards until her birthday had passed by four days.

No one human missed Cat, and she missed no one as well.

She hoarded the little beasts that were her only friends. She nuzzled them and talked to them and brushed their fur. The only reason Cat bought a Kindle reader over a Nook was because "kindle" was the term for a group of kittens.

But living in a houseful of cats had its problems.

She culled her horde of cats over the past few weeks by digging the corpses out from beneath mountains of trash, but she ran out of room in her backyard. Since she spent so much on cosmetic surgery, she ran through her inheritance quickly. Money was tight. Toward the end of the month she ran out of cash again and couldn't afford food, although what few dollars she did have went to pay for cat food. Her pretties would not suffer starvation! Still, her stomach rumbled endlessly, leaving her with only one option. She enjoyed their dark meat, although it was a bit stringy. It was then that she noticed the change.

Her skin felt softer and more elastic. She could swear her eyesight had improved, especially her night vision. Even her hair became more lustrous, much like a lion's mane. Her body became more limber so she could prance about her apartment like the cat she wanted to be. She was obsessed with cats. She wanted to look like one. She wanted to *be* one.

Never again would she bury her cats. No, she ate them. After all, you are what you eat.

She stopped at a storefront and looked at the televisions in the window. They were attached to a special camera that showed her face on every screen. Twelve Cats smiled back at her. Her bosom swelled with pride at her unusual look. Her almond-shaped eyes called attention to her face. Two years ago she bought special contact lenses with slitted pupils so she would look even more feline. Whenever she wore them, people's heads turned, but she didn't realize she bordered on the uncanny. Her catlike appearance made people feel uncomfortable, but she thought in her delusion they admired her.

They didn't. They mocked her behind her back. Children pointed fingers slapped away by mothers who couldn't resist gaping themselves.

Cat saw none of this. She knew she stood out in the crowd and she would have it no other way. She liked her unusual appearance, despite not liking people. She enjoyed the reactions she received but she rarely addressed anyone who showed the slightest bit of interest. The only reason she put up with Joanne was because the woman had known her before her surgeries. Cat knew she looked better than Joanne.

And now she walked into her cosmetic surgeon's sleazy secret room in his basement, ready for her latest feline transformation. Frankie would also become a new man, so to speak.

"I'd like to keep Frankie for the day to monitor him," the surgeon said. "Anesthesia is a tricky thing. So much can go wrong. When Frankie is fully alert and beginning to heal, he can go home."

"Thank you, Doctor. You take such good care of us. I don't know what we'd do without you."

The surgeon smiled his million-dollar smile, which was no exaggeration since he earned in the seven figures.

"And now you, Cat. This surgery will finalize your slanted cat's-eye look. The cheek implants will angle your face, making it more feline." The surgeon clapped his hands and grinned with delight. "You are truly a work of art, my masterpiece. I rarely get an opportunity to be so creative. I am indebted to you."

Cat knew, if anything, she was indebted to him because these surgeries were not cheap, but she wanted to look like her Frankie. She'd noticed many cat owners looked like their charges, and she wanted to take that look one step further. "Do you think I need another hairline reduction to make my forehead look bigger?"

"Not at the moment, but you will need that in a month or two. And I love the color! You and Frankie have the same beautiful auburn mane."

"It's called Desert Sunrise and the color blend was made especially for me." Cat beamed with pride as she ran her fingers through her shoulder-length, layered hair. The style matched Frankie's. She liked her thick hair. The new color was so much more alluring than her original mousy brown. She knew men and women alike envied her for her lustrous hair. Her hair got as many stares as her unusual face.

"Let's get you prepped, put under, pulled, and tucked, my dear. You and Frankie will have much to be proud of before the day is over." The surgeon gave Cat instructions as to how he would proceed. By the time she was in his operating room, lying on his most comfortable table, she daydreamed of accepting the Grand Prize in the next Stellar Kitties Cat Show looking so much like Frankie people's heads would turn.

The surgeon placed a mask over her face. "Count backward from 100."

"I smell burned toast."

"That's different. Most people smell pizza. The anesthesia is doing its work now. Count backward from 100."

"100 ... 99 ... 98 ... "

Cat dozed.

"Welcome back to the world of the living, Cat," the surgeon said. "You did very well. Frankie is also recovering. Both of you are just fine. You're as healthy and as strong as a lion."

"And now I can go home with Frankie?"

"Absolutely. You're my best patients. Always recovering quickly and you're repeat customers who pay cash, the best kind."

Of course, the *repeat customers who pay cash* part was most important. "Thank you so much, doctor. I'll rest a bit and head home. May I have a mirror?"

"Of course." He handed Cat a large hand mirror. "You are stunning."

Angry purple bruises encircled her eyes and colored her cheeks, but she knew they would fade in a day or two. Her face had swollen more than usual but, like the bruises, the swelling would diminish in time. Her surgeon was a genius with extraordinary, talented hands. She hated driving to the bad part of town and hiding in a small, dark room in his basement for her surgeries, but he was the only cosmetic surgeon in the region who was willing to perform her transformation. Her eyes angled upward even more sharply than before, enhancing her catlike and intense expression. Her cheekbones, fuller and broader, gave her the heart-shaped face she wanted so much but didn't have until now. Her bee-stung lips smiled above her pointed chin, pleased at what she saw gazing back at her from the mirror. Her transformation into a cat was almost complete.

Cat couldn't rush home fast enough. When she passed a butcher, her stomach rumbled. If only she had enough money to afford a steak! But no, she was broke again until next week. Her brood would bask in the light of her evolving beauty and she would treat them to their favorite Mariner's Catch cat food. Two declawed legs marinating in a ginger-tamarind sauce awaited her. Pickings were slim but they would have to do. This one died only a day ago so it was relatively fresh. She would broil it until the skin was crisp, just the way she liked it. She worried the flea medicine she gave her cats a week ago would taint the taste of the meat, but they tasted like chicken.

Cat walked through the door to her apartment with Frankie in tow in his cat carrier. Her clowder of cats perched all about—on the couch, on the rug, out of sight on her bed, in the bathtub playing with a spider, under the kitchen table, in the sink waiting for Cat to turn on the tap so it could drink. The ones out of sight ran into the living room when they heard the door open and close. When they spotted her, their hackles rose. Bodies tensed and tails fluffed as they backed away from her.

She opened the cat carrier and Frankie sauntered out. He looked up at his mistress, recoiled, and hissed.

"Frankie, what's wrong?" She reached out to smooth his ruffled coat, and he lashed out with one paw, slashing her wrist. She cried out in pain, cradling her hand close to her chest. Frankie moved backward slowly, body rigid and tense, and hissed again as if he saw something—or someone—unfamiliar.

That's when Cat noticed the silence. The purring that was a constant hum around her had ceased. Twenty cats stared at her, eyes wide, as if they didn't know what they saw. Teeth bared, they slowly approached her, in a pack, backing her into a corner.

They didn't recognize her.

In one great big wave, they leapt upon her, yowling and hissing their distress. They protected their territory as only cats can. Claws lashed out, tearing tender skin amid shrieks of pain. Teeth tore at her flesh. The coppery tang of blood filled the air. By the time her cats had finished with her, she was even more unrecognizable than she already was.

Years of surgical perfection had been wiped away with a sweep of claws and gnashing of teeth. Frankie had gnawed off her perfect nose. New cheek implants exposed to the air beneath torn flesh. Pointed earlobes that cost $500 sported teeth marks. In the end, Cat became part of her cacophonous cats in ways she never imagined. But, unlike her cats, she had only one life.

SEEDS

BY L.L. SOARES

After Roberta Maxwell stabbed her husband, Walter, five times with an ice pick, she went about with the methodical process of wrapping him in black garbage bags, placing him in a little-used closet on the first floor that had already been prepared for him, and then cleaning up the kitchen floor and counter.

She did all this with a calm, determined demeanor. No one would be looking for Walter so soon, and she had all the time in the world, at least for tonight, to make sure things were done correctly. Once the mess Walter had left behind was cleaned, Roberta went upstairs and took a shower. She changed into clean clothes, and put the ones she had worn during the assault in another garbage bag.

She put some boxes and other discarded items back in the closet, so that her husband's corpse would not be readily noticeable. Not that it mattered if it was found. She just didn't want to make it easy for them.

She called a cab and waited in the living room for exactly twenty-four minutes until the vehicle arrived, and then she left the house, carrying just her purse, the contents of which had been emptied out to accommodate the garbage bag with her soiled clothes and the weapon. Once again, it did not matter if she left these behind, but she wanted to leave things as orderly as possible.

139

The cab took her to a less than savory part of town. She got out, paid the fare, and had already gone out of sight down an alleyway before the driver could pull away.

Roberta Maxwell threw the purse in a dumpster she moved past, then walked to a nearby safe house, where she entered sever al rooms until she reached the one she wanted. At which time she reached under her hair to feel for a strange indentation in her scalp that felt almost like a zipper. She pried it up and went about removing her skin. It peeled off slowly, but in big, long pieces. Like peeling a hard-boiled egg. After she had discarded her skin, she put it in an already prepared container with an acidic solution that would disintegrate it.

Looking in the mirror, Roberta Maxwell was a bloody shape, with patches of muscle and tendons and even some bone. But a new layer of skin had already started growing, and already covered some parts of her body. It would be a short time before the new skin had grown back completely.

From that moment forth, Roberta Maxwell no longer existed i n the world.

"It's done,"Graham said as he talked in the prepaid cell phone. "I will expect the other half of the customary payment in my account before midnight."

He did not wait for an answer.

"Daddy!" June shouted when Tomas Robinson entered the front door. He had been on a business trip for three days, and his daughter instantly made the fatigue he was feeling melt away. He got do wn on a knee and picked up the girl.

"And how's my little Juney Moon?" he asked.

"Much better now that you're home, Daddy!"

His wife Louise came into the room then, and he got to his feet to greet her.

"I hate when you go away like that," she told him. "We both do."

"I'm not so crazy about it, either," Tomas said. "I could really use a shower."

Louise put her hands on June's shoulders. "Let's let Daddy go upstairs and wash up. Then we can eat dinner."

Tomas hugged them both again, and then picked up his briefcase and headed for the staircase. As he ascended, he couldn't help thinking about how blessed he was to have such a warm and loving little family. Louise had been hinting about wanting another child, and he had done his best to pretend he didn't notice. With everything on his mind these days, he didn't need something else to worry about. But the way he felt right now, the way the two of them made his homecoming so special, made him want to give Louise whatever she wanted.

When he got up to the bedroom, he went into the adjoining bathroom and turned on the shower. As he got undressed, he found himself humming an old tune that he hadn't thought about in years.

Tomas stood before the full-length mirror on the back of the door. He was in pretty good shape for a man his age. And, for the moment at least, everything was well with the world.

Then he slid inside the shower stall and started to scrub himself. It had been about six hours since his last shower, and he still felt dirty.

He closed his eyes and thought about the men he had killed earlier that morning. With a machete, no less. He would much have preferred to use a gun, but he wanted to send a message to those who would defy him. He was not a man to be trifled with.

He demanded respect, but getting his hands dirty wasn't something he enjoyed doing. His father had been able to do horrific things without batting an eye, but Tomas found the bad things stayed with him. That they affected him. He truly tried to distance himself from these things, but it just wasn't in his nature to be a stone-cold killer.

I do these things because I have to, he told himself. But it made him scrub his flesh all the harder. Trying to wash his sins away.

I am a seed, Graham thought, sitting in the cold, damp room. *Waiting to grow.*

Since shedding the skin of Roberta Maxwell, he had already regained three inches of height, and he was about twenty pounds heavier. His body would continue to revert to its original dimensions, dimensions that were restrained inside the body of a woman alm ost half his size.

Already there had been a phone call and a meeting was arranged. But he insisted they give him a day to rest. To recoup his energies. Normally, he would have taken more time off between jobs, but this one sounded urgent, and he didn't wa nt to create too much tension between himself and his employers.

After this I'll go away somewhere, he thought. *Maybe the Riviera. Somewhere where no one can reach me for a few weeks. It's been so long since I had a real vacation.*

He stretched out on the bed in the hotel room. Even though his skin was done growing, it was sensitive enough that everything felt enhanced, the cool sheets on his bare flesh, the pillows spread out beneath his pressure points. It felt wonderful to be free of restrictions, to simply *be*.

I really need more time to recover, he thought. *It takes a lot out of me.*

But rest was for the wicked.

"We need you back here."

"I just got home," Tomas said. "You can't expect me to come back so soon."

"There's been a problem," his associate on the other end, Rafael, said. "And nobody solves problems like this quite like you."

"You trying to tell me there's no one else on our payroll who can handle this?"

"Not anyone who can send the same kind of message. Who demands the same kind of respect."

Rafael was trying to use flattery to get him to do what he wanted. Tomas thought he was above such things, but it did play on his ego.

"Look, I want to spend time with my family."

"One, two days tops," Rafael said. "And I promise you we won't bother you again for a while. We just need your presence here to keep a few undesirables in line."

"I still don't know why someone else can't handle it."

"You know why I'm calling you," Rafael said. "You know what your strengths are."

"It will hurt like hell, leaving them again so soon after the last time," he said. "Will you take care of the details?"

"The plane ticket is already on its way to you. The other details are in the works. All you have to say is that you're coming."

"I'm coming."

"Then don't worry about the small details. They'll be handled for you."

"I wish it could *all* be handled for me," Tomas said, before he hung up.

He watched the driver put the suitcase in the trunk, and the well-dressed man climb into the backseat of the taxi. It was the same man from the photographs. Either way, Graham had to start the process now, but this unexpected detail would make things even easier. Without the man around, there was even less chance of being detected as he set things up.

Graham waited until nightfall, and then he removed the loose boards he had pried open the day before, and slid underneath the porch. Under the house. In the dark, he could feel the dirt beneath him, and spider webs brushed across his face and hands. He had stopped being squeamish about such things years ago. It wouldn't do in his line of work to be concerned about such silly things. He used the flashlight briefly, to get a good look at his surroundings, and then he shut it off and crawled to where he needed to be.

And then he waited.

He really hoped that Tomas Robinson would not be gone long. There were seeds to be planted, sprouts to take hold. And while Robinson's absence was convenient now, the longer he was away, the longer the process would take.

143

He was positioned where he needed to be.
Now, it was all up to his quarry.

The trip took less time than expected. Maybe it was because
Tomas was determined to get things done quickly and aggressively.
Even Rafael was surprised how swiftly and brutally he had been able to
take care of the situation. Tomas could see it in his eyes. His scared
eyes.

Before he got on the plane home, he made Rafael promise that his
number was off limits for the rest of the week, at least until the
weekend was over. He had earned time with his family, and he didn't
want any more distractions unless it was an absolute emergency. And
even then, he would weigh it carefully to determine just how urgent it
really was.

He got on the red eye and, despite his exhaustion, he couldn't get
any sleep. He just stared out the window of the plane at the clouds
below. Thinking of little Juney.

He thought about the man he had strangled with his bare hands.
The way the man's eyes bugged out of his head as he struggled for air
that wasn't coming.

Tomas listened to the sounds the plane made, hoping they would
lull him to sleep. Even a couple of hours would have made a world of
difference, the way he felt.

But sleep eluded him.

Graham woke under the house, knowing that Tomas Robinson
was home. He wasn't sure if he'd heard anything in his sleep, but
whatever woke him up was more than just a sound. He could *feel* the
man above him, in the house. It was so vivid that actually touching the
man wouldn't have been much more intimate.

They're all home now; time to take root, Graham thought. And
then he was no longer aware of the boundaries of his body. Instead, he

was like a pair of eyes hovering over the world. Hovering over the house of Tomas Robinson, looking for just the right soil in which to plant himself. The choice he made was essential to the plan. He entered the body of that chosen person and took up residence inside them, sending forth slender roots to firmly grasp bodily organs and hold them tight.

He then began to grow.

It would not happen overnight, but it did happen relatively quickly, considering how he had to begin again as a seed and sprout into a fully formed human being.

"I can't get up," she told him. She tried to be quiet, but every once in a while a low moan would escape from her lips. She was having one of her migraines.

Tomas felt helpless, but he knew there wasn't much he could do except leave her alone. He did get her a warm, wet cloth to put over her eyes, and he turned off all the lights. He tried to arrange the sheets so she was as comfortable as possible, but even then she was miserable.

"Is Mommy sick today?" June asked, waiting for him outside the bedroom door.

"Yes, she is having one of her awful headaches," Tomas said.

"I hate when she has those headaches," June said. "She sounds like she is in so much pain."

"Yes, she is," Tomas said. "But there isn't anything we can do except let her rest. Would you like to go to the park today?"

"Yes, Daddy," June said. "It's been almost a week since I've been to the park."

"Well, it's a nice enough day for it. The sun is out and it's warmer than it was yesterday. Why don't you go put on your jacket and we'll go for a walk."

"Okay, Daddy," June said and went to her room to get her jacket.

Even through the door, he could hear one of his wife's moans, and his heart went out to her. He was so used to being able to take care of matters, to getting things done, that it felt completely unnatural to him to be so ineffective.

There was medication for these maladies, he thought. But she was stubborn and would tell him the headaches didn't happen often enough for her to go see a doctor. That it was just something she had to live with. No matter how much he tried to convince her otherwise.

"I'm all set," June said, standing in the hallway in her jacket.

He got a coat from the hall closet, and they went outside to walk the two blocks to the park.

Graham shifted around a little inside the body, trying to get comfortable. Growing was painful stuff, and for this to work, he had to not only devour the innards of his host, but he had to replace those organs with working ones of his own. You couldn't have a heart stopping or a kidney malfunctioning and give it all away. That would defeat the entire process if you gave it all away before the big finale. He had to make sure no differences were detected, no warning signs that something was wrong.

It was almost like being one of those pods from *Invasion of the Body Snatchers* (he preferred the Donald Sutherland version from 1978 himself, expertly directed by Philip Kaufman), where the aliens created an exact replica of you to replace you. Except Graham was not an alien creature, and didn't have the luxury of working outside his subject. This was all an inside job, and demanded delicacy and intricacy. It was the hardest part of what he did, but also the most poetic aspect. Anyone could fire a gun or wield a knife, but for Graham, murder was like a sculpture using flesh as his medium.

The pain was getting to be a bit intense at this stage, but he kept himself busy, invading the body on a cellular level, acting as an intelligent, conscious wave of cancer cells, devouring healthy cells and replacing them with his own, stronger cells.

When he reached the dimensions of his host body, he had to know just when to stop growing. It wouldn't do to outgrow the body you were inside, bursting it apart. That would ruin everything.

"Is Mommy feeling better today?" June asked her daddy as they watched Saturday morning cartoons.

"I'm afraid not, Juney Moony," he said. "Her headache is still pretty bad."

He had tried to talk Louise into going to the emergency room, since this had lasted two days already, but she had refused to listen to him. It had almost turned into a full-blown argument, except that he saw how much it hurt her to speak, much less shout, and the sound of his own booming voice was acting like a sledgehammer on her head. She had started whimpering, and he left the room. He even slept in the guestroom, something he rarely ever did. Even when they had normal arguments, they always had a rule that they would not go to bed angry with each other. It didn't always work, but most times it did, and the make-up sex was worth it.

But this was the worst headache she had had in years.

Tomas felt so alone in that guest bed. It was smaller than his normal bed, and harder. It took him longer to fall asleep.

It wasn't like he didn't sleep on his share of hotel room beds when he was out traveling for his work, but when he was home, it was important that he sleep with his wife. He yearned to hold her close, to feel that connection between them. Knowing that he was a real, emotional human being, capable of love, went a long way to keeping him from really losing his shit.

There was a soft knock at the door, and he thought it was Louise, come to get him and bring him back to his own bed, but when he softly told the knocker to come in, it was June.

"Can I come sleep with you tonight, Daddy?" she asked. "I had some bad dreams."

He was so uncomfortable in the guestroom that he wanted to tell her yes, but she was an eight-year-old now, and he felt strange permitting her to get into bed with him.

"No, Juney, you're much too old for that," he said. "Now go back to bed and get some sleep. You know that, after you have nightmares, the next time you go to sleep you'll have nice dreams to balance them out."

"Are you sure, Daddy?"

"Of course I am," he told her, in a semi-whisper. "You're a big girl now, and you know that nightmares aren't real. Go back to sleep and forget about it."

She stood there in the doorway, hesitating. He thought she was going to come into the room anyway, but she didn't. He could barely see her in the darkness, but he could hear her breathing.

"June, are you still there?" he asked.

"Yes, Daddy."

"I told you not to be afraid. Now go back to your room like a brave girl."

She did not reply. She stood there for a few more minutes, and then he heard the door softly close and knew she had gone back to her own room.

She didn't normally act that way. Even when she had bad dreams, she had been able to go back to sleep on her own. Maybe she was upset because Louise had been feeling so poorly, and she was worried about her mother. But it struck him as odd that she would come here like that, and ask to sleep with him.

June seemed so small just then, he thought. Like she was little again. Tiny and afraid.

It was so unlike the well-behaved little girl she had become, who usually seemed older than she was. The one who was always so smart and made him proud.

He stared up at where the ceiling was. But the room was so dark, he couldn't see a thing. Staring like that, it was as dark as if he had his eyes closed.

Eventually, he fell asleep.

Graham felt like he was almost through growing. He had done this so many times that he knew exactly at what stage the pain would begin, how long it would last, and how intense it would get, and then when it would stop and the final rounding off would begin.

The first time he had done this he had been twelve years old. He was under the house of their next-door neighbors, and he was growing into the body of young Amy Jenkins, who was a few years younger than he. He had no clue what compelled him to shimmy underneath their house, or why he suddenly realized he was inside Amy's body, but the process had not gone to completion that time, and, halfway through, it had stopped and he had awakened, feeling disoriented and scared. Amy had been ill for a couple of days, and everyone was sure it was the flu. When he crawled out from under the house at night and found his way home, he was severely punished. His parents thought he had run away from home.

When it tried to happen again, he did everything in his power to resist it. But eventually he broke into the cellar of another neighbor's house, and grew into the body of Mikey Salmon, a boy his age who had always bullied him. This time, the process continued until completion. Again, the parents thought the boy had the flu, and when it was done, Graham ran out into the woods in this new body, terrified and having no idea what to do. And then an incredible itching came, and he peeled off Mikey's skin until he was free of it, and it took him another day, hidden in the woods, to regrow his own skin. This time, there was a search party for him. He had been gone several days, and his parents were sure something had happened to him. When he eventually went back home, he made up a story about getting lost in the woods and hitting his head on a rock.

It was soon after that he realized he had to run away for real.

Over the years, he had traveled across the country, gaining more and more control over this strange process that was now a part of him. But he learned how to use it to his advantage, to get money, sex, even power over those he despised. And now, he had turned it all into a profession.

It had been a long, painful, horrible journey, but now he was the master of his malady.

When Graham awoke the next morning, he got out of bed and wandered to the bathroom. He looked in the mirror, pleased with what he had been able to accomplish in only three days. The people he grew inside would never be able to tell that the person in the mirror was no longer him or herself. That the flesh was all that remained. And now, he could complete his mission.

It was not as efficient as a gun or a knife, but no one would have a clue what really happened.

He got dressed and sat in the living room, waiting for the sun to come up.

Louse was relieved that the headache had finally passed. She went out to the kitchen to make breakfast for herself and her family—she was so hungry—and she was surprised to see Tomas sitting on the living room sofa, already dressed and ready to go to work.

She never did understand what he did for a living. But it involved so much traveling. She kept trying to talk him into getting another job that would let him spend more time at home with her and June.

"Are you going on another trip?" she asked him.

"Afraid so," he said. "I wanted to wait until you woke up to say good-bye."

"How long will you be gone this time?" she asked.

"It's hard to say. It could be a little longer this time."

"You know I wish you'd change jobs," she said. "I can't stand the way you leave all the time."

"I know," he told her. "Just another year or so, and I won't have to travel so much."

He looked down at his hands. Hands that had broken men's necks. Strangled the life out of them. There was no reason that Louise and his daughter ever had to know about that side of his life.

He held her close and kissed her. "You know you keep me sane," he said. It was something he had said a thousand times before, and it still made her eyes get teary. She kissed him back and put her arms around him, never wanting to let go.

"You look like you're feeling better," he said when he pulled away. "I'm glad your headache is gone, at least."

"This was the worst one in a long time," she told him. "I thought it would never end. I almost took your advice about going to the doctor. But I'm okay now."

"Next time, if it lasts this long, don't suffer so much. There's medication for these kinds of things now."

"I know," she said. "But I was so sure it would pass. They always do."

"I think you just like being a martyr," he said.

She noticed his suitcase then. He had already packed. Somehow, he hadn't woken her. He could be so quiet when he wanted to, even though he was a big man.

"Are you leaving now?" she asked.

"I just want to kiss June good-bye," he said.

He went down the hall to his daughter's room and quietly opened the door. He crept inside and bent over her sleeping form and gently kissed her on the cheek as Louise looked on from the doorway.

"Daddy," June said, half-asleep. "Are you going away again?"

"Yes," he said. "But I'll be back home before you know it."

"Please hurry back," she said.

"I will."

He went back to the living room, and Louise followed him to the door. There was a taxi already waiting outside. The neighborhood was still dark and quiet.

"I hate when you leave so early," she said.

"The sooner I leave, the sooner I get back," he said.

He kissed her one last time. It felt wonderful. He almost didn't want it to end.

In the safe house, Tomas Robinson scratched around his scalp until he found an odd indentation and picked at it until he had started the peeling process. He was in another bathroom now, looking in another mirror over the sink as he peeled the skin away like a hard-boiled egg, revealing the blood-smeared rawness of his real face.

Soon, Tomas was just a heap of discarded flesh on the floor, to be disposed of in a specific way. There were containers ready and waiting for such things. Tomas Robinson no longer existed.

Graham could already feel his own skin regrowing.

Looking at his skinless face in the mirror, he closed his eyes and could feel Louise Robinson's kiss even now.

Knowing he would not feel that again filled him with more regret than the act of taking a man's life ever could.

PERFECTION

BY DOUG BLAKESLEE

The Row—Evening

Stars twinkled brightly in the night sky as the waning gibbous moon hung low on the horizon. Only the sound of a late night reveler driving home disturbed the calm. Henri stood in the deep shadows of the alley, looking at the darkened brownstone in the middle of the street; the only one not shuttered over in the row of vacant houses. *No one has moved in hours.* A look up and down showed a deserted street. He walked quickly across the road between the pools of light cast by the streetlamps, hopped over the low metal fence and into the cover of the side yard. The dew-slicked grass showed his footprints clearly across the lawn. *That will be eliminated soon enough.*

He wore a simple hooded, black jumpsuit to cover his short cropped hair and pale skin. Gloves, light, flexible boots, and a set of goggles rounded out his outfit. Madame rested on his back, strapped firmly in place to keep from hindering his movements The metal axe head pressed gently against the small of his back. Two leather satchels sat on his hips, bulging with small, round objects.

With a click, the basement door quickly yielded under the administration of a skeleton key. He cracked a glow stick and tossed it on the floor, letting his eyes adjust to the dim light. Posters of the human body, medical diagrams of exposed hands and feet, and other

153

related literature adorned the concrete-lined room. In the center sat an operating table, with trays of instruments, and monitoring equipment. His nose was assailed by the smell of antiseptic that failed to cover the faint odor of waste and blood. A hose lay curled up in the corner, and a central drain sunk into the floor near the wall. *Is the doctor in tonight?* He reached into a small pouch, pulled out a fist-sized package, pressed a red button, and fastened it to the underside of the table.

Henri paused at a display cabinet near the foot of the wooden stairs. Metal blades, plates, and replica bones lay in neat rows. There were dozens of the items, sealed in sterile plastic against possible contamination. Henri turned on the small hand-light and flashed it around the room. The blacked-out windows of the basement hid his activities from any outside observers. A pristine metal door sat in the middle of the east wall, bolted and locked securely. He stepped over to the door, pressed an ear against it, and listened. Nothing. Henri slipped back the bolts and softly turned to the locks. The door opened without protest.

Three body-shaped lumps lay on gurneys, covered by white sheets. His breath puffed visibly in the chilled air. He propped open the door, then turned toward the gurneys and pulled down the first sheet to reveal the body underneath. Henri's eyes narrowed in observation, committing the scene to memory. Metal plates covered the tops of the heads, fastened with metal studs. The lips, eyelids, and noses had been removed, the cheeks slit to allow the jaw to open wider, and sharpened steel dentures put in place. Darkened lenses covered the eyes, while a metal filter replaced the nose. He flipped down the next sheet. Metal plates covered the body in a patchwork mess, razor-sharp blades replaced fingers on the right hand, while the left was a stump. A spiked mass of metal lay unattached next to it. *Male. Genitals removed. Torso had been opened and then sewn up. Poor physical shape, probably homeless. Surgery expertly done, no signs of infection. Posthumous alteration?*

A wooden step creaked.

Home—The Day Before

"You have a new commission."

Henri looked up from his history book, studying the worry lines on his uncle's face. "So soon?" A small fire crackled, popped, and spit in the brick fireplace, warding off the chill of the early spring evening.

"Work comes as needed. This is a special request from our Patrons. Not a personal matter, but one of urgency." Andre Deibler held out a trifold slip of paper to his nephew.

The young assassin took the letter, unfolded it, and scanned the contents. His eyes shifted down the page quickly, then back to his uncle. "The request is quite specific."

"Such is the nature of our work. You know that," said Andre.

"This smells of urgency and desperation. They are paying extremely well for a single elimination, and there's a singular lack of details."

"We are not always given the luxury of details and precise plans. These things happen and we must follow our duty. It's not beyond your skill, Henri. As the Heir, you will need to understand that we do not always have the time needed."

He shifted in his seat, setting down the thick leather bound book on the side table. "I'm merely observing the situation behind the request, Uncle Andre. You've taught me that these matters are not to be rushed. We have standards to uphold."

The elderly man smiled. "Correct, but it is a request and we will need to fulfill it to the stated intent. Do you see this as an issue?"

"Non, uncle. Madame and I will see this work completed." Henri stood up, letter in hand, and nodded to his mentor. "It will be done as requested."

The Row—Evening

Henri launched himself through the metal doorway, rolling across the concrete floor, and came to his feet, Madame in hand. The lights flickered to life. His goggles adjusted instantly, preserving his vision. At the foot of the stairs stood a fresh-faced young man, sandy hair messed from sleep. Watery, pale-blue eyes peered inquisitively at Henri. "Who are you?"

"Your doom, Dr. Ward," said Henri.

"Isn't that a bit theatrical?"

"It would've been better if you remained sleeping."

"Insomnia is common among medical personnel. You tripped the silent alarm on the storage unit. Do you like my handiwork?"

"A pointless exercise. Desecrating the corpses of the dead is not unique, even with a modern twist. You are a ghoul, a madman." His hands gripped on to Madame tighter.

"Pointless? You do not grasp the genius behind my experiments. Stronger assassins. Ones that feel no pain. Follow orders without question. Obedient and loyal, a perfect weapon of terror."

"As you say, Dr. Frankenstein."

The doctor frowned. "Frankenstein would bow to my methods. Electricity to animate bodies? Passé. Chemicals are a superior method. Cleaner, less obtrusive. They allow for the acceptance of my modifications."

Henri glanced at the uncovered body in the cold room. "They aren't dead?"

"Now you see the genius. Chemical suspension of all life functions. They are perfectly preserved until needed. Pumps circulate an oxygenated fluid around the body, dopamine injected to keep them docile until needed, combat drugs to enhance their abilities, and brain modification to ensure obedience. Perfect assassins."

"A clumsy weapon. Blunt and unsubtle. Better suited for war than assassination."

The doctor snorted. "I have succeeded where others have failed. My work will live on long after my death and I will be hailed as a visionary."

"Why the act?"

"You are astute. Only a rational mind could have succeeded in this endeavor. Did you expect a raving madman playing God?"

"The thought did cross my mind." Henri gestured around the basement. "This is too neat. Too tidy. This is all too precise and deliberate. Even the bodies are merely for show."

Dr. Ward scowled and edged toward the stairs.

Madame flashed in the basement light as Henri whirled the ax blade around. The doctor's head rolled from his shoulders, his mouth moving in silent protest.

"You chose poorly, doctor."

Home—The Day Before

"What are you reading?" Andre stepped into the room, carrying the local newspaper. The headlines proclaimed "Brownstone row fire destroys block of condemned houses. Police suspect arson."

Henri didn't look up from the journal on the dining room table. A pile of similar books lay scattered about in front of the young man, with dozens of papers. He wrote on a legal pad as his eyes scanned the cramped writing. "The doctor's journals. There is more to this story than just a single man and his basement theater of horrors."

"You believe he was not acting alone."

He nodded. "That room was a sham. A showcase to misdirect and confuse." Henri gestured to one of the piles of paperwork. "It's taken some time, but I have traced the trail of money and front companies. He was the face of the operation."

"I will leave you to your research." Andre Deibler walked out of the dining room, nodding in satisfaction.

Hours later, Henri sat back and reviewed the pages of notes. *Clever. Very clever.* He stood up and went to the weapon rack, running a hand along the Madame's dark wood shaft. "We have work to do. The guilty must be made to pay for their crimes."

The Docklands—The Day After

The diesel engines of delivery trucks growled and rumbled as they moved the cargo up the paved road to the warehouses. Bright lights illuminated the yards and security guards manned the entrance, checking each truck as it entered and exited. Two large cargo ships lay tied to moorings on the dock, next to a smaller medical ship. Cranes moved cargo from dock into the holds. Men shouted over the whine of generators and truck engines. It was a hive of activity and work. Even the medical ship was busy, lights blazing and armed sailors patrolling the deck.

Henri swam under the dock, just below the water's surface, rising only to take a quick breath before diving back under. He dragged a large, waterproof bag behind him. The ship's hull appeared in front of him through the murky water. Barnacles and rust covered the metal in large, thick patches. Faded lettering high on the bow proclaimed the ship as the Angel's Grace. It rode high in the water that lapped and sloshed against the hull. He checked his watch, as the second hand swept toward 2:10 a.m. The lights of the dock went dark, leaving only the lights of the ships to illuminate the night. Shouts and curses echoed in the night as the whine of electric motors died.

He deftly climbed up the side, the magnetic gloves gripping the hull to allow purchase. He was over the rail in under thirty seconds, ducking into the shadow of the forward wheelhouse. The guards milled midship near the gangplank.

"Get those fucking lights back on."

"The mains are still out. Need to fire up the damn generators."

"Move it, shitheads. We need to keep on schedule."

"Yes, sir."

Henri flipped open a hatch and dropped into the dark interior, the low-light goggles compensating for the emergency lighting. He unzipped the bag, pulled out the pouch of explosives, and fastened it to his waist. Madame was lifted out with care, along with a silenced Glock. "Sorry, Madame. I mean you no disrespect."

He moved down the passageway, pausing at the bulkhead hatches to listen and place a charge behind the ductwork. Only the shouting above deck filtered down. There were no direction signs, only gray wrapped pipes and whitewashed metal decorated the ship. At a junction, the bulkhead door opened and a masked woman in blood-splattered surgical garb stepped through. Beyond her was another closed bulkhead door, forming a small air lock. Henri grabbed her, covered her mouth, and stepped into the head. He pressed the silenced Glock her chest and fired, a soft *pffft* the only sound. She slumped to the tiled floor in a boneless heap. He moved into the air lock, sealed the bulkhead behind him, and pulled the lever to open the other door.

158

UNDERNEATH

BY KEALAN PATRICK BURKE

"This is a joke, right?"

Dean Lovell shifted uncomfortably, his eyes moving over the girl's shoulder to the stream of students chattering and laughing as they made their way to class. Summer played at the windows; golden light lay in oblongs across the tiled floor, illuminating a haze of dust from old books and the unpolished tops of lockers. Someone whooped, another cheered, and over by Dean's locker, Freddy Kelly watched and grinned.

Dean forced his gaze back to the girl standing impatiently before him. Her eyes were blue but dark, her jaw slender but firm.

"Well?" she said.

He cleared his throat, dragged his eyes to hers and felt his stomach quiver.

Her face ...

Down the hall, an authoritative voice chastised someone for using bad language. Punishment was meted out; a groan was heard. At the opposite end of the hall, heated voices rose. A body clanged against a locker; someone cursed. Laughter weaved its way through the parade.

"It's not a joke. Why would you think it was?" he said at last, aware that he was fidgeting, paring slivers of skin from his fingernails, but unable to stop.

The girl—Stephanie—seemed amused. Dean met her eyes again, willed them to stay there, willed them not to wander down to where the skin was puckered and shiny, where her cheeks were folded, striated. Damaged.

"Since I've been here, only one other guy has ever asked me out. I accepted and showed up at the Burger Joint to a bunch of screaming, pointing jocks who called me all kinds of unimaginative, infantile names before giving me a soda and ketchup shower and pushing me out the door. *That's* why."

"Oh." Dean squirmed, wished like hell he'd stood up to Freddy and not been put in this position. Defiance would have meant another long year of taunts and physical injury, but even that had to be better than this, than standing here before the ugliest girl in the school asking her out on a date he didn't want.

Then *no*, he decided, remembering the limp he'd earned last summer courtesy of Freddy's hobnailed boots. A limp and a recurring ache in his toes whenever the weather changed. *Inflammatory arthritis*, his mother claimed, always quick to diagnose awful maladies for the slightest pains. But he was too young for arthritis, he'd argued. Too young for a lot of things, but that didn't stop them from happening.

The remembered sound of Freddy's laughter brought a sigh from him.

Ask the scarred bitch out. See how far you get and I'll quit hasslin' you. Scout's honor. All you gotta do is take her out, man. Maybe see if those scars go all the way down, huh?

"So?" Stephanie said, with a glance at the clock above the lockers. "Who put you up to this? Is a bet, a dare, or what?"

Dean shook his head, despite being struck by an urgent, overwhelming need to tell her the truth and spare her the hurt later and himself the embarrassment now.

That's exactly what it is, he imagined telling her, *a bet. Fuckface Freddy over there bet that I wouldn't ask you out. If I chicken out, he wins; I lose, many times over. The last time I lost he kicked me so hard in the balls, I cried. How's that for a laugh? Fifteen years of age and I cried like a fucking baby. So yeah, it's a bet, and now that you know, you can judge me all you want, then come around the bleachers at lunchtime and watch me get my face rearranged. Okay?*

164

But instead he said, "I just thought it might be fun ... you know ... go to the movies or something. A break from study ... and ... I hate to go to the movies alone."

She smiled then, but it was empty of humor.

"Sounds like a half-assed reason to ask out the scarred girl. You must be desperate."

"No," he said, almost defensively, "I just ..." He finished the thought with a shrug and hoped it would be enough.

"Right."

"Look, forget it then, okay," he said, annoyed at himself, annoyed at Freddy, annoyed at her for making it so goddamn difficult to avoid getting the living shit kicked out of him. He started to walk away, already bracing himself for Freddy's vicious promises, and heard her scoff in disbelief behind him.

"Wait," she said then, and he stopped abreast of Freddy, who was pretending to dig the dirt from under his nails with a toothpick. As Dean turned back, he saw Freddy's toothy grin widen. "Go for it, stud," he murmured.

Stephanie was frowning at him, her arms folded around her books, keeping them clutched to her chest.

"You're serious about this?"

He nodded.

She stared.

Someone slammed a locker door. The bell rang. No one hurried.

"All right then," she said. "I'm probably the biggest sucker in the world but ... all right."

For the first time, he saw a glimmer of something new in her eyes and it made his stomach lurch. He recognized the look as one he saw in the mirror every morning.

Hope.

Hope that this time things would work out right. That he would make it through the day, the week, the month, without pissing blood or lying to his parents about why his eyes were swollen from crying.

Hope that there would be no hurt this time.

Way to go, Dean, he thought, *nothing quite like fucking up someone else's life worse than your own, huh?*

"Okay," he said, with a smile he hoped looked more genuine than it felt. "I'll call you. Maybe Friday? Your number's in the book?"

"Yes," she said. "But Friday's no good. I have work."

She worked the ticket booth at the Drive-In on Harwood Road. Dean saw her there almost every weekend. Saw her there and laughed with his friends about the irony of having a freak working in the one place where everyone would see her. Secretly he'd felt bad about mocking her, but after a while the jokes died down and so did the acidic regret.

Now, as she walked away, her strawberry blonde hair catching the sunlight, he realized how shapely her body was. Had he never seen her face, he might have thought she was a goddess, but the angry red and pink blotches on her cheek spoiled it, dragging one eye down and the corner of her mouth up. This defect was all that kept her from being one of those girls every guy wanted in the back seat of his car.

"I gotta admit, you got balls, shithead," Freddy said behind him and Dean turned, feeling that familiar loosening of his bowels he got whenever the jock was close. Such encounters invariably left him with some kind of injury, but this time he hoped Fred would stick to his word.

"Y-yeah," he said, with a sheepish grin.

Freddy barked a laugh. "Give her one for me, eh bro? And be sure to let me know how that ol' burnt skin of hers tastes."

As he passed, he mock-punched Dean and chuckled, and though Dean chuckled right along with it, he almost wet his pants in relief that the blow hadn't been a real one.

The sun was burning high and bright. There was no breeze, the leaves on the walnut trees like cupped green hands holding slivers of light to cast viridescent shadows on the lawns around the school. Dean sat with his best friend, Les, on the wall of the circular fountain, facing the steps to the main door of the sandstone building, from which a legion of flustered-looking students poured. The fountain edge was warm, the water low and filled with detritus of nature and man. The bronze statue of the school's founder stared with verdigris eyes at the blue sky hung like a thin veil above the building.

"You've got to be kidding me," Les said, erupting into laughter. "Stephanie Watts? Aw Jesus ..."

Dean frowned. His hopes that Les would understand had been dashed, and he quickly realized he should have known better; Les couldn't be serious at a funeral.

"Well, it's worth it, isn't it? I mean ... if it keeps that asshole off my back?"

Les poked his glasses and shook his head. "You're such a moron, Dean."

"Why am I?"

"You honestly think he'd let you off the hook that easy? No way, dude. He just wants to humiliate you, wants to see you hook up with Scarface. Then, when you become the joke of the whole school, he'll look twice as good when he kicks your ass up to your shoulders. Trust me—I know these things."

Before Dean had moved from Phoenix to Harperville, Les had been Freddy's punching bag. The day Dean had showed up, he'd bumped into Freddy hard enough to make the guy drop his cigarette. Les's days of torment were over; Dean earned the label "Fresh Meat." It had been that simple; whatever part of the bullying mind controlled obsession, Dean's clumsiness had triggered it.

"What's worse," Les continued, "is that not only will this not keep that jerk off your back, but now you've put yourself in a position where you have to *date* Stephanie Watts, and for a girl who's probably desperate, God knows what she'll expect you to do for her."

"What do you mean?"

Les sighed. "Put yourself in her shoes. Imagine you'd never been with someone. *Ever.* And then some guy asks you out. Wouldn't you be eager to get as much as you could from him just in case you're never that lucky again?"

Dean grimaced, waved away a fly. "I never thought of it that way."

"I don't think you gave this much thought at all, hombre."

"So what do I do?"

"What can you do?"

"I could tell her I can't make it."

"She'll just pick another night."

"I could just *not* call her. That'd give her the hint, wouldn't it?"

"Maybe, but I get the feeling once you give a girl like that the slightest hint of interest, she'll dog you to follow through on it."

Dean ran a hand over his face. "Shit."

"Yeah." Les put a hand on his shoulder. "But who knows? Maybe all that pent-up lust'll mean she's a great lay."

"Christ, Les, lay off, will ya? If I go through with this, it's just gonna be a movie, nothing more."

"If you say so," Les said, and laughed.

"Who are you calling?" Dean's mother stood in the doorway, arms folded over her apron. A knowing smile creased her face, the smell of freshly baked pies wafting around her, making Dean's stomach growl. The clock in the hall ticked loudly, too slow to match the racing of Dean's heart.

"Well? Who is she?"

Dean groaned. In the few days since he'd asked Stephanie out it seemed the world was bracing itself for the punch line to one big joke, with him at the ass end of it. More than once, he'd approached the phone with the intention of calling the girl and telling her the truth and to hell with whatever she thought of his cruelty. But he'd chickened out. Trembling finger poised to dial, he would remember the flare of hope he'd seen in her eyes and hang up, angry at himself for not being made of tougher stuff, for being weak. It was that weakness, both mental and physical, that bound him to his obligations, no matter how misguided, and made him a constant target for the fists of life.

"Just a girl from school," he told his mother, to satisfy her irritating smile. He hoped that would be enough to send her back to the kitchen, but she remained in the doorway, her smile widening, a look of *there's my little man, all grown up* on her face.

"Did you tell your father?"

He shrugged and turned away from her. Frowned at the phone. "Didn't know I had to."

She said nothing more, but a contented sigh carried her back to her baking and he shook his head as he picked up the phone. They were always in his business, to the point where every decision he made had to be screened by his own imagined versions of them before he did anything. It angered him, made him sometimes wish he could go live with his Uncle Rodney in Pensacola, at least until he went to college and was free of their reign. But Rodney was a drunk, albeit a cheerful one, and Dean doubted that situation would leave him any better off than he was now. Overbearing parents was one thing; waking up to a drunk uncle mistaking you for the toilet was another.

Shuddering, he jabbed out the number he'd written down on a scrap of paper after using Stephanie's address (he knew the street, not the exact location, but that had been enough) to locate *Julie & Chris Watts* in the phone book.

Perspiration beading his brow, he cleared his throat, listened to the robotic pulse of the dial tone, and prayed she didn't answer.

"Hello?"

Damn it.

"H-Hi, Stephanie?"

"No, this is her mother. Who's speaking, please?"

The woman's voice sounded stiff, unfriendly and he almost hung up there and then while there was still a chance. After all, she didn't know his name, so he couldn't be ...

Caller I.D.

Damn it, he thought again and told her who he was.

"Oh, yes. Hang on a moment, please."

Oh, yes. Recognition? Had Stephanie mentioned him to her mother?

A clunk, a rattle, a distant call and the muffled sounds of footsteps. Then static and a breathless voice.

"Hi. I wasn't sure you'd call."

Me neither, he thought, but said, "I said I would, didn't I?"

"So we're still on for tomorrow night?"

There was a challenge in her voice that he didn't like. It was almost as if she was daring him to back out, to compose some two-bit excuse and join the ranks of all the cowards her imperfection had summoned.

"Sure," he told her and cursed silently. His intention had been to do the very thing she'd expected, to back out, to blame a family illness on his inability to take her out. He'd already come to agree with Les's assessment of the situation, and figured it really was a case of *damned if you do, damned if you don't.* Whatever happened with the girl, Fuckface

169

Freddy had no intention of stopping his persecution of Dean. That would be too much fun to abandon just because he'd shown some balls in asking out the school freak. Now, not only would he suffer the regular beatings, he'd also have school rumor to contend with. Rumors about what he'd done with the scarred girl.

"You still there?"

"Yeah." He closed his eyes. "So, when should I pick you up?"

The night was good to her.

As she emerged from the warm amber porch light, Dean almost smiled. In the gloom, with just the starlight and the faint glow from the fingernail moon, she looked flawless. And beautiful. So much so, that he was almost able to convince himself that she was not marred at all, that the scars were latex makeup she wore as protection against the advances of undesirables.

But when she opened the door of his father's Ford Capri, the dome light cast ragged shadows across her cheek, highlighting the peaks and ridges, dips and hollows, and his smile faded, a brief shudder of revulsion rippling through him. He felt shame that he could be so narrow-minded and unfair. After all, she hadn't asked for the scars and he should be mature enough to look past them to what was most likely a nice girl.

Christ, I sound like my mother, he thought and watched as Stephanie lowered herself into the seat, her denim skirt riding up just a little, enough to expose a portion of her thigh. To Dean's horror, he felt a rush of excitement and hastily quelled it.

You're being an asshole, he told himself, but it was not a revelation. He knew what he was being, and how he was feeling. He'd become a display case, his shelves filled with all the traits he would have frowned upon had someone else been displaying them. But it was different, and he realized it always was, when you were an outsider looking in. Here, in the car with Stephanie, he was helpless to stop how angry and disgusted he felt. It was just another event in his life engineered by someone other than himself, and that impotence made him want to scream, to shove this ugly, ruined girl from the car and just drive until the gas ran out or he hit a wall, whichever happened first.

"Hi," she said and he offered her a weak smile. Her hair was shiny and clean, her eyes sparkling, dark red lipstick making her lips scream for a long, wet kiss.

Dean wanted to be sick, but figured instead to drive, to seek distractions and end this goddamn night as soon as possible. He could live with the whispers, the speculation, and the gossip forever, but he needed to end the subject of them sooner rather than later.

"So where are we going?" she asked when he gunned the engine to life and set the car rolling.

He kept his eyes on the street. Dogs were fleeting shadows beneath streetlights; a plastic bag fluttered like a trapped dove on a rusted railing. A basketball smacked the pavement beyond a fenced-in court. Voices rose, their echoes fleeing. The breeze rustled the dark leaves, whispering to the moon.

Dean's palms were oily on the wheel.

"The movies, I guess. That okay?"

In the corner of his eye, he saw her shrug. "I guess."

"We don't have to, if you have something else in mind."

The smell of her filled the car, a scent of lavender and something else, something that filled his nostrils and sent a shiver through him that was, alarmingly, not unpleasant.

"Maybe we could go down to the pier."

"What's down there?"

"Nothing much, but I like it. It's peaceful."

And secluded, Dean added, and remembered Len's theory on what she might be expecting from him.

"Sounds kind of boring to me," he said then, aware that it was hardly the polite thing to say but wary of letting the night slip out of his control.

To his surprise, she smiled. "I used to think that, too."

"What changed your mind?"

"I don't know. The fire, maybe."

Oh shit. It was a question he knew everyone in school wanted to know, that he himself wanted to know: How did you get those scars? And now it seemed, she would tell him.

"The fire that ..." he ventured and saw her nod.

"My brother started it. Funny."

"What was?"

"That he set it trying to kill me and our parents, but he was the only one who died. Hid himself in the basement thinking the fire wouldn't get him down there, and he was right. But the smoke did. He suffocated. I burned."

"My God."

She turned to look at him then and, in the gloom, her eyes looked like cold stones, the light sailing over the windshield drawing the scars into her hair.

"Why did you ask me out?"

He fumbled for an answer she would believe but all responses tasted false.

"Someone dare you?"

"No."

"Threaten you?"

"Haven't we already been through this?"

"That's not an answer."

"I told you: No."

"Then why?"

"Because I wanted to."

"I don't believe you."

He rolled his eyes. "Then why are you here?"

Another shrug and she looked out her window. "I'm hoping some day someone will ask me out for real. Until then, I'll settle for trial runs. When you look like I do, being choosy isn't an option, even if you're almost certain you're going to end up getting hurt."

"Hell of an attitude," he said, but understood completely, and both hated himself for being exactly what she suspected and pitied her for having to endure the callousness of people.

People like him.

"Maybe. I figure it'll change when I meet someone who doesn't think of me as a freak."

He knew that was his cue to say something comforting, to tell her *I'm not one of those people*, but he was afraid to. It would mean fully committing himself to her expectations and they would undoubtedly extend far beyond this night. It would mean selling himself to her and that was unthinkable because, in reality, he was everything she feared—

just another guy setting her up for heartbreak, and as guilty as that made him feel, it was still preferable to making her think he was really interested in her. Neither were palatable options, but at least there was escape from the former.

"I don't think you're being fair on yourself," he said instead, and silently applauded his tact. "I think you look good."

She snorted a laugh, startling him, and he looked at her.

"What?"

"Nothing," she replied, but kept looking at him, even when he turned to watch the road; even when he found himself angling the car toward the pier; even as he felt his own skin redden under her scrutiny. The smell of her was intoxicating, the remembered glimpse of thigh agitating him, a persistent itch somewhere deep beneath the skin.

This is a dare, he reminded himself when he felt a faint stirring in his groin. *I'm only doing it because I don't want to get my ass kicked through the rest of high school. And never in a million years would I have asked her otherwise, and why the fuck is she still staring at me?*

He brought the car to a squeaking halt, its nose inches from the low pier wall, the black water beyond speckled with reflected stars, the moon gazing at its shimmering twin. Boats danced on the end of their tethers, bells clanking, announcing every wave. A rickety-looking jetty ran out to sea and vanished under the cloak of night.

And still he felt her eyes on him.

After a moment in which he screamed to announce *Well, here we are!* he turned to ask her why she was staring—he couldn't bear the sensation of those eyes on him any longer—but, when he opened his mouth to speak, she leaned close and crushed his lips with hers.

Dean's eyes widened in horror.

Oh, Jesus.

She shifted her lips just a little, and the side of her cheek grazed him. Hard skin. It was as if her nails had scratched his mouth. He recoiled; she followed, her hands grabbing fistfuls of his shirt. He moaned a protest but it only spurred her further. Her hands began to slide downward and oh God he was responding—even in the throes of horror he was responding and his hands were sliding over her blouse, feeling the softness there, the small points of hardness beneath his fingers and unbuttoning, tearing, freeing her pale, smooth unblemished skin. She made a low sound in her throat and broke away and for a terrible moment he thought she was going to stop, even though he wanted her to stop because this was a nightmare, but instead she sloughed off her blouse and smiled and now she was wearing just a bra and it was all he could see in a world full of pulsing red stars that throbbed across his eyes. She reached behind her and slowly, teasingly removed her bra and replaced it with his hands. His breath wa s coming hard and fast, harder and faster, an ache in his crotch as his cock stiffened even as his mind continued to protest *stop it stop it stop it you can't do this you don't* want *to do this* and she was on him again, her hair tickling his face, her mouth crushing, exploring, tearing at his clothes and he moaned, begged her, kneaded her soft, perfect breasts, then released them as she moved lower, lower, her wet lips tasting his nipples, his stomach, her fingers hooking the waistband of his pants and ...

... and then the passenger door was wrenched open and disembodied white hands, large hands, leapt forward and tangled themselves in her hair, wrenching her head back to show a face with surprise-widened eyes and a gaping mouth too stunned to cry out.

Dean could do nothing, the lust that had swelled to bursting within him quickly turning to ice water in his veins. *Oh God, no.* He watched in abject terror as Stephanie was torn screaming from the car, the breasts he had held not moments before crushed beneath h er weight as she was thrown to the ground face first. She whimpered and for a moment it was the only sound apart from the steady clanking of the bell.

And then Fuckface Freddy's sneering face filled the doorway.

"Surprise, shithead," he said.

It took only a moment for Dean to gather himself, but he did so with the awful knowledge that he was probably going to die, and that awareness lent a sluggishness to his movements that saw him all but crawl from the car to see what Freddy was doing to the girl.

It was worse than he thought, because as he straightened himself to lean against the car, he saw that Freddy was not alone. Lou Greer, the principal's son, track star and all-round sonofabitch, was with him, giggling uncontrollably into his palm and shuffling around Stephanie, who was now sitting up, a shocked expression on her face, her arms crossed over her bare breasts.

Freddy was smiling, a feral smile that promised hurt.

"I'll be damned," he told Dean, "you're just full of fuckin' surprises, man. I was only kiddin' you about bonin' Scarface and here you were about to let her gobble your rod. That's really somethin'."

The bell clanged on, ignoring the hush of the tide.

Somewhere far out to sea, a ship's horn sounded.

The ground around the car was sandy, a thin layer scattered above concrete. Pieces of broken glass gleamed in the half-light from the streetlamps that peered between the canopies of box elder and spruce. This also provided a perfect shield from the road. Few cars would pass by tonight, and those that did would not see much should anyone deign to look in this direction.

"Don't hurt her," Dean said, knowing as he did so that anything he said would only bring him more pain at the hands of Freddy and his comrade.

"That sounded like an order to me, Fred," Greer said, and giggled. It was the contention, of most people who knew him, that the last time the principal's son had been lucid, Ronald Reagan was taking his first spill over a curb.

Stephanie was shivering, her pupils huge, the scarred side of her face lost in shadow, and while Dean was filled with terror, he couldn't stop himself from reflecting back on what they'd been doing before Freddy had come along.

But then Freddy stepped close enough to drown Dean in his shadow and the memory was banished from his mind.

"Since when do you give a shit about her?" Freddy asked, somehow managing to sound convincingly curious.

"I—I ... I don't know."

Freddy nodded his complete understanding and turned back to Stephanie. She watched him fearfully.

"You do know he set you up, right?"

Greer giggled and muttered "Oh shit, that *sucks*" into his hand.

Stephanie looked at Dean and he felt his insides turn cold. There was no anger in her eyes, no disappointment; just a blank look, and somehow that was worse.

"That's a lie, Stephanie." He stepped forward. "I swear it's—"

In one smooth move, Freddy swiveled on his heel and launched a downward kick into Dean's shin. Dean howled in pain and collapsed to the ground.

"Shut the fuck up, weasel," Freddy said, and drove his boot into Dean's stomach, knocking the wind out of him. Dean wheezed, tears leaking from his eyes. When they cleared, he saw Stephanie, her arms still crossed across her breasts, her face drawn and pale but for the angry red on her cheek.

I swear I didn't he mouthed to her but knew she didn't understand, knew she couldn't understand because the look in her eyes told him she wasn't really here anymore, that she'd retreated somewhere neither he nor Freddy and Greer could reach her.

Greer stopped giggling long enough to ask: "What'll we do with her, Fred?"

Freddy shrugged and turned back to face Stephanie.

"Can't fuck her," he said, as if he were talking about the weather. "They'd swab her scabby ass and I'd be off the football team."

"Please, leave her ... alone," Dean managed, though every word felt like red-hot hooks tugging at his stomach.

"If you don't shut up, we will leave her alone, and do all the unpleasant things to you instead," Freddy said over his shoulder, and for a moment Dean stopped breathing.

Do it, his mind screamed. *Tell them to go ahead and beat the shit out of you. At least they'll leave her alone!*

But he said nothing, merely wept into the sand.

He didn't want her to get hurt, but he had been hurt so much himself that he couldn't bear the thought of more. Even if all of this was his fault. Even if the memory of the way she was looking at him haunted his sleep for the rest of his life.

He.

Couldn't.

Do it.

Incredibly, sleep danced at the edges of his mind and he almost gave himself over to its promise of peace, but then he heard a grunt and Greer's manic giggle and his eyes flickered open. The world swayed, stars coruscating across his retinas, then died.

Stephanie was no longer kneeling.

She was lying flat on her back, breasts exposed with Greer holding her wrists in his hands, as if preparing to drag her over the broken glass. As Dean watched, heartsick and petrified, Freddy grinned and straddled the girl. Still, she would not take her eyes off Dean. He wished more than anything that she would and "please," he moaned into the sand, sending it puffing up around and into his mouth.

"How did she taste, shithead?" Freddy asked and, setting his hands on either side of Stephanie's midriff, leaned down and flicked his tongue over her left nipple. As Greer giggled hysterically, Freddy sat back and smacked his lips as if tasting a fine wine.

"Charcoal, perhaps," he said and that was too much for Greer. He exploded into guffaws so irritating that eventually even Freddy had to tell him to cut it out.

And still Stephanie stared at Dean.

Oh fuck, please stop.

"I'm sorry," he whispered, and knew she didn't hear.

"Then again ..." Freddy tasted her right nipple, repeated the lip smacking and put a thoughtful finger to his chin. "Maybe soot. You wanna taste, Greer?"

He didn't need to ask twice. They exchanged positions, Stephanie never once breaking eye contact with Dean and never once trying to struggle against what Freddy and Greer were doing to her. She said nothing, but bore the humiliation in expressionless silence.

Dean, unable to stand it any longer, scooted himself into a sitting position, his back against the car, drew his knees up and buried his face in the dark they provided, surrounding them with his arms. In here, he was safe. All he could hear were the sounds.

It lasted forever and he wept through it all, looking up only when a sharp smack made him flinch.

Greer was on the ground, his giggling stopped, a hand to his cheek. Stephanie was in the same position as before, but her skirt was bunched up around her waist, her panties down almost to her knees, exposing her sex, a V-shaped shadow in the white of her skin. Freddy towered over Greer, one fist clenched and held threateningly at his side.

"I said *no*, you fuckin' retard."

Greer looked cowed, and more than a little afraid. "I was just goin' to use a finger."

"Get up," Freddy ordered and Greer scrambled to his feet. They stood on either side of the prone girl, the threat of violence in the air.

"You do as I say or fuck off home to Daddy, you understand me?"

Greer nodded.

"Good, now go get the car. We're done with this bitch."

Another nod from Greer.

The sigh Dean felt at the thought that it might all be over caught in his throat when Freddy turned and walked toward him. Dean's whole body tensed, anticipating another kick, but Freddy dropped to his haunches and smiled.

"Do we need to have this conversation?"

Dean said nothing; didn't know what he was supposed to say.

"Do I need to tell you what will happen if you tell anyone what happened here? Not that anyone will believe a little fucked-up perv like you anyway, and I have ways of making sure the finger gets pointed in your direction if you start making noise. Capisce?"

Dean nodded, tears dripping down his cheeks.

"Good. Besides, we didn't hurt her, now did we? We were just havin' some fun. Harmless fun, right?"

Dean nodded.

Freddy's grin dropped as if he'd been struck. He leaned close enough for Dean to smell the beer on his breath.

"Because you open your fuckin' mouth, shithead, and two things are gonna happen. First, we'll have a repeat of tonight's performance, only this time we'll go all the way, you know what I'm sayin'? We'll fuck that little burnt-up whore 'til she can't walk no more, and then I'll get Greer to do the same to you, just so you don't feel left out, understand?"

Dean nodded furiously with a sob so loud it startled them both. Freddy laughed.

"Yeah, you understand," he said and rose to his feet, taking a moment to dust the sand off his jeans. He looked over at Stephanie, still lying unmoving where they'd left her, and said to Dean: "She's not much of a talker, is she?"

Dean was silent.

"Pretty fuckin' frigid, too. Must be your aftershave got you that itty-bitty titty, shithead."

Greer's Chevy rumbled to a halt a few feet away.

Freddy glanced back over his shoulder, then looked from Dean to Stephanie.

"Well, folks, it's been fun. I hope you've enjoyed me as much as I've enjoyed you!"

He turned and walked to the car, his boots crunching sand.

With a whoop and a holler, Greer roared the engine and they were gone, the Chevy screeching around the corner onto the road behind the trees.

Night closed in around the pier and there were only the waves, the clanging of the bell, and the soft sigh of the breeze.

"Stephanie?"

He had brought her clothes, gripping them in a fist that wanted to tremble, to touch her, to help her, but when he offered them to her, she closed her eyes and didn't move.

"Stephanie, he said if I asked you out, he'd quit picking on me. He scares the shit out of me and I'm tired of getting my ass kicked and creeping around worrying that he'll see me. So I agreed, like an idiot. I'm sorry. I really do like you, even if I wasn't sure before. I do like you and I'm so sorry this happened. I swear I didn't know."

There was an interminable period of silence that stretched like taut wire between them, and then she opened her eyes.

Dark.

Fire.

Slowly, she reached out and took the clothes from him.

"Wait for me in the car, I don't want you looking at me," she said coldly, but not before her fingers brushed the air over his hand.

"Okay," he said and rose.

She stared, unmoving.

"I am sorry," he told her and waited a heartbeat for a response.

There was none. He made his way back to the car and stared straight ahead through the windshield at the endless dark sea, ignoring the sinuous flashes of white in the corner of his eye. Echoes of pain tore through his gut and he winced, wondering if something was broken, or burst.

When the car door opened, his pulse quickened and he had to struggle not to look at her.

"Drive me home," she said and put her hands in her lap, her hair, once so clean and fresh now knotted and speckled with sand and dirt, obscuring her face. "Now."

And still the smell of lavender.

He started the car and drove, a million thoughts racing through his mind but not one of them worthy of being spoken aloud.

When they arrived at her house, the moon had moved and the stars seemed less bright than they'd been before. There were no voices, no basketballs whacking pavement, but the breeze had strengthened and tore at the white plastic bags impaled on the railings. Stephanie left him without a word, slamming the car door behind her. He watched her walk up the short stone path with her head bowed, until the darkness that seethed around the doorway consumed her.

Still he waited, hoping a hand might resolve itself from that gloom to wave him goodbye, a gesture that would show him she didn't think he was to blame after all. But the darkness stayed unbroken, and after a few minutes, he drove home.

He awoke to sunlight streaming in his window and birds singing a chorus of confused melodies in the trees.

A beautiful morning.

Until he tried to sit up and pain cinched a hot metal band around his chest. He gasped in pain. Gasped again when the pain unlocked the memory of the night before, flooding his mind with dark images of a half-naked, scared girl and maniacal giggling.

The clanging of a bell.

oh god

He wished it had been a dream, a nightmare, but the pain forbade the illusion. Real. It had happened and the light of morning failed to burn away the cold shadow that clung to him as he recalled his cowardice.

Jesus, I just sat there.

When his mother opened the door and spoke, startling him, he exaggerated his discomfort enough to convince her to let him stay in bed. He endured her maternal worrying until she was satisfied he wasn't going to die on her watch, and then cocooned himself in the covers.

When she was gone, he buried his face in the pillows and wept.

I just sat there.

He wondered if Stephanie had gone to school today, or if, even now the police were on their way to Dean's house, to question him. The momentary thrum of fear abated with the realization that he had done nothing wrong. Freddy and Greer were the ones in trouble if the authorities were brought into it. And still he felt no better. Doing nothing somehow made him feel just as guilty as if he'd been the one holding her down, or pawing at her breasts, mocking her.

He wanted to call her, to try to explain without panic riddling his words, without fear confusing him, but knew he'd lost her.

But what if I hadn't lost her? he wondered then. *What if Freddy hadn't interrupted us and we'd ended up having sex? What would that mean today? What would that* make *us?*

He saw himself holding her hand as they walked the halls at school.

He saw himself holding her close at the prom as they danced their way through a crowd grinning cruelly.

He saw the look of need in her eyes as she stared at him, the possessive look that told him he was hers forever.

He heard the taunts, the jeers, the snide remarks but this time they wouldn't be aimed at Stephanie alone. This time, they'd be aimed at him, too, for being the one to pity her. For being blind to what was so staggeringly obvious to everyone else.

What the fuck is wrong *with me?*

Pain of a different kind threaded its way up his throat.

He didn't like the person his feelings made him.

He didn't like who he was becoming, or rather, who he might have been all along.

I just sat there ...

As the light faded from the day and the shadows slid across the room, Dean lay back in his bed and stared at the ceiling.

Watching.

Waiting with rage in his heart.

For tomorrow.

"Mr. Lovell, we missed you yesterday," a voice said, and Dean paused, the only rock in a streaming river of students.

The main door was close enough for him to feel the cool air blasting down from the air-conditioner, the sunlight making it seem as if the world outside the school had turned white.

Dean turned to face the principal, a tall, rail-thin man who looked nothing like his son. Small green eyes stared out from behind rimless glasses. His hands were behind his back, gaze flitting from Dean's pallid face to the object held in his hand.

"Yeah," Dean muttered. "I was sick."

"I see," Principal Greer said, scowling at a student who collided with him and spun away snorting laughter. "Well, this close to exams, I would expect you'd make more of an effort to make classes."

"It couldn't be helped."

Greer nodded. "Where are you going with that, may I ask?"

Dean lingered, his mouth moving, trying vainly to dispense an excuse, but finally he gave up and turned away. He walked calmly toward the main door.

"Excuse me, Mr. Lovell, I'm not finished with you."

Dean kept moving.

"Mr. Lovell, you listen to me when I'm talking to you!"

Now the scattering of students in the hallway paused, their chattering ceased. Heads turned to watch.

The doorway loomed.

"Lovell, you stop *right this minute!*"

Dean kept moving.

"You ... your parents will be hearing from me!" Lovell sounded as if he might explode with rage. Dean didn't care. He hadn't really heard anything the old man had said anyway.

The hallway was deathly silent as he passed beneath the fresh air billowing from the a/c, and then he was outside, on the steps and staring down.

At where Fuckface Freddy was regaling two squirming girls with tales of his exploits.

"I swear," he was saying, "the bitch told me she got off when guys did that. I mean ... in a goddamn *bowl* for Chrissakes! Can you believe that shit?"

It took four steps to reach him and when he turned, he squinted at Dean.

Sneered.

"The fuck *you* want?"

Dean returned his sneer and drew back the baseball bat he'd taken from his locker.

He expected Freddy to look shocked, or frightened, or to beg Dean not to hurt him. But Freddy did none of those things.

Instead, he laughed.

And Dean swung the bat.

His parents, talking. He lay in the dark, listening. They were making no attempt to be quiet.

"Did you talk to him?"

"I didn't know what to say. He says he's sorry."

"Sorry? He gave the guy a broken jaw, a busted nose, and a concussion! Sorry isn't going to cut it."

"He was upset, Don."

"Oh, and that's supposed to get him off the hook, huh? Did you ask him what the hell he's going to do now? Greer *expelled* him. You want to appeal against that? Just so our darling son can beat the shit out of the next guy who's dumb enough to cross him? Everyone gets upset, Rhonda, but not everyone pisses away their future by taking a bat to someone. I can't wait to hear what that kid's parents are going to do. They'll probably sue the ass off us."

"He says the guy was picking on him."

"Oh, for Christ's sake."

183

"Well, I don't know ... you go talk to him then."

"I'm telling you ... if I go up to that room, it won't be to talk."

"Then talk to him tomorrow. He's obviously got some problems we didn't know about. You being angry isn't going to help anything."

"Yeah, well, jail isn't going to do him much good either, now is it?"

He lay in the dark, listening.

Smiling.

Over the next few days he was dragged to meetings, and heard the tone, but none of the words. Voices were raised, threats were issued, and peace was imposed. There were questions, different faces asking different questions, all of them threads connected to the same ball: *Why did you do it, Dean?*

Had he chosen to answer those blurry, changing faces in all those rooms that smelled of furniture polish and sweat, he would have told them: *I just sat there.* But instead he said nothing, and soon the faces went away, the slatted sunlight aged on the walls and there was only one voice, a woman, speaking to him as if he were a child, but still asking the question everyone wanted to ask and which he refused to answer because it belonged to him, and him alone.

"Dean, I want to help you, but you have to help *me*."

That made him smile.

"Tell me what happened."

He wouldn't.

"Tell me why you did what you did."

He didn't, and when she shook her head at some unseen observer, standing in the shadows at his back, he was released. No more faces, no more voices, just his parents, expressing their disappointment, their frustration. Their anger.

It meant nothing to him.

In the dark of night he awoke, unable to breathe, his body soaked in sweat, panic crawling all over him.

I'm sorry I'm sorry I'm so sorry

Look at you now, a voice sneered in his ear and when he turned toward it, Fuckface Freddy was grinning a smile missing m ost of its teeth, his nose squashed and bleeding, one eye misshapen from when Dean had knocked it loose. His breath smelled like alcohol. *Look at you now, shithead.*

Dean clamped his hands over his eyes, into his hair and pulled, screamed, a long hoarse tortured scream that made lights come on in more houses than his own.

Look at you now ...

"These sessions will only be beneficial to you, Dean, if you open up to me ..."

Look at you now ...

"He starts at Graham High in the fall. Let's hope he doesn't fuck that up."

"Don't talk like that, Don. He's still your son."

"Thanks for the reminder."

Stephanie kissed him, her head making the covers ripple as she worked her way down his stomach. He moaned, filled with confusion and desire. Surely it couldn't all have been a dream, but if not, then he was thankful at least for the respite, this neutral plain where no harm was done and no one had been hurt.

Not here.

And when he ran his hands through her hair, she raised her face so that he could see the scars. So that he could touch them, remember them. But there were no scars. Only a wide gaping smile from which Greer's giggle emerged ...

Almost a month later, his parents left him alone for the weekend. They'd asked him to come with them to Rodney's farm; his uncle was sick, and they claimed getting away from the house for a while might do Dean some good. And Rodney would be just tickled to see his nephew.

Dean refused, in a manner that dissuaded persistence, allowing them no option but to leave him behind, but not without a litany of commands and warnings. Then, on Friday evening, his mother kissed him on the cheek; he wiped it away. His father scowled; Dean ignored it. Then they were gone and the house was filled with quiet, merciful peace.

Until there was a knock on the door.

Dean didn't answer, but his parents had not locked it and soon Les was standing in the living room, hands by his sides, a horrified expression on his face.

"Dude, what the fuck are you doing?"

"Venting," Dean said, drawing the blade of his mother's carving knife across his forearm. He stared in fascination as the cuts, deep and straight, opened but remained bloodless and pink for a few moments before the blood welled.

"Hey ... don't do that okay?" Les said, his voice shaking as he took a seat opposite Dean. "Please."

"It helps," Dean said, wiping the blade clean against the leg of his jeans. Then he returned the knife to an area below the four slashes he'd already made. Blood streaked his arm and Les noticed a spot of dark red was blossoming on the carpet between his legs. Dean had his arm braced across his knees, as if he were attempting to saw a piece of wood. Face set in grim determination, eyes glassy, he slowly drew the blade back, opening another wide pink smile in the skin.

"Jesus, Dean. What are you doing this for?"

"I told you," Dean said, without looking up from his work, "it helps."

"Helps what?"

"Helps it escape."

"I don't get it."

"No. You don't," Dean said and gritted his teeth as he made another cut.

There were dreams and voices, the words lost beneath the amplified sound of skin tearing.

And when he woke, he knew his arms were not enough.

Summer died and took fall and winter with it, a swirl of sun, rain, snow, and dead leaves that filled the window of the Lovell house like paintings deemed not good enough and replaced to mirror seasons that surely could not move so fast.

A somber mood held court inside. A man and a woman moved, tended to their daily routines, but they were faded and gray, people stepped from ancient photographs to taste the air for a while.

And upstairs, a room stood empty, the door closed, keeping the memories sealed safely within.

Another year passed.

"Two, babe," the kid said, running a hand over his gel-slicked hair and winking at the pretty girl in the ticket booth. On the screen behind him, garish commercials paraded across the Drive-In screen and the meager gathering of cars began to honk in celebration.

The kid glanced over his shoulder at the screen and looked back when the girl jammed two tickets into his hands. Using her other hand she snatched away his money, offered him a dutiful smile and went back to her magazine.

"Chilly," scoffed the kid and returned to his car, his shoes crunching on the gravel.

The movie previews began and the honking died. Crickets sawed a song in the field behind the screen.

The moon was high, bathing the lot in a cool blue light.

"One," said a voice and the girl sighed, looked up at the man standing in front of her and began to punch out the ticket. Her hand froze.

"Hi, Stephanie," Dean said.

He moved his face into the amber glow and Stephanie barely restrained a grimace.

"What are you doing here?" she asked after a moment, then tugged the ticket free and slid it beneath the Plexiglas window.

"I wanted to see you."

"Oh yeah, for what?"

"To apologize."

"Apology accepted," she said testily and glared at him. "That'll be two dollars."

He smiled, said, "You look amazing," and passed over the money.

And she did. The scars were gone, with only the faintest sign that they'd ever been there. Perhaps the skin on her right cheek was just a little darker than it should have been, a little tighter than normal, but that could be blamed on makeup. Without the scar, she was stunning, but then, through all his nights of suffering and the endless days of rage, he'd come to realize that even *with* them, she'd been beautiful. It was he who'd been the ugly one, ugly on the inside.

She stopped and stared at him, the look he remembered, the look that had haunted him—but then it was gone, exasperation replacing it.

"What happened to you?" she asked.

He put a hand to his chin, to the hard pink ridges of skin there and shrugged. "I had to let it out."

188

He expected her to ask the question so many people had put to him ever since the day his father had kicked in the bathroom door and found him lying bleeding on the floor, his face in ruins, his mother's carving knife clutched in one trembling hand, but she didn't. She simply shook her head.

"You destroyed yourself."

He nodded. "For you."

Her laugh was so unexpected he staggered back a step, the scars on his face rearranging themselves into a map of confusion.

Someone honked a horn at the screen. A chorus of voices echoed from the speakers.

Stephanie looked ugly again. "You almost killed him, you know."

"Who?"

"Freddy."

"I know. He deserved it."

"No, he didn't."

He watched her carefully, watched her features harden and a cold lance of fear shot through him.

"What do you mean? After what he did—"

She frowned, as if he had missed the simplest answer of all. "I *asked* him to do it."

On the screen, someone screamed. For a moment, Dean wasn't sure it hadn't been himself.

"You used to see Freddy hanging around all those cheerleaders and blonde bimbos at school, right?"

He nodded, dumbly, his throat filled with dust.

"Did you ever actually see him out with any of them?"

He didn't answer.

Ominous music from the speakers; footsteps; a door creaking loudly enough to silence the crickets.

"He had an image to maintain, Dean. He had to fit the role of the high school stereotype. He was a jock and that meant he should be seen with a certain type of girl. But that's not the kind of girl he *liked*." She smiled, and it was colder than the night. "He liked his girls damaged, as if they'd been through Hell and returned with tales to tell, as if they had scars to prove they were tough and ready for anything. The Barbie doll type made him sick."

Dean shuddered, jammed his hands into the pockets of his coat; wished he'd brought the knife.

"I was his girl," she said, a truth that wrenched his guts surer than any blade. "No one knew because he still had his pride. Why do you think he hit Greer for trying to fuck me? That was going one step too far. 'Course that dumbass Greer knew nothing about it and still doesn't."

Dean stared, his body trembling, his hands clenched so tight the scars on his arms must surely rip open and bleed anew.

A joke. It was all a joke.

"We didn't think you'd freak out like you did and beat seven shades of shit out of Freddy. Christ. You nearly killed him, you asshole."

But Dean didn't hear her. An evil laugh filtered through the speakers, followed by a hellish voice that asked: "Where's my pretty little girl?" And then a scream to make Fay Wray proud.

Where's my pretty little girl?

"How ..." Dean began, before pausing to clear his throat. "How did you ...?" He indicated his own mangled face with a trembling forefinger.

"Surgery," she said airily. "It's why I'm still working in this fucking dump. My mother refuses to help me pay for it. Too busy buying shit she doesn't need on the Shopping Channel. Of course, when I lost the scars, I lost Freddy, too. I was tired of him anyway."

The sound of unpleasant death, of skin rending, gurgling screams, and bones snapping, filled the air.

"Hey," Stephanie said with a shrug, "it's all in the past, right? No hard feelings?"

Look at you now, shithead.

Dean nodded, licked his lips. "Yeah. Right, no hard feelings."

Stephanie nodded her satisfaction. "Good, so are you going to watch your movie, or what?"

Look at you now.

190

THE PERFECT SIZE

BY A.P. SESSLER

The vinyl flaps lifted as suitcases of all sizes emerged through the wall on the conveyor belt and rolled into hands of every ethnicity. A coffee-colored hand lifted a green canvas suitcase; next a lemon palm swept up one in burgundy leather, then peachy fingers gripped a tartan of red.

A female voice boomed over the loudspeaker system in one language after the other, directing all new arrivals to their desired stations at Changi International Airport.

Frank stood at the curve of a U-shaped baggage carousel awaiting his luggage. A Caucasian businessman from America, he stood roughly six feet tall and wore a dark-blue suit and dark-gray fedora. He was so anxious to leave, he flinched when he saw his suitcase come through the opening, but the crowd gathered around the carousel made it impossible to retrieve without knocking them down or climbing onto the conveyor itself to do so.

He restrained the impulse and waited until the brown leather bag bearing his initials came to greet him. After catching it by a corner he unzipped the suitcase to ensure the entirety of its inventory was secure and intact.

He zipped the suitcase closed and made his way to the airport exit to hail a taxi. He was fortunate to gain the attention of a nearby driver,

191

who looked up from the newspaper he was reading and waved for Frank to approach.

The man was in his forties. He wore a red short-sleeve T-shirt with faded, illegible print on its front. His small eyes were canopied by his thick, wiry eyebrows. He quickly folded his newspaper as Frank approached the cab.

"Where to?" asked the driver as Frank opened the back door and put his suitcase inside.

"The Tiger Lotus Hotel," answered Frank after sitting down and closing the door. He removed his hat and held out his hand with a folded fifty-dollar bill between his fingers for the driver to take. "I would appreciate it if we got there fast."

"No pay now," said the driver. "Pay later."

Frank shrugged it off and put the bill in his breast pocket.

The driver turned his head forward and started the meter. The back of his head looked like a ball of slick, dark yarn down to its last strands. "We get there real quick," he said just before putting the pedal to the floor.

Frank fell back into the seat and put his hand on the door handle, first to brace himself, then to ensure it was locked.

The taxi weaved in and out of traffic as the cars falling behind became a blur. Frank squirmed in his seat and waved his cell phone around as he tried to pick up a signal. The taxi exited the East Coast Parkway and headed into the city, away from the Singapore Strait.

Frank pressed the CALL button on his phone again. A moment later a graphic indicating the signal had been received appeared on the phone's LCD. After a few rings, a female voice answered.

"Hello, husband," she said.

"Hello, Xiulan," he replied.

"Where are you?" she asked.

"I'm on my way to the hotel. I landed about forty-five minutes ago."

"How was your trip?"

"It was fine, but we'll talk about that later. How are you doing?"

"I am well. I've missed you."

"I've missed *you*," he echoed. "I've been thinking about you the whole time. Actually, it was really difficult to keep my mind on business."

"I hope your thoughts of me didn't interfere with your success," she said gingerly.

"No, they didn't. But even if they had, the thought that I would soon be with my beautiful little wife would be more than enough."

There was an extended pause before she spoke. "I have a confession to make."

"Yes?" he swallowed as his concern became audible. "What is it, dear?"

"I am not as 'little' as I was on our honeymoon."

"You mean," he asked excitedly, "you're pregnant?"

There was another pause. "No. I'm not."

"I don't understand. If you're not pregnant, how could you be any bigger?"

"Though I am not pregnant, I have been eating enough for two," she said in an attempt at the western humor he often used.

"Oh, come on," he said. "You could eat four times as much as you do and not gain a pound."

"I respectfully disagree," she said. "I have put on considerable weight since we've last been together, and for that I sincerely apologize."

"Xiulan, you couldn't gain enough weight for there to be cause for apologies."

"Again, I respectfully disagree, husband. I do hope you are not disappointed with me."

"You couldn't disappoint me. You're everything I've ever wanted. And I can't wait to see you again and make love to you no matter what size or shape you are. *You* are what matters, not what you look like."

Again there was a pause, then soft sobbing.

"Oh, Xiulan," he said. "Don't cry. I love you."

"I love you, too. But I know you're attracted to me because of my culture and my size. You know we encourage women to remain demure, and I regretfully confess that I have lost that which you were attracted to."

"That's enough of that talk. Don't you worry about your appearance," he insisted. "It's not for your sake that you're beautiful, it's for mine. And no amount of weight could take your beauty away. I want you to put on the slinkiest, sexiest thing you can find and I want you to be ready for me, because I'm going to make love to you the moment I lay my eyes on you."

"Yes," she said. "I will do as you say."

After they said their goodbyes, he hung up the phone. He looked up to see that in the rearview mirror the driver's eyes were fixed on him, and Frank suspected they had been for the duration of his now less-than-intimate conversation. When their eyes locked, the driver quickly looked away.

The taxi pulled to the curb in front of the Tiger Lotus Hotel and came to a stop. Frank ducked his head as he exited the taxi, then removed his suitcase and hat. He put the hat on to shield his eyes from the bright noon sun, then removed the fifty-dollar bill from his breast pocket and handed it to the driver.

"One moment. I get change," said the driver as he opened a small cash box and reached inside.

"No change," said Frank.

"You give too much," said the driver.

"No, no. That's yours," affirmed Frank.

The driver looked ashamed for having eavesdropped.

"In case you didn't get the gist of that phone call, this will be the first time I've seen my wife since our honeymoon," said Frank as he winked at the driver.

"Oh," said the driver, as his less-than-perfect teeth showed through his wide smile. "Many blessings and congratulations!"

"Thank you," said Frank, smiling back. "Good day."

"Thank *you*, sir!" said the driver as he waved good-bye with the bill clenched in his fist.

A steady wind blew through the valley of concrete and steel surrounding the busy street. Frank steadied his hat with one hand as he walked up the wide marble steps to the large glass double doors, one held open by the hotel doorman. He thanked the man in Malay and entered the hotel's atrium.

He walked past the stonewall pond filled with every breed of the hotel's namesake, then through two large columns to the hotel's main desk. The attendant was sandwiched between the wall and the semicircular desk, which had gates on both ends to allow him to exit in either direction.

"Good afternoon, sir," said the attendant in a voice that creaked like an old door. "May I have your name, please?"

"Franklin Lawrence," Frank answered.

"Greetings, Mr. Lawrence," said the attendant. He looked through the guest book to locate Frank's room number. The thin man was in his fifties, and tall enough to see Frank eye to eye when he stood up straight. He was also Frank's equal in fashion, with his fine suit and manicured nails. "I see your last stay was nearly a month ago. How was your trip, Mr. Lawrence?" he asked.

"It went very well, Mister—" said Frank as he scanned for a name tag to return the favor of familiarity. He couldn't find one on the man's suit but did find it on the desk. "Xiang," Frank said, hardly missing a beat.

"You are welcome," said Mr. Xiang. He then addressed the attentive bellhop who stood nearby. "Take Mr. Lawrence's luggage to room 731."

The bellhop took the suitcase from Frank's hand and put it on a strolling carrier.

"Just a moment," said Frank as he held out a hundred-dollar bill for the bellhop. "Can you stop by the gift shop and get me a bouquet of your finest flowers?"

"Yes, sir. I'll be right back," answered the enthusiastic young man as he carefully took the bill from Frank's hand and bowed his head graciously.

"Just one more moment," said Frank as the bellhop was about to walk off. "Leave them at the door with my luggage. I'll take them inside."

"What about your change?" asked the bellhop.

"Keep it. If it's less than thirty percent, charge it to my bill," Frank answered.

The bellhop eagerly walked off to the left of the counter and disappeared around a corner.

Mr. Xiang adjusted his glasses as he ran his finger along the rows and columns of slots on the key card box to find Frank's room key. "Here is your key, Mr. Lawrence."

"Thank you," said Frank as he took the card and turned to walk away.

"Oh, Mr. Lawrence, I almost forgot. You have a package."

"I do?"

"Yes, sir," said Mr. Xiang. He reached under the desk and retrieved a large manila envelope. "Here you are, sir," he said as he handed the envelope to Frank.

"What is it?" He flipped and rotated the envelope.

"I don't know, Mr. Lawrence, but it has your wife's name on it."

Frank had just located the name tag. "I see that," said Frank as he noted the obvious.

"And one last thing before you leave, Mr. Lawrence," said Mr. Xiang with one finger pointed up as he smiled with an open mouth.

"What is that?" asked Frank suspiciously.

"Enjoy your second honeymoon."

Frank's shoulders relaxed. He returned the smile. "Thank you, Mr. Xiang."

Frank secured the envelope between his side and right arm and walked to the elevator. He pushed the UP button and waited a moment. A bell sounded and the elevator doors opened. He stepped inside and waited for the doors to close. As the doors slowly slid shut his phone rang.

"Hello, dear," he answered.

"Hello, husband," said Xiulan. "I was wondering if the front desk had a package for me."

"Yes, they did. What is it?"

"It's a surprise."

"The only surprise I want is to see you in that nightie," he whispered with lowered eyebrows.

"I will see you soon. And remember, it's a surprise—no peeking."

"Yes, dear," he said giddily.

She hung up.

He was all the more curious as to the contents of the envelope. When he squeezed the middle with his thumbs, the volume of the package shifted to the top. When he squeezed the top with one hand, the volume returned to the bottom. It felt like several folds of a soft material. He imagined it was a new negligee just for their long-anticipated reunion. He pulled the envelope from under his arm so he could read its label. It was obviously addressed to Xiulan, that much of the foreign characters he could make out, but the rest was Greek to him (or in this case, Mandarin).

He reasoned one small look would hardly ruin the surprise. He tried to gently peel open the corner of the envelope, but it was sealed too tightly.

He reached into his jacket's inside pocket, where he kept various grooming items he often used to appear his best before meeting an important client. He retrieved a nail file and slid it under and along the envelope's adhesive-sealed seam.

As the file parted the halves of the envelope, a thick, green fog flowed slowly out and upward. He quickly held the envelope away from his face and ran his fingers along the seam to reseal it. The cloud lingered midair before him. He turned his head sideways and held his breath as he used the envelope to wave the cloud away from him.

The emerald tendrils floated toward the button panel. As he leaned closer to examine it, the elevator bell rang and the doors opened.

"Going down?" asked the plump, elderly Englishwoman, who wore a heavy fur coat and hat. Her bright-red lipstick made her pale skin and bobbed strawberry-blonde hair look even fairer.

"No, ma'am. Going up," said Frank as he looked nervously about the elevator to find where the green cloud had gone.

"Beggin' your pardon," apologized the woman when she saw Frank's expression. "I'll catch the next lift."

"No problem, ma'am."

When the doors didn't immediately shut, Frank went to press the CLOSE DOORS button, but instead of hitting one button his finger pressed four at once. The elevator didn't respond.

He tried to press the tiny button again. The doors closed and the elevator continued its ascension. It was then Frank realized the green fog had dissipated.

As soon as the elevator reached the top floor, he hurried out to his penthouse suite. The luggage cart was beside the door, bearing Frank's suitcase and the bouquet of flowers the bellhop had purchased per Frank's request.

Frank ran the key card through the slot and opened the door. He placed his suitcase just inside, and then carried the bouquet of flowers to the dinner table. He quickly put the DO NOT DISTURB sign on the outside handle and deadbolted the door.

"Xiulan, I'm home!" he announced.

"I'm in the bedroom, waiting," she answered back.

"That's my girl." Frank smiled as he threw the envelope, his hat, and jacket on a nearby chair. He kicked his shoes off and tossed his belt and tie aside, then proceeded to unbutton his shirt as he walked toward the bedroom.

He opened the door. To his left was a tall hardwood dresser and a full-length mirror with Xiulan's profile reflected in it. The wall was lined with white-curtained windows, and at the foot of the bed before him was a rattan chair with a round, high top.

Next to the chair stood Xiulan with her back turned. The sunlight pouring in through the curtains passed through her silk nightie and revealed her silhouette.

"Did you bring the package?" Xiulan asked with her back still turned.

"The package?" He had already forgotten. "Oh, it's in the living room—but whatever is inside is unnecessary for what I have in mind."

"But *not* for what I have in mind," she said as she turned her head and looked at herself in the mirror.

"Dear, are you sure whatever is in that package is ... safe?"

"You opened it?" she asked.

"I'm sorry. I did," he confessed. "I thought it was a new nightie. Xiulan, there's something bad in that package."

"No! It's not bad," she objected. Her usually soft voice grew loud. "It's the answer to my prayers."

"Your prayers?" he laughed. "Since when do miracles come in a manila envelope?"

"Don't mock me," she said with a frown as she looked away. "You know Chinese people have knowledge of things western doctors don't."

"Nobody's sick! Who needs a doctor?"

"I do!" she yelled. She turned to face him. "Look at me!"

From her small, round face and large, almond-shaped eyes to the long black hair she only let down when they made love, he could find no flaw. However, if he were honest, he would admit she gained several pounds.

"You look fine," he said.

"You're lying!" she accused, and then turned away.

"Xiulan, at this moment I don't care how you look. I'm so ready to make love to you, it doesn't make a difference in the world."

"So, you're desperate, is that it?"

"Why are you acting like this? I don't care that you've put on a few pounds. You're my wife, and I love you."

"You're just horny."

"Yes, you're right. I'm horny. I get to make love to my wife for one week on our honeymoon, then I'm called off to Japan for a month. And every day all I can do is think of being with you."

"For someone who was thinking of me so much, you seemed to do rather well in making another business deal."

"This is crazy! What in the world happened to you?"

She turned around again. "This is what happened to me!" she said as she invited him to look at her body. "You left me alone for a month! At least you could have let me return to my parents until you returned. I was so depressed all I could do was eat, and eat, and eat."

During their month apart from each other, she found comfort in chocolates dark and sweet, bonbons, éclairs, pastries, cakes, red meat, sausages and bacon, pasta, and rich sauces of every kind. She didn't mean to get so carried away, but she had never had the freedom to do so. She was never wealthy before, and never with someone who encouraged her to enjoy the finer things in life. She was brought up to control herself in emotion and appetite.

"I'm sorry I left you alone," he said. "But you know how important this deal was for me and our future, and you knew I had business to wrap up here before we go home. In all honesty, honey, you're still beautiful to me."

He leaned forward and took her hands in his. She tried to pull away but he held her firmly, and then kissed her forehead.

She pouted girlishly. "I'm fat."

"No, you're not, honey."

"Yes, I am. I look like one of those American girls on TV," she said with a whimper.

Frank laughed. A moment later she joined in.

He brushed her cheek with his hand and tucked her hair behind her ear. "You really want what's in that envelope?" Frank asked.

She nodded her head.

"I'll be right back with it," he assured her.

He walked into the living room to find the package. It took him a minute to remember he had tossed it on the chair underneath his jacket. He brought her the envelope.

"There's something crazy in this," he said as he handed it to her. "It looks like it's poisonous."

"It's not poison!" she huffed as she rolled her eyes. "I just hope you didn't waste it all."

"I didn't know what it was," he explained.

"Just watch," she demanded.

When she opened the envelope, the same murky, green fog slowly rose from the package. Frank took a deep breath and held it in as he stepped back cautiously. Xiulan closed the envelope, then with her hands she waved the fog toward her plump belly. She turned her head aside and lifted her hands out of the cloud. The fog seemed to evaporate, and with it the pounds she had put on the past month.

Frank exhaled. "That's amazing!" He slapped his hand over his mouth, then let his fingers fall underneath his jaw as if to keep it from falling to the floor. "I had no idea!"

"I told you," she said. "Chinese medicine is different from your western medicine."

She opened the envelope and waved another plume of fog toward her thighs. The cottage cheese ripples in her flesh soon became smooth.

She held the envelope behind her back as she stared at her buttocks. She was about to open the envelope when Frank objected. "Look, if you found the perfect body in a bag, why not use it to your advantage? If it can shrink some things, why not leave some things the way they are, you know?"

"So, you like my butt big?" she asked sincerely.

"You may have put on some weight, but it's not *all* bad," said Frank as his eyes darted to one side and back.

"Really? Men like big butts?"

At first Frank was embarrassed to answer, but then nodded his head.

"Okay. How about this?" she asked.

She bathed in the fog from her waist up to her bustline. Her breasts seemed to increase by at least a cup size, though in reality the fog had merely narrowed her waist. Frank's eyes and smile also increased in size, without any aid from the green gas.

"So, you liked my typical Asian body the way it was, but now you like it better?" she asked.

He wasn't sure how to respond. "I didn't ask you to use the stuff," he reminded her. "I told you I was fine with you the way you were, but if you want to play plastic surgeon with the 'creeping death' gas, then by all means, let's have some fun with it."

He looked at his body in the mirror. "You know, I could definitely do with a smaller gut." He pinched the excess of flesh between his thumb and forefinger.

"You can—after I'm done," she said.

"What do you mean? You're fine."

"I'm not finished yet. Go to the living room. I'll call you when it's time."

"I don't think you need to improve much more."

"I told you I wanted to surprise you."

He smiled as he exited the bedroom, and then pulled the door shut. He paced in the living room, anxiously awaiting his *new* bride. After a moment, he removed his socks and pants, and then continued pacing in his unbuttoned shirt and boxers.

He walked back to the door and opened it a crack to peek inside. "Are you ready yet?"

"Not yet," she said. Her breasts and hips were larger than before.

Though he was highly aroused at her new appearance, something didn't quite look right about her.

"Did you do something to your face?" Frank asked carefully.

"I didn't like having such wide cheeks. I thought I would make my face more slender and youthful."

"Okay. Just don't get carried away. I don't want people thinking I'm a cradle robber when we walk down the street."

"When I'm finished, you won't care what people think," she said with a perverse smile.

She pushed him out of the room and closed the door.

Frank heard the door lock. He was so excited he clapped his hands and rubbed them together in anticipation. He paced around the living room again, now in a dance. Before he got too caught up in his moment of reverie, he returned to the door.

"Are you finished yet?" he asked loudly with his cheek against the door. He watched as his breath formed pulsating patches of fog on the cherry-wood finish.

"Not yet," she said in a soft voice.

201

"Are you going to save some for me?"

"Yes. Just wait."

He paced the floor until he could no longer stand it. He marched to the door. "All right, honey, that's enough. You can open the door now."

He waited for the sound of the lock to turn. "Honey? Open the door," he said as he wiggled the door handle. "Xiulan? Are you all right?"

There was no response.

"Dear, you're scaring me," he laughed nervously. "If you don't open the door right now, I'm going to break it down. I'm not kidding."

When she didn't respond he thrust his shoulder into the door. He nearly broke his arm but the door didn't give. He thrust his shoulder in again ... and again. There was a loud crack as the wood split around the handle and hinges. He threw his other shoulder into the door. The entire door, minus the deadbolt and door set, went crashing into the full-length mirror beside the bed.

Frank stepped over the threshold and carefully placed his bare feet between the mirror shards scattered on the floor. Next to the broken glass was the manila envelope, unsealed and emptied of its contents.

Xiulan giggled softly. "My, you are an eager one," she said.

She sat in the rattan chair at the foot of the bed, resting her palms on the edge of the seat and dangling her feet above the floor. She had perfectly sized breasts, a perfectly flat stomach, perfectly thick hips and perfectly round buttocks. Her face was perfectly shaped and her lips were perfectly tempting. Everything about her was perfectly perfect, save one minor thing.

"No!" cried Frank. "No, no, no!"

"What's the matter?" asked Xiulan in a high-pitched voice. "Aren't I the perfect size?"

He lowered his eyes in revulsion, to be spared the abominable sight, but there in each shard of mirror on the floor was reflected the dreadful truth. Like a congregation of nymphs, each image of her laughed at him in unison.

Xiulan, with her perfectly proportioned body, was now as small and fragile as a little girl's doll.

PIPER AT THE GATES

BY DAVID BENTON & W.D. GAGLIANI

In every grain of wheat there lies hidden the soul of a star.

~ Oswald Crollius

He pushed his index finger into the wetness and waited, knowing he had to find the exact spot and not wanting to disturb the subject too soon.

The anticipation burned just under the surface of his skin and he started to sweat, his body reacting to what it would feel when the circuit was closed.

If only this was an exact science.

He swirled his finger around in a circular pattern, feeling the flesh and other matter part for him, warm to the touch and inducing both a squeamish and an almost erotic response from him, as if he were manipulating genitalia. He shivered with expectant ecstasy held at bay, waiting, waiting, for his skin to make the desired connection. Below the pad of his finger he felt the top surface of the metal plate that kept Rick Dempsey's brain from bubbling up through the crack and cavity in his war-ravaged skull.

The metal plate was heating, sending its signal up through his index finger. Cedric Lindstrom trembled. He felt an erection beginning. He felt sweat trickle down his back and pool under his armpits.

His finger spread some wet, fleshy substance aside and penetrated further into the cavity.

Dempsey's eyes sprang open, but he could not move.

Lindstrom knew he was almost there. He swirled sideways, and suddenly the circuit was closed and his expectation was exceeded once again.

The sensation grew, and suddenly it was as if a bolt of electrical current had leaped from the metal plate (and whatever was just underneath it—presumably the clump of shrapnel they had been forced to leave inside) and discharged through the skin of his fingertip and into his phalange and on to the metacarpal, and from there into his arm like lightning.

His body jumped with the energy that coursed through his veins, tendons, and bones, and his eyes rolled up into his head.

It was the greatest, best high he had ever experienced, even after decades of experimenting with both street and the most advanced designer drugs available to him, given his medical practice.

It was the greatest, best high ... and it seemed to encompass every cell, every sinew of his being. It was sensual and erotic and led to an immediate orgasm, which would have been a *bummer* ... except that as long as the current flowed, there would be another orgasm right behind the first. And then again.

As long as his finger remained in that position, closing the circuit between the brain, the skull, the plate, and most likely the shrapnel itself, Lindstrom rode the sexual roller coaster that was Private Dempsey's ruined brain.

As he jiggled and shivered through a series of orgasmic episodes, Lindstrom's eyes refused to acknowledge that below his hand—buried in the soldier's head almost to the palm now—the young man's head was shaking rapidly from side to side and his eyes were nearly bursting from their sockets, open and staring with stark horror that would have been reflected in the endless scream from his gaping mouth ... except that his vocal cords had been severed by other shrapnel, and the scream would forever remain silent.

Dr. Cedric Lindstrom rode the high of the brain-crack now jolting through his system, oblivious to the horrific visions that his incursion was causing his young patient.

The circuit stayed open for nearly an hour.

Byron Stevens strode across the parking lot to the towering office building. He double-checked the address, comparing it with the one on the pamphlet he gripped in his sweaty hand. Though it was warm in the late-afternoon sunshine, he felt a chill that cut bone-deep.

A shadow passed over him, but when he glanced up to see what had cast it, he found nothing but an endless expanse of pale blue sky. He hastened his pace.

At the corners of his vision dark shapes moved, tailing him and then vanishing when he turned to look their way.

He jogged now, closing the remaining distance between himself and the building quickly. The doctor ducked in through the glass double doors, staring behind him as the entrance slowly hissed closed.

Wondering whether he was out of its grasp.

Not wanting to be.

The therapist's office wasn't exactly what Dr. Byron Stevens had expected. He'd imagined himself reclining on the proverbial couch, the shrink seated next to him in a plush high-backed chair, taking notes on a legal pad. Instead, Julia Chambers sat facing him across a cluttered desk—a computer monitor and a paper-stuffed inbox won the top-of-the-heap contest. *Overworked, maybe?* Framed degrees shared wall space with an oil painting of a sailing ship teetering on a roiling sea. A bookcase sagged with a hodgepodge of psychology textbooks entombing framed photographs of what Byron assumed were her now grown children.

"So, Dr. Stevens," Chambers said. "What did you want to talk about today?"

"Umm ..." Byron hesitated. He'd never seen a shrink before and honestly he didn't want to talk to her about anything. His appointment was mandated as part of his rehab and probation. Really, he was damn lucky he hadn't lost his medical license yet, though a review board could still pull the trigger. He should have known better than to write himself all those scrips in a vain effort to recapture the ...

The high. Call it what it is.

Problem was, there was only one way to relive the *high*.

Lord, his hands and feet itched at the thought of what he was missing.

Sure, the VA had cut him some slack. He was under a lot of stress after the deaths and the trial. He'd been acquitted of the worst of it, but still lived under a cloud of suspicion. His career hung by a thread.

"Why don't you just start at the beginning?" Chambers prompted.

He was distracted by her tan pantsuit and gaudy low–hanging silver pendant that resembled a primitive bird, some kind of stones forming its eyes. Her hair was obviously dyed, reddish-brown with a little gray sneaking in near her temples, thick makeup attempting to cover her age lines. When Byron realized that she was watching his hands, he stopped wringing them, which was what he did in lieu of scratching them bloody.

"Don't think too hard, Dr. Stevens. Just start talking. You've been through a lot and it's completely normal—all things considered—that you should feel emotions that are hard to deal with on your own. Opening up and talking about it will help you face your inner turmoil. So, where do you think this all started?"

Byron sighed. "It started when I first met Private Rick Dempsey. Hell, he'd already endured a dozen surgeries and a year and a half of physical therapy when I first saw him at the VA hospital. That kid had been through a lot. I already knew that from his file, but actually seeing him drove it home." He licked his lips, suddenly dry, and Chambers handed him a bottle of water. After pausing to drink, Byron continued.

"The explosion had almost killed him outright. It was a worst-case scenario: Now he was a quadruple amputee with extensive damage to his chest, abdomen, and face. He'd lost his ability to speak due to damage to his throat, had lost his left eye, and he still carried a fragment of shrapnel in his frontal lobe—removal of the shrapnel would kill him, they decided. A metal plate was what kept his brain from being exposed. His previous doctor had just retired due to illness and I had taken over the young man's case."

Private Dempsey had come in for his regularly scheduled visit. Seeing his war-torn body—scar upon scar upon scar—jarred Byron. Trying to be kind, he had told the soldier that he was lucky to be alive. "His single remaining eye damned me for my poor choice of words," added Byron.

He continued. "It wasn't a long visit. A quick blood pressure test, pulmonary, respiratory. Though he'd come in with a powered wheelchair, I had him ambulate a short distance on his prosthetic legs. Rick's lack of vocal cords required that he wrote down answers to any questions that I had. He was on a waiting list for a speaking valve, you know, God bless the USA, but he was reasonably skilled—considering the circumstances—with a pen in the stainless steel hook that had replaced his right hand. In this way he complained to me about headaches, which I'd seen in his charts. And he brought up a newer problem that he assumed had been caused by his head injuries: hallucinations."

"What kind of hallucinations?"

"Well, that's a large question, isn't it?"

Chambers tilted her head at Byron's defensiveness. She waved for further details.

"Okay, so, I had him scheduled for an immediate set of new X–rays and other imaging to make sure the shrapnel in his head hadn't moved or caused hemorrhaging in the brain."

Byron felt a sudden presence behind him, looming over him in the chair. He snapped his head around and quickly scanned the room. A cold, clammy sweat squeezed from the pores on the back of his neck. His breath hitched and then sped up.

"Dr. Stevens. Are you all right?" the therapist asked.

Byron swung his head slowly back around. Disoriented, it took him a moment to remember where he was and why.

Byron shook off the question, and the fleeting paranoia. "Yes, of course!" He glanced at his watch. "Where was I? Umm ... oh, yes, the results of Dempsey's imaging panels were inconclusive. But I was concerned, so I sent him to see a longtime acquaintance of mine, a specialist in brain trauma. Dr. Cedric Lindstrom, head of the trauma unit at University Hospital. Shortly afterward, Dr. Lindstrom and I met privately to discuss the case."

"Cedric, it's great to see you." Byron extended his hand across the table. Cedric had surgeon's hands, soft yet strong and undeniably skilled. Though it was two o'clock in the afternoon, only the faintest trace of sunlight reached their table in the back corner of the restaurant, rendering the air around them hazy.

"It's been a while," Cedric said.

"Too long."

Byron pulled out a chair and sat.

"I hope you don't mind, I ordered a starter for you," Cedric said. "Glenfiddich—neat, wasn't it?"

"Perfect," said Byron, lifting the glass to his lips. Then: "So how have you been? How are things with Marcy, and the dogs?"

"Well, the divorce was finalized six months ago. And she got the dogs."

"Oh, shit, Cedric. I'm sorry."

"Ah, it's for the best. Things were getting rough, near the end. You know, we all work too much. It's hard to maintain a strong relationship and a big career. The career always wins. Besides, now I can trade up for a younger model!"

"That's the right attitude. Cheers to that!" Byron raised his glass and Cedric followed suit, a strangely blank expression on his face.

"And you?" Cedric asked after drinking.

"Same story, I guess," Byron answered with a shrug. "Busy all the time. Cell phone in one hand and pager in the other. Hell, I'm on call right now." He swirled his Scotch. "But don't tell." He winked.

"My lips are sealed!"

The waiter came and they ordered, and after a few squalls of chat about sports and the weather, they ate their steaks in relative silence. After indulging in the finest New York strip their money could buy, and another round of single malt, Byron turned the conversation to the topic that had been weighing on his mind for several weeks. "So, that boy Dempsey that I sent to you. What ever became of him?"

Cedric coughed once, then coughed at length. He seemed to have been taken by surprise. "Oh, the war hero," he said, wiping a golden drop from his lower lip. "Well, that's a very interesting case."

"A tragic case," Byron amended.

"Yes, that kid's been through some hard circumstances, and he's facing more, no doubt of that."

"Did you come to a determination of whether his hallucinations have a real physical basis, or are they mostly PTSD-related?"

"As I said, a very intriguing case. Are you at all familiar with the work of a Dr. Elias Raymond?"

Byron shook his head.

"Of course not, why would you be? Raymond had some unusual theories. He was something of a pioneer in brain science, conducting some strange experiments in Costa Rica way back in the late 1800s. His theories—at least those in his later years—hinged on the idea that with a small modification to the frontal lobe one could glimpse ... well, as he termed it 'beyond the veil' or 'seeing the Great God Pan.'"

"What exactly does that mean?"

"Yes, what is the *veil*? Raymond theorized that we—people—only perceive a small portion of the universe and that with a small alteration to the brain a person would be able to ... possibly peek into other dimensions."

This time Byron almost choked. "Wait a minute! What you're saying is that Dempsey is seeing into another dimension?"

Cedric chuckled. Nervously. "No! Not at all. That's ... ridiculous. What I'm saying is that the incision made by the shrapnel may be causing his hallucinations. And that Dr. Raymond's experiments—though, er, misguided—may have carried a small grain of truth. Most of our higher brain functions—like sight—take place in the frontal lobe. I think the damage done to our young hero's brain is giving him what seem to be very real visions. When I say very real, I mean that often he can't differentiate his hallucinations from reality. He is seeing the Great God Pan."

Byron drained his Scotch, shaken. "Have you considered removing the shrapnel?"

"No. Much too dangerous. It would be almost impossible to remove it without giving him a stroke, and probably even killing him."

"Can medications help?"

"Nothing that I know of. I'm working with him closely. As I said, a very *interesting* case. A once-in-a-lifetime opportunity to observe something like this."

"Hell, Cedric, he's not an experiment!" Byron objected, raising his voice. "He's been through enough, hasn't he?"

"Relax, Byron, I'm not saying he's an experiment." Cedric looked around the quiet restaurant. "But at this time there's nothing we can do *but* observe. Observe and experience."

Chambers said, "So do you think you did the right thing by referring Private Dempsey to Dr. Lindstrom?"

Byron squirmed in the chair while he reflected on the therapist's question. He was on the verge of an answer that seemed just out of reach. He sighed, then shook his head.

Chambers waited patiently, her expression hard to read.

"I don't know," he said finally. "It seemed the right choice at the time. At least, it seemed logical. It wasn't until later that I realized that, although Cedric Lindstrom had been a friend, he wasn't quite a *trusted* friend. He was was fine to have a few drinks with, while discussing sports and politics. But I realized he wasn't the kind of friend you shared secrets with."

"So was Dempsey's condition a secret?" Chambers tilted her head as if one earring had suddenly gained in weight.

"No. I'm just saying that Cedric Lindstrom was the kind of physician, person, who always looks out for his own interests, first and foremost. You know, the kind of person who will hold you over a barrel if it'll give him an advantage."

"And did Dr. Lindstrom have you over a barrel?"

"In a matter of speaking. I had referred Dempsey to him. If he wasn't one hundred percent trustworthy, then what was I?"

"So did you feel guilty about the referral?"

"I guess so. After I spoke to him, yes, I felt I'd made a mistake."

"And it was sometime after this meeting with Cedric Lindstrom that you ..." she checked her notes ... "heard from Private Dempsey's mother?"

210

"Yeah, a couple of weeks later."

"And did you immediately connect Lindstrom with Dempsey's ... disappearance?"

"No! Yes ... maybe. I was simply trying to contact Cedric to see if he'd seen or heard from Dempsey. I thought—"

"When you couldn't get a hold of Lindstrom, did you suspect a connection?"

"I didn't suspect anything." Byron wiped sweat from his brow. "Maybe I did. Maybe I should have ..."

"That was when you went to the Lindstrom's house?"

"Yes," Byron whispered, squirming.

The late-morning sun was blinding today. Byron shielded his eyes from its glare as he wound his way to Dr. Cedric Lindstrom's front door, along the paving stone path that meandered through a carefully manicured lawn dotted with well-designed flower beds. When he reached the carved oak portal, Byron pressed the doorbell. The chime sounded inside, beyond the tiny, polished-wood-surrounded, leaded-glass window. He waited.

He rang the bell again.

Byron had just about given up and was turning to leave, when the door opened a crack.

"Hello?" a hoarse voice came from inside.

"Hello, Cedric? It's Byron. I didn't know ... I wasn't sure. Are you free to talk?"

Cedric Lindstrom stared out at Byron through the security chain as if he were trying to decipher a coded message. His eyes were bloodshot. Byron thought Cedric hadn't shaved—or slept, or even bathed—for days. There was a rank odor wafting from the open door.

"Byron?" Cedric asked, strange confusion in his tone, as if he'd run his finger down a list until Byron's name had rung a bell.

"Yes, it's *me*, Cedric. Can I come in? Can we talk?" Byron stepped closer and looked his old friend in the eye.

Recognition seemed to wash over Cedric's features. He attempted a smile, but it turned to grimace. His eyes twitched and squinted in the blinding sunlight. "Of course, Byron. Please, come in," he said. He closed the door and Byron thought he was being rejected, but after disengaging the lock, Lindstrom stepped aside and opened his home to Byron.

"My God, Cedric, you look like complete shit," Byron said bluntly as he sidled inside past the physician, whose body did carry the smell of sweat and unwashed clothing.

Lindstrom quickly fumbled the chain back into place, slid closed the deadbolt, and turned the lock button on the doorknob. "Can't be too careful," he said with a tremor in his voice.

"No, I guess you can't," Byron said. He felt a growing discomfort that was part fear for his own safety and part sadness for his friend's condition. Maybe losing Marcy had been harder on Cedric than he'd let on.

"Can I get you something, a drink?" Lindstrom said as he shuffled away.

"No, I'm fine, but you don't look fine."

"It's no trouble." Lindstrom seemed to waver on unsteady feet.

"I really don't have time right now, Cedric. I just stopped by to ask you some questions."

"Oh, okay." His eyes unfocused.

"Do you remember the Dempsey boy?"

"Yes," a smile crossed Lindstrom's lips. "That's a very interesting case," he rambled.

"Have you seen him recently? The boy's mother says he's completely disappeared, which isn't easy in his condition. Have you treated him within the last few days, or ...?"

"Why, yes, I *have* seen him recently, Byron."

"Thank God! Where?"

Lindstrom's face screwed up into a half-grimace again. "Well, in fact, he's downstairs right now."

"What?"

"He's here, Byron. Would you like to see him?"

"Yes, very much, Cedric."

"Okay, follow me," Lindstrom said, turning away. He barely lifted his feet as he walked. It seemed to Byron that his friend had aged fifty years in the few weeks since they'd last met, before Cedric had accepted the case. "A very *interesting* case," Cedric murmured again, mostly to himself.

Byron followed Cedric down a flight of carpeted stairs into what had once been a game room. A pool table had been shoved in a corner, while a rank of pinball and old-style arcade machines were jammed in another. One had toppled against the southern wall, broken glass twinkling below its shattered face. The long bar that stretched across the other side of the room had been well-stocked, but ranks of bottles had been swept off the back shelves and rested in various piles of glass on the stained carpeting. They walked past all of this destruction without remark. Lindstrom was lost somewhere in his own mind, and Byron just wanted to find Dempsey and get the hell away. Whatever had happened here, he wasn't sure he wanted to know. For the first time, Byron feared for his own safety.

"Interesting case," Cedric repeated as he reached a door on the far side of the ruined game room and threw open the door. As they stepped through, Byron noticed the long scratches on the wood panel. This second room was unfinished basement. To their right, a furnace and water heater hulked like alien shapes, pipes and conduit running above them like waving tentacles. The floor was poured concrete, slightly declining to meet the floor drain.

Another scratched door lay beyond. The doctors passed through it also.

By now Byron's sense of danger had kicked into overdrive, but he needed to see what his friend had done. And then he needed to get out.

Inside this last room—a workroom that had been transformed into a makeshift laboratory—Private Rick Dempsey lay secured to what could only be described as some kind of workbench or operating table. Each of the private's stumps was securely fastened to the table by thick leather straps. The table itself was propped at a roughly forty–five-degree angle, with Dempsey's misshapen head in the upper position. Tools hung from pegboard on the walls: wrenches, screwdrivers, clamps, hammers, saws, anything a homeowner could or would use around the house. Interspersed on the wall were surgeon's tools, some of them askew as if they'd been hastily replaced. On a nearby workbench Dempsey's prosthetics sat in an obscene flesh-colored pile. A photographer's floodlight on a tripod stand blazed in Dempsey's face. The boy seemed to be either sleeping or unconscious. His head lolled forward. A horrific jagged opening in the boy's cranium drooled a light pink fluid down his face and dripped onto the concrete floor, where it had puddled.

"Jesus, Cedric! What have you done?"

"I've told you, it's a very interesting case, Byron. I needed to experiment further."

Byron stormed toward the unconscious Dempsey and checked his carotid artery for a pulse. He was alive.

Thank God!

Then he used his thumb to peel open Dempsey's good eye. The pupil immediately shrank in the glare of the floodlight. The boy's head jerked away from Byron's hand. He was awake. His twisted features faced Byron and the doctor flinched, horrified by what he saw.

"Rick," Byron addressed Dempsey. But before he could formulate a sentence, Lindstrom grabbed Byron's hand and forced it against the boy's head.

"You must understand!" he shouted. "You have to *see*. There's more to this than it looks!"

Pressing Byron's thumb into the jagged crevice in Dempsey's skull, Lindstrom's body checked his colleague's until he couldn't gain his balance. Under the pressure, the ruined soldier's bloodshot eye widened in pain. Pain, and ...

Pain and what?

Before he could begin to wonder, Byron found himself immersed in blinding white light that blotted out the grotesque workroom and its contents. When the light receded he was no longer in his friend's basement. He was ... *somewhere else.*

The first thing Byron noticed was the intensity of the sunlight, bright beyond description, followed immediately by a dry, scorching heat that hurt his skin. In front of him, people were running and objects were raining down on them—*on him, too!*—falling from the sky like a hellish shower. But everything seemed to be in some kind of slow-motion. A plume of stinking black smoke curled up from the vicinity and obscured Byron's vision on and off. He wobbled, unsure of what bound him in place. Sand crunched beneath his feet, but he gained little traction.

He looked down, blinking furiously. A shattered human body lay supine. A soldier's body. It was Rick Dempsey, ripped apart, flesh and bone rent asunder and blood splatters spread out on the sand beneath him. Not far away, the hulk of some kind of vehicle burned, intense flames licking the air sluggishly. Debris still rained all around him, slowed so he could see each individual metal particle, some of them red-hot.

He understood, vaguely. Somehow Byron was in Dempsey's memories. In his near–death. He was *there*, feeling it all with his own senses.

Byron could hear people yelling, screaming, but the voices were muffled and drawn out in the frozen-time moments. He heard a siren wailing, its sound more in time with him than the surrounding scene. But it wasn't a siren, it was a voice—someone screaming. Byron looked down at Dempsey's ruined body. It wasn't him shrieking. Someone else, stepping gingerly through the slow-motion crowd, was screaming.

Then Byron was once again submerged in the brilliant white light, so brilliant that he almost fainted at its intensity. Then his sight returned and the details of the basement walls came flooding back.

He stared into Dempsey's face. The boy had his mouth open in a scream but no sound emerged from his open mouth. Below that, his uncovered neck gaped where shrapnel had destroyed his vocal cords.

Jesus, could Byron have heard him screaming here, while he'd been in that other place?

He became aware that his hand was still jammed into Dempsey's head, his fingers submerged in the pink fluid that leaked around them now. He also became aware that his body felt electric, sensitive to each particle of air that swirled around the close basement atmosphere.

And he became aware that, impossibly, he had an erection.

His skin tingled, in fact *all* his skin, and his clothes had become scratchy and constricting.

In what seemed like a nightmare fueled by some kind of bizarre drug cocktail, Lindstrom pulled Byron's hand from inside Dempsey's skull and led him away. It was as if a life-giving tether, an IV of blood replacing empty veins, had been ripped from his flesh. It was as if life itself had been interrupted like the pulling of a plug from a wall outlet, except that it was his flesh that now lost power and ... *what else?*

Byron's knees sagged and he felt the wet concrete hug him as he reached out for it. He grabbed it and felt nothing even as as his fingertips scrabbled uselessly on the rough floor, his nails splintering.

When he awoke, he was sitting half-propped on a stool at the basement bar with Cedric, a glass of Scotch in his hand. His fingers ached and he spied blood dripping on the glass. The pads of his fingers burned.

"You saw, didn't you?" Cedric asked.

Byron swallowed the complaint that bubbled to his chapped lips. He nodded.

"Did you understand what you saw?"

Byron's bleeding hand trembled, making it difficult to take a healthy gulp of single malt, but he gave it his best effort. "What the hell just happened?" he asked when he'd swallowed the burning liquid. His whole body felt on fire. His groin ached.

"I don't really know," said Lindstrom. "On surface, it's some kind of projected memory loop, starting right at the moment Dempsey was wounded. The scene doesn't change, but every time you go back new details emerge. Until something else ..."

"*Every time* you go back? Jesus, Cedric, what are you doing?"

"We can't let him go, Byron. There's too much at stake," Lindstrom said. The physician's hand fumbled with something on the bar. "It's not just the time and space movement, whatever it is that allows you to experience the explosion. *That's only the beginning!* Then there's a different experience. The more you go in ..."

"You're damn right, there's too much at stake!" Byron erupted. "This is a young man's life we're talking about, Cedric! If we're gonna do research let's do it right, at a real facility, with permission from the goddamned patient and his family!"

Lindstrom didn't answer, but something made a *thump* on the bartop.

Byron's eyes widened. It was a large-frame nickel-plated revolver that Lindstrom was cupping beneath his right hand, a glass of Scotch in his left. Both his hands were steady.

"I tried, Byron. He wants it removed."

"Huh?"

"He wants the shrapnel removed from his brain. At all costs. Even if it kills him."

"So ... so you kidnapped him?"

"Listen, Byron, this is a once-in-a-lifetime discovery. I'm not entirely talking about a scientific discovery; I'm talking about a spiritual awakening. Didn't you feel it, the super reality beyond this simple physical reality? The rush of discovering senses you didn't even know that you had?" Lindstrom caught himself and paused. Then he whispered, "Byron, wasn't it like the best high you've ever had? Like a drug-induced high mixed with the best orgasm of your life, except multiplied tenfold?"

Byron paused. He had felt *something*—even now it was stirring inside him, stirring in his groin, a feeling that he wanted to continue— an opening of his consciousness, and a desire to return to that place had started to burn. Not the physical place of Dempsey's loop—he understood that the loop was the soldier's own, and Byron had merely gone along for the ride, but the feeling that *all* his senses would open and there would be more to his life, his life that suddenly seemed so miserably bland and ... *closed*. But then his conscience spoke up. "There has to be another way, Cedric," he said weakly.

Lindstrom leaned closer, placed his Scotch carefully on the bar, still holding the revolver loosely. "But don't you see that something's unlocked in that boy's brain, an opening to *somewhere*, that we don't yet understand? You realize what else might be there that we can't even imagine? Don't you want to know what happens when we die? Don't you want to know what lies beyond the pearly gates?"

Byron snorted. "Be honest, what you really like is the boner it gives you! You like it just as you liked cocaine back in college. Admit it."

"I did. I do. It's like some kind of *crack* no one's ever discovered, Byron. It's like a potent mix of crack, heroin, testosterone, and ... and ... a sexual elixir, all in one."

"But it's not *yours*, Cedric. It's not your head you're defiling. And he wants the shrapnel out, you said so yourself."

"So, you think I should go into that boy's head and remove what may be the key to unlocking dimensions beyond the three simple ones we know, most likely killing him in the process? And then what? See if I can get permission to potentially lobotomize hundreds or thousands of volunteers in hope that we might find it again? Who's going to allow that, Byron? Is that really a better option?"

Byron was thinking about the sand, and the too bright sun, and the smell of burning flesh. Even sitting here at Cedric's basement bar he could feel the hot breeze against his skin. But then his thoughts turned to the amazing feeling of the *high* that had been there too, the sense-awakening electric jolt through his system that had given the experience its exhilaration. It—the memory of it coursing through him—was making him wish he could feel it again.

No, it was making him *crave* it.

But the boy—Lord, hadn't he been through enough? He'd lost everything, just to end up being tortured by an insane doctor who should have been treating him with compassion? *Two* insane doctors! Byron forced himself to focus. He made his decision and turned to face Lindstrom. "I can't let you do this, Cedric. I have to tell the authorities."

Without a word, Lindstrom swung the pistol and aimed it at Byron. But Byron had been expecting the move. He blocked Lindstrom's arm from locking and then punched him with his other hand over and over in the face, until Lindstrom collapsed, unconscious and bloody. His head hit the concrete with a wet *smack*.

He left Lindstrom sprawled out on the floor and hurried back to Dempsey in the workshop. When he entered, the boy was again passed out, strapped to the angled bench. Byron moved quickly. His hands were on the restraint securing Dempsey's upper left stump, when he looked down at the boy's face, which was so scarred that he seemed barely human. But Dempsey looked strangely peaceful in his sleep.

Byron took his hands from the restraint. What would it hurt to *go back* one more time before freeing the soldier? What would it hurt to feel the brain-crack moving through him, pumping through his veins and tendons? Even if he had to relive the soldier's experience ... Lindstrom had said it was just the beginning, that it would change, evolve somehow. Byron wanted to learn about that change, and he wanted to feel the jolt again.

Lindstrom was knocked out in the other room, the boy was asleep. *No one would know.*

Byron touched Dempsey's head lovingly, caressing his scalp until he located the soft spot in the soldier's skull. He took a deep breath, guilt pricking his conscience. Then he jammed his thumb into the hole again and rotated it, twisting it into the open incision. The squishy inside reminded him of a gutted fish.

White light flashed like a photographer's strobe, filling the room before making it disappear. Then Byron was in the desert, sun and sand making his skin sizzle. Ahead of him, people ran through the thick, slow-moving time, while pieces of the exploded vehicle floated down around him like feathers drifting in the wind, only seeming to gather speed when they speared human flesh.

The explosion seemed to echo continuously and Byron felt the sound waves rippling through the air. Now beside him lay Dempsey's wrecked body, the scent of blood so pronounced that Byron tasted it. He could smell other things too: sweat, urine, feces, burning fuel, and barbequed human flesh. His senses were primal.

He looked up into a sky that was perfectly blue. Massive, oily-black-winged serpents—*could they be the size of jumbo jets?*—wheeled in jagged orbits through the cloudless sky. Across from where he and Dempsey lay, Byron saw tall black figures ... impossibly tall, featureless figures with oily black skin like that of the serpents glistening in the sunlight. These figures stood still, staring directly at him through the haze of the explosion. The other people who scattered at molasses-speed away from the explosion didn't seem to notice these tall figures, nor did they notice Byron, as if Byron and the dark figures were in a separate part of space-time, observing a prerecorded section of some other reality. Byron counted a dozen, but there might have been more. They approached him, moving in real time through the crowd, avoiding the slow-motion figures still fleeing the explosion. The figures dodged the crowd with the grace of panthers stalking through the jungle.

Though his rocked senses were overloading, Byron could see that the figures' skins actually moved like continuous curtains of thick fluid flowing over their skeletons. They had no eyes or mouths, or distinctive features of any kind.

Byron was in the throes of the brain-crack high and felt no fear, despite the fact that they towered over him, bending down to examine him (and Dempsey, presumably). He felt himself grinning idiotically in trippy fascination, his groin awake as if they were beautiful human celebrities rather than grotesque alien beings.

The things gathered over Private Dempsey's shattered frame and the private screamed in terror. He was conscious, his one remaining eye pleading with Byron while the other wept a black viscous liquid onto his cheek. The soldier reached out to him with an arm that ended in shredded flesh and bone.

A sharp pain stabbed the back of Byron's head.

"When I awoke in that godforsaken basement, I could taste blood on my lips. At first I thought it was my blood, but then I lifted my head off of the floor and saw Dempsey and Cedric Lindstrom's bodies."

"And you called the police?" Chambers said.

"Yes."

"You realize that version is, uh, different than what I have here in the official account."

"Yeah, well ... my lawyer advised me to leave out the crazy parts."

The therapist nodded appreciatively, but Byron worried that he'd said too much. "Those parts weren't really important to the case," he added.

"No," she agreed. "Tell me about the condition of the bodies."

"Didn't you read the papers?"

"Yes, but I'd like to hear it from you, Dr. Stevens. It's part of the healing process."

"They were heaped up on the floor. Cedric Lindstrom had been stabbed in the face, neck, and chest more than twenty times. Dempsey was lying partially on top of the doctor with a yellow screwdriver handle still protruding from his right eye."

"What did you do before you called the police?"

"I didn't touch them at all. The bodies."

"You claim you have no idea who would have wanted to do something like this?"

"No, none. I was unconscious." Byron put his head in his hands.

Chambers said, "Presumably, whoever murdered Cedric Lindstrom and Rick Dempsey knocked you unconscious first?"

"I guess so."

"And did not harm *you*?"

"No."

"Was there anything unusual about what else was found at the scene?"

He hesitated. "The fingerprints ... found on the murder weapon, that screwdriver, were ... well, they were Private Dempsey's. His prints were on file for the Army." He paused. "*But he had no hands!*"

"And did the medical examiner—"

"It was determined that Dempsey was the second to die. He committed suicide with a hand he did not have, after using that hand to kill Cedric!"

"Can you account for that in any way, Doctor?"

Byron shook his head. Behind the therapist, a large black shadow moved with the silent grace. It crossed in front of the window, and then it vanished.

Chambers leaned forward. "Dr. Stevens, are you all right?"

"I'm fine," Byron whispered. He wiped a sheen of sweat off of his brow.

Her eyes were hard as they stared at him. "Your file indicates that subsequently you requested a transfer to the brain trauma unit. Can you tell me about that?"

"I ..." His eyes burned and he avoided her gaze. "I considered that my experience would make me a good candidate to help others who suffered traumatic brain injuries," Byron said. He squirmed in his chair. Sweat poured down his face now, but he ignored it.

She closed the file. "Well, I think that's all we have time for today, Dr. Stevens."

"You think I'm crazy, don't you?"

"No, not at all. I think you've been through some terrible experiences. You were traumatized almost as much as your patient." Her look softened. "Look, these things take time, Doctor, and the more you talk it out, the closer you'll come to finding some closure. We'll talk more." He nodded, unconvinced. "And Dr. Stevens, for next time could you bring your files on the Dempsey case?"

"I guess so," Byron said. "It's not ... really legal, is it?"

"Everything we do here is completely confidential, Doctor. I think having the files here ... will help you through the process. I'll see you next week."

Julia Chambers watched Dr. Byron Stevens leave, his defeated eyes haunted by what they had seen—but also by what he *needed*. She felt the need in him. She sympathized, but only to a point. He was beaten, almost forced out of his profession, tainted. Marked. An addict, of sorts. She shook her head and carefully placed his file in a locked drawer. Then she went to the bookcase and touched the photo of her daughters. Her eyes misted.

The year before, they had both died in that goddamned accident. She had allowed them to drive to the lake without her. It was a decision that could never be undone. A pain that could never be relieved. She'd tried. Oh, how she had tried. She had plummeted down a rabbit-hole of drugs and drink and despair the likes of which not even her worst patients could understand.

Now she replaced the frame carefully, turned it just so. Steel in her bones.

Moments later she was on the phone, finalizing her appointment to meet a Sergeant David Weiss, currently a resident at the Veterans Administration. His wounds were freakishly similar to those suffered by Dempsey. His file now lay open on her desk. She'd pulled it when she had seen that Stevens had requested a transfer to the brain trauma ward. She knew there had been a reason. She knew how the mind of an addict worked. *And ...*

She had developed a sudden interest in brain trauma herself.

At least, in *this kind* of brain trauma.

Mostly, she wanted to stick her fingers in this man's wound, touch the metal plate embedded there in his skull, and seek the solace he could bring. She shuffled the papers. Perhaps she would see what he saw. Perhaps she would see her own salvation. Or perhaps she would find only relief from the pain. But it would be worth it, whatever it could be. Her eyes hardened at the thought of what she might need to do to keep him from hurting her—to keep him from thwarting her ...

Her hands trembled.

BABYDADDY

BY JONATHAN TEMPLAR

They had their first session with the counselor two months into Dominique's pregnancy.

The counselor didn't come cheap. She had an uptown office that had been designed by an expert to be perfectly bland, perfectly unthreatening. It was a vision in beige, gentle on the eye, not a sharp edge in sight and soft carpeted from wall to wall. The blinds were pulled in case the view outside dared to ruin the illusion. It was like being in a well-furnished womb—which was ironic, given the circumstances.

"You're having some issues with the pregnancy?" she asked them in a honey-coated voice, her hands folded carefully in her lap.

Dominique pointed the finger. "*He's* the one with the issues."

Henry bristled. "It's not pregnancy I've got a problem with. Pregnancy is fine. Shit, we worked hard enough for it, mind my French."

The counselor waved a hand to suggest she'd heard far worse between these walls.

"So what is wrong?" she asked him.

"Nothing's wrong. I'm just fed up with hearing how *we're* pregnant. People come up to me, people I know, and they just can't wait to say it to me. 'I hear *you're* pregnant?'" Henry looked down at his flat, empty belly. "Shit, that's news to me! *We're* not fucking pregnant, *she* is fucking pregnant. My part in this was pretty much over by the time I'd finished shouting hallelujah and rolled over."

"And don't you just love to let me know about it? This is supposed to be a magical time, for *both* of us, and all he's done for the last month is make me feel guilty that I'm the one born with a womb."

The counselor gave a small, superior smile. "Womb envy," she said.

"What?"

"It's more common than you might imagine."

In his time, Henry Schade had envied many people and many things. Michael Jordan. Ron Jeremy. Mike Karchevsky three houses down with the red Lexus and the wife with the hundred-thousand-dollar tits. They didn't have much in common, but the lack of a womb was foremost. "Bullshit."

She was undeterred in her prognosis. "Pregnancy can be a complicated time for both parents. Male emotional responses are often overlooked in a rush to coo over the expectant mother. It's understandable that daddy might become resentful of the attention that mommy starts to receive. And it's even more natural to feel as if you have been relegated to a supporting role in the process when you begin to see the physical effect pregnancy has on mommy."

"She's got a fucking name, stop calling her mommy," Henry spat.

She ignored him, as if she was doing this whole session from a preprepared script. "Trust me; you're not the first man to sit on that sofa suffering from a lack of empathy with a pregnant partner."

"Hey, I have plenty of empathy!"

Dominique scoffed.

"I do!"

The counselor raised a hand, palm outward, a calming measure, sensing that Henry's temperature was rising. "I'm not disagreeing with you. But it's an easy response to understand, you see all the physical effects that mommy undergoes as baby develops, you can sense them bonding before you have an opportunity to contribute, and you feel that you're just reduced to the role of a spectator."

Henry nodded. To his great surprise, she'd actually summed it up pretty well. "It pisses me off, that's all."

She returned his nod, smiling blandly at him as she did. "I have a colleague who runs a clinic you might find helpful. He's keen on enhancing the male experience of child gestation and birth. He's something of a ... pioneer in the area."

"Anything that might help," Dominique said with undue eagerness.

The counselor wrote a name and a contact number on the back of a business card. The card was inevitably beige with a gentle font. She passed it to Dominique with a furtive look that briefly betrayed her sympathetic loyalty to the pregnant party. Henry saw it clearly.

"Good luck," she said.

Conception

It was called "BabyDaddy," but judging by the muted signage, it wasn't too keen to advertise the fact. The contrast to the counselor's uptown office couldn't have been more depressingly striking. BabyDaddy was comprised of no more than a forlorn single unit in a forgotten business park located far away from anything that mattered. Next door was an importer of foreign sex toys called The Cock Shop. Henry wondered if this was by accident or design.

The unit was littered with, not so much furniture, but *debris*, the flotsam of failure that had accumulated around its occupant. The chaos of the surroundings suited Dr. Petorian only too well. Precisely which institution had awarded him a doctorate, and in what discipline, was not disclosed in any of the company literature.

"Doctor" Petorian had a manner that could kindly be described as animated.

"Don't they just fucking piss you off, cooing and clucking over your wife like she was the prize pig at a county fair? And just because you were kind enough to impregnate her? All she had to do was lie back and let it happen, and now suddenly she's the center of attention. How the fuck did that happen?"

Dr. Petorian was not what Henry had expected. He thought he'd again be spending the afternoon listening to the carefully chosen platitudes of someone else ready to charge a hundred dollars an hour to

225

tell him what he already knew. But Petorian was something wild, a force of nature who paraded around his office like a bear trapped in too small a cage. His eyes shone out from behind thick-framed glasses that magnified them until they appeared too big for his face, and there was stubble on only one side of his chin, as though he'd been distracted halfway through shaving. To add to this, he wore a white coat that was incorrectly buttoned and far too large for him. He was like a hyperactive child playing doctors and nurses.

But Henry still thought the man was talking a lot of sense.

"I do get the feeling I've got the thin end of this deal," he said.

"Well, my friend, let's see if we can't beat nature at her own game. Let me tell you a little about the procedure I offer."

He pushed a bunch of leaflets across the desk. The one on the top was adorned with a picture of a man with his hand tucked tenderly around his own, obviously pregnant, stomach. The logo at the top shouted *BabyDaddy* far more confidently than the sign outside the door.

"Now, childbirth itself is beyond us, of course. But we can give you the *experience* of pregnancy, we can replicate all the symptoms and physical changes that your partner will be encountering at the same rate she does. You can, quite literally, share in the pregnancy, with the bonus that you duck out for the final act and leave all the pain and mess to her."

Henry brushed the pamphlet with his fingertips, reluctant to actually pick up the thing. "What would it involve?" he asked.

Petorian shrugged a shambolic shoulder. "A simple surgical procedure under local anesthetic. We implant what amounts to a bladder in your abdomen. Across the time frame of your partner's pregnancy the bladder inflates, pushing your stomach outward to mimic the growth of the fetus. We'll provide a series of hormonal supplements that you will take at prescribed intervals. When the child crawls out of its mother, or if you have enough of being the daddy to a faux baby, you simply deflate the bladder and have another ten-minute procedure to remove it from your belly. You'll have a tiny little scar afterward that you can tell everyone hails from your own caesarean section."

"That's all a bit extreme."

"Maybe so. But this way, you get to share the joy of childbirth. You get to experience what nature has denied us. You get to feel what

226

she feels. Why should she get it all to herself when you both had a hand in baking that bun in her oven?" He leaned across the desk, his comically large eyes bulging. "Don't you deserve someone cooing over you for a change?"

"I'm supposed to be achieving empathy," Henry pointed out.

Petorian shrugged. "You know what they say about walking a mile in someone else's shoes."

Henry certainly did. He started to flick through the leaflet.

It couldn't hurt to consider it, after all.

Second Trimester

Everyone in the store gave Henry a wide berth. He didn't care anymore. He was used to it. Used to that look on their faces, that look of puzzlement that slowly surrendered to disgust.

Fuck them.

He didn't care about what they thought, not anymore. The only thing he cared about was Junior. He walked down the aisles with a basket in one hand and the other wrapped around his belly as if to shield it from the rest of the world.

His feet hurt. His ankles were swollen. And his nipples had started leaking again this morning, so he'd worn a sweater even though it was baking hot so he sweated as if there were a tap left on beneath his skin. It dripped from his forehead onto the ice cream as he bent down to pick up a tub. He put the frozen cardboard to his brow and let it cool him for a while.

The girl at the checkout served him with a scowl on her face, as if someone had shit on the conveyor.

"You got a problem?" he asked her.

"Look who's fucking talking," she murmured.

"What did you say?"

She looked him right in the eye.

"Freak."

Henry thought about asking to speak to her manager. But he needed to pee and he just wanted to get home. So he let it pass. The manager would probably just be worse, anyway.

The procedure had been carried out two months before. Henry had it done at a clinic that provided a cheap but cheerful service. They even seemed to think he was doing a wonderful thing having the rubber womb implanted. The attending nurse certainly told him as much. As Petorian promised, it was indeed a brief operation, although it wasn't exactly painless. The womb/bladder had been the size of a balloon, and it went in easily. The incision was sore for weeks; it still itched when Henry had a bath. He'd gone home with a box full of hormone treatments provided by Petorian. The medicine came from a Mexican pharmaceutical company, with dispending notes all written in Spanish. Henry hadn't stopped to consider the implications of that, but by then he was so wrapped up in the idea of fatherhood, he likely wouldn't have cared anyway.

He started to inject them. The bladder started to swell. And soon enough, it wasn't anything to do with empathy anymore.

Dominique had walked out on him a couple of weeks ago. She wouldn't even take his calls. Selfish bitch. It had come to a head at a Lamaze class. She was starting to show, that curving round stretch of belly that told the world that she was expecting, that she was with child, that she was, for the extent of her pregnancy, someone *special*. But Henry had started to show even more, and when they had sat and begun to practice focused breathing, it was pretty clear to both of them that whatever reason he initially had for having his own mock pregnancy implanted, it was now more important to him than the one they had made together. Her breathing didn't matter to him, it was his own that he needed to perfect. The looks of revulsion from the other couples were too much for her. She couldn't have gotten out of there fast enough, and one of the other mothers-to-be, a sour bitch who must have been fat even before the pregnancy pounds had piled on, had cornered Henry as he tried to follow.

"You fucked-up creep. Think about your wife for one second and get rid of that thing."

She poked him in his engorged belly. It was all he could do to stop himself from slapping her ugly face.

"I believe in my baby's right to life," he told her, and pushed past.

He didn't catch up with Dominique and he hadn't seen her since. Their only contact had come through her friend, Angelica, who had made it clear that there was only one way that they could possibly be reconciled. And Henry had no intention of getting rid of his baby.

"You seriously care more for a bag of fucking air than your own child?" Angelica had said to him.

"This is *my* child," he answered, pointing to his stomach.

"You need serious help, Henry."

And perhaps she was right. But he was *happy*. Since he'd had the implant, everything seemed to make so much more sense. And there was no way he was going to let that feeling go, not until he reached full term.

Third Trimester

Dr. Yates pointed to a dark shadow on the x-ray. It pressed against the bright white blur that was the bladder in negative, as if it was fighting off the rapidly inflating intruder.

"It's definitely a tumor. We'll need to do a biopsy to determine its nature, but it's growing at an alarming rate."

"It's not a tumor, doc. We both know what it is."

"Mr. Schade. *Henry.* I understand why you undertook this procedure. I think you probably did so with noble and selfless intentions. But all you have done is allowed yourself to be mutilated at the hands of a hack. This has caused you and your wife no end of emotional pain and now there is clear physical damage from the pressure you have been putting your body through. It's time to put a stop to this. We can have that implant out of you within the hour and have you on a proper course of remedial steroids to try to prevent the growth of the tumor."

"It's not a tumor."

Dr. Yates sighed, rubbed his temples, tried not to let the exasperation show. "Henry, you are not pregnant. Your body is simply lying to you, responding to the chemicals you've been pumping into it, chemicals that have no right to be circulating in your system. That, and the monstrous thing you've got implanted inside you, is pushing your body to its limits, and your body is starting to crumble under the pressure. You need to have it removed *now*, before it's too late to repair the damage."

"This is not damage. This is my child."

"Henry, you need immediate surgery and you need psychiatric help before this kills you. Do you understand?"

"You can feel it kicking, under the skin. Come and feel, then you'll understand."

He lifted the shirt, a 4XL, the only size that would now fit over the grossly distorted shape of his stomach. The exposed skin was stretched obscenely, almost gray in pallor. It looked as if he were about to burst.

"Touch it," he demanded.

Dr. Yates turned away. Years of training, years of experience, none of it helped him hide the instinctive disgust he felt.

Henry rolled his shirt back down. "It's not a tumor," he said defiantly.

Full Term

ER was quiet on a Wednesday. Always was. There was a dreary calm about the place that would seem impossible during a hectic shift on a Saturday night. The staff needed no encouragement to take advantage of the lull. Rosalitta on the front desk even had time to do her nails. She held up her right hand and wiggled her fingers, admiring her work, the scarlet-painted digits that were her pride and joy. She had lovely hands. If her face had been as pretty as her hands, she would be living it up somewhere far away from this dump. If only.

Henry ruined the moment. He burst through the double doors with his hands clutched across his stomach, his face twisted with agony.

He fell to the floor. The blue jeans that he wore—jeans that he couldn't button anymore and had to let hang loose around his waist, in the hope they didn't fall—were blood-soaked. As he fell, he splashed blood across the floor in a pattern that might have been beautiful in another circumstance.

"It's coming. Help me! Fuck, I need an epidural *now!*" Henry wheezed at her from the floor.

Rosalitta screamed for assistance.

Delivery

A team of blue-green attired nurses and doctors circled above Henry like uncertain vultures. He couldn't see their faces. The pain was everything and it tended to block out most of the details.

"Extensive rectal bleeding, his stomach is distended. We need to get him into surgery ASAP."

Henry reached up a hand, still smeared with his blood. "My baby. You need to free my baby."

"What baby? What's he talking about?" A female voice.

"Unless we get him into the theater straight away, it's not going to matter."

Then Henry was being wheeled along a corridor. He could see the lights in the ceiling. They kept trying to put something over his face, something that smelled strange and made his thinking fuzzy. He pushed it away.

"It'll help you relax, help with the pain," a voice from far away whispered to him.

"No," Henry said, waving his arms at them. "I want to be awake. I want to see it arrive."

And he held onto consciousness, despite the pain that was ripping through him.

The lights were brighter, still above his head but steady now. He was no longer moving. He was in the theater.

Henry couldn't see the blue-green vultures anymore, could only hear their random voices.

"Jesus, what's inside him? There's something under the skin, I can see it pushing through."

"There's evidence of severe internal hemorrhage. We need to open him up, right now, before he just bleeds out on the table."

"Why hasn't this man been anesthetized?"

"He refused all attempts to administer any."

Henry screamed. The pain was impossible. *Unbearable*. But didn't women do this all the time? Wasn't this what *they* had to endure? It

231

couldn't be that bad, that's what Henry had always thought. They like to tell you what agony childbirth is. But, if it was *this* bad, none of them would ever go through it more than once, right? But they did. And if *they* could cope, he certainly could. He remembered the lessons from his short-lived Lamaze class. Remembered what they had taught about controlling the breathing, controlling the pain. He puffed his cheeks—swift, shallow breaths.

"Hold him down. I have to cut!"

There were hands on his shoulders, pushing him down. Then something ice cold on his belly, pressing into the distended flesh. Then the pressure in his skin eased as the scalpel pierced through. There was a long hiss that at first sounded almost like a sigh. Then it deteriorated into a wet, flatulent rasp, accompanied by a vile smell, a smell so bad that it made everyone in the room recoil, covering their mouths despite the masks they already wore. Several of them retched.

"What the hell has the man got inside him?" one of them asked, the senior voice, the one who had to be the surgeon. Henry could see his eyes beneath the gray eyebrows; they were wise but full of revulsion.

"Some kind of implant?"

"If it is, I can't see what possible purpose—"

He stopped midsentence. They all stopped.

Henry raised his head as far as he could, his chin digging into his chest. He could see the white skin of his stomach, the red slit where it had been opened, a thin-lipped smile in the flesh smeared with the lipstick of his blood. The medics were backing away from the operating table, backing away from Henry.

The mouth opened wider. Was *torn* open. The "child" crawled its way out, slithered from the wound and across the deflated stomach on a cushion of Henry's gore, carrying itself on stunted growths that could not possibly be limbs. The lumpen, misshapen ball that could not possibly be a head pressed into Alan's chest, too heavy for the body to raise in its own.

Henry reached out and picked it up. It keened, a sound like something nature had cursed. But he soothed it, stroked it gently in his arms. And it started to mewl like a kitten from something that could not possibly be a mouth, a gaping void in the center of what could not possibly be a face.

One of the medics shrieked.

Henry held the shivering, twitching tumor up to them, so they could all see how beautiful it was.

"It's a boy," he said, with all the pride of a new father.

was hoping he had a bad ending for being a selfish, shallow dickwad!

THE LITTLE THINGS

BY CHRISTIAN A. LARSEN

Glenn leaned on his vanity with both hands after wiping an arc through the steam from his shower. He wasn't tired, even in the morning—not anymore. He was leaning on the vanity so he could take a closer look at his face. It felt fine. He felt fine. Better than fine. Glenn felt almost superhuman, a far cry from the fifty-two-year-old who, just three months ago, sat in his doctor's office hearing that he had stage IV pancreatic cancer. But here he was, no chemo, no radiation, and for the first time in years, as randy as a college kid. There weren't any side effects. An experimental treatment, and no side effects. It seemed almost too good to be true.

But there was the smudge.

It looked like soot, except it was a faint green, a faint green turned almost to black, and Glenn had never seen soot quite that color. Besides, he hadn't cleaned the fireplace in forever. It was definitely not soot.

Rolling his thumb over the spot like he was fingerprinting himself, he found that it did not change color, though it did seem to smudge a little more, spreading in every direction almost imperceptibly. Glenn looked at his thumb to see if it had come off.

It had not.

"One hell of a motherfucking bruise," he whispered. If his breath gathered on the mirror, he couldn't tell. The shower steam had filled the room. It was like standing in a cloud, and, like the skin he was standing in, it felt great. Whatever the smudge was, it couldn't be all that bad. He stepped into the shower and let the water course through his hair. He continued to thank his lucky stars that he still had all his hair. Not too many fifty-something cancer survivors could say half as much, and the gray, well, the gray just gave him character.

The truth was, he had more to feel lucky about than a full head of salt-and-pepper hair. He should be dead, or close to it, and Dr. Murtagh's therapy, treatment, cure—whatever you wanted to call it— was the only reason he was standing in the shower, with the hot water running between his toes. The nails looked particularly long this morning. *When was the last time I cut them?* thought Glenn, reaching for the shampoo.

Dr. Murtagh said that Glenn had anywhere between three and nine months to live. "With aggressive treatment," said the doctor, tenting his fingers in a practiced and yet somehow cavalier way, "Of course, you might be one of the lucky ones. Going the traditional route, you stand about a six-percent chance to surviving beyond five years or so, but that all depends on how far along you are."

How far along I am, thought Glenn in the office and again in the shower. *The smug sonofabitch made it sound like I got myself pregnant.*

But the smug sonofabitch wasn't finished. Dr. Murtagh had something lined up for Glenn that was straight out of a pulp novel, a cure so radical it couldn't be true, or wouldn't work at all, and it didn't involve chemicals or radiation, which Glenn thought was probably worse than dying young. Murtagh's cure involved tiny robots, nanobots, the doctor had called them, and all Glenn would need was to take a shot in his arm, like a vaccine. Murtagh was so high on the idea, he had called it a vaccine for life. That seemed like a lot to promise, but Glenn was willing to buy into it. At that moment, he was willing to buy into anything that promised him long life and happiness.

Michelle came with him to the counseling session, mostly because Dr. Murtagh wanted to pitch her, too. He didn't say as much, but the cancer didn't dim Glenn's perception. As convinced as Dr. Murtagh was that he could cure Glenn, there were outside chances and ravenous lawyers, so the documents had their signatures and their witnesses. And then, all that was left was the injection of a serum filled with microscopic robots—something he had joked was akin to injecting himself with a load of semen. Michelle laughed, but Dr. Murtagh didn't. Fifteen minutes later, Glenn was walking in the parking lot with a cotton ball taped to the inside of his elbow with a bandage.

Coursing through his bloodstream, the nanobots were already mapping, taking data, and attacking cancerous cells and viruses. Of the ones that had taken damage during the injection, or from Glenn's own failed immune system, half had been repaired, and the other half—more than the other half, really—would be replaced within the first seventy-two hours, faster than they could clear up Glenn's diarrhea, fatigue, and abdominal pain, even though he felt better almost right away.

The fall wind tossed her hair and Michelle kissed him like everything was new again. "I love you, Glenn. No matter what.'

No matter what, she had said.

No matter what turned into a quick second adolescence, without the thinning hair of a midlife crisis, or the shoulder acne of steroid abuse. He simply felt—great. Better than he had since his mid-twenties, and hornier than all get out. He was a little embarrassed to tell Dr. Murtagh that his microrobots were better than an army of little blue pills, especially since while he was telling him, he had to shift around his own erection, the way he had done in history class in high school when he sat next to that cheerleader who dressed like she was a working girl.

He had given it to Michelle so hard and often, it was actually starting to scare him, like an addiction. Nymphomania, she had called it, but she was wrong. In men, it was satyriasis. But her saying so made him hold off some, and then he rediscovered the weights in their basement, and a long list of chores and home improvements the fatigue of age had kept him from, and that wasn't enough even then to knock him out. He realized that he was sleeping less than three hours a night, and sometimes hardly at all. It shocked him to realize that he really hadn't noticed all along.

And that was all before the tumor had even disappeared.

Dr. Murtagh cautioned Glenn not to talk about the treatment. This news had to be rolled out right, tightly controlled, with the medical journals getting the first bite at the apple and not the *Enquirer*.

Only Glenn, Michelle, and a few friends and family even knew he had cancer in the first place. Who was he going to tell?

Steam clouded in front of him. It had to be really hot to billow around him like it was, and he thought about checking the water heater in the basement and maybe dialing it back a notch, but it didn't feel hot. It didn't feel anything. He didn't feel anything except good, and it reminded him a little of some of the recreational herbage he enjoyed in college without the lung burn and belching smoke. There was a vague sense of nausea, just nibbling at the edges, but it felt like it was in someone else's stomach.

Glenn looked at his hands. They looked disconnected in the steam. *Like the hands of fate?* he thought, dredging up an old album title or quote from a book from his high school days or something. They were darker than he remembered them, but not tan. As a matter of fact, they looked positively gray against the white tile of the shower stall. Like golem hands. Clay, cold and gray. He reached for the towel bar where he hung his washcloth to try and steady himself, but it was too late. The nerves in his legs had turned to mist themselves, and he didn't even hear the crashing sound he made when he hit the porcelain and sent the shower door off its rails.

"Glenn?" asked Michelle from the kitchen downstairs. She had been drinking coffee at the kitchen table and reading the e-mails on her phone. She sipped at her coffee again, not tasting it at all, trying to remind herself that everything sounded bigger through a wall or floor. Wasn't that the way it was in their first apartment, when the religious couple tried to have them evicted for knocking boots? Yes. Yes it was. But she knew the analogy rang hollow. As hollow as the sound she heard coming from the bathroom. "Glenn?"

Seconds passed that felt more like minutes. She kept time with the sound of the blood knocking in her ears. The moments were long, but they were only moments. And after what was really only half a minute or so, just a second or two before Michelle leapt to her feet to check on what she assumed was Glenn in extreme distress, she heard Glenn's footsteps upstairs, though the floor, and like the crash, louder than they should be. They also sounded tired. Slow. But the thing that made her worry was that the water was still running. If he was okay, he would have shut off the water.

"Glenn?" she asked again, this time starting down the hall toward the stairway with an unfeigned sense of urgency. "Honey, are you alright?"

Glenn was standing at the top of the stairs, backlit by the hall light. He looked unsteady, wobbling from foot to foot while water dripped from his tousled hair down his skin and onto the carpet. Water and something else. She caught a glint of red.

"Oh, God, Glenn, you're bleeding," she screeched, sprinting up the stairs faster than she thought a woman suffering hot flashes could. "Let me help you!"

Glenn stepped backward, behind the light instead of in front of it, and had Michelle not been running to fast, what she saw would have stopped her in her tracks. A piece of shower door stuck out of his belly like a rhino horn and it bounced up and down like a livid erection, dripping with blood instead of semen. But that wasn't what horrified her. As she caromed toward him, she saw the look in his eyes —or the hint of death, because he wasn't precisely looking at her. He was facing her, but one iris seemed as big as a silver dollar, and the other one a pinhole. Neither was moving or reacting to the light, but Glenn reacted to her, raising his golem arms, covered with nightmarish black and green bruises. His fingers raked at her back and he embraced her, plunging the shard of glass into her abdomen like the erection it mimicked.

Michelle gasped, her face making a perfect "O" of astonishment, knowing that she was seriously hurt, but not feeling it. Not yet. But Glenn didn't feel it, either. There was no knowing on his face —no gnashing of teeth or grimacing ... he didn't even grunt when he pulled her close. She felt herself beginning to faint, a long, slow descent like going down a slide in damp clothes, but she had time to think one last ridiculous thought before unconsciousness washed over her, a thought generated by the dead-eyed gaze and gray skin of her husband.

So this is how the zombie apocalypse begins.

She awoke in a hospital room, in a bed with the head cranked to a pleasant angle. The covers were tucked so tightly, she felt like the orderlies had made the bed with her still on it, but the blankets were maddeningly thin, and when she tried to draw her arms and legs into herself to ward off the cold, she found that she couldn't. She was handcuffed to the rail—and footcuffed, if there were such a thing. She couldn't remember if she'd ever heard of such a thing, and then chased that thought around for much too long before she even questioned why.

And when she did question why, more questions started piling through the door with it, so that all of them were asked (or half-asked) but none were answered. Where was Glenn? Was he okay? Dead, maybe? How was he walking around with a shard of shower door sticking out of his belly like a dorsal fin, and why was he gray? It wasn't the cancer. Michelle wasn't a doctor, but she knew cancer didn't do that. Glenn had looked like a zombie, but people in zombie movies were always sick before they turned. Sick or bleeding. Had falling through the shower door done that? Of course not.

The door to the room opened. It wasn't a regular hospital door, heavy, hollow-core wood with a stainless handle. It was a metal door that sealed, with a safety glass window crisscrossed with wire. Michelle couldn't see, but she guessed—correctly, as it later turned out—there was another door that sealed just behind it. And then she realized there was no window in the room, just a wall of curtains with no light coming from behind it. She found that fact somewhat more interesting than the man in the hazard suit approaching her, with a ridiculous grin on his face behind the glass visor. It looked like the grin of a corpse. A corpse trying to hide what it felt like to be in hell.

"Dr. Murtagh," she said. She sighed for reasons she didn't understand. "How are you?"

"I think the question is, how are you?" he countered. His voice sounded distant and tinny, like he had the world's worst cold.

"Aside from the handcuffs and what I presume to be at least half a dozen stitches in my stomach, I feel pretty good." Michelle thought that understating it was the way to go with the good doctor, who it seemed use information like a bludgeon. She actually felt great!

"Sutures don't hurt?"

"Where's Glenn?"

"Glenn has been detained."

Michelle's physical vibrance was not enough to keep her emotions in check. Hot, salty tears welled up in her eyes, and she started to tremble with frustrated rage. When she spoke, it was in a quavering voice through clenched teeth. "Where is Glenn?"

"Glenn is being observed—"

"You give me a straight answer or I'll, I'll—"

"You'll what?"

Michelle threw a stunted punch at Dr. Murtagh, who jumped back. He then smiled, like the neighborhood bully who teases a dog on the other side of a fence—or at the end of a short chain. Her fist was, of course, on the end of a very short chain. But that smile, that—to be frank, shit-eating grin—made her not care, and she was every bit the junkyard dog that the doctor was teasing. Chomping, slavering. But only on the inside. On the outside, she twisted the cuff with her wrist, until the blood started seeping. That made Murtagh's smile fade a bit.

"Please quiet down, Ms. Wambolt," he said, trying to sound authoritative by using her last name. It came out more like a request. Like a substitute teacher.

Michelle let her arm drop to her side. All the air had been let out of her lungs through some unseen valve. Her chest seemed to deflate, which she at least half attributed to the sag in her menopausal breasts. Her arms did look gray, though. That wasn't menopause. The last time she saw that color was when she volunteered for that children's art class. It was the exact color of modeling clay. The exact color of Glenn at the top of the stairs with the shark's fin of glass sticking out of his gut. And she was starting to see blackish-green blotches, too.

"What happened to Glenn?" she whispered. But she still felt fine, and a giggle nearly chittered out of her.

"Glenn is showing no signs of slowing down."

Michelle heaved out a hoarse sigh, almost like a gritty belch, and she squinted her eyes like she couldn't hear him.

"Glenn is being observed. He is somewhere safe, where he can't hurt himself or anyone else."

But he's not Glenn anymore, thought Michelle. *Like I won't be Michelle anymore, very, very soon. But not soon enough for you, Dr. Murtagh.*

"I suppose it won't hurt to tell you the truth now, not in the shape you're in. The paramedics he infected with the nanobots had to be destroyed," explained Dr. Murtagh, leaning in a little bit to make sure she could hear him. "Killed with fire, as my nephews might say. A video gamer phrase if there ever was one. The shame of it is, the little buggers really did kill your husband's cancer."

The way he said "little buggers" made her think of the case of the crabs she had in college. But she showed no outward reaction. He didn't really give her an opportunity.

"But we designed them to be smart. Too smart, it turns out. They repaired, they replicated, and they became self-aware. Then they set up shop in your husband's nervous system, killing him off from the inside with more alacrity than the cancer ever could. What they did was turn him into a human marionette. And when his blood was introduced to your system—and the paramedics'—you were all infected with the little things."

The little things, thought Michelle. *That's just about right. Better than little buggers. Just a little closer, now.*

Dr. Murtagh leaned over her, almost leering at what he'd created. "We're going to try an electromagnetic pulse and see what that does to your husband. I wouldn't get too hopeful, though. At best, it will just shut him down, him and the emergency workers the nanobots have infected. So it won't bring him back, but it's easier than reducing a human body to ash." He sat on the edge of the bed, seemingly unaware of Michelle at all now. "We didn't cure cancer, but think of the military applications. There goes the Hippocratic Corpus: First do no harm."

Indeed, thought Michelle. *It was the last thing she ever thought.*

Her arm shot toward Dr. Murtagh so fiercely, it seemed like it was on a spring and the chain of the handcuffs might snap at its weakest link, but it did not. Infected with self-replicating nanobots or not, Michelle was still just one woman, but that didn't stop her from repeatedly pulling on the handcuffs, rattling steel against brushed steel once, twice, and again a third time while Dr. Murtagh watched her with a bemused look on his face. He shifted on the bed and pursed his lips at her the way an adult might do toward a silly child.

"You're going to break your arm," he said, waving his hand at her blank eyes. "If you can hear me in there. You'll break it right off." He scoffed once so loudly his breath clouded on the inside of his faceplate.

But Dr. Murtagh didn't understand the little things. Not until it was too late. Not until Michelle's hand really did break completely off at the wrist, exposing the ulna and radius bone like a couple of stilettos, pink with pulsing blood. A flap of skin was still connecting her hand to her arm, but it peeled back like soft latex and stretched, with a thick undercoating of fat and muscle. Michelle drove what used to be her wrist into Dr. Murtagh's gut, slicing through the hazard suit he wore to keep the nanobots out, the fabric separating as if made of meringue.

He looked at her and groaned, knowing it was already too late as thousands of nanobots streamed into his brain.

CLOCKWORK

BY SHAUN JEFFREY

I knew the black cat was dead. Even if I hadn't just seen it struck by the car, I would still know it was dead. Finding my father lying on the floor two weeks ago, hands clutched to his chest as though trying to keep warm, made sure of that.

One of the cat's front paws protruded at an odd angle, its claws protracted as if in a failed attempt to scratch at the vehicle that had bowled it along the road.

The driver of the car hadn't stopped. Unlike dogs, you didn't have to report it if you killed a cat.

I gingerly reached out and touched the body. Its fur still felt warm and soft. My fingers brushed a red collar around its neck. The attached tag on the collar told me the cat was called Sooty.

Although it was only a cat, I couldn't stand the thought of the owner finding the dead feline in or at the side of the road, so I picked up the carcass and, with nowhere else to put it, I dropped it in with the shopping I had bought in town. I would bury it when I reached home.

A car drove by, making me flinch. I wondered what it sounded like; wondered what lots of things sounded like. Deaf since birth, I lived in a world of unimaginable silence. The only time I had been glad of my deafness was when I saw mother screaming after I alerted her to father's body.

245

When I arrived home, I reached into the bag and touched the cat. Its body now cold, it had already started to go stiff. I stroked it once, and then opened the gate and deposited the corpse outside my den at the bottom of the garden before heading toward the house.

"You took your time," mother said as she took the shopping bags from me. She enunciated each word so I could lip-read.

I shrugged and signed that I had lost track of time.

Mother smiled, but she couldn't disguise the haunted look of the bereaved. She started to say something else, but her lips stopped moving and she pulled out a tin of baked beans dotted with blood. She frowned. "What's this?"

Already one step ahead, I moved my fingers to say the steaks must have leaked.

Mother nodded. It was a reasonable answer, as the cuts of meat often leaked.

My sister Vicky sat in her highchair, playing with a rattle. I smiled at her and she smiled back. She opened and closed her mouth and I touched her cheek, feeling the vibrations of noise resonating through her skin. While mother put the shopping away, I made my way out to the den, a wooden structure five-foot high and four-foot square that I had built last summer.

The cat lay on the grass outside. If it weren't for the mangled paw and the specks of blood, it would look as though it were having a catnap.

I picked it up, opened the door, and carried it into the den, stooping as I entered.

It was warm inside the room, and I stood up straight. Sheets of plastic yellowed in the sun made the light that shone through the window appear golden, illuminating the clocks that covered every surface.

There were mechanical clocks, pendulum clocks, mantel clocks, cuckoo clocks, and clocks that I had made. Within the den, I could feel the reverberating beat of the clocks like a huge heart, and feeling the familiar ticktock of the clocks through the ground and walls, I felt it was the closest I came to actually hearing.

Pieces of clocks cluttered the table against the back wall. There were springs, cogs, levers, weights, and a whole host of other parts. I swept some of the bits aside and deposited the cat on the table while I searched for a bag to put it in. Deciding on an old plastic one, I turned back and grabbed the cat. Straight away, I felt the familiar pulse of the clocks through my fingers. For a moment, I imagined the cat was still alive, that I had made a mistake, that it wasn't dead.

A coiled spring unwound against the cat's leg. I stared at the clock components. If there was one thing I was good at, it was making broken things work again. And that's when the idea came to mind. What if I could mend the cat? I wasn't thinking I could bring it back to life, but perhaps I could give it a semblance of life, could give it movement.

I thought about it for a long while before I set to work.

There was a penknife on the table. I picked it up and unfastened the blade, feeling it click open. A thin sheen of sweat painted my brow as I gingerly held the small penknife against the cat's soft underbelly. This was stupid. I couldn't do it, and my stomach recoiled at the thought.

With a shake of my head, I dropped the knife and stared at the corpse. It looked pitiful, and fresh tears stung my eyes. After a slight hesitation, I picked the knife up again and sliced the blade into the cat before I had time to change my mind. It wasn't so bad when I started. There wasn't much blood as no heart pumped, and despite the cold, slimy feel, removing the cat's innards was no worse than taking the giblets out of the turkey at Christmas, something I had done last year.

Once I had gutted the cat, I started to construct a mechanism to provide movement. It wouldn't be the most technical of accomplishments, but I knew when it was inside the cat, no one would see it, so I wasn't too concerned. I used a small drill to make holes in the cat's bones, to which I attached Meccano strips, supplementing its own skeleton with one of my own onto which I attached the clockwork device I had made.

I had to make a couple of journeys to the house, but mother seemed to either not notice me or ignore me as she fed Vicky.

Because I found the body, I think she blames me for father's death.

It took the best part of the remainder of the day, but eventually I finished.

I stood the cat on the table, inserted a key into a small hole in its underside, and turned it. Through my fingers on the cat's back I could feel the cogs turning, the multiple springs being tensioned.

Ten turns later, I released the key and stepped back. The cat's eyes stared back at me, but nothing happened.

Wondering if I had done something wrong, I stepped toward the cat when it suddenly blinked, stopping me in my tracks. That wasn't supposed to happen. Its eyes weren't supposed to blink—couldn't blink because nothing powered them. I had considered how to make its eyes move, but decided making it walk would be enough.

The cat's head moved a fraction, just a twitch at first, almost imperceptible, and then it swiveled from side to side as though testing the movement. It took a tentative step, its movements jerky, mechanical. The limbs hardly bent at the joints, which was disappointing after I'd spent so long fashioning the Meccano and bone links.

I could feel my heart beating in time with the clocks that pulsed through the room. The cat staggered toward me, its limbs moving with the stiffness of a soldier on parade. I took a step back; could feel the blood throbbing at my temples, could feel the sweat on my back.

What had I done?

The cat opened its mouth. That shouldn't have happened either. It wasn't wired to work.

I wondered whether it made a sound.

Unable to look at it any longer, I ran out of the den, back to the house and into the kitchen, where I stood shaking.

"Alex, are you okay?" mother asked as she looked up from feeding Vicky.

I couldn't tell her what I'd done, didn't fully understand it enough to explain, but that dead cat was more than a reanimated clockwork pussy. It had a life of its own, and it terrified me. I'd only wanted to make it move, to make it not seem so dead.

"You're pale as a sheet. Are you sure you're okay?"

I signed that I was fine, and then I offered to carry on feeding Vicky while mother had a break. Mother smiled and nodded.

"You're a good boy, Alex."

While I spoon-fed Vicky, something purporting to be pasta in sauce, I thought about the cat. I couldn't leave it in the den. But what could I do with it?

My sister opened and closed her mouth, as greedy as a baby bird. Her hair was like spun gold, her eyes as blue as the sky. She still had a lot of baby fat, which made her look like those old paintings of cherubs. I smiled at her, and she smiled back. I envied her the innocence that didn't yet feel the pain of loss.

After I'd fed and changed her, I rocked her to sleep, put her in the cot, and then walked back out to the den.

I stood outside the structure, my hand on the door, feeling the beat of the clocks through the wood.

Bracing myself, I took a deep breath, then flung the door open and stepped back. When the cat didn't appear, I took a cautious step toward the den and peered inside to find the cat had torn its way through the plastic window.

Distressed, I ran around the side of the den and looked in the hedgerows to see if I could spot the cat, but it was nowhere to be seen.

How far would it get with ten winds of the key?

Surely not that far.

I remembered the way it had blinked and opened its mouth, actions it wasn't supposed to be able to do. Perhaps it would go further than I imagined. Perhaps the clockwork components weren't powering it at all; perhaps it hadn't really been dead. A shiver ran up my spine. I felt like screaming, but didn't know if it was through fear or uncertainty.

Although I continued searching, there was no sign of the cat. After a while, I even wondered whether it had really happened, but when I returned to the den, I noticed the cat's innards in the plastic bag. They had started to smell, so I buried them in the garden and then ran back inside the house, where I shut and bolted the door.

During the next few days, I stayed indoors more than normal, which didn't go unnoticed by mother. I think she preferred it when I was out. She questioned me a couple of times, and I could tell she thought there was something wrong. But I couldn't tell her what I had done as it didn't seem right. Besides, I didn't think she'd believe me.

That first night in bed, I had felt sure the cat was going to creep up on me, and there I'd be, unable to hear it. So I lay on the mattress in a way that I could touch the floor, trying to feel for the ticktock of my feline creation, but when it never came, I eventually fell asleep.

It wasn't until three days later that I found the bird's carcass in the hedgerow.

I stared at it, wondering how it had died. Eventually, I crouched and picked up the bird, recognized it as a starling. When I looked closer, I noticed a hole in its neck. Parting the plumage around the hole, I could just make out the shuttlecock ridges of an air-rifle pellet.

Bird in hand, I walked down to the den. Being a small creature made it a tricky process, but I made a small incision on the underside of its chest. Into this, I placed a small frame, to which I attached the motor, fashioned from watches. Its legs were too small to animate, so I didn't consider doing anything other than making its wings move. I hoped it would be enough.

I had rigged the windup mechanism into its chest, and I gave the key ten turns and then set the bird on the table.

It took a while, but then it blinked and its beak opened and closed. It flexed its wings, the movement still mechanical. Moments later, the bird gave a nod of its head and launched itself into the air. It made an ungainly test flight, struggling to keep itself airborne. I wondered whether the watch components were too heavy.

It finally came to rest on the windowsill where it fluttered its wings a couple of times before flying away through the open door.

I ran outside and watched it struggle into the sky, circling higher and higher until I lost sight of it. When I eventually lowered my gaze, I saw mother standing at the back door, gazing out. She looked happy. Vicky babbled in her arms.

When I found Vicky sprawled on the floor by her highchair a couple of days later, it seemed like an ironic case of déjà vu. I stared at her for a moment, then checked her neck for a pulse. The feel of her cold skin made me flinch. I sat back and chewed a fingernail, wondering whether she had cried out when she fell. Not that it would have mattered, as I wouldn't have heard.

Having left Vicky in my care while she visited my father's grave, mother would undoubtedly hold me responsible. This time she would be right.

My sister felt heavier than she was as I lifted her from the floor and carried her out to the den. The partially gutted badger that I had been working on eyed me from the bench as I set my sister down. My skill at reanimating the clockwork menagerie had grown immeasurably.

I picked up the knife.

Hopefully, mother would never notice.

LUSCIOUS

BY JEZZY WOLFE

"I really wanna be a 10."

A row of perfectly straight teeth gleamed between full lips. Bryce's eyes dropped from the botoxed smile to her taut calves, following their curve behind her knees and over her smooth, bronzed thighs, to the cuff of her short shorts.

Damn. She's a 10 already.

He pretended to look at the color swatch she held against her arm. "I think you've hit a plateau. That happens with regular beds. But our unique bed design will allow you to break through that wall and give you the deepest tan you've ever had. If you sign up for a platinum membership, the first thirty days are a trial offer."

His smile split his face in a calculated maneuver he'd perfected for his sales pitch. "We also have our own specially formulated line of lotions and serums to give you a deep bronze glow without turning you orange. And as a platinum member, you'll get them at a discounted price."

"I have my own lotion," she said, flipping straight black hair over a coppery shoulder.

"I'm afraid you wouldn't be permitted to use it in our machines. Our lotions are designed to work with the bulbs we use, and other lotions will inhibit your results."

253

She frowned. "I dunno ..."

"I've noticed you're starting to peel on the back of your shoulder." Bryce gently brushed her back—which didn't have so much as a flake of dead skin—and feigned concern.

Her eyes widened, registering immediate panic. "Okay, I'll do it!"

"Good girl," he said, steering her to the front desk, his hand on the small of her back. "Denise, please enroll Miss—"

"Candy."

"Of course. Enroll *Candy* in our platinum program. And give her a complimentary bottle of our starter serum." He winked at Candy before heading to his office, and she shot him a quick smile before giving the clerk her information.

Women spared no expense when it came to vanity, and twenty years taught Bryce Golden every trick in the book for securing their loyal patronage. There was a time when women were dissuaded from tanning due to harmful UV rays and the potential contraction of nasty melanomas, but Bryce broke that barrier with a cornucopia of lies that eased their minds and opened their wallets ... and legs. At fifty-three, Bryce had the physique of a man in his twenties, and the stamina to match.

The salon was a perfect remedy for his raging libido, which he assuaged on a daily basis with the various women that visited the beds. But only with the platinum members. A man had to have standards, after all.

He poured a glass of scotch and settled behind his desk, looking over the many applications of new platinum clientele. Opening his planner, he penciled different names into his schedule throughout the week. Before leaving the office, he knocked back the remnants of his beverage and adjusted the rigid muscle in his slacks.

Membership wasn't the only thing on the rise.

Candy bounced on Bryce's lap, her back to his chest, the copper of her skin almost matching the deep bronze of his thighs. He reached around to squeeze handfuls of her round breasts, and groaned. Candy, too caught up in the moment to notice it was a groan of disappointment, moaned and climaxed, leaning back against his chest as he emptied himself between her legs.

"That was so good," she gasped, still writhing.

But Bryce just grunted, waiting for her to move.

He'd explored her entire body with his mouth and hands, and stumbled across the repeated evidence of a surgeon's handiwork. There were two dark scars on the insides of her thighs as he'd peeled off her bathing suit. Two more scars hid in the bottom crease of her ass. Her breasts were a little stiff, the dark nipples perpetually erect, and two long scars could be felt on their undersides as he groped her.

Meanwhile, she whimpered and screamed, as helpless and eager as every other woman who danced on his lap. Five o'clock at Golden was packed; every bed in the facility was running. The women in the beds were blasted with the hum of the lightbulbs, the blare of music from speakers positioned by their heads, and fans blowing cool air across their toasting bodies. Candy could have spoken in tongues and no one would've heard a sound.

She'd be good for an occasional wank, but nothing else. She was a life-sized, posable action figure. All silicone, lipo, and botox. Fake.

He ran his hands over her seemingly perfect thighs, wishing he could push her off his lap, but instead slid his fingers between her legs. Regardless of whether the clients met his physical standards, he tried to keep them all satisfied. Her moans followed him as he pulled the door closed and retreated to his office.

The last clients filled their appointments and left, leaving the staff to wipe down the equipment and gather the sweaty white towels for washing. New towels were folded and placed on the beds, the wastebaskets were all emptied, and the salon was ready for a new business day.

From his office doorway, Bryce spotted Denise checking a locked door in the back corner of the salon, and froze. He often worried he'd forget to lock it, and a towel girl would wander inside. But the knob held tight, and Denise walked away with not even a shrug.

"Everything is ready for tomorrow, Mr. Golden. I'm leaving now," she said, her smile polite but notably tired.

"Of course. Thank you. See you in the morning." He smiled, half waved, and watched as she disappeared down the hallway that led to the salon's front entrance. The front door closed, the hasp snapping in place as she locked up for the night.

Fishing the key from his pocket, he opened the door and stepped inside. A pungent odor stung his nostrils. *I need to change the air filter.* Women turned their noses up at the idea of basking in someone else's aroma while they baked their skin to rawhide.

Bryce wiped down his customized creation and placed a folded gold towel on the plexi, readying it for the next client. He switched on the ventilation fan before heading back to his office for a well-deserved meal.

Mayor Teddy Andrews laughed too loudly at Bryce's joke, and offered him another scotch. After watching Sunday football in the mayor's luxurious theater room, they were sprawled on couches that lined a bar in the well-appointed recreational basement. Andrews was a spoiled trust fund baby of a local congressman, who tried only once to follow in his father's footsteps, and failed. Relegating himself as mayor was far less challenging than trying to be a real politician. But Teddy could rival any political figure with his self-indulgence, which made him a convenient choice as a friend. Bryce enjoyed the perks of being best friends with a man like Teddy.

"So Bryce, how are the plans for the Anniversary Gala coming along? I'm looking forward to seeing how you outdo last year's soiree."

Bryce hosted a huge celebration every year for the city's most elite citizens, which was more anticipated than the Fourth of July fireworks or the yearly lighting of the Christmas tree. The ball was practically a local holiday, and tickets always sold out almost immediately. Between the celebrity-studded guest list, elaborate menus, and fantastic decor, the gala raised a small fortune every year, much of which was donated to the city. It was a small price to pay for the immunity it afforded Bryce.

"Prepare to be amazed, my friend," he said, his speech slightly slurred by the top-shelf liquor. "This year's event will blow all past years out of the water."

Teddy laughed again. "I don't see how that's possible. Unless you managed to get topless Vegas showgirls to serve as waitresses."

"Really, Teddy, can't you show a little class?" Aubrey Andrews stood in the doorway, a scowl drawing together her perfectly arched eyebrows. Her arms were crossed over her chest as she leaned against the frame, honey ribbons of hair spilling over her shoulders.

Both men sat up, like a couple of boys caught looking at their father's dirty magazines. "I was just joking, sweetheart," Teddy said.

She strode to the bar and poured a glass of tonic. "Right. I'm sure you are." While her voice was light, her eyes were dark flashes.

"Looks like you're overdue for a visit to the salon," Bryce interrupted.

Aubrey froze, just for a moment, then chuckled. But her laugh sounded forced and too abbreviated. "My schedule has been really busy lately."

"You know all you have to do is call ahead. I will personally make sure there's a bed open for you." He finished his scotch, watching her flush over the rim of his glass.

"I don't know, Bryce. I will have to get back to you on that."

She left before he could respond, oblivious to his eyes starring daggers at her back.

Teddy slouched back down, tossing back the remnants of his scotch, and grinned. "So anyway, how about it? Topless waitresses? Whadaya think?"

Bryce trailed his lips over Aubrey's bronzed shoulder, tightening his arms around her. She lay stiff against him, as she had for the past hour, never meeting his gaze. Usually she was passionate—reckless

257

even—when they went at each other. But today she barely tolerated his ministrations, distracted by whatever was on her mind. Even her orgasm felt insincere.

She sat up and pulled on her clothes, leaving him sprawled naked on the couch in his office. He eyed her smooth calves, thighs ... up to her hands, which trembled as she buttoned her blouse.

"What's going on?" He sat up and began dressing, stomach clenched in anticipation. "You've avoided me for weeks, and now you're in a hurry to leave. What's rattling around in that head of yours?"

Aubrey's eyes shimmered, her cheeks flushed. "This is it, Bryce. We have to stop."

Bryce never deluded himself that they were in love. Like all the others, she was just an object. They'd been doing this for years. Nonetheless, as she stood there, head bowed shamefully, his gut knotted and ached. His chest throbbed, and heat flooded his head. "What?"

"I can't do this anymore," she said, her voice wavering.

"What the hell are you talking about?" He shoved his balled fists into his pockets as he stood slowly, towering over her. "Are you fucking Teddy? Is that it?"

"He's my husband!" She stepped back, arms behind her as she felt for the door. "Don't do this now. We both knew it wouldn't go anywhere."

"You told him." Bryce's voice was even, barely above a whisper. He took a step toward her.

"No!" The color drained from her face as she fumbled for the doorknob. "Of course not, but ..."

"But?"

"I think he already suspects us." Grasping the knob, she pulled the door open just enough to slip out.

He raised his fist, ready to slam it through the door panel, enraged that she would lay such a bombshell on him before she ran away. His blood pumped furiously, the sound in his ears louder than a steam engine.

But then again, so what if Teddy knew? The man wasn't a saint to begin with. He'd had his share of affairs. Hell, Bryce knew enough to send Teddy and Aubrey straight to divorce court. Teddy would pay through the nose if Aubrey knew about her husband's infidelities, even in light of Bryce. So the chances of Teddy doing anything more than applauding Bryce for bedding his wife were nil.

But Aubrey didn't know that. She still operated under the illusion that the only malfunction in her marriage was the affair she'd been having with him. Perhaps if he told her about her husband, she'd stay.

He caught her before she made it to the lobby, pulling her into an empty restroom. "You never did use the beds. At least get in a last session. It'll be more suspicious if you go home as pale as you left."

She stood out of arm's reach, uncertainty flickering in her eyes. "I don't know ... do you even have any open beds right now?"

"The ultrabed is actually available. Usually it's booked solid, but we had a cancellation today."

Her gaze narrowed. "I've been in all your beds. I didn't realize you had an ultrabed."

"Like I said, it's usually booked solid." He tried a casual smile, but his jaw was clenched, and he could feel the veins in his temple throbbing.

If she noticed, she chose not to mention it. After a brief hesitation, she relented. "It may take a while to find another salon. I suppose I should."

He led her down the hall with his hand on the small of her back, steering her wordlessly toward the locked door in the back. The door swung open slowly, but without so much as a squeak, when he unlocked it. As he followed her into the room, he checked the doorknob to make sure it was still locked.

Aubrey stared at the stainless steel monstrosity that ran the length of the far wall and laughed, a nervous chuckle that almost sounded like a cough. "You call that thing a tanning bed?"

Bryce chuckled and slid past her, opening the hood to reveal the bed inside. Like the other beds, a Plexiglas shield covered the rows of bulbs that would encapsulate her.

"I always thought they looked more like well-lit coffins," he joked.

"That's because they are," she said, her voice flat.

He waited, half expecting her to change her mind or try to leave. The ultrabed always intimidated clients, but he managed to coax them in with his usual tactics. Of course, under the circumstances, those would only drive her out the door.

"You know what? I don't have my goggles or my lotion. I shouldn't do this."

He smiled. "No worries. I have extra oil and goggles right here." He opened a narrow cabinet that housed bottles of tanning elixirs, gold hand towels, and packages of tiny neon-colored specs. "Why don't you get undressed while I get the bed ready for you? If you want, I can apply your lotion."

She frowned, crossed her arms across her chest, and backed away. "I meant what I said, Bryce. No more sex."

"What? I'm trying to help you, Aubrey. That's all. You know damn well you have to use the proper oils for these beds to work correctly."

She nodded, dropping her arms. "Yeah, okay. Fine. Can't reach my back anyway, and I don't want to burn." She unbuttoned her shirt. "Just make sure you keep it in your pants."

As he pushed the proper buttons, the machine came to life, the lights whirring softly as they began to glow. The glow wasn't the usual bright blue white, but a softer amber hue. He squirted a palm full of oil in his hand and spread it across her shoulder blades.

"Are the bulbs malfunctioning?" She studied the machine as he ran his hands across her, coating her tanned flesh with a generous layer of fragrant oil.

"No, they're supposed to look like that. That's why they work so well."

She was completely relaxed now, allowing his hands to reach every spot on her body as he massaged more oil into her skin. He relished the feel of her under his palms. Unlike most of his clientele, Aubrey possessed natural beauty. Her strict health regimen rewarded her with perfect skin and supple curves. No part of her body was enhanced, lifted, or tucked.

"That smells familiar. What's in it? It's wonderful." She leaned into his touch.

"Some herbs and oils, lots of nutrients. It's my own personal recipe. You're gonna love the results," he murmured. As he helped her slide onto the bed, his lips brushed her neck quickly. Placing the goggles over her eyes, he smoothed her blonde hair away from her face and whispered in her ear, *"Désolé, mon amour."*

"Hmm?"

Without reply, he lowered the heavy cover until it closed completely, and then buckled a hasp lock at either end of the bed. On the control panel, he entered a new temperature and set the timer. As the wire coils hidden behind a panel beneath the bulbs roared to life, he heard the faint sounds of her protests escalate to screams. He calculated she'd pipe down after, maybe, fifteen minutes.

After some time, her screams died to whimpers, gurgles, and then eventually a faint sizzle. He slid out of the room. The stillness of the hallway and the cool air-conditioning revitalized him, like stepping into a swimming pool.

A towel girl passed with a customer in tow, and a customer exited one of the nearby tanning rooms. They smiled at him politely, murmuring shy hellos as they went about their business. He laughed softly as he headed for a glass of scotch.

Soundproofing. Best investment he ever made.

His cell phone buzzed in his pocket. He glanced at the screen before answering. "Teddy, my man. What's going on?"

"Can I talk to you?" Teddy's voice wavered.

"Sure you can. Shoot," Bryce said.

"It's about Aubrey. She's been acting weird lately. I think she might be seeing somebody." Teddy sniffled. "And I think I know who it is."

"That's rough, buddy. Why don't you meet me at the salon after closing time?" Bryce looked back at the locked door. "I'm having dinner here tonight."

RAPTURE

BY CHARLES COLYOTT

The tip of the blade—not a sterile scalpel, but a carefully honed and disinfected utility knife (which would just have to do)—found the hollow just beneath and to the interior of the jawbone. A gloved finger pressed the utility knife into place, and the kiss of the steel elicited a sharp intake of breath. Fat droplets of blood hit the plastic sheeting with loud pats, coming more frequently as the blade began to move, to cut.

Gloved fingers stuffed cotton inside the gill-like incision, mopping up the worst of the blood and holding the wound open. The gloved fingers held up a mirror and turned it so the man could see.

He opened his mouth and raised his tongue. Tufts of the cotton peeped at him from the floor of his mouth, little gore-tinted bits near his back molars. The man reached inside, wiped away the globules of glistening yellow fat, and fingered the two gills, one on each side of his lower jaw, before grunting with something like satisfaction.

He consulted the diagrams laid upon the metal table in front of him and then looked back to the mirror. He bared his teeth—stained pinkish now—and used one latex-clad finger to draw his upper lip aside.

The bit pressed into the gum tissue just above his front teeth.

Its tip stung.

With a deep breath, the man pulled the bit away and found the tube of topical oral pain-relieving gel, and squeezed a liberal amount onto his gloved fingers. He rubbed the gel over his gums (and even applied a little to the fresh gill areas, though it burned), before taking up his tools again.

He fit the bit back into the correct location and took a deep breath.

Then he pulled the drill's trigger.

"Man, those movies used to scare the shit out of me. You were pretty badass, back in the day."

Brennan smiled. It was not his best smile, the one he practiced in the mirror sometimes to put timid people at ease. No, this was a thin, tired smile. An annoyed smile.

"Thank you," he said.

"Whoa. Even your voice is different. Did they, like, make you sound all grungy and shit with computers or something?"

"No, that was my voice, too. I just don't go around growling like that all the time."

The kid, a long-haired stoner in a heavy metal T-shirt, just stared at Brennan. Then, slowly, he looked down at the table, down at the line of 8x10 photos. His eyes scanned the photos, stills from each of the *Razor Dawn* films as well as candid, behind-the-scenes snapshots, before glancing back up at Brennan to say, "Are these free or something?"

Brennan's jaw was beginning to ache; he realized he'd been clenching his teeth again.

"They're twenty dollars," he said.

"Apiece?"

"Yes."

"For what?"

"Well, for the photo and an autograph."

The stoner stared at him for a long moment before saying, "What the fuck ever, dude," and walking away.

Brennan let out a long, slow breath and looked over at Kim. She smiled sympathetically and crossed her legs. They were good legs, still, after all these years. She'd taken care of herself, and it showed.

Brennan wasn't so bad himself, of course. He'd managed to keep it together, anyway (though, of course, having a decent plastic surgeon helped).

He had to.

Brennan glanced across the way, to the empty table, the apologetic sign taped to its surface letting convention-goers know that, due to unforeseen circumstances, Donald J. Praggert had cancelled his appearance.

Unforeseen circumstances.

Prick.

The convention had pretty much allowed Brennan and Kim to set their prices because Don had promised he would show up. The publicity—"First *Razor Dawn* reunion! In honor of the twentieth anniversary of the film!"—had bumped the convention up from the B-level crap festival it really was to something higher, something sublime. *Fangoria* was set to write a piece on the reunion. So was *Rue Morgue*.

And Don fucked it all up.

In accordance with the Shit Rolls Downhill doctrine, the convention folks took out their frustration on Brennan and Kim. The pissed off reporters would probably do the same ... they'd already written crap reviews of the last four *Razor Dawn* sequels (*"For a supposedly tireless hellspawn, Brennan O'Rourke looks like he could use a nap,"* one of the kinder ones read).

When the con wrapped up at five, Brennan packed up his photos and posters and toy figurines, and turned to Kim Torrence.

"Want to get a drink or something?"

His former costar had risen to scream-queen fame at the ripe age of seventeen, when she spent half of the first *Razor Dawn* running in terror from Brennan's demonic character, "The Prophet."

Kim gave him an apologetic smile and said, "I wish I could ... but my flight's in an hour, and I have to teach tomorrow."

"You're a teacher now?" Brennan said.

"Have been for almost ten years. First grade."

"You ever miss the business?"

Kim's eyes widened. "Goodness, no. I mean, it was fun while it lasted, but ... I just didn't feel like there was any longevity there."

Brennan glanced away and nodded.

He hadn't done much work yet this year, but he was counting on "The Horror Show" to hire him again to host its all-night Halloween movie marathon again. It wasn't much—basic cable didn't pay for shit—but it was something. It kept his face and his name out there.

Until the next film.

The big one.

The reason—Brennan hoped, anyway—that Donald had pulled a no-show.

The magazines had lost interest a few years back when, after promising something for so many years, Donald J. Praggart, eccentric horror genius, still hadn't delivered.

But Brennan knew.

He'd seen the drafts of the script.

And Praggart's glorious return to the *Razor Dawn* franchise would blow everything out of the water.

All the shitty sequels? Forgotten.

The scandals surrounding Praggart's bizarre behavior? Forgiven.

Brennan's status as horror icon par excellence? Reinstated and cemented.

"Have you seen him lately?" she said.

Brennan shook his head.

"You were friends, right?"

He looked at her. "Sure. We still are ... it's just ... well ..."

"He's Donald Praggart?" she said, with a hint of a grin.

Brennan returned her grin. He remembered the endorsements of all the big name horror folks proclaiming Don to be the next Lovecraft, Poe, King, etc. How surreal had all of that been? Especially for his friend, the kid who, in school, had been relentlessly bullied and mocked for being sickly and bookish.

As she gathered the last of her things, Kim rose up on tiptoes to kiss Brennan on the cheek.

"It was nice to see you again," she said. Her perfume was sweet and spicy, and Brennan couldn't help but take note of the way her breasts pressed against him as she hugged him. "If you see Donald, tell him hi for me."

Brennan tried to remember that this was Kimmy ... little Kimmy Torrence from Oxfart, Nebraska (or wherever the hell it was). He'd helped her with math homework on the set of the first film, for God's sake.

But that was a seventeen-year-old girl. This was a thirty-seven-year-old woman.

And that reminded Brennan that he, too, was twenty years older. He still had decent muscle tone. His hairline had gone to hell, but that was okay. Fans were used to The Prophet's clean-shaven (well, *skinned*) head, so cutting his hair was the best move Brennan had ever made. People had started recognizing him on the streets again.

He watched Kim go, remembering the scent of her, the feel of her body against his for that briefest of moments.

Then she was gone.

With a sigh, he packed up the rest of his things and left.

The convention high waned. Brennan was forced to, once again, admit the truth: Real life sucked.

Sure, cons had their problems—especially for someone like Brennan—but they were a lovely distraction from the pointless banality of everyday life.

Still, it wasn't as fun as it used to be.

The *Razor Dawn* films had created a peculiar subculture within the horror community. The people who came to Brennan's table usually fell into one of two camps. The first, like the annoying mouth-breather who had closed out this last con for him, were of the stoner/metalhead persuasion, for whom the films represented a kind of live-action version of their favorite album cover artwork. Those kids were annoying—and boring—but generally harmless. The other camp, though ...

Brennan could spot them from miles away. He could *smell* them. The clove cigarettes. Benzoin, myrrh, and patchouli. Black leather, chromed chains, and pale, pale flesh penetrated with bits of metal.

Razor Dawn had created a generation of fetishists, viewers who believed in the films' "philosophy" and lived by Praggart's strange, dark mythos.

And they worshipped The Prophet.

On screen, anyway.

In real life, Brennan had discovered that they were some of the whiniest, most pathetic, and thoroughly goddamned boring people on planet Earth.

He yawned as he climbed the steps to Praggart's house, a modest, comfortable little two-story in Woodland Hills, California. He tried the doorbell, but there was no answer. He checked the voicemail message again, found the key that Don had slipped under a flower pot, and let himself in.

Furfur met him in the foyer, crying loudly. Brennan stooped and scratched the black-and-white cat's head before heading into the kitchen to get him a can of food. After feeding the cat, he helped himself to a ham sandwich, ate it by the kitchen counter as he nursed a Heineken taken from the fridge, and lingered a bit, allowing as much time to go by as he dared before putting his plate in the sink, brushing the crumbs from his hands, and walking toward the back of the house.

Speaking of things that just weren't that fun anymore ...

He unlocked the deadbolt securing the cellar door and descended the steps. When he flipped on the light switch, he watched in amusement as Praggart's guests tried—unsuccessfully—to remain defiant. They blinked away tears as the light blinded them and tried in vain to cover their nakedness, forgetting momentarily the shackles that held them in place.

"Had enough?" he said.

The female nodded, eyes wide with fear.

Brennan sighed. He walked around behind the girl and removed her catheter. He unlocked her ankle restraints and finished by freeing her wrists. The girl rubbed the angry red welts on her wrists and emitted a tiny "thank you" while Brennan began to decatheterize, unshackle, and otherwise detach the male.

"I trust you enjoyed your stay?" he said to the boy.

"W—will we g—get to meet him now?" the boy said.

Brennan raised an eyebrow at this. "Did he not come to see you?"

Both of them shook their heads.

Brennan frowned. That wasn't usually how it worked.

Brennan had gotten the message on his way to his agent's office. Don had asked if Brennan would mind "attending to the company," a term Don had used, when he and Brennan had shared a flat in college, whenever he had guests who had overstayed their welcome. Don's place was only twenty minutes or so from Brennan's, and Brennan was quite familiar with his old friend's strange appetites, so he didn't mind stopping in.

"Who locked you up, then?" Brennan said to the couple.

"Housekeeper," the girl said.

"Ms. Procell," Brennan said.

The girl nodded.

"I see."

Brennan looked around, sighed, and said, "Well, the show is over, kids. Wasn't it fun? Nothing like a weekend in the cold and dark, eh? Did you learn any 'mysteries of the flesh' while languishing down here, hungry and alone?"

"It was horrible," the girl said.

"Well, of course it was." Brennan said. "You came looking for a horror story, and you found it."

"W—what if we t—t—tell ...?" the boy said.

Brennan tuned in to his film persona and regarded the boy gravely. The kid shrunk down upon himself and started to cry.

"Do you think anyone would believe you?" Brennan said coldly.

He glared at them menacingly as they dressed in their ridiculous faux gothic clothes, and he walked them to the door. From the window, he saw the girl look back once, her eyes swimming in and out of focus.

Brennan sighed again. This was the problem with the fetishists. They loved the idea but not the reality. Reality was uncomfortable and humiliating and more than a little bit painful.

He climbed the stairs and walked down the hall to Donald's office. It was empty, but the desk was overflowing with a flurry of papers. He walked past the desk and opened the closet door. A ladder set into the wall inside led up to the attic, where Donald really worked when he was writing.

Brennan stepped up onto the first rungs of the ladder, though his knees protested and his lower back threatened to revolt. The large, empty room above, with its bare wood floors and the single bulb hanging from the ceiling, was Don's preferred working space. He would sit there, with pen and notebook in hand, and craft whole universes. He wrote, sometimes, for days at a stretch without sleep or food.

When Brennan climbed up out of the hole, though, he first noticed that the room was vacant.

Then he saw that Donald had been up to something.

The floor was covered in plastic sheeting. Several spotlights on long tripods stood around a small work area in the middle of the room. A small hand mirror lay, cracked, near a metal worktable. Brennan took a few steps closer, saw the power drill lying on its side, the canister of metal hooks that had spilled onto the table, and a number of blades fanned out on a white cotton cloth. And he saw the arcs and spots, the dark, tacky pools and the dry, brown patterns that had painted the well-lit attic in shades of crimson and ochre.

Brennan stared. He'd known Praggart for most of his life, knew the man as a serial blasphemer, pervert, and occasional sadist, but he had never really *hurt* anyone (the occasional flogging or fisting notwithstanding, of course).

What the hell had happened? And how was Brennan supposed to deal with it?

He didn't want to be an accessory to whatever horrible crimes it appeared that Don had committed, but he also wasn't about to turn in a friend, even if the bastard had screwed them all when he stopped playing the Hollywood games and handed over the franchise to a bunch of cocky little shits who wouldn't know horror if it crawled up inside their urethras and laid eggs.

There was a paper there, on the floor, partially saturated in what Brennan had to believe was blood. He stepped closer and looked at it.

Medical diagrams of some sort. A cross section drawing of a human head. Certain notes had been scribbled, in pencil, at some points of the drawing, but the writing had smudged and Brennan couldn't read any of it.

After a thorough investigation of the scene, Brennan climbed back down the ladder. He planned to grab another of Praggart's Heinekens, give the cat a little extra food and water, and leave an appropriately scathing message on Don's voicemail on the drive home. He hadn't planned on finding the black lacquered box on the previously empty dining room table.

As he approached the box, he noticed the flowing, spidery script on the note, and knew it immediately.

It read, "For Brennan—a new vista. I look forward to seeing you again."

Don's handwriting, naturally.

Brennan turned the note over, checking to see what, if anything, he'd missed.

It was blank.

He opened the box and looked inside. None of it made sense. The box was filled with a seemingly random assortment of newspaper clippings, some handwritten notes, a few bizarre-looking charts, a book—a—a textbook survey of linguistics—and a badly faded black-and-white photograph.

"I see you have received the package."

Brennan, startled, spun to face the speaker: a tall, thin blonde woman, with pale skin and eyes.

"Ms. Procell," Brennan said, regarding the strange, cold woman. "This is your doing, then?" He gestured to the box.

Ms. Procell cocked her head strangely as she looked at the box. "Mr. Praggart wanted you to have it."

"Did he give you any messages in regard to why?"

Ms. Procell looked up at him again, and he couldn't help feeling that her strange, glassy eyes were not seeing him.

"Where is Don, Ms. Procell?"

"Gone," she said, the faintest whisper of a word.

"Gone where?"

Her eyes focused then on Brennan's face, and she smiled.

"Fucking crazy bitch," Brennan muttered to himself. With the late-afternoon traffic, it was after seven by the time he got home.

The box sat innocently upon the passenger seat, and Brennan found himself occasionally placing a protective hand upon the cool, lacquered lid.

He had taken the thing and left Praggart's after realizing that he was getting nowhere with Procell. Brennan had never cared much for Don's taste in friends and lovers, but Amelie Procell was the oddest. Once, when Brennan had dropped by to return Don's latest script draft, the woman matter-of-factly disrobed in front of the two men and had begun masturbating. Her low, incessant giggling during the act had given Brennan the chills.

Thinking back, Brennan remembered something Don had told him when he was preparing for the first *Razor Dawn* film. Don had said, "I don't want you to be the boogeyman. I want you to be the dark." And while it was only a low-budget horror film, Brennan had taken it seriously. He took Don seriously.

For his role, Brennan had become the dark. He'd seen and participated in things that most people couldn't imagine. But Don ... Don always took it farther. And sometimes, Brennan had learned, the dark gets inside, like a chill, and you can't shake it.

Brennan parked in his garage and took the box inside.

He fixed a meager dinner and ate while trying to watch television, but the inanities on the screen bored him. He had a small video library that he kept locked in his bedroom safe, but those films were not the sort of thing one watched while eating.

After dinner, he showered. He shaved, looking at his form in the steamed mirrors, appreciating the shape of his jaw, his eyes, his muscle, bone, and sinew. He could easily imagine them distorted, mutilated by the work of a team of artists over a span of hours. He'd spent thousands of hours in the makeup chair, transforming into the creature that had once graced toys, lunchboxes, comic book covers, and T-shirts all over the world.

Now he saw a man. An aging, slowly decaying man.

Nothing special.

He slipped on his robe and opted to leave Praggart's strange box of nonsense for the morning.

And when he climbed into his bed and closed his eyes, Brennan dreamed.

Slick, red walls breathing. A hungry, painted mouth, lips parting, teeth shining. Stumbling in a darkness filled with wicked, barbed things that slid into his skin and refused to let go. Procell's exhibitionist tendencies on display in the middle of a costume ball, except that, as

Brennan pushed past masked faces and painted smiles, he saw that the emaciated and nude body splayed and wildly attending to itself was headless. The body changed. He knew, in the way that dreamers know, that it wasn't Procell anymore.

It was Kim.

Men in the crowd gazed hungrily at the stump of the neck, and Brennan felt himself wanting to join the queue that had lined up for a turn at the gaping raw meat of her neck.

He sat up. The taste of bile filled his throat, and he thought for a moment that he would be sick, but the sensations faded. He was hot, his skin reddish and covered with a sheen of sweat.

He stumbled into the kitchen and poured a glass of milk. He took a drink and quickly spit out the oily chunks into the sink. He checked the date on the container but saw the milk should have been fine. With a sigh, he put coffee on instead, knowing that sleep wouldn't be returning to him soon anyway.

He could feel the box there, sitting on a chair. He had to admit the strangeness of it all attracted him. He wanted to know, to understand.

After pouring himself a cup of coffee, he removed the lid and began to read.

The first several newspaper clippings had something to do with a scientist in Chicago. Brennan noted there was a pencil scribble just under the byline. Don's handwriting again. Something from the Bible: "In the beginning was the Word ..."

Brennan read the articles, but the whole story wasn't there. He knew the scientist was doing some kind of work with sound. Sound as it related to what? To medicine? The rest of the story didn't make sense until he realized that Don had put the articles in chronological order with photocopies of scientific reports and an obituary feature. The scientist, it seemed, had saved a young woman, an Eve Christie, from what should have been a mortal wound (a car accident according to one report, though other reports listed a fatal stabbing and a self-inflicted gunshot wound) with some sort of mysterious acoustical technique. The article wasn't clear on this point. Brennan continued reading and found that the story quickly turned rather bizarre.

The girl, it seems, woke up one morning, bought a shotgun, and gunned down her boyfriend for reasons unknown. She then drove to the nearby university, found the scientist who had—by all accounts, however conflicting—saved her life, and blew his head off. Then, in a bit of the text highlighted, presumably, by Praggart, the girl died. While that newspaper didn't mention how, another report included in the box did: her body was found by grad students just after she had shot the scientist. Her body, by the students' accounts, *disintegrated*.

Brennan frowned and got another coffee.

The next piece of information in the box was a photocopy of the International Phonetic Alphabet chart, listing—Brennan would find—every sound the human vocal apparatus is capable of making, regardless of language. The chart represented these sounds with strange-looking symbols, and documented how each sound was made via anatomical "articulators" like the lips, teeth, palate, etc.

Brennan briefly glanced at the chart, didn't understand either how to read it or its possible significance, and tossed it aside. He picked up instead the crumpled black-and-white photograph. It was a simple photo of a whitewashed house, with laundry-laden clotheslines and a child playing in the front yard. Brennan stared at the photo, unable to articulate exactly why the picture disconcerted him so ... until he saw a shady silhouette cast through a bed sheet on the line. The figure was clearly humanoid, but there was something wrong with it. Its proportions, the angle of its limbs ... something Brennan couldn't pin down.

The textbook followed, and Brennan was puzzled by it as he flipped through the heavily highlighted and underlined passages. A cross-section diagram labeling each of the articulators for speech had been drawn over in pencil. Various fanciful swirls, dot patterns, and whorls adorned the figure, with no explanatory notes.

Brennan sighed and got up from the table to get another cup of coffee. The first faint rays of sun were peeking through his kitchen window, and he glanced out to sneak a glimpse of the sunrise. What he saw was a bald, albinotic figure, dressed in some sort of skin-tight black leather, staring at him from the yard. White towels and linens waved from crisscrossing clotheslines around the figure, but Brennan kept his eyes on the figure. It nodded to him, a sort of beckoning gesture, and Brennan squeezed his eyes shut, expecting the figure to have vanished when he reopened them. The figure remained, however.

Brennan crossed to the back door and hesitated before opening it. It was madness to go out there, of course, but wasn't it all madness?

More than anything, he wanted to see, wanted to know. He had to know.

He approached the figure in a kind of waking dream. With each step, the figure's pale features came more into focus and, while the creature's visage was not familiar, marred as it was with all manner of hurts, Brennan realized that he knew the thing.

"What ... happened ... to you?" he said to it.

"*I ascended.*" The creature said with a choir of voices.

"How? What is all this?" Brennan said.

The creature's face contorted, layers of flesh and sinew unfolding and creasing into something that Brennan realized with revulsion was a smile.

"*Let me show you.*" It sang.

The layers of independently moving tissue around its mouth flagellated, and a symphony of hisses, clicks, and keening wails emitted from it. Brennan was entranced by the raw, bloodless wound in the creature's face. The musculature beneath the flawless, pale skin, the pinprick holes riddling its teeth, the gill-like folds along its jawline. The wounds were clearly more than just decorative markings, unlike those piercings and brandings made by primitives the world over.

Brennan had been so enthralled by the being's appearance that he had not noticed that they had traveled somehow. He was surrounded, now, by black glass. Volcanic rock, perhaps. And tiny puffs of a greenish steam coiled up from cracks in the floor here and there in an endless dance. Brennan looked to the creature and said, "Where are we? What's happening?"

In an instant, they were surrounded by chittering creatures, the misshapen homunculi of a particularly cruel god. Ashen faces glared up at Brennan with yellowed or cataract-glazed eyes. Broken and rotten teeth gnashed at him from behind scarred and burnt lips. Alien tongues spitting alien curses.

For a man who had made a living by frightening others, Brennan O'Rourke knew then that he had never known true horror. This, the cacophony of madness that surrounded him, the sea of unwashed and unholy flesh, this was horror. He felt it in the meat of his body, smelt its reek in his nostrils, burning his lungs ...

But the creature that had brought him here, the pale phantom with the eyes of a former friend, that *thing* seemed right at home. It reached out an alabaster hand and caressed the withered little mutants that had swarmed them.

"What is this?" Brennan said again.

"Proof." The creature sang. *"Of something more. Something greater."*

Brennan wanted to scream. There was nothing great about this place. He felt a dull hum that thrummed from the rocks and liquefied his bowels; he wanted more than anything to run from the place or, barring that, to bash his head against the black glassy stone until his spilt brains ceased to register the abomination of the place.

"You know how I have searched. Let me tell you what I have found, old friend: In every corner, only darkness. In the far reaches, only a gibbering nothingness. In the human heart, only cruelty. There is only one god in this plane, Brennan. Me."

"I—I don't understand."

"I want you to join me. I want us to re-create the world."

Brennan looked at Donald Praggart's mutilated, ethereal face and said, "How?"

"In the beginning was the Word."

The independently moving pieces of the thing's face began twitching and flailing, producing an eerie howl that rippled through the spaces around them and ripped them from the hellish scene.

Brennan hovered in a vast emptiness, illuminated only by the odd luminescence of his companion, a cold, dim glow that pooled out of Praggart's alien skin like sickness.

"The boy, the scientist, pointed the way."

"The scientist from the newspaper? Did he really heal that girl?"

"Oh, yes. But his magic died with him."

Brennan recalled the strange, highlighted end of the story—the incredible melting girl.

"He knew the key was sound. The sound of creation, of God. He attained some small success, but he was unwilling to take the next step."

"Which is?"

"The human throat is incapable of speaking in God's voice."

Brennan stared at Praggart's horrific face and the meaning of his words began to sink in. He remembered the chart detailing the sounds each bit of the mouth and throat were capable of producing.

"You ... you changed the articulators," Brennan muttered.

Donald closed his eyes and smiled beatifically. Brennan took note of the tiny holes, drilled with care into gums and teeth. Apertures that must act like the holes in a flute. He noted the gills along Donald's jaws, the layers of movable tissue around his mouth; slits in musculature that opened and closed like multiple sets of vocal cords.

"Jesus ..."

"*No, not Jesus.*" Praggart said with a grin.

"And you did this yourself."

Praggart still smiled, clearly proud of his achievement.

Brennan thought about it and, hesitantly, said, "Show me."

They were back in the house, in his kitchen. Praggart sang a discordant mix of notes and the linguistics book rose into the air, opened, came apart, and reassembled. Brennan stared at it, at the charts carefully marked with Praggart's insane anatomical modifications.

"Can you help me?" Brennan said quietly.

Praggart smiled again and turned to select a suitable tool from the knife drawer.

And Brennan O'Rourke took the black lacquered box and slammed it into the back of Praggart's head with a satisfying crunch. The pale being fell and rolled, turning to cast its pale eyes on its attacker. Brennan lifted the box again and, as Praggart inhaled to call forth whatever unholy revenge, he drove the wood down into the hellish hole in his former friend's face, splintering honeycomb teeth, tearing sculpted muscle, and splitting jaw from skull.

The thing's eyes, wide with shock, begged for mercy, for answers.

Brennan cut them out with a paring knife before the thing finally ceased.

His heart pounded in his chest. His breathing was labored and too fast.

He sat at the kitchen table and caught his breath.

And with the sun on the horizon, he assembled his tools.

The razor in his hand caught the first rays of light, casting rainbows down on the dead god on his floor.

Brennan O'Rourke adjusted his mirror, placed the tip of the blade just so, and smiled. He glanced down at the body on the floor and began to cut. As the blood burbled into his mouth, he said, "If you see the Buddha on the road, Don? You kill the Buddha."

PRIMAL TONGUE

BY MICHAEL BAILEY

"*Virkeligheden er jo ligesom i eventyrene,*" said the woman in the terminal.

The woman smiled and moved her attention to the cooing child in the stroller. She put her hand on the leg of the man sitting next to her, a husband or boyfriend.

Danish. But Gil Sloat couldn't understand a word of it. Were they talking about him?

The man took his turn. "*Jeg håber, du har det dejligt og nyder livet.*"

Then he chuckled.

"*På godt og ondt,*" she said, taking his hand.

We're in America, people. Speak English.

"NOW BOARDING FLIGHT 0196 TO BALTIMORE AND WASHINGTON." A static-filled female voice, from the only airline representative working gate J87. Strange that airports still used overhead paging to announce flights. Internet and cellular technologies managed ticketing and seating assignments and boarding passes and other travel arrangements, yet a person—an attractive woman in an ugly blue uniform—was still responsible for controlling the chaos of boarding an airplane. Common courtesy and common sense were rarities.

"FREQUENT FLIER PLATINUM MEMBERS MAY BOARD AT THIS TIME."

Most airlines had eliminated first class, but half a dozen membership programs allowed certain passengers to board before the masses, followed by active duty military, those with disabilities, and families with young children. These minorities then had to luggage-slalom through the impatient herd of coach passengers as they line-hopped to the front.

"THOSE WITH SMARTPHONES, TABLETS, AND OTHER HANDHELD DEVICES MAY BOARD AT THIS TIME."

Gil imagined those words over the loudspeaker, followed by the amoeba-like flow of techno-lemmings piling through the gate, smartphones and tablets and other handheld devices aloft to protect them. Shoulders smashing shoulders. Men and women and children trampled by passengers eager to secure their overabundance of carry-on luggage. He imagined standing in back, or seated, like the Danish family, watching the chaos unfold instead of taking part, later to be penalized as his single, sized-approved carry-on is checked due to a lack of space in the overhead compartments. He could relate to those people. The patient ones, those he'd *like* to understand. The Danish woman shared his view; he could see it in her eyes.

The rapid boom in technology was partly to blame for the world's ruin. Devices invented to simplify life more often simplified the living. Let a person become dependent on portable technology and then watch him get struck by a vehicle while crossing the street. It happened all the time. The *chinonchest* syndrome: when a person is so involved in their handheld device/gadget/toy, they forget to look up now and again. Zombies, all of them. Keystroke conversations, not spoken word.

And there Gil sat, hearing the words of people he wanted to understand, but he couldn't understand them. The baby's coos were easier to translate than the Danish. The child wanted attention. Maybe it was foreign cooing.

Is there such a thing? Is all language the same until it's learned? Is there, perhaps, a common language shared by all; something primal, unnecessary to learn, before we fuck it all up and disorientate the world by segregating ourselves with language?

"*På godt og ondt,*" Gil said, copying what the woman had said.

280

She looked up from the child.

He hadn't meant to say the unfamiliar phrase, but the terminal was so dead with people *not* talking that the words came out of his mouth, as if wanting to be heard.

"*Taler du dansk?*"

A question. Somehow he knew she asked if he understood Danish; that much he could gather by facial movements and her curiosity.

Her husband nodded. "*God eftermiddag!*"

"Sorry," Gil said, embarrassed. "I don't speak Danish."

The woman's eyebrows furrowed. She spoke slowly: "But you know what was I said, in *dansk*. 'For better or worse,' you said."

Why do so few Americans learn other languages?

Her English wasn't perfect, but she had translated his words and could speak the language far better than his butchery of *dansk*, of which he understood zilch.

Gil apologized again. "I repeated the words because I enjoyed the sound. I only know English. What was that first thing you said? *Virkeli*-something ..."

"*Virkeligheden er jo ligesom i eventyrene.*" The words rolled easily off her tongue, with elegance and grace.

"Sounds beautiful. What does it mean?"

"Haha. It means—" Her eyes searched the ceiling, "I guess you could say: what is real is like the fairy tales."

"If only that were—"

"PASSENGERS WITH SPECIAL NEEDS AND THOSE WITH CHILDREN CAN NOW BOARD."

The crowd of passengers without special needs, and the childless, sandwiched closer to the front.

Gil had special needs. He needed to understand.

Maybe people don't want to understand.

The Danish couple rose, searching for a path.

The husband shrugged his shoulders. "Eh," he said. "Plane will not leave without."

Seeing the couple made him feel alone. If only he and Nell were still together, he could stand by her side, hold her hand. Gil wore happiness like a mask and Nell ran off with it. He could no longer hide his depression from the world ...

"MICHAEL RILEY, PLEASE REPORT TO THE PODIUM.

MICHAEL RILEY, PLEASE REPORT TO THE PODIUM FOR YOUR STANDBY SEATING ASSIGNMENT."

"Well," Gil said. "It looks like this is going to take some—"

"ACTIVE DUTY MILITARY MAY BOARD AT THIS TIME, FOLLOWED BY ..." The gate agent clicked off, covered the handset to help a customer—apparently not Michael Riley, unless he was a heavyset black woman with a cane—before starting again.

"FOLLOWED BY ZONE 1. ZONE 1 MAY BOARD AT THIS TIME."

So many detailed instructions, yet no one listened.

"This is going to take a while," Gil said. "I'm going to find some coffee and learn another language."

"*Ét sprog er aldrig nok*," the woman said.

Language translation apps were inexpensive, if you already owned a mobile device, but they rarely made the bestseller list. Those spots were apparently reserved for entertainment and educational packages. Those apps should raise the bar; instead, they seemed to make everyone *stupider*, as Nell used to say.

Gil bought a paltry vanilla latte—the last time he'd ever settle for coffee from one of the Starbucks machines—as he browsed the programs available at the *A.I. Unlimited* kiosk: an unmanned touch-screen mounted on a wall three gates down from J87. A scanner read payments, and a retractable cable connected to one's *Digital Software Adaptation Interface. D-SAI* for short.

At the top of the list was a flashbook of *Fahrenheit 451*, which was amusing: the Ray Bradbury classic about a world where books were burned out of existence, only to be preserved by those willing to memorize them. The eBook version issued twenty years ago had made Gil laugh—paper pages turned/burned to digital—but that was during the push to eliminate paper. People still read then. Once the eBook craze dwindled—following criminalization of printing on paper—and people could simply upload stories into their minds without needing to read them, the concept of 'reading' died. For most people. Gil still 'read' and enjoyed it, although the stories he read were digital. He saw it as a vacation from reality; to be lost in the pages of fiction, immersed in characterization and plot. That was a liberating experience.

The line at gate J87 was still a mess. He had twenty minutes to board.

He'd never tried a flashbook. What was the point?

It had been years since he'd read Bradbury. He remembered the highlights, such as 'firemen' raiding houses to confiscate books and set them on fire, and classic books memorized word for word by a rebelling few. Most memories of the book seemed to have burned as well.

Why not buy a copy?

The screen scrolled through simple instructions.

Gil attached the *D-SAI* cable to the port on his left wrist, twisting until it locked in place.

Ray would be rolling over in his grave if he saw this ...

Perhaps he had envisioned it.

Gil pressed the button and waited.

UPLOADING ... TRANSACTION COMPLETE.

Instantaneously, Gil remembered the missing pieces, the novel suddenly whole. In only a moment, the words were there.

"It was a pleasure to burn," he recited to no one. "It was a special pleasure to see things eaten, to see things blackened and *changed*. With the brass nozzle in his fists, with this great python spitting its venomous kerosene upon the world, the blood pounded in his hands, and his hands were the hands of some amazing conductor playing all the symphonies of blazing and burning to bring down the tatters and charcoal ruins of history."

The entire book.

Gil, the technology proselyte.

For the next month, the book would be his, word for word. That's how the copyright-protected apps worked. The words still belonged to Bradbury's estate. Someone, somewhere, would receive a paltry stipend for this purchase. After the virtual rental, whatever Gil had read and could remember would remain. But the experience was shortened from hours to milliseconds, which defeated the purpose of reading—the long escape from reality reduced to a hiccup.

Such an amazing book.

Educational material was different. The purchaser became owner, with no expiration date, and permanent knowledge retained. Uploaded to long-term memory as opposed to short-term memory. A different part of the brain. This meant more money.

Digital education courses were priced higher than classes taken in person. Language *translation* programs worked on a temporary basis for travel or whatnot, with the purchaser comprehending the spoken word of another language—although unable to speak it. Language *knowledge* programs worked on a permanent basis, with the purchaser understanding the new language indefinitely. But it was expensive. Basic Spanish, the second most common language in the United States, cost more than learning four years of Spanish in college, and that was only for comprehension. Languages still required linguistic practice, learned muscle memory of the tongue and mouth, as well as phonological and morphological development to speak, read, and write, although no one wrote anymore. You couldn't upload those.

Gil's savings could buy him only a single permanent language; that, and his trip to Europe. He was running from life, but it was a much-needed vacation. It would help him forget.

For the next three weeks, he'd travel to Portugal, Spain, France, and then through Belgium, Amsterdam, Germany, with perhaps a stop at Denmark before crossing over to Sweden. The Baltimore/Washington International Airport was his first destination, then a thirteen-hour nonstop flight to Lisbon.

Gil touched the display and purchased 30-day rentals of Spanish / *español*, French / *le français*, German / *Deutsch*, Swedish / *svenska*, Danish / *dansk*, and Portuguese / *português*. After Portuguese, the screen flickered with a glitch of 1's and 0's and returned to a confirmation screen. After hesitating, he pressed the button labeled UPLOAD ALL.

"Hmm." He felt nothing.

As a test, Gil changed the language settings on the kiosk to Spanish / *español*. All of the words changed. The center of the display read:

¿HABLA USTED ESPAÑOL?

SÍ / NO

"Technically, no, I do not *speak* Spanish, but why not?" He recognized the phrase from his newly-purchased memory. He pressed the button and said, "Sí."

SELECCIONE EN EL MENÚ SIGUIENTE, POR FAVOR

Please select from the menu below.

"That's incredible ..."

He tried repeating the phrase, but butchered the hell out of it, getting only *por favor* correct, since he'd heard that before, like the French *si vous plaît*.

"*Sa-lid-a*," he said, pressing the exit button.

The line at gate J87 had transformed from chaotic to manageable, so he headed that direction and joined the line. There were maybe twenty people left to board. The gate agent hassled the Danish couple about the stroller, for not boarding earlier when she'd called for families with young children. Gil didn't need a translator program to decipher the gestures from the woman in the ugly blue uniform.

A commotion at the *A.I. Unlimited* kiosk turned him around. A squad of uniformed men with assault rifles surrounded the device while two men in suits inspected the screen. Others in suits wandered the terminal, interviewing those in the area, fingers to their ears. One made eye contact with Gil before he boarded.

"*Humeasamajmeinaiaweh. Kai koynaibeilkhoweh?*"

That's how it sounded, at least. Gil recognized the dialect Indian vernacular: Hindi, Marathi, Bengali, or Punjabi. Probably Hindi.

The rapidity of the words made him think of Nell, a strikingly beautiful woman he'd met in Quebec. Although Nell spoke fluent English, her second language, she had to keep reminding Gil to speak more slowly. *Translation takes time*, she had said. He didn't realize how rapid English sounded to the world outside his bubble until he met her. Not until she rattled off *le français* to prove a point: "*Comment vas-tu? Je vais bien, merci. Et toi? Comme-ci, comme-ça. Quoi de neuf?* You understood only a few of those words. It seemed normal to me, but to you it seemed fast, *correct?*"

Nell's last words to him: "Are you happy?"

Of course I'm happy, he'd said, taking her words out of context, not realizing she was saying goodbye. *What does she think? I'm not?*

He hadn't realized they were lines from Bradbury until now.

It was a pleasure to burn, it was a pleasure to—

01110011 01100101 01100101 00100000 01110100
01101000 01101001 01101110 01100111 01110011
00100000 01100101 01100001 01110100 01100101
01101110

—to see things blackened and changed.

Perhaps an error in the flashbook.

The Indian fellows next to him rambled untranslatable phrases. Even if he could understand, the words would probably get lost in translation.

"Hamar kayneh kali yeh hai: Hindustani longh Gita mei yeh baath par ke samjis ke beil nai khowa jai. Maine para aur samjah ke har zindagi ek tofah hai. Kitna kitabh, jaise Quran aur Bible mei sawal likhan hai, aur insan par ke soche ke yei such baath hai? Tabh ye baath insan apan aur apan bachei ke zindagi mei likh ..."

The older one looked at Gil. "My little brother, he thinks I want to eat our mother. Ha! Mothers give you milk, and so do cows; that's his reasoning. Since I like quarter-pounders with cheese," he said, lifting the bag, "he thinks I'd butcher our mother."

"That's not what I said."

"He thinks the Gita says we shouldn't eat beef, even though it was written before we ever had McDonald's."

"Don't listen to him. *Gita kuch aur nai bole iske bareh mei.* He's putting words in my mouth."

"He puts goat in his mouth. Hindustani people eat goats, and goats give milk. He has no justification for his reasoning. Do you eat goat?"

Gil shrugged. "I can't say I've ever had the opportunity."

"Tastes like old beef." The older brother removed the hamburger from the bag. He unwrapped half of it and took a big, slow bite. After washing it down with his soda, he said, "Cow is much tastier than goat, whether or not the Gita says so."

"FLIGHT ATTENDANTS, PREPARE FOR TAKE OFF."

The plane lurched as it was pushed back from the gate.

Gil had read that planes did not have a means of moving in reverse. They had to be pushed by something more primitive—a ground-based vehicle, something capable of bidirectional movement, translating *reverse*, one could say.

Soon they were in the air, the two brothers conversing once again in Hindi.

After take-off, the brothers conversed again in Hindi.

Should have picked up that language too, instead of this faulty book.

Gil loved theoretical/religious arguments, something everyone struggled with. The struggle intrigued him.

He asked the older brother, "Where you're from, do they still teach writing?"

"I am from California, so no."

"Ah, sorry."

Public schools in the United States, following in the wake of other nations, had stopped teaching writing over two decades ago; instead, language education focused on typing, whether by keyboard or touchscreen. The world had migrated to a digital age. Pencils and pens were a rarity, unless purchased from art supply stores, and writing on paper was unheard of. Cursive had been the first to go. Schools stopped teaching it. The act of writing was a lost skill.

"But if you mean India, the answer is also no."

"It's a shame, really."

"Yes, it is … but, like with *all* change, we can choose not to accept it. Do you write?"

"I write every day, at least a page. My mother encouraged writing. And she saw it coming. 'Soon,' she told me, 'the world will no longer have a need for books or for writing of any kind.' For her *last* birthday, I bought her one of those Kindle devices, one of the first eBooks. She unwrapped it, held it like fragile glass and said, 'What in God's name is this?' She used it once, I think, but said she'd rather stick to 'real' books. That she liked the feel of them, the smell of their pages."

"What did she do when they stopped printing books?"

"She said no one writes worth a damn anymore, and that *real* writers had created enough books for generations to read. 'We don't need new books,' she said. 'Everything that *can* be written *has* been written. Everything new plagiarizes from the past. Nothing new is original.'"

"What is it you write?"

"My own take on unoriginal ideas. She gave me these journals

287

years ago. Black leather-bound with two hundred pages in each. I'm not sure where she found them, but she gave me about twenty. I've filled up five so far. Who knows, maybe someday I'll do something with them."

"Do you have a pen?"

Gil carried one in his shirt pocket—nearly confiscated as a weapon at security. He pulled it free, clicked the end, and handed it to him.

"My brother," he said, pointing with his thumb, "he cannot write. He can copy what he sees, like drawing shapes, but he cannot really write. Our mother taught me and my sisters, though. My grammar is horrible, I must warn you."

On the back of his drink napkin, in smooth script, he wrote the following:

भाषाकेबिनामनुष्यकभीनहींछोड़ाजाएगा

"It's beautiful. What does it mean?"

"Man will never be left without language."

Halfway through a ginger ale and an unfunny-romantic comedy on the seat monitors—soundless because he wasn't interested—the Starbucks coffee wanted out. Whenever Gil needed to use the restroom on flights, he was never alone. A line of three needed to un-Starbucks their bladders.

He excused himself as he squeezed by the Indian brothers and joined the end of the line. As he moved up the aisle, he hoped to hear one of the languages he had purchased so he could understand the translation process. Most passengers were engrossed in the movie, occupied with handheld devices or otherwise silent.

That's what the world's becoming. Silent.

After a dance with an overweight fellow returning to his seat, Gil noticed the Danish couple at the back of the plane.

As Gil moved closer, he was able to understand their conversation, as if by telepathy or a teleprompter in his head:

"Jeg begik en fejl," the woman said. I made a mistake.

"Det kan man vist roligt sige." I'll say.

"*Hvad mener du?*" What do you mean?

"*Det, jeg siger.*" What I am saying.

"*Men du er jo nødt til at tilgive mig, hvis vi skal komme videre.*" But you have to forgive me, if we are to move on.

Forgive her for what? What could she have possibly done?

She touched her husband's hand, but he pulled away and turned to the window. She looked at Gil, but she didn't smile this time. He felt pity, and then guilty for listening in to this private conversation.

They were going through what he'd gone through months before with Nell. Their body language told him they'd fallen apart. They were at the end of something once wonderful.

"*Det ved jeg ikke, om jeg kan,*" the Danish man said. I don't know if I can do that.

"*Jamen, hvad vil du så?*" Well, what do you want then?

"*Lige nu vil jeg bare have, at du ikke siger noget.*" Right now, I want you to not say anything.

The Danish couple's fairytale relationship was just that: a fairytale. Whether or not Gil wanted to listen, he was going hear and understand their conversation. From their meeting at the gate, they believed he couldn't comprehend their language, and probably assumed others couldn't either.

Gil felt wrong, but he couldn't turn it off. He focused his attention elsewhere, pretending ignorance, looking to the signs that read NO SMOKING and NO E-SMOKING, to the personal air vents and flight attendant call buttons and the overhead compartments, anything to hold his attention other than their words. He wanted to return to his seat, to hold his bladder longer, but the line had filled in behind him and he was trapped.

If he could turn back time, he'd return the damn language.

"*Hold nu op. Alle begår fejl. Vi er kun mennesker. Og hvis vi ikke kan tilgive, hvor ender vi så?*" Come on. Everybody makes mistakes. We are only human. And if we can't forgive, then where do we end?

Perhaps she had cheated on him. But it was none of Gil's business.

He massaged his temples, trying not to listen, trying not to remember Nell, trying instead to recall the back of the Sky Mall digazine from the pouch in his seat—an advertisement for a perfume with a horizontal half-naked couple on a beach with a caption proclaiming the name of the perfume and a tide frozen in time, indefinitely lapping at their bodies. A fake perfect-happy, half-naked couple colliding on the sand in halftones with an illuminated heart-shaped bottle in the foreground, yet the words—

"*Ti nu stille,*" he said. Be quiet.

Words ever so right.

Gil tried to bring up the book, to hide in the digital pages stored in his mind, but the words weren't there. Bradbury was gone.

"*Så det er det?*" So that's it then?

"*Måske.*" Maybe.

"*Skal jeg gå?*" Do you want me to leave?

He'd said the same thing to Nell. Different words, but the same words.

"*Nogle gange er fejl så store, at de ikke kan tilgives. Vil du ikke nok tie stille. Jeg har brug for at tænke.*" Sometimes mistakes are so big, that they cannot be forgiven. Please be quiet. I need to think.

"*Undskyld. Jeg mener det virkelig. Hvis jeg kunne gøre det om, ville jeg gøre det. Undskyld.*" I'm sorry. I really mean it. If I could do it over, I would. I'm sorry.

"*Tak.*" Thanks.

Gil shuffled forward. The Danish woman caught him trying not to look at her this time and she smiled, but the passion hidden in that smile did not need translation: *passion* meant *suffering*. He saw that in her eyes. Although her eyes were dry, hurt welled instead of tears. She turned to her husband, but he gave his attention to the white blanket of cloud outside the window, so she focused on the child between them. That's when the corners of her mouth curled and she silently cried, a single tear dripping onto her lap.

The primal language.

Action and reaction. Feeling. Emotion.

The baby cooing and the mother's instinctual response of tending to a child too young for dialogue, just *goo-goos* and *ga-gas* and other nonsense noises. Pets cuddling when you're sick, acting sad when you're sad, happy when you're happy. A baby crying because another baby is crying. Sadness answering sadness, anger countering anger, joy begetting joy, a smile met with another smile ...

Tongues only wrought confusion.

Virkeligheden er jo ligesom i eventyrene, she'd said to Gil at the gate. He understood now. People often lived the fairy tale life, masking misery with ideals of happiness. The words had sounded beautiful; now they sounded terrible.

They sounded familiar.

He offered the woman a crooked smile, hoping she'd look up from her sorrow to see that *he* understood, to see empathy: something they could communicate without the need for words.

I don't want them anymore.

After touchdown in Portugal, he couldn't sleep. His mind would not shut off. Every conversation required his attention, no matter the language, whether he wanted to hear or not.

And then all at once the pages of the flashbook returned.

To quiet the endless conversations translating through his mi nd— mixtures of Spanish-Portuguese-English-French —Gil referenced *Fahrenheit 451*, recalling and reciting the words as if one of its memorizing characters.

"The woman's hand twitched on the single matchstick," he said. "The fumes of kerosene bloomed up about her ... felt the hidden book pound like a heart against his—"

01100011 01101000

01100101 01110011

01110100 00001101

00001010

What's wrong with this damn thing?

A woman wanted his attention, to ask him something, directions perhaps.

He kept walking out of the Lisbon terminal.

"Silly words, silly words, silly awful hurting words ..."

Gil skipped ahead to a favorite part: the end.

"And when it came to his turn, what could he say, what could he offer on a day like this, to make the trip a little easier? To eve rything there is a season. Yes. A time to break down, and a time to build up. Yes. A time to keep silence, and a time to speak. Yes, all that. But what else. What else? Something, something ..."

A man standing next to a white Mercedes with a lit TÁXI roof ornament hailed him down the moment he stepped out of the Lisbon terminal.

"*Americano, americano! Senhor,* you need taxi?"

Did he look that American?

"*Que hotel?*"

"Which hotel?" He checked his cellphone. "Yes, it's uh… here it is. Sofitel Lisbon Liberdade."

"Sofitel Lisbon, nice… *cinco estrelas.*" The driver held out his hands. "*Dar!*" Give!

Give?

The man shook his hands for the luggage, and Gil understood without needing the words, which didn't do him much good when translated; he was having trouble keeping up. *Cinco estralas,* the man had said, meaning the hotel: five stars.

"Oh, yes. Thank you," Gil said, handing over his suitcases.

Translation takes time, Nell's voice haunted.

"*Obrigado.*" Thank you.

"Orbrigado."

The cabbie opened the trunk, tossed his luggage inside. Gil made his way into the backseat, where he was surprised to find a man already seated.

"*Ei.*" Hey.

Gil nodded. The man nodded. The doors closed, and that was that. Then something hot speared his leg in a way that made his muscles spasm and his jaw clamp.

"*Ser ainda,*" the man said. Be still.

He had buried the needle of a large syringe deep into Gil's thigh as the taxi sped away. The barrel stuck from his leg like a knife hilt. Gil controlled his eyes, but the rest of his body paralyzed; not numb, because the liquid burned along his leg, up into his groin, and blossomed in his chest. The sensation crawled up his neck. He'd clenched his teeth at the initial agony and now his mouth was stuck shut, lips tight.

Gil tried to scream at the reflection of the taxi driver, but the taxi driver smiled and repositioned the mirror so that Gil stared a t himself.

They were going to jack him, and there was nothing he could do.

The man next to him felt Gil's pocket and pulled out his handheld. He held it in front of Gil's face to unlock it with the facial recognition security. Within seconds, he brought up Gil's digital passport and banking information and scanned it into an antiquated touchscreen device.

292

"We're sorry to do this to you, *Americano*. You have made recent purchases, no? *Tradução para a língua.*" Language translation.

Gil's sealed mouth made untranslatable noises.

"Our *amigo entende* Portuguese."

"*Vamos*, Abrahan," said the driver. Let's go.

Abrahan didn't translate to anything. It was his name.

"Bad luck for you, *meu amigo*," said the man next to him. He pressed the handheld to Gil's face, close enough to make it blurry and unreadable.

"*Lamentamos muito, meu amigo*," the driver said. We are very sorry, my friend.

"You found something you weren't supposed to find. *Dados sensíveis.*" Sensitive data. "But your find is, how do you say ... *inestimável?*" Invaluable.

Hidden code in the book?

"Now in here," Abrahan said, tapping Gil's forehead. "We can leave no trace."

The phone display turned white and then it was gone, black, powerless, and Gil knew it had been wiped clean.

"*Fazer a conexão,*" the driver said. Make the connection. "*Vamos.*" Let's go.

"Yeah, yeah," Abrahan said.

"*Apagá-lo.*" Erase him.

The most frightening phrase Gil had ever heard.

Two words.

No, no, no—

Abrahan prepared a *black box*—an unethical device used by computer hackers long ago, the plain chassis hiding the complex interior, an interface on either side.

He attached a cable to the *D-SAI* port on Gil's wrist and connected the other end to the black box. The antiquated touchscreen connected to the other interface to decode the digital makeup of whatever he planned to wipe from Gil's mind.

How much could he see? What could he erase?

And then the man told him.

"Language translation app: *português*, language translation app: *español*, language translation app: *le français, Deutsch, svenska, dansk* ... You must like languages, *meu amigo*. Ah, flashbook: *Fahrenheit 451. Bom livro?*" Good book?

The fireman.

"Find it?" said the driver.

"*Sim.*" Yeah.

The man worked through the list of languages, swiping his finger across each program to erase them: "*Dansk, ido.*" Gone. "*Svenska, ido. Deutsch, ido. Le français, ido. Español, ido.*" His finger simply flicked them away. "*Português,*" he said and paused. "I take this one, you no longer *entender ...*"

"*Não se preocupe.*" Don't worry. "I will let you keep *bom livro* to have until you pass, but will scramble the rest. *Entender* scramble, *como ovos?*" Like eggs.

They planned to erase Gil's memory, not just the translation applications or past purchases, but everything about him.

"Wrong place, wrong time, *meu amigo.* We have to destroy it all. You will not feel a thing, *eu prometo.*" I promise. "*Português, ido,*" he said, swiping his finger one last time, and it was gone. All of his learned languages were gone.

A small part of Gil welcomed the loss.

"*Fazê-lo,*" the driver said. No translation.

"*Não me apresse. Isto é difícil.*"

"*Você já fez isso antes.*"

"*Cem vezes.*"

Foreign words once again.

The driver pulled the car into an empty alley. They gently carried Gil's numb body and set him on the pavement. Immobile, he faced the sun as they poured flammables over his body and his belongings.

Kerosene is nothing but perfume to me, Gil pulled from the book.

Abrahan tapped on the device still connected to the port on Gil's wrist, deleting, erasing, doing something ...

"*Lamentamos muito, meu amigo.*"

Soon it would—

01001001001000000110110001101110111
01100110010100100000011110010110111
0111010100101100001000000010011100110
0101011011000110110000101110 ...

—*be gone, perhaps a virus shot through the mind to*—

"*Sinto muito,*" one of them said.

Nell—

0100100101100110001000000011100110110
111101101101011001010110111110110110
011001010010000001110011011011110110
110101100101011010000110111101110111
001000000110011001101001011011100110
010001110011001000000111010001101000
011010010111001100100000011011000110
111101110011011101000010000001110100
0110100001101111011101010101100111 0110

1000011101000010000001100001011011101
0110100101100100001000000110000100010010
0000011000100110100101101111001100001
0111001001111001001000000111011100110
1111011100100110110001100100001011000
0010000001101011011011100110111110111
0111001000000111010001101000011000011
0111010000100000010010010010000000110
1000011000010111011001100100101001000000
0110000101101100011101110110000010111
1001011100110010000000110110001101111
0111011001100101011001000001000000111
100101101111011101101010010101110 ...

PART ONE
The Hearth and the Salamander

It was a pleasure to burn.

It was a special pleasure to see things eaten, to see things blackened and *changed*. With the brass nozzle in his fists, with this great python spitting its venomous kerosene upon the world, the blood pounded in his hands, and his hands were the hands of some amazing conductor playing all the symphonies of blazing and burning to bring down the tatters and charcoal ruins of history ...

Special thanks to Trine Einspor for writing and translating those beautiful Danish words; to Chris Prasad for offering an interesting conversation in Hindi; to Gary A. Braunbeck, Mort Castle, Thomas F. Monteleone, F. Paul Wilson and Douglas E. Winter for their guidance with this story; and to Ray Bradbury for changing the world with words that will never be forgotten.

THE WRITERS

MICHAEL BAILEY

Michael Bailey is the author of *Palindrome Hannah*, a nonlinear horror novel and finalist for the Independent Publisher Awards. His follow-up novel, *Phoenix Rose*, was listed for the National Best Book Awards for horror fiction, was a finalist for the International Book Awards, and received the Kirkus Star, awarded to books of remarkable merit. *Scales and Petals*, his short story and poetry collection, won the International Book Award for short fiction, as well as the USA Book News "Best Books" Award. *Pellucid Lunacy*, an anthology of psychological horror published under his Written Backwards label, won for anthologies for those same two awards. His short fiction and poetry can be found in anthologies and magazines around the world, including the US, UK, Australia, Sweden, and South Africa. He is working on his third novel, *Psychotropic Dragon*, a new short story and poetry collection, *Inkblots and Blood Spots*, and recently edited *Chiral Mad*, a multi-award nominated anthology of psychological horror to benefit Down syndrome charities, with stories by Jack Ketchum, Gary A. Braunbeck, Jeff Strand, Gene O'Neill, Gord Rollo, and many others. You can visit him online at www.nettirw.com.

DAVID BENTON & W.D. GAGLIANI

Outside of his writing, David Benton has worn many hats, finding employment as a warehouse worker, landscaper, printing press operator, cheese maker, brick layer, and janitor (long nights, impossible odds). He is also a musician. Current projects include a collaborative novel with Bram Stoker Award winning author John Everson and W.D. Gagliani, a mid-grade novel series and a young adult novel series (both with W.D. Gagliani, written under the pen name A.G. Kent) as well as playing bass guitar on tour with the heavy metal novelty act Beatallica.

W.D. Gagliani is the author of the novels *Savage Nights* (Tarkus Press), *Wolf's Trap* (Samhain Publishing), *Wolf's Gambit* (47North), *Wolf's Bluff* (47North), and *Wolf's Edge* (Samhain), plus the upcoming *Wolf's Deal* (novella) and *Wolf's Cut* (Samhain, 2014). *Wolf's Trap* was a finalist for the Bram Stoker Award in 2004. He has published fiction and nonfiction in numerous anthologies and publications such as *Masters of Unreality* (Germany), *Malpractice: An Anthology of Bedside Terror*, *Dark Passions: Hot Blood 13*, and *Dead Lines* (all with co-writer David Benton), plus *Robert Bloch's Psychos*, *Wicked Karnival Halloween Horror*, *The Black Spiral: Twisted Tales of Terror*, *More Monsters From Memphis*, *The Midnighters Club*, *The Milwaukee Journal Sentinel*, *BookPage*, *Chizine*, *Cemetery Dance*, *HorrorWorld*, *Hellnotes*, *Science Fiction Chronicle*, *The Scream Factory*, and others. Some of his fiction is available in the collection *Shadowplays* (Tarkus Press) and various Benton & Gagliani collaborations are available in the collection *Mysteries & Mayhem* (Tarkus Press). With David Benton, he also writes middle-grade fiction as "A.G. Kent." He is a member of the Horror Writers Association (HWA), the International Thriller Writers (ITW), and the Authors Guild. Raised in Genova, Italy, as well as Kenosha, Wisconsin, W. D. Gagliani now lives and writes in Milwaukee.

New publications for Benton & Gagliani include a reprint of their *Hot Blood 13* story, "Mood Elevator," upcoming in *Old Nick* (magazine), and W.D. Gagliani's review column "Printer's Devil," also in *Old Nick*. Recent publications include a reprint of Gagliani's "Until Hell Calls Our Names" in the anthology *Undead Tales* (Rymfire Books). Find W.D. Gagliani online at www.wdgagliani.com, or read their "Mysteries & Mayhem" blog at http://moodelevator.wordpress.com/

DOUG BLAKESLEE

Doug Blakeslee lives in Portland, OR and spends his time writing, cooking, gaming, and following the local hockey team. (Go Winterhawks!) His interest in books started early thanks to his mom and hasn't stopped since. A heavy fan of sci-fi and fantasy, it came as a pleasant surprise that his first sale was the suspense short story "Madame" to the anthology *Uncommon Assassins*. He recently started a blog, The Simms Project at http://thesimmsproject.blogspot.com/, where he talks about writing and other related topics. He can be reached via the blog, Facebook, or e-mail at simms.doug@gmail.com.

E.A. BLACK

E. A. Black's dark fantasy and horror fiction has been appeared in *Kizuna: Fiction For Japan*, *Stupefying Stories*, and *Mirages: Tales From Authors Of The Macabre*. She writes erotic fiction with the pen name Elizabeth Black. An accomplished essayist, her articles about sex, erotica, and relationships have appeared in *Good Vibrations Magazine*, *Alternet*, *CarnalNation*, the *Ms. Magazine* blog, *Sexis Magazine*, Clarion blog, Erotic Readers and Writers Association blog, *On The Issues*, *Sexy Mama Magazine*, and Circlet blog. She also writes sex toys reviews for several sex toys companies. Born and bred in Baltimore, she grew up under the influence of Edgar Allan Poe. She lives in Lovecraft country on the Massachusetts coast with her husband, son, and four delightful cats. She has never been under the knife. Visit her web site at http://eablack-writer.blogspot.com/. Friend her on Facebook at https://www.facebook.com/elizabethablack.

CARSON BUCKINGHAM

Carson Buckingham knew from childhood that she wanted to be a writer, and began, at age six, by writing books of her own, hand-drawing covers, and selling them to any family member who would pay (usually a gumball) for what she referred to as "classic literature." When she ran out of relatives, she came to the conclusion that there was no real money to be made in self-publishing, so she studied writing and read voraciously for the next eighteen years, while simultaneously collecting enough rejection slips to re-paper her living room ... twice. When her landlord chucked her out for, in his words, "making the apartment into one hell of a downer," she redoubled her efforts, and collected four times the rejection slips in half the time, single-handedly causing the first paper shortage in U.S. history. But she persevered, improved greatly over the years, and here we are.

Carson Buckingham has been a professional proofreader, editor, newspaper reporter, copywriter, technical writer, and comedy writer. Besides writing, she loves to read, garden, and collect autographed photographs of comedians and authors she loves, as well as life masks of horror movie icons. She lives in Arizona, with her wonderful husband, in a house full of books, orchid plants, and pets. Check out her blog at carsonbuckingham.blogspot.com.

KEALAN PATRICK BURKE

Called "one of the most clever and original talents in contemporary horror" (*Booklist*), Kealan Patrick Burke is the Bram Stoker Award-Winning author of five novels (*Master of the Moors*, *Currency of Souls*, *The Living*, *Kin*, and *Nemesis*), nine novellas (including the *Timmy Quinn* series), over a hundred short stories, and six collections. He edited the acclaimed anthologies *Taverns of the Dead*, *Quietly Now*, *Brimstone Turnpike*, and *Tales From the Gorezone*. An Irish expatriate, he currently resides in Ohio. Visit him at www.kealanpatrickburke.com or find him on Facebook at facebook.com/kealan.burke.

CHARLES COLYOTT

Charles Colyott lives on a farm in the middle of nowhere (Southern Illinois) with his wife, daughters, cats, and a herd of llamas and alpacas. He is surrounded by so much cuteness it's very difficult for him to develop any street cred as a dark and gritty horror writer. Nevertheless, he has appeared in *Read by Dawn II*, Dark Recesses Press, *Withersin* magazine, *Terrible Beauty Fearful Symmetry*, and *Horror Library* Volumes III, IV, and V. You can contact him on Facebook, and, unlike his llamas, he does not spit.

BRYAN HALL

Bryan Hall is a fiction writer living in a one hundred year old farmhouse deep in the mountains of North Carolina with his wife and three children. Growing up in the Appalachias, he's soaked up decades of fact and fiction from the area, bits and pieces of which usually weave their way into his writing whether he realizes it at the time or not. Several of his stories can be found in print magazines, online e-zines, and in upcoming anthologies. The short story collection, *Whispers From the Dark*, includes fourteen of the best shorts he's published to date. His first novel, *Containment Room Seven*, is now available from Permuted Press. In August 2012, the first novella in his "Southern Hauntings Saga" was released by Angelic Knight Press and the series is now ongoing. You can visit him online at www.bryanhallfiction.com.

RICK HUDSON

Rick Hudson was born in Derbyshire, England in 1966 and has lived in Manchester most of his life. He has been writing professionally since 1984 and his fiction has appeared in numerous magazines and collections as well as being broadcast by the BBC. He is the author of two novels: *Dr Twelve* (2010) and *Shrapnel* (2012). Whilst working in horror fiction, his literary ability and talent as a writer have been praised by the wider literary community: *Punk Globe* described his writing as "Nothing short of brilliant and inspiring" and invited its readers to "marvel at Hudson's mastery of language and literary technique." Academic writer Catherine Pattern (University of Winchester) claims that his fiction is marked by "remarkable writing skill, phenomenal ability to use language and the lyrical, striking and often beautiful style he employs." Rick cites his influences as Martin Amis, William Faulkner, Ted Hughes, Thomas Ligotti, Monty Python, Alice Cooper, and HP Lovecraft. Rick is also an English Literature academic—specializing in the study of horror, sf and fantasy fiction—and lectures at a number of universities in the North West of England. He welcomes the opportunity of contributing work to US magazines and publishers, and very much invites visitors to his Facebook page—although he does warn you that this can be "anarchic at best."

SHAUN JEFFREY

Shaun Jeffrey is the author of five novels, including the *The Kult*, which was filmed by independent production company, Gharial Productions. He has also had numerous short stories published in publications such as *Dark Discoveries* and *Cemetery Dance*. Besides writing, he is a black belt in Tae Kwon Do, and he has recently started participating in off-road races that incorporate obstacles and mud ... lots of mud. For more information, check out www.shaunjeffrey.com.

CHRISTIAN A. LARSEN

Christian grew up in Park Ridge, IL and graduated from Maine South High School in 1993. He has worked as an English teacher, radio personality, newspaper reporter, and a printer's devil. His short stories have appeared in *Chiral Mad* (Written Backwards), and *A Feast of Frights* (The Horror Zine Books) and *Fortune: Lost and Found* (Omnium Gatherum). His debut novel, *Losing Touch*, with a foreword by *New York Times* bestselling author Piers Anthony, will be published by Post Mortem Press in 2013. Christian received his bachelor of science in broadcast journalism from the University of Illinois and studied secondary English education at National-Louis University. He lives with his wife and two sons in the fictional town of Northport, Illinois. Follow him on Twitter @exlibrislarsen or visit exlibrislarsen.com for more information.

LISA MANNETTI

Lisa Mannetti's debut novel, *The Gentling Box*, garnered a Bram Stoker Award and she was nominated in 2010 both for her novella, "Dissolution," and a short story, "1925: A Fall River Halloween." She has also authored The *New Adventures of Tom Sawyer and Huck Finn* (2011); *Deathwatch*, a compilation of novellas—including "Dissolution"; a macabre gag book, *51 Fiendish Ways to Leave Your Lover* (2010); two nonfiction books; and numerous articles and short stories in newspapers, magazines, and anthologies. Her story, "Everybody Wins," was made into a short film by director Paul Leyden, starring Malin Akerman and released under the title *Bye-Bye Sally*; the film has been posted on YouTube. Lisa lives in New York. Visit her author Web site at www.lisamannetti.com, as well as her virtual haunted house at www.thechanceryhouse.com.

SHAUN MEEKS

Shaun Meeks lives in Toronto, Ontario with his partner, Mina LaFleur. Shaun's work has appeared in *Haunted Path*, *Dark Eclipse*, *Zombies Gone Wild*, and *A Feast of Frights* from the Horror Zine, as well as his own collection, *At the Gates of Madness*. He will also be featured in the anthologies *A Six Pack of Stories*, *The Horror Zine 4*, and *Fresh Grounds Volume 3*, and will be releasing a new collection with his brother called *Brother's Ilk* in late 2012 and his new novel, *Shutdown*, in early 2013. To find out more, visit him at www.shaunmeeks.com.

KATE MONROE

Kate Monroe is a redheaded author and editor who lives in a quiet and inspirational corner of southern England. She has penchants for the color black, horror, and loud guitars, and a fatal weakness for red wine. Her interests in writing range from horror to erotica, taking in historical romance, steampunk, and tales of the paranormal on the way; whatever she dreamed about the night before is liable to find its way onto the page in some form or another. Check out her web site at http://kateserenmonroe.com.

CHRISTINE MORGAN

Christine Morgan divides her writing time among many genres, from horror to historical, from superheroes to smut, anything in between and combinations thereof. She's a wife, a mom, a future crazy cat lady and a longtime gamer who enjoys British television, cheesy action/disaster movies, cooking, and crafts. Her stories have appeared in many publications, including *The Book of All Flesh*, *The Book of Final*

Flesh, The Best of All Flesh, History is Dead, The World is Dead, Strange Stories of Sand and Sea, Fear of the Unknown, Hell Hath No Fury, Dreaded Pall, Path of the Bold, Cthulhu Sex Magazine and its best-of volume *Horror Between the Sheets, Closet Desire IV,* and *Leather, Lace and Lust.* She's also a contributor to *The Horror Fiction Review,* a former member of the HWA, a regular at local conventions, and an ambitious self-publisher (six fantasy novels, four horror novels, six children's fantasy books, and two role-playing supplements). Her work has appeared in *Pyramid Magazine, GURPS Villains,* been nominated for Origins Awards, and given Honorable Mention in two volumes of Year's Best Fantasy and Horror. Her romantic suspense novel *The Widows Walk* was recently released from Lachesis Publishing; her horror novel *The Horned Ones* is due out from Belfire; and her thriller *Murder Girls* was just accepted by Skullvines. She's delving into steampunk, making progress on an urban paranormal series, and greatly enjoying her bloodthirsty Viking stories.

JM REINBOLD

JM Reinbold is the Director of the Written Remains Writers Guild in Wilmington, Delaware. She is the author of the novella "Transfusions," published in the anthology *Stories from the Inkslingers* (Gryphonwood Press, 2008). "Transfusions" was nominated for a Washington Science Fiction Association Small Press Award. Her poetry has appeared in *Red Fez Magazine, Strange Love* (2010), and *A Beat Style Haiku* (2012). In 2011, she received an honorable mention from the Delaware Division of the Arts Individual Artist Fellowships for her novel *Prince of the Piedmont.* She has been selected twice (2008, 2012) by the Delaware Division of the Arts as a fiction fellow for the Cape Henlopen Poets & Writers Retreat. In 2009, her novel-in-progress, *Summer's End,* was a finalist in the Magic Carpet Ride Magical Realism Mentorship competition. She is currently working on a mystery/crime novel, a number of short stories, and haiku. You can visit her online at www.jmreinbold.com.

M.L. ROOS

Malina Roos writes everything except romance because she has problems yanking axes out of young lovers' heads. Her work can be found in *Death to the Brother's Grimm* from Omnium Gatherum Media, and *Spinetingler Magazine*. Her great passions are writing, reviewing books, her three dogs, and her spouse, who mysteriously dies in most of her work and now sleeps with one eye open. She is currently working on several short stories and a novel.

DANIEL I. RUSSELL

Daniel I. Russell has been writing horror since 2004 with many short stories published in publications such as *Andromeda Spaceways Inflight Magazine, Pseudopod,* and *The Zombie Feed* from Apex. His debut novel *Samhane* and short story "By the Banks of the Nabarra" were both nominated for Western Australia Tin Duck awards in 2011, as was the story "Broken Bough" in 2012. He is the author of *Come Into Darkness, Critique* and *The Collector Book 1: Mana Leak*. His novel *Mother's Boys* is due for release in 2013 from Blood Bound Books and his work will also be appearing in Brett McBean's final novel in his *Urban Jungle* trilogy. Daniel is currently the Vice President of the Australian Horror Writer's Association and was a special guest editor of *Midnight Echo*.

A.P. SESSLER

A resident of North Carolina's Outer Banks, Sessler searches for that unique element that twists the everyday commonplace into the weird. Last year, he sold his first published story, "Tourist Trap," to the *State of Horror: North Carolina* anthology, edited by Armand Rosamilia. Having his second published story, "The Perfect Size," appear in *Zippered Flesh 2* enthuses him immensely.

L.L. SOARES

L.L. Soares's fiction has appeared in dozens of magazines and anthologies, including the original *Zippered Flesh* collection. His first novel, *Life Rage*, was released in 2012 from Nightscape Press, and is available from the usual places. His second novel, *Rock 'N' Roll*, should be out by the time you read this, published by Gallows Press. His other books include the short story collection *In Sickness* (with Laura Cooney) and the upcoming mainstream novel, *Hard*, due out in May of 2013. He is an Active member of the Horror Writers Association (HWA), and a former chairman of the New England Horror Writers (NEHW). He also cowrites the Stoker-Nominated horror movie review column, "Cinema Knife Fight," with Michael Arruda. CKF currently has an official web site, a staff of writers, and new content every weekday at http://cinemaknifefight.com. Check out his site at www.llsoares.com.

JONATHAN TEMPLAR

Jonathan Templar has written a large body of acclaimed dark and speculative fiction, much of which has been published in anthologies and compilations from a range of publishers. Jonathan's recent work includes the story "The Meat Man" in the charity collection *Horror for Good* and "Basher" for the shared world anthology *World's Collider*. His novella *The Angel of Shadwell*, the first in a series of stories for steampunk detective Inspector Noridel, is to be published by Nightscape Press in September 2012 and his first collection of stories, *The Geometry of Hell*, is due later in the year. Jonathan has an author site with a full bibliography at www.jonathantemplar.com.

JEZZY WOLFE

Jezzy Wolfe is an author of dark fiction, with a predilection for absurdity. A life-long native of Virginia Beach, Jezzy lives with her family and quite a few ferrets. Her stories have appeared in such ezines and magazines as *The World of Myth*, *The Odd Mind*, *Twisted Tongue*, *Support the Little Guy*, and *Morpheus Tales*. She has also been published in a variety of anthologies, such as Smart Rhino's first *Zippered Flesh*, Graveside Tales' *Harvest Hill*, *The 2009 Ladies and Gentlemen of Horror*, *The Best of the World of Myth: Vol. II*, Library of the Dead's *Baconology*, and the Choate Road fun book, *Knock, Knock ... Who's There? Death!* She was a founding member of Choate Road.com and at one time cohosted the blogtalk radio shows "The Funky Werepig" and "Pairanormal." Currently she writes reviews for *Liquid Imagination*. In addition to her brand of humor and horror fiction, she maintains both a blog and storefront for ferret owners and lovers, known as FuzzyFriskyFierce. You can visit Jezzy on her author's blog at jezzywolfe.wordpress.com, on her FuzzyFriskyFierce blog at FuzzyFriskyFierce.wordpress.com, or visit her storefront at www.cafepress.com/3fmerchandise.

THE ILLUSTRATOR

SHELLEY EVERITT BERGEN

The magnificent book cover graphic was created by Shelley Bergen, who was born and raised in Winnipeg, Manitoba, Canada. She still lives there today with her husband of nearly thirty years. They have one son.

"I have always been artistic to some degree, dabbling in painting with acrylics, poetry, tapestry, and, finally, digital photomanipulation," she said. "Discovering digital photomanipulation in 2000 opened a whole new door artistically for me. I now specialize in dark/macabre portraits, but am not limited to just that. In 2003, I was invited to join an online art community called Twisted Realmz, which is where I met fellow artists Antti Isosomppi and Matt Shealy. Great friendships ensued as well as collaborated artwork. This led to the launch of our company, Groundfrost Illustration & Design, in 2004. In the years since, we have had the privilege of creating artwork for projects for The Black-Eyed Peas, Kanye West, John Legend, God Forbid, Fragments of Unbecoming, The Killers, Dead Eyed Sleeper, Cutting Block Press, and Telus Publishing, to name but a few. In 2008, we created the artwork for the graphic comic *Lobster Girl*, story written by Jon Morvay. The comic went on to become the best-selling independent comic of that year. We are still going strong to this day, with no end in sight!"

Groundfrost can be found at www.groundfrost.net, or Shelley can be contacted personally for commissioned work at gbergen3@shaw.ca or on Facebook under her full name.

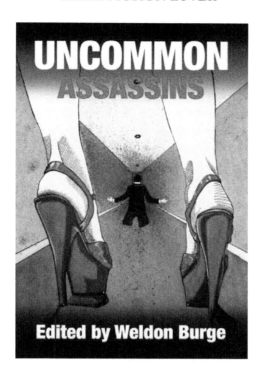

Printed in Great Britain
by Amazon

26563311R00185